# Diary of the Reluctant Duchess

## *Becoming Fancy*

### Sharon K. Middleton

Black Rose Writing | Texas

©2020 by Sharon K. Middleton
All rights reserved. No part of this book may be reproduced, stored in a retrieval system or transmitted in any form or by any means without the prior written permission of the publishers, except by a reviewer who may quote brief passages in a review to be printed in a newspaper, magazine or journal.

The author grants the final approval for this literary material.

First printing

This is a work of fiction. Names, characters, businesses, places, events, and incidents are either the products of the author's imagination or used in a fictitious manner. Any resemblance to actual persons, living or dead, or actual events is purely coincidental.

ISBN: 978-1-68433-569-5
PUBLISHED BY BLACK ROSE WRITING
www.blackrosewriting.com

Printed in the United States of America
Suggested Retail Price (SRP) $19.95

*Diary of the Reluctant Duchess* is printed in Adobe Caslon Pro

\*As a planet-friendly publisher, Black Rose Writing does its best to eliminate unnecessary waste to reduce paper usage and energy costs, while never compromising the reading experience. As a result, the final word count vs. page count may not meet common expectations.

# Praise for
## *The McCarron's Corner Series*

"A tale with an intriguing historical setting and time-travel premise…"
–*Kirkus Reviews*

"…weaves vivid descriptions of the Revolutionary War era."
–*IndieReader*

"A richly imaginative series."
–Bruce Logan, author of *Finding Lien*

"Middleton writes different historical eras with ease."
–John Hazen, award-winning author of *Fava*

*McCarron's Corner* has won multiple awards for Historical Romance.

# Acknowledgments

I again want to thank my family and friends for their encouragement and support as I continued Fancy's story. I could not write without the support, encouragement and love of my husband, Gary.

For several years now, Dawn Anderson patiently listened to me read manuscript after manuscript out loud at lunch each day. Dawn was my secretary for years, but more than that, she was my friend. She died unexpectedly in April 2019, and she left a huge empty spot in my heart and in my law practice.

Since her death, several other friends have come to the rescue to help me proofread and edit. I give special thanks to Judy Broussard and Maureen Maskell. These two ladies ply at the thankless task of helping me catch errors in manuscripts. I am eternally grateful for their help and their friendship.

I give special thanks to Reagan Rothe, my publisher. Thank you for your faith in me, Reagan. You will never know how much your trust and faith means to all of us you represent through Black Rose Writing. I hope Diary of the Reluctant Duchess does as well for us as it does for Fancy in this story.

Diary of the Reluctant Duchess is the story of a young woman as she becomes all that she can be and finds her happy-ever-after. I dedicate it to all who struggle to overcome their inner demons, to become stronger, more beautiful, and more interesting humans. May we all become strong at our broken pieces.

Kintsugi.

Diary of the Reluctant Duchess

# Prologue

Ernest Hemingway once wrote, "the world breaks everyone, and then some become strong at the broken pieces." The Japanese repair things with a process they call Kintsugi. They repair broken pottery with a strong adhesive and sprinkle the adhesive with gold dust. The resulting piece is stronger, more beautiful, and more interesting for having been broken and repaired. Richard says people are a lot like those Japanese vases. We can also become stronger, more beautiful, more interesting when we become repaired after we break down. Instead of trying to hide the flaws and cracks, they accentuate and celebrate as they become the most substantial part of us.

When I first heard about Kintsugi, as it applies to people, I felt despair. I knew I was too broken, too shattered, to be repaired, much less strengthened or more beautiful. I viewed myself as not worthy of being restored. But now, I think I'm like one of those magnificent Japanese vases. I love the idea that each of us can mend and become stronger than we were in the first place through the help of the Almighty.

I was born long ago, longer than you could imagine. I have some cracks in my surface and some on my heart. Some you can see. Others, not so much. But they repaired me. I hope they strengthened me, made me more beautiful, more interesting, with each glimmer of gold from the refiner's fire.

Our lives don't go backward. We don't get to redo the past. I have learned there is no sense in lingering over 'what-if's' about our history. Life is like a road map. We learn and grow from the wrinkles on the map. Thank heaven, I am learning how to let those things go and to move on. We become more interesting with the accumulation of dings and scars along our journey through life. Our perceptions write timeless poetry upon our flesh and our minds with a quill dipped in the refiner's gold. Our wounds become scars, which create art as our genuine beauty emerges.

This journal is my story of how Plain Fancy Selk became more than merely the Duchess of Ranscome. I was always most reluctant to assume the role of a duchess. It was never a suitable fit for me. I will start my story with Richard. Without Richard, I would never have become who I am today. Richard is who told me about the process of Kintsugi. In that respect, this story is as much his as it is mine.

# Part 1
# Before

# Chapter 1
# Richard
# November 1782

I love her with all my heart. I traveled back in time nearly 240 years to find her, and she chose another man over me. How do I survive? How do I go on?

How did this all go wrong?

My name is Richard Owen Winslow. I am 30 years old. My mother conceived me in Boston, Mass., and gave birth to me in San Antonio, Texas. My dad was white, and my mom was black. Half-black, or 'mulatto,' to use the terminology used in 1782. That makes me a 'quadroon,' or one-fourth black. No biggie from the period in which I lived. Here, it's an enormous issue. More than a drop marks me as black in Colonial Virginia. Go figure.

I was a doctor in the third year of my residency before I came searching for Francesca. I abandoned my studies for the promise of love and a happy-ever-after ending with this exceptional young woman. I had lived in Texas, Massachusetts, Virginia, and Georgia before I came to this time in search of love. Since then, I have been to the Indian Territory, Georgia, the Carolinas, Virginia, up to New York, and then to Ireland, Britain, and Barbados. Now, we are back in Virginia, and I am a broken man.

I did not know love could hurt so damned horribly.

Mom says Francesca and I belong together. She contends I need to hang on and keep the faith. I thought we belonged together, too, before Barbados, but then Francesca told me she would marry that sorry rat bastard Kirk O'Malley. In my mind, O'Malley is not much better than the godforsaken men who kidnapped and sold her to him. It would have been kinder for Francesca to cut my heart out instead of telling me she chose Kirk over me. Then, to top it, she told me she would have his baby.

I will never forget that excruciating pain until the day I die. The carpal tunnel of love trapped me.

I feel numb. I will admit an occasional shot of Marc McCarron's excellent corn whiskey helps numb me. I don't know what to think. I don't know what to believe. I feel so damned empty, alone, and defeated. I don't know how I feel anything because Francesca broke my heart when she chose O'Malley.

I learned I could cope with most things here in this era. I can live without flushing toilets and toilet paper. I deal daily with filth and disease. I manage without cell phones and cars. I wear a long-sleeved shirt, coat and tie even on the hottest of days, and that was hard to do in Barbados. I survived the Battle of Yorktown, where I sawed shattered limbs off teenaged boys without anesthesia. I will never forget their screams of agony or the hideous smell of gangrene and death. Hopefully, I will never be in a battle situation like that again. However, I am young enough that I could live through the War of 1812, in another 30 years. I can adjust to just about anything if I am where I am supposed to be, and I'm with the person I am supposed to be with for the rest of my life.

But, I no longer know where that would be. I thought it was with Francesca. Was I wrong?

My Mom, Sassy, adopted me after she married my dad. My birth mom, Kathryn, died of a drug overdose when I was 8. My Mom came to this era after my Dad died. Sassy found a second chance at love and happiness with William Selk. She figured out she could send letters to her ancestors in San Antonio. Their descendants kept those letters until last year when they sent them to my Uncle Jim and me.

In her letters, I fell in love with Mom's stories of the new United States of America, and of Will's baby sister, Francesca Marie, who they call Fancy. After a trip to Ireland to scope out more information on my Mom and her new family, I knew my future was in the past when I found the painting at Ranscome Manor of Lady Francesca Selk. The description beneath the portrait said she was the First Duchess of Ranscome and the beloved wife of Dr. Richard Winslow. Wow, talk about winning the jackpot! I went back home and had a ring made like the one the beautiful woman wore in the painting, a large, oval aquamarine surrounded by rose-cut diamonds, set in yellow gold. I left home in 2015, and arrived here in 1781, ready to find my future.

I thought I had it all figured out. Boy, I was in for a surprise.

First, Francesca Selk married Sir Calvin Hobbs. That old codger hated me from the minute he laid eyes on me. He didn't want another living man to look at Francesca the way I looked at her. You know, like she was the most gorgeous, special woman in the entire universe.

Well, old man Hobbs died at Yorktown, and I figured the path to our happiness was secure. Wrong again, Winslow. I screwed up big time and almost blew it with her when I blurted out secrets she wanted no one else to know. God, if looks could kill, I would have dropped dead on the spot that morning. We finally worked through our problems related to my basic stupidity when an effing British Colonel kidnapped her in NYC. Now, there's a sorry excuse for a human being if one ever lived. It took six freaking months to hunt her down, only to have the woman I love more than life itself tell me she intended to marry another man. Jesus, take me now.

I Am Broken.

I told Will and Mom a jillion times I think I came at the wrong time. Maybe I jinxed everything coming when I did. I never expected the woman I followed through time and all over the freaking planet to marry another man when I finally found her the second time.

Mom smiles and says it will all work out. Sheesh, no wonder she and Dad used to fight. Sassy is enough to drive a saint to suicide.

In 1782, Mom wrote she was expecting twins. I arrived here in 1781, and now it's 1782. She told us last week she is expecting. Will and she are delighted. She seemed disappointed she didn't surprise me.

"I knew you would be pregnant in 1782." I gave her a smug smile.

Mom looked startled. "How did you know that?"

"You wrote Uncle Jim and told him."

She grinned ear to ear. "*M'hijo*, my son, why hadn't you told me?"

"Wasn't my place to tell you the future."

She laughed and made that little 'psst' sound that annoyed Dad to no end. "I tell General Washington the future all the time."

I shrugged. Mom's view is that it is okay to talk about the future if it doesn't change the future. I worry telling people about the future might cause inadvertent changes. I sure as hell would have warned her if I had known Bloody Ban Tarleton would come to Belle Rose and hurt my Mom, and I would never have let Francesca out of my sight if I had any idea Tarleton would kidnap her, beat her, and sell her as a slave.

Hell, maybe I came here to punish Tarleton. That might help assuage some of my guilt over Francesca's abduction, as well as some of my anger towards O'Malley. Maybe.

But, seriously, what if I arrived too soon? Did I mess up the time-space consortium, or whatever the hell it is, by arriving too early? I know Lily McCarron came when she was a kid and went back until it was the right time. What if I arrived at the wrong time and it screwed up our future?

Dammit, I want our happy-ever-after. I ache with longing for our happy-ever-after.

Will I ever be Francesca's choice? How long do I have to wait for it to be the right time for us?

Yeah, I know. Don't make permanent decisions based on temporary feelings. Mom has told me that as long as I have known her. I'm trying.

I told Mom maybe I should go back Beyond and return here later. Perhaps I came at the wrong time. But does she listen to me? No, of course not. Once Sassy Selk gets something in her head, there is no changing her mind. She is the most stubborn, hard-headed, obstinate, inflexible woman you could ever meet. And she thinks I make rash, emotional decisions?

So, now we are all going to Ireland for Christmas, weeks after we got back to the Belle Rose Plantation. Really? Now? I think my Mom flipped her noodle.

Will grins at me and laughs like he knows some master plan he hasn't shared with me. Hell, maybe he does. "Don't buck her, son. You know she won't give up on this. She's like a hound dog with a bone. Once that little gal makes a decision, it's as good as done."

"But, Will, this is wrong on so many levels…"

He grinned at me even broader and shook his head. "You might as well give up, Rick. Arguin' with the moon makes more sense than arguin' with my little Sassafras. You know her. Just reconcile yourself to the fact we are going to Ireland for Christmas. Pack warm."

"But—"

"Pack warm, son." He again laughed at the joke they have not bothered to share with me.

I must be missing something. Or perhaps Mom and Will both went wackadoodle. So, I'm packing warm for Ireland. We leave in the morning at the ass crack of dawn.

I don't think I can bear to see Francesca with that man, growing great with his baby inside her.

Oh well, this won't hurt very long. It's no worse than a broken arm.

Hell, who am I kidding? It's a thousand times worse. And I have no control over this crap with Francesca.

I looked down and realized I rubbed the scrape on my wrist raw again. Blood is seeping onto my cuff.

*Way to go, Winslow.*

"Aren't you packed yet?" Sassy frowned at me as she tapped her foot in my doorway.

I looked up from my writing, startled by her voice. I turned my hand a little, so the new bloodstain on the cuff would not show. "I'll be packed by time to leave, Mom, but—"

"*Bueno.* Now, quit your dawdling."

I shook my head in exasperation. "Mom, I'm not dawdling. I'll finish packing before morning. Now listen to me. I'm convinced that I came at the wrong time."

She tossed her head, her eyes flashing emerald sparks of anger. With one hand on her hip, she stomped her foot, twirled her hand, and pointed her forefinger on her other hand at me. She stood there, tapping her foot. Dad used to call that pose her Sassy Stance. She intended to intimidate me, but it no longer works with me. I tried to bite back a grin, but she caught it and frowned even more.

"Nonsense, Rick. *Escuchame, m'hijo.* Listen to me. We have been through this before. You know you belong here. You could not have come if you don't belong here."

I shook my head again for the umpteenth time. "Mom, you need to listen to *me*. We all know Lily McCarron came at the wrong time. I think I did, too. I can go back home. Come back here in a few years—"

She shook her head. "Oh, no, Richard Winslow. You are not slinking back to Atlanta like a whipped pup. You belong here. And we are—"

"Going to Ireland for Christmas. Yeah, I got it the first 4,735 times you told me. Great. Kirk ought to be over-freaking-joyed for me to show up for their first Christmas together in Ireland, as his wife nears her delivery date of their baby. I can't get over how rash and impetuous *you* can be at times."

I shook my head in disgust.

She tilted her head, unsure if she would glower or grin. "Me? Rash? Impetuous? Ha! I'm the ultimate conservative. You must mean someone else."

I shook my head. "No, I mean you. You are no longer a conservative. The word means 'holding to traditional attitudes and values and cautious about change or innovation, typically concerning politics or religion.' Think about it. Our founding fathers aren't career politicians. The British consider the founding fathers and all those we call patriots to be outlaws. They view us as angry extremists who refuse to quietly submit to an elite political establishment's oppressive rule over their lives. They are *not* conservatives. You and Dad taught me that. You jumped right into the fray. You are actively working to create a fresh form of government, the Constitutional Republic, 'a more perfect union.' You conspired against the status quo, the Constitutional Monarchy. Hell, you were one of Washington's spies. You are helping to craft a Constitution for the brand new United States of America. And if that isn't enough to show you are *not* a conservative in *this* day and age, then think about this. You are pro-abolition of slavery and pro-women's rights. You are encouraging Will to free the rest of the Belle Rose slaves—"

"And you know that will happen by year's end since the Virginia Legislature has passed laws allowing an owner to free his slaves. We have prepared the paperwork to free everyone and are awaiting the signatures of the Virginia Legislature for approval. We paid all the requisite fees." She glared at me, hands on her hips again with that little foot of hers tapping impatiently, daring me to contradict her.

I chuckled again. I'm always amused when Mom's Hispanic accent sneaks out when she gets angry or upset. Her Hispanic roots showed right then. "Oh, yes, I know, and I'm thrilled. You have urged Will to be sure all the slaves and former slaves learn to read and write and have a skill. And you know that's still illegal in Virginia."

She tossed her head again, shrugged her shoulder, and sniffed. "It's a stupid law."

I laughed out loud at that one. "I agree, but my point is, it's the law, and you are seeking to change it. That is not conservative action, by definition. I also know you believe women should have equal rights as men and women should have the right to vote, which women won't have until 1919. By law, women are little more than chattel. I hate to tell you this, Mom, but *you* are the quintessential progressive of 1782."

She looked shocked. She hyperventilated. I laughed again.

"That's not funny, *m'hijo*."

"Probably not, Mom. I didn't intend to be funny. It's true."

She frowned and started to say something. She apparently had second thoughts, frowned again, and whirled around to leave without another word.

I chuckled. It's nice to get the last word in an argument with Sassy Selk now and then, especially when I am right.

But, honestly, why couldn't it have been *my* baby Francesca is carrying? Oh, yeah. *Mr. I'll Take the High Road* here insisted we used birth control when we were intimate. Well, except for that one time. At least it isn't Tarleton's baby if she's sure it isn't mine.

No sense crying over spilled whiskey, as Dad used to say. It looks like I'll be there to help Lily in case anything goes wrong. Francesca has a leaky heart valve secondary to a near-fatal case of rheumatic fever as a child. Dan could repair her heart, Beyond. Not easy-peasy, but a competent cardiovascular surgeon like Dan could fix it, *no problemo*. No way we could do that surgery here. For starters, Lily is not nor am I a cardio specialist, although I took the cardio residency when Dan offered it to me. Now, I wish I had finished it before I came. Dan always told me my future was in cardiovascular surgery. At least I only took a leave of absence from the program. I can still go back and finish it. Nor do we have electricity here to operate a heart and lung machine, if we even had one. Nor a skilled cardio team. Hell, we don't have access to a sterile surgical field where I would want to attempt that surgery *if* I had the knowledge, training, equipment and *if* all the other variables were in my favor. Which they are not.

Shit, the only reason I gave in at Barbados about dueling O'Malley was that Francesca had a heart attack and almost died right there in front of me. Imagine a twenty-two-year-old woman in full-blown cardiac failure. I was never so frightened in my entire life. The whole concept still boggles my mind. Otherwise, I would have been able to choose weapons. I may be a doctor, but I'm a damned fine shot, thanks to all those hours on the range with Dad, especially armed with the high-powered rifle and the tactical shotgun I brought from Beyond. Will could have bought O'Malley's estate, including Francesca, he could have freed her, and we could settle into Ranscome Manor now as Doctor and Mrs. Winslow, also known as the Duchess of Ranscome, for our happy-ever-after.

Huh. It just hit me. I've been to Ranscome Manor before Francesca or O'Malley. Back in the future.

I folded the rest of my shirts and a heavy woolen sweater Sassy knitted for me last winter and tucked them into the trunk. I added socks and underwear, or as they call them here, drawers. I already had another chest packed with my suits. After all, the upper-class man must dress appropriately at all times. I stopped folding the next pair of drawers in mid-air and laughed out loud.

I've been to Ranscome Manor and Waterside, too, when we all went to Cork last summer while we searched for Francesca. I'm crazy about her Grandpa. Lord Micah Fitz Simmons is one rad old fellow, but I would expect no less from Marc's father. Marc is uber cool himself. Maybe you have to be easy-going and flexible to cope with travelers, as he calls Lily, Sassy, and me. I can tell Marc is cut from the same cloth as his dad. Lord Fitz Simmons seemed to like me a lot, too, even if he doesn't know I came here from the future. We had many talks while I was there. I loved the way his eyes would sparkle when I would talk about his granddaughter.

I noticed the same sparkle in his eyes when I would catch him looking at Francesca's mom. Tamsin Fitz Simmons is still a beautiful woman. She's about the same age as my Mom. It's a shame Tamsin never married again after they lost Jay Fitz Simmons at sea all those years ago. She says she would have everything she wants now if Francesca came home.

Of course, Cork has never been home to Francesca.

Hmm. I wonder how Lord Fitz Simmons is getting along with Kirk O'Malley? I began laughing again as I envisioned suave, sophisticated, Lord Fitz Simmons butting heads with the blunt, outspoken, less-than-tactful sailor. Kirk O'Malley is rough as a cob. It ought to be something to behold when Lord Micah Fitz Simmons takes on Captain Kirk!

I was still laughing as I finished packing my things. Who knows? This cluster f— might be fun. Like Dad used to say, every problem in life contains the seeds of its solution. If life gives you lemons, make a whiskey sour. Oh, yeah, I could almost taste one.

We started for Ireland bright and early the next morning. Will said it would take us about 40 days to get to Cork.

I frowned. "I thought you said that it would take that long to sail to Ireland from Barbados?"

Will nodded. "The Revenge is a faster ship than is the Revelation. Revelation is more substantial and slower. More what your Mom calls 'old school.' But the Revelation is steady and reliable. I prefer to cross the Atlantic in Revelation at this time of year. Plus, pirates will be less inclined to try to take us than if we're on the Revenge again. There are reports that Captain Davy Jones is in the waters off the coast of Ireland."

My jaw dropped. "Pirates? Are you serious? Davy Jones? You sure he doesn't sail on The Flying Dutchman?" I asked, chuckling as I remembered the character from the Pirates of the Caribbean movies. "I kinda expected pirates in the Caribbean, not near Ireland."

Will nodded, all serious. He looked grim to me. "Yes, there are multiple reports that Captain Davy Jones of the Bonne Homme Robert is terrorizing Irish waters. The Flying Dutchman is one of his ships, but he is usually on Robert. I more than half expect to run into the old reprobate." He gave me a sharp look. "How do you know about him?"

I didn't want to explain those crazy *Pirates of the Caribbean* movies to Will. "Wow. I guess Dad must have mentioned him."

He gave me a long, appraising look before he responded. "Humph. Yeah, sure, that must be it. Ireland has been home to pirates for many centuries. Piracy is almost the Irish way of life. I reckon it began way back in the 400's, with raids to Britain for slaves. Today, pirates ravage British shipping in aid of our war for independence. And lots of Irish pirates hail from the Cork area. Anne Bonny was from Kinsale. Peter Roach was from Cork. Davy Jones hails from Bantry."

"Great," I muttered. Would names from the future continue to pop up in the past? First Calvin Hobbs, then Captain Kirk of the Enterprise, and now Captain Davy Jones of the Flying Dutchman. Who on earth would come next? Jack Sparrow? Sophia Loren? Jack Kennedy? Thomas Magnum? Or maybe Marilyn Monroe?

"They say Jolly Johnny England is actually from Ireland, not England, but no one knows for sure. He has an upper-class English accent. If I had to worry about any of them, he's the one I would fear the most. He will laugh, joking, acting like he's your new best friend, and then he will shoot you right through the eye while still laughing over a shared joke."

"Why do they call him Jolly Johnny?" The information about a pirate I had never heard of before intrigued me.

"He'll be laughing and joking with you and then shoot you without batting an eye. They say he always smiles afterward and says, 'Jolly good.' He's a cold one. He's the Arch Pirate. No matter who might troll these waters, it puts us in an awkward position. If we fly the British flag, pirates may attack. If we fly the American flag, the British may well attack."

"Dammit Will, I do not want to be in a battle at sea or anywhere else!"

Will looked grave. "Nor do I, Rick. Nor do I, especially with your mom and the babies on board."

I frowned. "So… What do we do?"

His smile was taut. "Carry both flags. Hope the Brits don't catch us. Just like we did last summer."

That rattled me. "Wait… do you mean we pulled that stunt when we went to Ireland, England, and Barbados earlier?"

Will finally broke out the famous Selk smile. "You betcha, son. How else did you think we took an American ship to London in search of Tarleton and Darlington?"

Sheesh. Just what the blazes were we doing?

# Chapter 2
# Fancy
# 1782

The sky was red that morning.

"Always be grateful for the terrible things in life, Fancy. They open your eyes to the best things you hadn't noticed before." Kirk sighed as he lowered the spyglass.

"Isn't that kind of like saying, 'if it weren't for bad luck, I'd have no luck at all'?" I retorted. "You don't think it's Davy Jones, do you?"

Kirk half-way grinned as he tousled my hair. "Ah, lass, I would hate to think I have brought naught but poor luck to you. Right now, you might well be correct. I meant perhaps things are not so bad as we might think. I damned sure hope it's not *that* sorry bastard. Get below deck with Lily and the bairns. This fight could get nasty before it's over."

I shook my head. "No, if they want to take this ship, we will all meet the sorry whoresons fighting. We won't go down without a struggle. They are fools if they think taking this ship will be easy, especially with them flying the red sail."

Kirk frowned as he shook his head and handed me a loaded flintlock pistol. "Stubborn wench. Jo was right. You might be little, but by damn, my Wee Duchess is fierce. Then arm yourself, lass, and hang on for the ride. It will be a rough go if we are to outrun yon scalawags."

I slipped the pistol into my belt and chewed my lip as I stared at the enormous ship looming on the horizon. I realized my hands were shaking as my heart began thrumming fast like it does when I get scared. We saw the pirate ships behind us most of the past two days. Kirk was concerned but not too worried until the other vessels began gaining on us this afternoon. And now, they had hoisted the red flag. We knew they were pirates from the Jolly Roger they flew. The red flag they now raised meant they would give no quarter, and they would take no prisoners. They wanted the Enterprise, reputed to be the fastest ship on the seven seas. If they could mount her, we were all good as dead.

It had been a fractious six weeks since we left Barbados. First, we caught a late-season hurricane. Marc said they hit a similar storm eighteen years ago on the way to Ireland. We finally escaped that to find ourselves followed by this pirate ship. And now, they had replaced the Jolly Roger with the red flag of death.

Some days, you wondered if it was all worth it. And to think we could have just gone to Belle Rose. We would be home by now.

"Who do you think captains her?" I hung tight to Kirk's waist, rubbing the fabric of his shirt back and forth between my fingers. I realized I shook less if I hung on to him, and my heartbeat began slowed a bit, almost back to normal.

Kirk shrugged. "I don't know. I hadn't expected pirates just off the coast of Ireland. We will run hard, darlin'. Marc tells me there's a deep-water pier at Waterside. I'm hoping to sail straight there. Now, let's pray yon blaggard is not Captain Davy Jones of the Bonne Homme Robert."

I frowned. "Why not the Bonne Homme Robert?"

"She's a frigate with 40 guns and a crew of 370 of the bloodthirstiest bastards that ever roamed the seas."

My heart began to beat hard and fast again. I pressed a trembling hand to my chest as if to calm my racing heart. "Oh, dear."

"Aye. Oh, dear, indeed. If it is Robert, she sails with four other warships. He took those ships the way he hopes to take this one."

I gulped and wiped a sweating palm on my skirt. "Can the pirates outrun us?"

Kirk was silent as he studied the ship on the horizon. "I hope he can't. We will find out if the Enterprise is as canny as she is supposed to be. But raising the red flag means he's damned sure going to try to take the Enterprise. You sure you want to stay on deck with me?"

Wordless, I nodded. He bent over to kiss me.

"Then steer for me for a few minutes while we adjust the rigging. Creeps and Marc, help me. We need to get the sails trimmed as neat as possible right away if we're to outrun that one."

First Mate Anthony 'Creeps' Francisco nodded and hurried to help Kirk trim the sails to catch more wind. My father nodded and pushed with a half dozen other sailors up into the rigging. I knew Marc used to sail some for Ranscome shipping years ago, and he was always a dutiful man in a pinch like we were in now. He might no longer be young, but my Daddy was still agile. In no time at all, the men efficiently trimmed the sails. Soon, I could tell our sleek schooner was edging further away from the warship following us.

It did not surprise me. I knew the Enterprise was a new adaptation of a schooner. Sassy said this design would develop in the mid-nineteenth century and would be called a clipper. She insists those clippers will be the fastest, wind-driven ships on the seven seas. The Enterprise was our experimental design, and she had given superlative performance since first put into the water eighteen months ago.

Today would tell the tale whether this ship was the fastest and most maneuverable ship on the seas. If we won this race, we would live. If we lost, we would lose our lives, including the lives of my Bella, Charles, and the precious cargo I carried in my womb.

Suddenly, I awoke, the scream still lingering on the air even as Kirk shook me. "*Mo leannan*, wake up. It's just a dream, darling."

I gasped as I struggled to focus and then pulled him close, still trembling. Once again, sweat had drenched my gown, sour with the rank smell of fear. "Damn, why do I keep dreaming this nightmare?"

He shook his head. "I don't know, my love. What do you say? If it weren't for bad luck, you would have no luck at all?"

I trembled again and laughed. "That's what I say every time I dream about the red sky and that blasted ship."

He shook his head again, this time in disbelief. "And this makes how many times you've dreamed it now?"

I clamored to peer out the porthole. "Three. Why do you ask?"

"Portents come in three's, lass."

I swear a whole family of possums must have climbed over my grave then by the shivers I had when he said that. I rubbed my arms and noticed the little hairs were standing straight up. "What's that poem you say about red skies?"

"Red skies at night, sailors' delight. Red sky at morning, sailors take warning."

I turned back to him. "The sky is red this morning."

He nodded. "Aye, as your Da pointed out to me. We've taken warning. But there is no pirate ship looming on the horizon flying the red sail, *mo leannan*."

I stared into the horizon. "Well, at least not yet. I reckon that's something."

But had we been given a warning, first by my dreams and then by the red sky of the morning? Were we headed for pirates as we approached the coast of Ireland?

Kirk raised his spyglass and then grinned as he lowered it to hand it to me. "Look there, my love. I think there will be no pirates today. We're at Waterside."

"What is it that Sassy says? Oh, my God, Rebecca? Well, Rebecca, I reckon we are here!" I threw my arms around his neck to hug him close.

Marc entered the room in time to hear me. "Aye, it is somethin' like that. And there before ye, Fancy, is the most beautiful home in all of Ireland, including Ranscome Manor. Of course, Waterside is newer and more modern than Ranscome Manor, although Ranscome is bigger. The gardens here alone are breathtaking. My father built it for my mam, ye know. He built the gardens on a formal plan which you can see well from the house looking towards the water. There are more gardens on the other side which ye see travelin' here from Cork. I remember my mother loved those gardens that open right down to the sea, which is why they named the house *Waterside*. My Da is the First Earl of Waterside."

Marc was right. Waterside was so beautiful it took my breath away. With my heart in my throat, I hurried to sponge off before I grabbed my clothing. I ran the brush through my hair before I deftly re-braided my waist-length tresses. I tossed the long braid over my shoulder before I rushed out of the captain's quarters and across the deck of the Enterprise, where I stared, mesmerized, by the view of the exquisite manor house Micah Fitz Simmons built for his bride, Meara McCarron Fitz Simmons, over fifty years before.

I realized I was still trembling, and my hands were again wet with nervous sweat. I felt calmer as I rubbed my hands back and forth across the fabric of my skirt. The repetitious movement of the fabric rubbing across my skin always seemed to calm my nerves.

And then I saw the people approaching the dock. My heart lurched. The elderly, silver-haired gentleman leaned on the arm of the slender, dark-haired woman I had thought I would never see again. It had been a lifetime since I last saw her, but I would have known her anywhere. She raised a hand to shield her eyes and jumped up and down. I never dreamed I would live to see Tamsin Selk jump up and down in apparent excitement. Even though the Enterprise was still on the water, I heard Tamsin's excited voice. "Papa, they've brought my baby home! Oh, sweet Jesus, they brought my Fancy home!"

My heart lurched with unexpected emotion at sight and sound of my mother, excited I was coming to Waterside. I pressed my hand to my mouth as if that might help keep me from crying, but the tears were already stinging at my eyes.

I couldn't hear what the older man said. She kissed his cheek with great tenderness and then ran to the dock where she continued dancing up and down as Kirk brought the elegant ship to moor.

I never saw my mother act this way before. Lord knew I never saw her jumping with excitement when I was a child. Energy radiated from Tam. She was enthusiastic and seemed happy to be alive. It had been nearly twenty years since I last saw her, but I could not remember ever seeing her look so happy. Life in Ireland appeared to agree with her.

"I can't do this." I was suddenly terrified. I blinked those damned tears back, and I clung to Kirk's waist in terror.

He tousled my hair. I've noticed he does that a lot, usually when I am stressed, and he is trying to lighten my mood. "Of course, you can. You're the Duchess of Ranscome. You can do anything you set your mind to do."

Marc turned to smile at me. "Aye, lass, Kirk is right. You can do this. And we are all here to give ye encouragement and support."

Mouth dry with terror and longing, I glanced up at my father. "I'm scared. What if she doesn't like me, Daddy?"

My father bent to kiss the top of my head. "Not as scared as Tam is. Besides, what's not to like about you, lass? You're the most likable person I know. It will be fine. You'll see."

"She looks well." I cringed at the bitter note in my voice as I again wiped my sweat-soaked hands on my skirt.

"Aye, she does. Ireland has been good for her. But I promise ye, lass: she's more afraid of the meeting to come than you are. She has a ton of guilt about leaving ye all those years ago at Belle Rose."

I said nothing. It didn't seem appropriate to say, 'Tamsin should have a ton of guilt over abandoning me' right then. I stared wistfully at the beautiful woman waiting impatiently at the dock. I realized with a start that I was chewing on a fingernail, and I forced myself to drop my hands. *Don't bite your nails, Fancy. You're a duchess. Ladies don't rip at their nails.*

Creeps jumped to the dock, and Kirk threw the line to him. As Creeps tied off, Kirk coaxed me over to the dockside to help me off the schooner. Marc, Lily, Fitz, and the children rushed ahead of us down to the elderly gentleman standing alone on the dock. I saw Marc throw his arms around my grandfather and gather him into a loving embrace.

I took a deep breath and squared my shoulders as I reached for Kirk's hand. I felt calmer as he took my trembling hand into his own. "Okay. Let's do this."

We started down the gangplank, but Tamsin wasn't waiting another minute. Halfway down, she met me, and after just the slightest hesitation, she threw her arms around me. I stood rigid, unsure what to do, and then I slowly felt my tension, no, my years of pent-up anger and hurt melted out of me. Eighteen long years of pain and rage came flooding out of me from the loving grasp of my mother. Unbidden tears welled up in my own eyes again, and then the tears spilled over. I could not prevent my rush of tears any more than I could stop my hands from creeping up to cling to the sobbing woman holding me tight in her arms.

"I didn't think I would ever see you again," she gasped as she stroked my face. "Oh, my God, Fancy, you're all grown up. You're so beautiful."

"I didn't think I would ever see you again, either." My voice sounded shaky with emotion as I laid my face into her hands.

She looked at me, anguish all across her beautiful face. "Fancy, I'm so sorry."

I put a finger up to her lips. "It's okay, Mama. It's okay. I'm here now."

Her eyes bright with tears, she nodded and then hugged me close as I remembered the mantra I repeated over and over during those long, painful years. Tamsin left me when I was four years old to chase after an Irish lord. It turned out her Irish lord was the half-brother of my father. She left me to be abused by a man who thought I was less than him because of the blood I got from her. I had no interest in going anywhere near her, I told myself many times over those long, lonely years of abuse.

For the first time, I realized I lied to myself all those years. I wrapped my arms around my mother and clung tight to her as I cried my heart out. I would never tell her about all the hell I endured after she left. She didn't need to know.

Hopefully, no one else had told her. I could tell by her body-racking sobs she carried enough guilt about abandoning me.

And somehow, a bit of the pain I carried all those years seemed to disappear right then. The mark might always be there, like a scar, but the old, raw wound was no longer there, weeping bitter, angry droplets down over my aching heart. Each tear I shed seemed to wash healing balm over the old injury that resulted when my mother abandoned me. I had a fleeting thought of the gold epoxy Richard told me they use to mend broken pottery in Japan. Perhaps our tears were a kind of emotional gold epoxy sent by God above to help heal our broken hearts. I was sure I felt some of my shattered pieces mend with each tear shed by both Tamsin and me that day. I hoped Tamsin felt some healing, also.

Marc often asks me, "Are your next steps heading where you want to go? If not, step off the path and do something unexpected."

I think I stepped off the path I expected to take right then when I did something I never expected to do. I embraced Tamsin Selk Fitz Simmons and called her Mama. Miraculously, when I seized the moment, God rewarded me with healing I never expected to receive.

Kirk and I finally walked off the gangplank arm in arm to my grandfather. A smile broke across his face as his pale blue eyes filled up with tears. He gathered me into his trembling limbs and kissed both my cheeks. "I told ye she'd come home to us someday, Tammy."

She smiled and reached out to squeeze his hand. "Yes, you did, Papa. You never gave up hope."

I felt a pang of concern when I caught sight of the old fellow, stooped with arthritis and age. I knew he had been a tall man, maybe as tall as my Daddy, but now bent from rheumatism, he was a little taller than Lily. Lily is a tall woman, but she is still a good 7 inches shorter than Marc. My grandfather's skin looked parchment-thin. He had a good bit of snow-white hair, although you could see his pink scalp through the thinned strands on top. Wrinkles lined his noble face, and his hands shook with a palsied tremor. I straightened up, and remembering Kirk's constant urging I smile more, I pasted a shaky smile on my face. I quickly wiped my sweating palms on my skirt again before I extended my hand to him. "It's an honor to meet you, my lord."

"Ah, now none of that, girl. I'm your Grandpa. Come and hug me, good and proper!"

Suddenly, the smile on my face was real as I laughingly went into the open arms of the ninety-year-old man waiting for me to hug him for the first time.

Finally, we broke apart. My grandfather sniffed as if embarrassed by the show of emotion and then frowned as his eyes scanned the crowd on the dock. "Where's young Richard?"

Well, sure enough, I felt like the cat had plum dab got my tongue then. Kirk slipped up by my side, and I looked at him with dismay. I could see the shock flash across his handsome features. What would he say? How would he react?

Let's face it. My Captain has a temper. A bad temper. An Irish temper.

I slipped an arm around Kirk's waist. "Grandpa, Richard went back to Virginia with Sassy and Will. But I would like you to meet…"

He frowned and interrupted me. "What? He went back to Virginia? Why on earth would the man do that? He's sore in love with ye, girl."

I cleared my throat. "Grandpa, I'd like to introduce you to my *husband*, Kirk O'Malley. Kirk is the Captain…"

Tamsin gasped and threw her hands over her mouth. "Oh, Fancy…"

"I know who O'Malley is, lass. But why in the name of Saint Bride herself would ye marry the rapscallion who carried ye off to Barbados and then lied to William about you in July?" My Grandfather might be old, but he was still full of Fitz Simmons starch and vinegar.

I laid my hand on my growing belly and held my head high. I could feel my gut clench and my cheeks redden. Micah Fitz Simmons was not going to humiliate me on my first day in Ireland. By damn, I came too far to turn tail and run now. "I would have thought the answer to that was obvious, sir."

He paled as he realized what I meant. His head jerked up to my face again as tears of grief filled his eyes. "Oh, lass, you didn't have to marry the scoundrel."

I didn't even consider explaining I had to marry him if I wanted my baby born free. I swallowed hard and pulled Kirk closer to me. *Make it believable, Fancy.* I stood up as tall as I could and reached my arm around Kirk again. "But I had to marry him, sir. I love Kirk. And please, don't call my husband a scoundrel."

Damn, it was hard to say that, but somehow, I managed. But then, some days, I could almost believe I loved Kirk. And I felt safe with him. Kirk could calm the terrifying storms of fear when they raged through me, unbidden. I knew he had my six, as Sassy would say. He would watch my back.

But my grandfather's words angered me. Would Lily say his words triggered me? My anger flared, and I had to bite my tongue to keep from telling him what I thought of the real scoundrel, the one who spirited my mother to Ireland without me all those years ago, leaving me to the not-so-tender mercies of Tom Selk, a fate no four-year-old child should have to endure. I don't like to be in confrontational scenes. I feel threatened, unsafe, unwell when I wind up in situations like this one was fast becoming. I could feel my resentment swelling again. I might forgive Tamsin, but I could never be able to forgive Jay Fitz Simmons for convincing her to leave me in the Colony of Virginia when I was four-years-old. I wasn't sure I could forgive Micah Fitz Simmons for raising Jay to be the man he proved to be, the man who would sell his brother and sister to Barbary pirates, and then convince a woman to run off and leave her only child behind. Heck fire, the man who would rape a woman and leave her for dead when he kidnapped her baby.

*Wow. That would have been a mouthful if I said it out loud.*

Marc and Lily shuffled from foot to foot. My half-brother, Fitz, looked like he might either explode or vomit, I wasn't sure which. I knew how he felt. I was feeling mighty sick to my stomach about then, and God knew the whole situation was enough to puke a mule. Fitz had made a sort of peace with Kirk, also, but I knew he was far from friends with my husband.

Fitz's loyalty remained with Richard. I suspected Marc and Lily's commitment did.

Yet despite all Kirk's faults, he was good to me more than he was ever bad. He could calm the storms when they raged through my tormented mind.

Richard could, too. But he left. Twice. Both times without a word.

I'd had worse. Far worse. And at least my new husband wasn't anywhere near as low a dog as Jay had been years before when he raped and damned near killed Lily, kidnapped Michael and somehow convinced my mother to leave me behind when they fled to Ireland, like rats in the night. Jay Fitz Simmons was nothing more than a shameless bastard in my book. He never would be more than that to me.

Oops, my bad. I forgot Jay *was* a bastard, which was why he sold my daddy, the legitimate heir.

Tamsin looked shocked but quickly hid her dismay behind a practiced smile. *Hmm, could she teach me to do that? It could be a handy skill for the Duchess of Ranscome. And God knows, I don't smile enough.*

"Enough of this talking out here on the water. My heaven, it's mid-December. It's cold! I swear it will snow tonight. I can taste it in the air. I'm sure it was never anywhere nearly this cold in Barbados." Tamsin began to stammer.

I rubbed my hands up and down my arms, covered with only my dress sleeves and a light woolen shawl. "No, it was hot there when we left, and I have to admit, I am mighty cold. Perhaps we could all go inside this beautiful house and get warmed up."

Sassy does this thing with her fingers to her eyes that signifies 'I've got my eye on you.' It surprised me to see my grandfather make that sign at Kirk. As Kirk huffed up, I slid in between them and took each man by the arm. "Oh, now, enough of all that nonsense. You two men need to behave yourselves. Come on. Let's go in. I want to see this beautiful home."

Kirk held tight to my arm, his head high, bright pink spots on each cheek, and his nostrils flaring with each breath of the frosty air. His meaning was clear, at least to me. *She's mine. Don't feck with me, old man.* I'd seen him angry before, but I had only seen him this angry that day in Bridgetown when the wedding was interrupted. It impressed me he somehow held his temper in check. I slid my hand into his and squeezed it. He broke his gaze from my Grandfather to me. I smiled.

Kirk smiled back. "I love your granddaughter, sir."

Grandpa made a noise best described as a snort. "Of course, you do. Your great love for Fancy must be why ye lied to William. What's that wee Sassy says? Ah, yes. That was one strike."

I bit back the laugh at the reference to the game Sassy often told us about, and Richard was teaching the children. Now was not the time to laugh.

As Kirk's lips thinned with anger again, Marc spoke up. "Kirk and I had many long talks on this journey. He realizes he was wrong to lie to Will. And yes, I told him it's like that game Sassy says the children played in Mexico when she was a child. I think she called it baseball. I can't say I understand all about the game, but I remember Sass says 'three strikes and you're out.' Kirk understands the lie was his first strike. Three strikes, and like Sassy says, he'll be out. Forewarned is forearmed, aye, Kirk? But I have seen him with my daughter enough that I believe he loves Fancy. I think she loves him. Much like Tam loved Jay when they came here. I don't expect Kirk to get to the third strike."

Grandpa made that snorting sound again. "He'd best not, or there will be hell to pay. Wonderful. So, she's in love with a sailor when she could have had a doctor. With her title, she could have had a prince. Mark my words, he'll never stay home with ye for very long, lass. His first mistress is the sea…"

"Is that what you think of Will, too? Because he's been at sea longer than Kirk." I snapped the words out as my grip tightened on Kirk's arm.

Grandpa looked shocked. "No, but…"

And once again, my temper flared. "I mean you no disrespect, sir, but you know nothing about this man or all he has done for me in the past eight months. Please keep your opinions to yourself until you get to know my husband and me. And I will try to hold my tongue about your scoundrel son who brought my mother here long ago without me. How he convinced her to abandon me in Virginia when he brought Michael with them. And I remember the other things he did before they came here. I won't insult Lily by describing them…"

My voice broke with unexpected emotion.

"That's enough, Fancy. Stop it. Don't throw mud." Marc's anger was palpable. I cringed as he pulled a wide-eyed, pale Lily into the protection of his arms.

My Grandpa looked shocked. And hurt. His lip trembled a bit as we continued to walk towards the house. *Oh, great. I can usually control my temper. Why not today? Now I've hurt my grandfather's feelings.*

Plus, Fitz was Jay's son. I felt shame for having insulted his father, who Fitz never knew. My words about his father had to sting.

But as I glanced up to Kirk, I noticed the look on his face.

"Aye, that's my Wee Duchess. 'Though she may be little, she is fierce.'" My Captain beamed with pride.

My Grandfather looked at him sharply. "That's a quote from *A Midsummer Night's Dream*. Ye ken Shakespeare?"

Kirk smiled slightly. "Aye. We read a lot at sea. 'Oh, when she's angry, she's keen and shrewd! She was a vixen when she went to school. And though she is but little, she is fierce.' I believe it was Act Three…"

"Scene Two," Grandpa said, surprise clear in his voice. "Well, I'll be damned. Now I've seen everything. A sailor who quotes Shakespeare."

"Mister Jo taught it to me long ago. He taught me a lot about Shakespeare. He used that quote to describe Fancy even back then. T'was on the voyage from Ireland back to Virginia in late '64. He told me he was missing the lass somethin' terrible. I had just turned 20 and become the first mate on the ship. Mr. Jo told me his Wee Duchess was little, but she was fierce, and t'would take a firm man to husband her."

Grandpa looked surprised. "Jo Selk said that? To you?"

Kirk nodded. "Aye, sir, he did. He said, 'O'Malley, t'will take a firm man to husband the lass someday, for though she be but little, my wee lass is fierce.' I remember we both laughed when he said that. I never dreamed I would someday meet his wee, fierce lass, much less marry her. However, you'll find, sir, I am a far sight stronger man than is Dr. Richard Winslow. Jo Selk and the sea made me strong enough for *mo leannan*."

*It might depend on your definition of strength*, I thought, with more than a little resentment, but I bit my tongue. Now was not the time. That would come later. And besides, the story Kirk wove about Jo and him talking about me, was well worth hearing.

And then my Grandpa near ruined the moment when he made the 'eyes' motion again to Kirk, and then held up one finger before he silently mouthed, "Strike one."

I shook my head at him with a loud shush. My grandfather sniffed and then shrugged as if he couldn't care less whether he embarrassed Kirk or anyone. I shook my head, already frustrated at the outright animosity showed by my grandfather towards my husband in less than five minutes of our arrival.

We entered the house in awkward silence. I gasped as I looked around. Marc was right. The home was exquisite, probably the prettiest place I would ever see. As we entered the foyer from the garden, we could see through to the gardens on the other side of the house, the proper entrance. The way the sunlight filled the rooms seemed to pull the gardens inside the enchanting home. Off to the left of the foyer was the dining room, and to the right was the parlor. An elegant mahogany table with twelve matching claw-footed chairs filled the dining room. Gold and cream silk covered the chair seats. The most beautiful china I had ever seen adorned the table. Through an open door in the dining room, I peered into an enormous kitchen. After my look into the beautiful dining room, we entered the parlor, also decorated in gold and cream. A pianoforte and an exquisite harp sat across from a comfortable chair, covered in plush silk velvet.

My grandfather settled himself into the chair as Tamsin showed me around the rooms. I figured Tamsin often entertained my grandfather there. I remembered she could play both instruments and loved to sing, although I don't recollect her singing for the family much when I was small. She would sing me songs at bedtime. I sorely missed the nightly lullabies when she ran off with Jay. I could see another door at the back of the parlor opened to a room lined with books. *That must be his library, or perhaps his office.* The bedrooms should be upstairs unless they adapted the office into a bedroom for my Grandfather now that he was so old and frail. And in every room, the sun poured in to fill them with golden light.

Tamsin rattled on and on, trying to fill the uncomfortable silence. I forced a smile. "It is exquisite. I never dreamed people lived in anything so beautiful."

She beamed and reached out to squeeze my hand. "I'm so pleased you like it. Come on. I have so much more to show you."

Laughing at her unexpected exuberance and enthusiasm — not things I remembered about her at all — I let her lead me through the remaining rooms.

It was like a dream palace for the fey folk. The family says Ginny always planned to name her daughter Gentry, in honor of the gentry, which is the Irish name for the fey folk. That's how my cousin got her English name. Bright Star is her Cherokee name. She is petite with ebony hair and sparkling blue eyes, much like they say the fey folk look. All the 'English' relatives, as the Cherokees call the Colonists, refer to her as Gentry, although I called her Star when I lived at McCarron's Corner in '78 and '79 with Sassy. This home was fit for the gentry or any other royalty who might come calling. I can't think of a word better than exquisite to describe it. Maybe splendiferous, if that's even a word.

I have to admit that I tend to create words.

At last, Tamsin took me to a large bedroom upstairs overlooking the bay. Tamsin decorated the room in pinks and mauves, with a French-styled canopy bed and chest. A small, elegant writing desk sat before a window overlooking the water. A nightstand stood next to the bed with a rose-colored oil lamp atop it. A pale pink and cream rug covered the floor. It looked like it might be an Aubusson. There was a framed, needlepoint canvas of an adolescent girl dressed in pink hung on the wall above the bed.

"This is your room. I thought you would be much younger when you came. It seems a little young for you now. We can always change it."

My heart lurched. Tamsin sounded nervous, worried I might not like the room. It was the room she designed for her little girl. I realized with a start that the needlepoint resembled what I looked around the time she left. "Who did the needlepoint?"

She blushed. "I did."

My mouth went dry as tears welled up in my eyes at those two words. When Tamsin could not have me there, she painted me with wool and canvas to keep a memory of me alive forever in the room she decorated for me. Lord knows I would have dearly loved to have grown up in this setting. As my hands shook again, I squeezed her hand and forced a smile. "It's beautiful. I wouldn't want to change a thing here."

I frowned and then reached for the chatelaine hanging at my waist. On the writing desk sat a small painting that looked like the miniature of me in the chatelaine. I looked from one to the other, comparing the artwork. "Mama, did you paint this and the miniature in the chatelaine? Fitz said you painted the miniature."

She smiled. "No, Fitz is mistaken. Your Grampa did both. He used to be handy with a brush. Isn't it lovely? He painted it from memory based on the painting of you at Belle Rose. I must admit the hair color is a bit off. He wanted to make you look older than in the painting we saw when we came to Belle Rose right after Jo died. I thought your hair would have darkened over the years to the auburn in the painting. Oh, well, if that is all we got wrong, I guess we did well."

It amazed me that a man who had never met me nor seen me before could paint a projection of what I would look like in my teen years. It touched my heart. I could tell it meant so much to Tamsin for the old man to paint these for her. The resemblance in the needlework and the paintings was remarkable. You could tell it was the same girl, only older in the portraits than in the needlepoint. I studied the little painting for a minute before I squared my shoulders to broach the subject. I knew she would not want to hear this.

"Mama, you know we will go to Ranscome Manor soon—"

She grabbed both my hands and started shaking her head. I realized her hands were shaking with growing dismay and alarm. "Oh, no, Fancy, you must stay here, at least until the baby comes. You will want to remodel that musty old house before you move way over there. My heavens, they built it when Elizabeth was Queen way back in the 1500s. It's over two hundred years old! No one has lived there for ages. It needs all new bed linens and curtains, and my heavens, you'll want new furniture. Order those from London, or maybe even from Paris. Plus, Ranscome Manor is plumb on the other side of Cork, at least thirty kilometers from here. Please, baby girl, you must stay here. I just got you back. I couldn't bear for you to rush right off. You have to stay, at least for a little while."

I cringed as her voice broke, and a hand flew to her face to cover her mouth as she struggled not to cry. Oh, merciful heaven, I never expected the desperation in her voice, much less her clinging to me as if her life depended on it. As tears welled up in her beautiful Selk blue eyes, I forced another smile and pulled her close to hug her. "Maybe we better see if these two men of ours can get along without trying to murder each other first before we make any long-range plans."

She blinked a couple of times as she tried to control her disappointment and then smiled again. "Perhaps that would be best. But…"

"But what, Mama?"

"Know you are always welcome here, Fancy. Always. I can't believe you are finally here, after all those years."

As she pulled me back into her arms again, I noticed a little muscle twitched by the side of her mouth. Suddenly, I remembered it used to do that when something upset her. I patted her trembling hands, surprised they looked so much like mine. "It's okay, Mama. It will all work out fine. You'll see."

I had a lump in my throat about the size of a roasted turkey as we went back to join the others in the parlor. Lily says, 'the solution for tomorrow is in the bosom of the present.' Hmm. I wonder if that's why my heart hurts so much sometimes? Maybe some of those solutions are just too big for one little heart to handle. I reckon I must ask Lily about that.

Dinner was quiet as everyone was on their best behavior. It impressed me that Grandpa, as I had decided to call him, did not attack Kirk again. Kirk stayed on impeccable behavior without the slightest temper flare. I was proud of him, but it exhausted me, physically as well as emotionally. I turned in soon after the tense, uncomfortable dinner ended. The nanny had already fed the children and put them to bed.

I'm not sure what time it was when The Incident occurred.

I was sound asleep by the time Kirk came to join me. I awoke with a start as Kirk stumbled over the desk chair. I placed it by the side of the bed so he would have a place to sit and pull off his boots. I knew my husband had been drinking rum downstairs by the warm scent of the liquor that wafted into the room with him. I figured he felt more than a little 'frisky.' Plus, I knew he was feeling more than a little intimidated by the gorgeous manor house and the cantankerous elderly gentleman who owned it. I was sure Kirk tried to come in without waking me up to snuggle up and rouse me with fondling and kisses. As he tripped over the chair, he cursed at his clumsiness. "Dammit, I was tryin' to slip in here and see if ye might want to get naked."

I had grown great with my unborn child, but he still desired me, God bless his heart. How could I turn down a man who lusted for me in my condition? I raised, giggling as I lifted my night rail over my head. I dropped the delicate garment to the bed. "Let me light the lamp."

I reached for the pretty rose-colored oil lamp sitting beside the bed on the night table. I intended to turn the flame up so Kirk could see. Instead, I knocked the lamp off the table. I let out a brief shriek as Kirk and I both hustled to put out the fire on the floor. I slid off the tester bed, hit my face on the nightstand, and somehow, my long hair caught fire.

About the time we beat out the fire on the floor and on my smoldering hair, the bedroom door burst open. Marc glowered at us both. "What the bloody hell is going on in here?"

At that point, I didn't know whether to laugh or cry, so I did both. I laughed like a half-crazed loon, with tears running down my face, my hair still smoking from the fire. "It's okay, Daddy—"

Kirk realized I was lying on the floor naked as a jaybird. His face turned beet red as he jerked the quilt off the bed to cover my body.

Marc's eyes grew wide, and his expression changed from concern to fury as he looked at me, lying on the floor naked and sobbing. It seemed he crossed the room in a flash and grabbed Kirk up by his collar. As he began shaking Kirk, he demanded answers. "What the feckin' hell is going on, O'Malley? Why are my daughter's hair smoking and her face battered? So, help me, man, if you dared raise a hand to her…"

As Kirk paled and stammered, I scrambled up from the floor, clutching the quilt about me and threw myself between them. "No, Daddy, no, I knocked the lamp over and fell off the bed. Kirk never touched me except to help me!"

Marc's hands stopped mid-air. He was angrier than I had ever seen him in my entire life. "O'Malley, if you ever raise a hand to my daughter, I'll kill you. I don't care if you've had your three blasted strikes or not. You ever hurt my girl? So, help me God, you'll be dead. I'll tell God ye died, and he'll believe me."

Silent, eyes wide with shock, Kirk nodded. He began babbling something, but I have no idea what he was saying in Irish. Marc looked unimpressed as he continued to glower at Kirk.

"Daddy, I swear, he didn't hit me. I reached to turn up the lamp, I lost my balance, and I fell off the bed. I hit my face on the table. Let's face it; I'm not my most graceful self right now. My land, I'm as big as the side of a barn! The lamp hit the floor, and Kirk and I were trying to put out the fire. Kirk did not hit me."

Marc was breathing hard. He did not look like he was buying a word I uttered. As I clutched the quilt about me with one hand, I stomped my foot and gave Marc a little shake with my free hand.

"Marcus McCarron Fitz Simmons, have I ever lied to you? Do you think I would cover for Kirk or anyone if they hit me and set my hair on fire? For God's sake, Daddy, it was an accident. Look at his hands. He put the fire out with his bare hands!"

Marc's hands dropped. He took a couple of deep breaths to calm himself as Kirk took a couple of deep breaths to stay alive. Finally, Marc looked at me and then back to Kirk. It upset me when Marc made the same 'eyes on you' motion my Grandpa made at Kirk earlier at the dock. I realized I was crying.

"It still holds. You ever lay a hand on my girl, and I swear to the Almighty I'll kill you with my own bare hands. And believe me, I've lived with the Cherokees in Indian Territory long enough that I know ways to kill a man that you never want to consider. Not to mention the God-awful things I learned from the Barbary pirates. Understand?"

Eyes wide as saucers, Kirk nodded. "I understand, sir."

Marc looked from Kirk to me and then said, "Fancy, if this *man* ever hurts you …"

I cringed at the scorn in Marc's voice as he uttered 'man.'

I shook my head. "He did *not* hurt me, Daddy. He was hitting my hair to extinguish the fire. It's not his fault! For heaven's sake, Daddy, look at his hands. They're burned."

Lily entered the room and looked around with a shocked expression. She slipped up beside Kirk and took one of his large hands into hers. "He burned his hands, Marc. I need to treat this."

Kirk jerked his hand from her without taking his eyes off Marc. "I'll be fine, Lily. Don't waste your time worrying about the sorry likes of me. Check on Fancy."

She nodded as she moved to me. "Are you all right?"

I nodded. "Yes, Kirk put the fire out where my hair caught fire. We will most likely have to trim it some tomorrow. I imagine it looks like a hot mess right now. He burned his hands."

She nodded. "I can see that. Kirk, you need to ice your hands."

"I said, don't worry about me, Lily. I'll be fine," Kirk snapped, shaking with rage. 'Believe me; I've suffered worse before."

Marc looked mollified. "Fine. You say it was an accident, Fancy. I'll give him this one. But so, help me God, if this man ever hurts you…"

He didn't finish. He didn't have to. We all knew what was left unsaid. I could tell Marc still didn't believe me.

I held up one of Kirk's hands. "Look at this, Daddy. Kirk burned himself, saving me. He did not hurt me."

He blanched at the sight of Kirk's burnt hand, already forming large blisters across his palms and fingers. "Fine. I still meant what I said."

Kirk jerked his hand away from Marc and walked over to the window. He threw the window open and took deep breaths of the cold air as I hurried to his side to scoop up some of the new-fallen snow on the windowsill into the bowl that had been sitting on the desk. I heard him draw a breath in and felt him tense as I stuck his hands into the snow. I dreaded to think how bad it hurt.

"Keep your hands in the snow until the pain stops, Kirk. And you will probably need some medicine on those burns…" Lily began.

He nodded his head. "I'll be fine. My *wife* will tend to my hands."

His voice was terse, his tone clipped. His Irish temper was showing loud and clear. His meaning was unmistakable. He did not want Lily's help after Marc's attack.

Lily looked uncertain about what to do. "B-but—"

"I'll come to get you if I need anything else, Lily. Thank you." I tried to smile.

She nodded. "Keep them iced in the snow at least a half-hour. Tomorrow, we will find some Aloe Vera to put on his hands."

"Not butter? I always thought you used butter on a burn." Her instructions surprised me.

"No, the ice takes the heat out and stops the burn from worsening. Butter can make a burn worse. It's like buttering up that steak on the grill. Call me if you need me." After the slightest pause, she turned to push a glowering Marc out of the room.

Kirk bent to kiss my forehead. "I'll be fine."

"I know, but let me fuss over you. Usually, it's you worrying over me."

He smiled and then cringed at the cold on his burns.

"I can tell your hands hurt. Silly man, don't pretend those burns don't pain you something terrible." I scolded him as I gathered his burned hands into mine and bent to kiss them.

His eyes softened as he looked down at me. "Aye, a bit. Damn, it smarts."

Oh, yes, I could tell it would be a lovely visit to Waterside.

# Chapter 3
# And Then There Was the Weird Stuff Commencing Christmas 1782

"Mommy, Mommy, wake up, it's Christmas!"

I awoke, laughing. Two excited children climbed on top of me to awaken me. We had been at Waterside for the past two weeks since we arrived in Ireland. Kirk traipsed back and forth to Ranscome Manor to ready it for us to move, while I nested at Waterside to await the birth of my baby.

Kirk followed the children into the room, grinning as he carried in the tray of hot chocolate. Bella handed me my dressing gown as I arose from the bed, and I reached for the steaming cup of my beloved chocolate.

"Give Mommy a big hug and a kiss and then let me get dressed to come downstairs. Charlie, don't jostle the bed. I'll spill the hot chocolate." I tried to coax year-old exuberant Charlie to stop bouncing on the bed.

Kirk grabbed Charlie up off the bed mid-bounce and tickled the toddler until he laughed with glee. The children gave me wet, chocolatey kisses and turned to leave our room. I could tell by the loud footsteps that they rushed down the curved staircase towards the parlor below where Christmas awaited.

How could this man be wonderful one minute and *not* the next? I would never understand. He kept me in a constant state of confusion.

Kirk helped me dress in the blue velvet robe volante I made for Christmas. He laughed as I shook my head in disgust. The robe bulged over my belly in a most unladylike and unstylish manner.

"My land, if I get any bigger…" I grumbled with frustration growing as fast as my belly.

"You look beautiful, and you know it. Here, run the brush through your hair. God, I love your glorious red-gold tresses. Now, let's go downstairs before those children drive your grandfather crazy. He's close to losing his patience. They have been ready to rip into the presents for over an hour."

I quickly brushed the snarls from my hair. I tied a blue velvet ribbon into an enormous bow to hold my 'glorious red-gold tresses' back from my face before I slipped my aching and swollen feet into my matching slippers. Kirk helped me down the stairs to make our way to the parlor where the children were loudly singing Christmas songs as they waited for us. As we entered the room, Bella squealed with excitement and ran to hug me again.

"Can we open our presents now, Mama?" Bella bounced up and down, filled with Christmas excitement.

"May we." I gently corrected my daughter as I laughed.

She grinned. "May we open our presents now?"

"Ask your Grandpa." I smiled at my grandfather.

My grandfather smiled as he nodded. "Aye, you may start passing out the presents, Bella."

Charles and she both squealed with excitement and dove for the presents beneath the Christmas bough. This Christmas was Charles' first. He was little, but he understood what *presents* were. Bella began sounding out names and then carried the gifts to each of us. When the children handed out all the packages, we began opening our gifts. Each person opened one present at a time, so we could all see what was inside the gift before opening the next. The children opened their presents first. The beautiful doll Marc and I found in Cork thrilled Bella as much as I had been years before when Marc brought my Dara doll from Ireland. This pretty doll wore a red and green plaid dress. I chose this dolly because she had brown hair and blue eyes, like my beautiful child. Charlie began building a 'fort' with his new blocks. Bella squealed again with delight when she opened a present from me, a blue velvet dress like mine for her and a matching dress for her new doll. Charlie was oblivious to anything except the blocks Fitz crafted for him. My son sat building things as he sang off-key. His singing is so awful you would think he is related to Sassy. The child could not carry a tune in a bucket, but he loved to sing.

My grandfather seemed pleased with the dressing gown I stitched for him on the voyage from Barbados. I made it from a beautiful piece of indigo blue and white fabric Kirk swore came from India. I added a white cotton pique collar and cuffs, which I quilted with blue cotton embroidery floss. I was quite pleased with the result. I knew it was increasingly difficult for my Grampa to get out of bed some days. I thought the dressing gown would enable him to look handsome and well dressed, whether still in bed or sitting in his comfortable chair.

I nibbled on a fingernail as Tamsin opened her gift. I had not known what to get her until I saw the piano and harp. With a little stealthy snooping, I discovered what sheet music she owned. I could buy her the newest sheet music available at the music shop in Cork. Her eyes misted with tears as she beamed at me. "You couldn't have given me anything better."

I laughed. "Next year, I promise I will make you something pretty. My Mama taught me how to sew at an early age, you know."

She laughed as well. "You remember that?"

Wordless, I nodded. I got my love of needlework from her. She had me learning to sew when I was no bigger than Charles. She still did some of the prettiest needlework I ever saw.

And then I gasped as I opened the box from her. "Oh, Tamsin, I... I..."

I cried. It was a shift edged with the most exquisite, hand-tatted lace I had ever seen.

"Oh, baby girl, don't cry. It's just a little ol' shift..." Tamsin stammered with embarrassment.

"You tatted the lace yourself. Don't deny it. I've seen you working on that lace since we got here. Oh, Mama--"

I was bawling like a baby as she rushed to my side to wrap me in her arms. I rubbed the fabric of her sleeve back and forth as she comforted me. I wanted a memory of this moment imprinted in my mind forever.

Lily beamed at Marc, who once again bought her new medical books he had shipped from the Continent. I can never get over how this woman goes all gooey over the most boring old medical books. This year, she also beamed with excitement over the dried herbs I brought from Barbados, each with a description of its medicinal use on the island. Several of the herbs originated from Africa. I had it all put into a mahogany chest I obtained from the apothecary in Bridgetown. We soon lost Lily's attention as she investigated the box and its contents. The rest of us continued to open our presents. You would have thought I gave her a box of diamonds. Well, Marc calls her his Diamond Lil. She always laughs, like she knows some enormous joke about Marc calling her that which she hasn't shared with the rest of us. Hmm. Come to think of it, maybe she does.

Marc beamed over the linen shirts I made him, as did Kirk. "I didn't do as much for you two as I planned. I ran out of time and energy. I promise I will make you both something nice once the baby arrives."

Marc grinned and came over to kiss my cheek. "Girl, having you with us is all the gift I wanted."

I beamed at my Daddy. "You always know exactly what to say."

I opened boxes for the new baby of little gowns and blankets, all lovingly made by Tamsin and Lily. They touched me. As much as Lily hates to sew, she made things for my baby. I knew these were gifts straight from their hearts, especially for those two women to have worked on the project together for me. Let's face it: they have never been close. Thanks to them, my baby would have an elegant wardrobe.

My grandfather gave me the baby cradle, which had been Dara and Marc's, crafted of oak with Celtic knotwork carved into the back of it. "Long ago, I made that cradle myself."

I beamed with pride as I ran my hands over the beautiful oak cradle. "Oh, Grandpa, I love it. Thank you."

"Fitz used it as well," Tamsin said. "The carving is the tree of life."

I tilted my head at her, not sure what she meant.

"The knotwork on the cradle symbolizes the tree of life. Papa carved the cradle from oak, a sacred tree in Ireland."

She flashed another Duchess-worthy smile at me. It was a shame I was the Duchess instead of her. My mother would have made a fabulous Duchess of Ranscome.

I looked up, surprised at her words. "That makes it even more special. I will consider this to be on loan until Fitz marries and has children of his own. It should follow in the Fitz Simmons family."

Fitz turned beet red as we all laughed. "That may be awhile, you understand. I've not received an answer from Nicole yet. Mayhap she is hoping for a better catch than someone who will only be an Earl someday. Oh, here."

He shoved a package into my lap.

I grinned as I unwrapped the awkward box and then gasped. "Oh, Fitz, it's beautiful."

It was a carved mobile to hang over the new baby's crib. An Irish harp, a wise old owl, a ball, oak leaves, and blocks were all carved of oak wood and strung together with knotted lengths of silken cord. Fitz made each by hand and painted each with love.

"Ah, it's nothing, ye silly girl. Just some things I carved on the voyage home."

I laughed as he blushed beet red, and then I hugged him tight as I handed him his present. He beamed with pride at the hand-knit scarf, cap, and matching gloves. "Thank you, Fancy. I'll get excellent use of these at my next post."

We all grew silent at his words. Fitz had received official notification of his transfer to Canada. None of us were happy about it, even though it came with a promotion for Captain Winston Fitz Simmons. "Well, you need to go over there and see that girl and learn if she wants to go on a grand adventure to the New World with you. I reckon Canada would be the most exciting honeymoon."

He nodded. "Or whether Nicole wants to remain here while I go freezin' myself silly there."

Tam fussed, tears welling up in her eyes. "I still think Viscount Fitz Simmons should be exempt from going. He needs to be starting a family here at home."

Fitz cut his eyes at her. "Not now, Mam."

She frowned, but hushed. No one wanted to say my Grampa might not be around much longer, but we were all aware this would probably be the last Christmas he would be with us. He became more frail by the day.

Marc and Lily's gift to me was in a gigantic box. I gasped when I lifted the lid off and pulled back the layers of tissue paper covering the large Kinsale cloak made with an attached hood, constructed from soft, luxuriant purple and green Irish mohair wool and lined with purple silk. I had been complaining of the bitter cold ever since we arrived in Ireland.

"You'll be warm now." Lily grinned mischievously.

I nodded as I rubbed the fabric of the beautiful cloak against the side of my face. "I sure will. Thank you both."

My Grampa grinned as I opened a box with a matching mohair scarf and gloves. I rubbed the soft fabric against my cheek. I realized they might be the only gifts I would ever receive from him. "Thank you, Grampa. I will treasure these."

Finally, Kirk handed me a little jeweler's box wrapped in silver tissue with a blue velvet ribbon. I tried to frown. "This is all? It sure is little."

He laughed. "Aye, my Wee Duchess, but as they say, wonderful things come in compact packages."

I laughed. Kirk dubbed me that the first day at Waterside. I was just about to open the little box when there was a knock at the front door. As we all looked up, I realized we had unexpected company for Christmas.

The children jumped up and ran to the foyer to hug their cousins as Will and Sassy entered the room.

I paled and sat up a little straighter as Richard entered the room. I slipped the small box into my pocket. I could open it later. I held my new gloves in my lap, rubbing the luxurious fabric back and forth to calm myself as my heart clamored in my chest.

Richard looked nervous and uncomfortable. He went first to my grandfather, who hugged him like he was the Prodigal Son returned home. Richard next shook hands with Marc, who pulled him close to thump his back. Finally, he turned to me.

"Merry Christmas, Francesca." His eyes grew enormous as he noticed my enormous belly. He glanced back to my eyes, the unspoken questions all over his face. *When is this baby due? Whose baby is it?*

I gulped and looked away. I could feel the flush creep up my neck to color my cheeks with bright red spots. I couldn't face the query right then. I tried to paste a Tamsin worthy smile on my face as I looked back at him, and I held out my hand. "Hello, Richard. You are looking very well."

A grim look replaced Kirk's laughter and relaxed demeanor of a few minutes before Richard arrived. Kirk came over to stand beside me, and he draped a possessive arm around my shoulders. "My wife and I didn't expect to see you here, Dr. Winslow."

Kirk bent to kiss my cheek as he slowly trailed his hand down my arm. His unspoken warning was clear. *Mine, Winslow. Back off. She's mine.*

I flashed a quick smile up at my husband as I grabbed and squeezed his hand. I realized with dismay that my hands were shaking. "No, we didn't. But it's always good to see family, especially at Christmas."

Damn. How do I always marry jealous men? Then again, perhaps they both knew full well of whom they should be wary.

Bella bounded up to Richard and threw her hands up for him to lift her to him for a kiss. He smiled and laughed as he lifted her into his arms. She snuggled closer, but we could all hear her stage whisper.

"I knew you would come. Now Christmas will be perfect!"

*I wish you would have told me*, I thought, as my fingers rubbed the plush fabric of my gown back-and-forth between my trembling fingers, hoping the familiar back and forth pattern would soothe my frazzled nerves. Even the luxurious, silken nap of the velvet failed to help calm my emotions. The rhythmical movement of cloth against my fingers usually settles my nerves, but the old technique didn't work then. I realized I was doing what Lily calls 'disassociating' when I tried to distance myself emotionally from what was going on, but believe me, right then that disassociative thing, whatever it is, seemed appropriate. Sure enough, as I rubbed the velvet of my gown back-and-forth, the tightness in my chest slowly eased, my hands shook less, and I felt better in control of my emotions. My heavens, if you can feel that much better from just rubbing a little ol' bit of fabric back and forth between your fingers, why on earth wouldn't I do it?

We all engaged in idle chatter while the cook sat the food out in the dining room, and then we went into the sumptuous Christmas brunch. I had eaten goose before, and I usually like it. That day, I found it rich and greasy for my taste. I thought maybe Irish goose tasted richer. Lily thought my reaction to it was because of my advanced pregnancy. I cringed at her words and struggled not to glance at Richard. I lost the struggle. He was staring at me as if trying to read my thoughts. I dropped my eyes back to my plate and continued to piddle with the now cold slice of grease-covered goose. I pushed the dish back in disgust as I realized I had lost my appetite.

Finally, as they cleared the dishes, Kirk urged me to open my present. "Go ahead, my love. I think you'll like it."

Anything to change the subject, I thought with relief. I flashed Kirk a smile as I fished the little box out of my pocket. With a flourish, I untied the ribbon, removed the silver tissue, and opened the lid to the jeweler's box.

I blinked. I could feel the blood drain away from my face. Suddenly, the whole scene seemed unreal, more like something I was watching from a distance than something happening to me. I looked over to Kirk. No, he didn't seem to have a clue his gift might upset me. I struggled to keep the trembling of my hands from showing while I blinked the threatening tears back. Finally, I swallowed hard, and then somehow asked, "Where did you get this?"

He grinned and reached over for the box. I snatched it back from his hands.

"No, answer me. Where did you get this?" My voice wavered with emotion.

"Don't you like it? I thought you would love it." He looked concerned and hurt.

I slammed the little box down on the table so hard that he jumped. "Answer me, Kirk. Where did you get this?"

I then held up the box so everyone could see the beautiful ring in the box. Lily gasped and threw her hands over her mouth. Sassy's mouth fell agape and I could almost see the steam coming from Will's ears. Marc turned red in the face and he arose, but not before Richard was already across the table, grabbing Kirk up by the collar.

"God damn it, O'Malley, I want to know, too. Where the bloody hell did you get this ring?"

The men were close to blows when I banged my hands down hard on the table. I raised the ring box again. "Kirk, I'll ask it one more time. Where did you get this ring?"

Kirk looked stunned by not just my reaction but the reactions of Richard, Sassy, Will, Marc, and Lily. He swallowed hard several times before he answered. "I bought it in Baltimore ..."

I picked up the beautiful oval aquamarine engagement ring Richard gave me the night before my kidnapping in April. As tears filled my eyes to overflowing, I placed the ring back in the jeweler's box. "I can't accept this ring, Kirk. But I can return it to where it belongs."

I handed it to Richard.

Kirk turned purple with rage. "What the bloody... That ring cost a bloody fortune. Why are you giving it to him, of all people?"

I pushed back from the table and arose. "Because this is the ring Richard gave me on April 5th when he asked me to marry him. Since our betrothal ended without marriage, I think the least I can do is return the ring to Richard, especially considering he had it made for me."

"I had it made for *you*, Francesca. It's *yours*..." Richard protested.

I shook my head. "No, you gave it to me as an *engagement* ring to pledge our intention to marry. I need to return it to you." I tucked it into his outstretched hand and curled his fingers around the box. "Please, Richard, take the ring..."

Richard stared at me before he finally nodded and tucked the ring box into his jacket pocket.

Kirk looked stunned. "Fancy, I didn't have any idea. I bought it in Baltimore."

"Remember when I regained consciousness on the ship? You told me Tarleton sold me to you. I told you I was engaged to another man. I asked if I was wearing my engagement ring when the men brought me onboard your ship. You said you saw no such ring."

"You weren't..." he began.

"But here's the ring, Kirk. You claim you found it in Baltimore, the same town where you bought me. Did Tarleton sell you the ring when he sold me to you?"

"No, I swear, Fancy, I bought it in August when I sailed north. I found it in the shop named on the box. I knew you said you lost a blue ring..."

"An engagement ring," I interjected.

He swallowed hard. "I saw this one, and I thought you would like it. I never dreamed it was the same ring..."

"Strike two." Marc's low, quiet voice reverberated with menace.

Kirk looked at Marc in shock, stunned by his tone even more than his ominous words. "But Marc, I swear..."

Marc shook his head as he pushed back from the table to come over to me. As he gathered me into his arms, he repeated, "Strike two, Kirk. I warned you. Three strikes, and you will be out of her life. Forever. This is strike two."

Kirk looked around the table. He held his hands up as if imploring us to believe him. "I swear, I didn't know it was the same ring..."

My grandfather glared at him. All the men glared at him. Sassy and Lily looked shocked. Tamsin reached over and took one of my trembling hands into hers and began to gently stroke it, back-and-forth. The children sat silently at their little table at the end of the room. Their nanny cleared her throat and coaxed them out of the room.

As they reached the door, Bella turned back to Kirk. "I finally liked you." She put her hands on her hips, shook her head and looked at me. "I knew you should have married Rick."

Bella shook her head again and turned to walk on out of the dining room.

Out of the mouths of babes, as they always say.

Oh, yes, when he is good, he is wonderful, but when Kirk O'Malley is bad, he is an extraordinary ass.

# Chapter 4
# Fancy, Bonnie And Then Some
# 1783

As luck would have it, I went past January 5th. I hoped and prayed to deliver my baby nine months to the day after Richard and I last engaged in sexual intimacies, if not a tad early. It was not to be. My water broke on the morning of January 20th, halfway between the last time I was with Richard and the first time I was with Kirk. I gave birth to Dara Siobhan O'Malley Selk after a short, hard labor. We named her after both Marc's sister and Kirk's mother. We would call her Bonnie.

Fortunately, my heart held out. Lily said the murmur sounded worse, but somehow, I survived the birth. We both agreed I should not have another baby for a while, if ever, so she put this thing she called an IDU (or did she say IUD?) inside me to prevent me from conceiving another child soon. I did not understand how the tiny contraption worked, but Lily swore the small device Richard brought from Beyond would keep me from getting pregnant. A doctor must remove it *if* I ever want to have another baby.

Kirk would not know I avoided another pregnancy. I feared he might not take 'no' for an answer, and I wanted to prepare. Lily shook her head at that.

As expected, Lily blood-typed my baby. She types everyone's blood who allows her. It amuses me that while almost everyone will let a physician bleed them, some folks can be so suspicious of a bit of blood wiped on a piece of paper. My Bonnie was O negative. The news thrilled me. It must mean Richard was her father. And then Lily dropped the bombshell. Both Kirk and Richard have O negative blood.

"You mean either of them…" My voice faded off in horror.

She nodded, grim-faced. "Exactly. At that, she is a size that could be a small nine-month baby or a large eight-month baby. She could be Rick's baby and a little late, or Kirk's baby, and a little early. I'm sorry, honey, but the blood type alone won't get you where you want to be."

I jerked my head towards her, stunned by her comment, astonished she realized what I had hoped to announce. I swallowed hard and shrugged. "Well, I reckon that means Tarleton more than likely isn't her sire. Surely, he isn't O negative, too. But with no clear-cut decision based on her blood type, I guess that means I proceed with Plan B."

She looked stricken, if not downright horrified. She blinked twice and then took off her spectacles and wiped them slowly. "Oh, honey, are you sure you want to go through with this?"

I gulped. God knew this could get me killed, but what choice did I have? I had thought about this alternative since I talked with the minister that night in Barbados. He was the one who suggested it. Kirk could never know the minister helped me with this scheme. I later discussed the audacious plan with Marc and Lily. Marc was all for it, especially after Kirk's second strike. Lily, not so much. I squared my shoulders. "Nevermore so."

Marc and I consulted with an attorney in Cork after the Christmas debacle over the ring. Kirk was at Ranscome Manor overseeing repairs and did not realize Marc took me to see Mr. O'Halloran about anything but Betty. It surprised and pleased Kirk when I offered to adopt his daughter, Betty. The lawyer had already filed the petition for me to adopt her. The plan was we would bring Betty back with us when we went to visit his mother after I legally became Betty's guardian.

It outraged the elderly barrister when I told him how Kirk trapped me into indenture and forced me to marry him so my baby would not be born a slave for life. He then laughed when I told him how I connived to get Kirk to bring us back to Ireland, where I figured the Duchess of Ranscome could get the marriage annulled. I might be conflicted, but Christmas Day pretty well pushed any doubts I had about this out of my mind. When I saw that beautiful ring, I believed Kirk knew who I was from the 'get-go' when Tarleton sold me to him.

"Ah, but, your Grace, the marriage is already *void ab initio*. That means it was void, or invalid, from the outset of the marriage since it was illegal for Mr. O'Malley to marry a person of color such as yourself in Barbados. You were wise not to mention your status there, or the court could have determined you to be a slave for life. I am not at all sure it was legal to put a Duchess of the Realm into indenture."

I thought Marc's eyes might bug out of his head. I chuckled.

"I know. That's what the minister told me in Bridgetown. That's why I waited until we got back here to raise the issue."

I mentioned nothing that had happened since we arrived in Ireland.

He chuckled again. "Your Grace, you don't need an annulment. You need a legal declaration by the Court the marriage is void. That will get the scoundrel out of your house and out of your home."

He didn't say it, but I knew what he meant. *And out of your bed, Fancy Girl, if not entirely out of your conflicted heart.* I took a deep breath. "Fine. Then please prepare the paperwork. But don't mention this to my husband."

He nodded. "Of course, Your Grace. You are my client, not Capt. O'Malley."

He prepared a brief on the subject and a petition for declaratory judgment to have the chancellery court in Cork rule the marriage void. He assured me they would sign the adoption within days and without delay. I planned to adopt one orphan child known as Betty O'Malley, with a name change to Elizabeth O'Malley Selk. The papers did not mention Kirk at all. She would be *my* child. Kirk could *never* take her from me.

As soon as they signed the adoption, the attorney would move for Declaratory Judgment that the marriage was void.

It delighted Marc I had the marriage declared void. Kirk might not have received the third strike Marc was always talking about yet, but I was sure Kirk would get it once he received those papers. The lawyer knew not to serve him the documents unless I was safe at Waterside with my family and the children. He understood I would be far too vulnerable at Ranscome Manor, alone except for a passel of children. Hopefully, they could serve the papers on Kirk before he left for Barbados and the Caribbean. I convinced him not to require me to accompany him on the trip. He planned to leave by mid-March.

I never intended to return to Barbados. Likewise, he would never take one of my children, including Bonnie and Betty, to Barbados. None of us would wind up slaves for life on the hellacious Sugar Isle. I hated it that I could not take Betty to visit Dolly and Odo, but Betty's safety was more important.

As Marc said, nothing from nothing was nothing, and that was what Kirk O'Malley would get from this so-called marriage. A big fat nothing. Well, except for his ship. He could keep the blasted ship.

Three weeks later, with the adoption completed, Kirk and I left to go to Kinsale so Bonnie and I could meet little Betty and Kirk's mother. I don't think Bonnie cared. In contrast, I was terrified. I looked forward to this about as much as if I needed to have a wisdom tooth pulled. My heart was racing, my hands were shaking, and I was again chewing on my lip. *Damned nerves,* I thought.

It didn't take long to sail to Kinsale. Mrs. O'Malley moved there after her husband was drowned in a fishing boat accident years before. She lived with her daughter, Mary Kate, her son-in-law, Alan, and their four children and Betty. She disliked Kirk's 'half-breed bastard,' as Siobhan O'Malley scornfully called her much-resented, mixed-race grandchild.

I did not intend for Betty to grow up unloved and unwanted as I had.

Mrs. O'Malley oohed and aahed over Bonnie. She frowned at Kirk. "Now, here's the pretty girl to give ye babes. No more like that one." Her voice filled with scorn, as she jerked her head towards the filthy toddler cowering in the shadows behind her.

"Oh, no, don't be mean." I handed Bonnie over to Mrs. O'Malley, whose face softened into warm, grandmotherly mush.

As she cooed over my baby, I approached the toddler.

"Betty? My name is Fancy. Your Daddy and I want you to come and live with us. Would you like that?" I asked as I held out a bit of the candy I brought for her from home.

She snatched the treat right out of my hand and then cowered back from me again. I struggled to keep my face bland as she raised an arm protectively over her little face as if to ward off a blow. I could not believe how filthy she was, grubby with weeks if not months of neglect. I cringed because I could see bugs crawling in her hair. Her little dress looked like dirt held it together, and her bare feet were black with grime. She would be a pretty child cleaned up and dressed appropriately, but right then, she looked like what Sassy calls a 'hot mess.' I didn't want my newest daughter to be afraid of me because I blew up at her Gramma the first time we met. I sat there, squatting on my haunches in my beautiful silk dress, whispering to her until she finally came over to hold out her hand again.

She hesitated and cut her eyes towards her Gramma. Finally, she spoke. "More?"

My heart leaped. Betty would trust me, at least a little. I nodded and smiled at her as I fished another candy out of the small sack. "More."

She beamed at me as she stuck the candy and her grubby little fist into her mouth.

By the end of the visit, the child snuggled up close to me, sleeping as I combed the lice and nits out of her hair.

"I don't know why your botherin' to do that. The child will have the wee devils back in her hair in a few days." Mrs. O'Malley frowned in disapproval.

*Probably so, if you don't keep them cleaned out and if she sleeps in a bed filled with them.* I bit my tongue and shrugged again. "I enjoy combing her hair. Could I get a wet rag to wash off her hands and face? She's sticky from the candy."

Mrs. O'Malley made a sound like a horse snorting. "I'll fetch ye a rag, but I don't know why you would even bother. Betty is the messiest child I ever saw. Ye can't keep her clean. Oh, you'll have yer hands full with that one. With three weans of yer own, I do not understand why ye want *this* worthless child."

I held my head up, angry at her words. No longer could I hold back my anger. "Worthless? No child is worthless, and every child should feel wanted and loved. Every baby is a precious gift from God. Betty is Kirk's daughter, and she should grow up with his other child."

"Aye, my Wee Duchess can handle another child, Mam. We have a sizable house, a nanny and a governess. We will manage with one more."

Mrs. O'Malley looked startled. "A sizable house? A nanny and a governess? I didn't know ye were doin' so well, son."

He laughed. "I do well enough, but the house belongs to Fancy. Didn't you always tell me to catch me a rich bride?"

She nodded, her eyes narrowing speculatively. "Aye, I did, son. But how rich is your lovely wife?"

"Rich enough." I somehow kept my voice calm and low.

Kirk laughed. "Richer than Croesus. Fancy is the Duchess of Ranscome."

I felt my heart drop. *Just had to brag, didn't you, Kirk?*

She looked shocked. "*Ai, Dia*, son, what have ye done?"

"I fell in love with a beautiful woman who turned out to be rich. Why?"

She shook her head. "I thought I warned ye never to get involved with the English, son."

You would have thought he told her I was an ax murderess, or maybe the female equivalent of Banastre Tarleton.

I cleared my throat. "I'm *not* English. Both of my grandfathers were as Irish as you are. They were both born and raised at Cork. My father was born and raised in Cork as well. My mother lives in Cork. Besides, Kirk rescued me from a nasty situation last spring, Mrs. O'Malley. I am *not* English."

She shook her head, impatient. "Him helping you didn't require you to marry the man."

I sighed in exasperation. It would figure my difficult husband had an equally difficult mother. I swallowed hard. "No, it didn't. I married him because I love him."

It just about gagged me to utter those words.

Siobhan O'Malley blinked. "Love, eh? But do ye *suit* each other?" She shook her head. "The lad never had good sense about women. First, that one's mam," she said, with a toss of her head towards Betty. "And now the daft fool married above his station. He wed a blasted Duchess. How is a woman a Duchess, anyway? It makes no sense at all."

I was getting offended until Kirk looked at me, grinned, and winked. He diffused my anger with just that look. I felt some of my outrage leave my body as I stifled a laugh.

Mrs. O'Malley didn't look convinced we suited each other as we left. She seemed happy Betty was going home with us and grudgingly accepted me as Kirk's wife. She wished us well, although I was sure the words near choked in her craw.

Richard looked stricken when we returned with Betty. He paled when he realized I adopted the cute tyke. He pivoted and left the house to stare at the water.

It was all I could do not to rush after him.

"Oh, dear." Sassy twisted her handkerchief into a knot.

I glanced at Kirk and shrugged. I could not explain right then what my entire plan was. I loved Richard, but I dared not share my intentions with him. I might have to throttle him if he got mad and blurted it all out to Kirk before the judges signed the declaratory judgment. In less than a fortnight, everything would be in place, and Kirk would receive the papers. And then, these two men could woo me properly. Unless Kirk was so mad, he up and left for Barbados as I suspected he would do.

Yes, I was conflicted.

Kirk was the only person who ever comforted me when I had night terrors. He would hold me close, murmuring words of love to me in Irish and English. With him, I had just about quit having the horrible dreams I'd had since Tarleton. How could I contemplate leaving the man who freed me from those terrible memories I used to relive night after hideous night?

When he is good, he is very, very good. But when he is bad, my bold Irish rogue is horrid.

Tamsin used to tell me a poem about a little girl who had a little curl right in the middle of her forehead. Tam would always playfully curve one of my curls around her finger when she recited that portion before she continued to tell me when the little girl was good, she was very, very good, but when she was bad, she was horrid.

Kirk had the temper of the little girl in the poem, the horrid temper I had when I was little before Tom whupped the snot and my anger right out of me. It terrified me how Kirk would react to the news our marriage was void. I hoped and prayed his reaction would not be horrid. I feared it would be. His horrid Irish temper was a significant factor in my decision to do this. I was sick and tired of tiptoeing around him like I was walking on eggshells all the time.

The irony was, I had feelings for Kirk. Deep feelings. Powerful feelings. On one level, I loved him, but I was afraid of him. I asked myself repeatedly: *can you truly love a man who terrifies you*? I did not want to receive a repeat of the whipping I received in Bridgetown. Never. How would he react to learn I was mixed? But if we were to remain married, he would have to accept me for who I was, not just what I was. Or perhaps, he had to take me for all that I was. Kirk knew me as a rich Duchess. His Wee Duchess. Would he still want me when he learned his Wee Duchess was a woman of color?

And I would never dare tell him all my stories, about Tom or Simon or even all about Calvin. He had a hard enough time with Tarleton. He could never handle the fact other men used me poorly.

And then there was Richard. My dear, sweet, impetuous Richard.

I knew I loved Richard 110%. I wanted to be with him. I longed- yearned- to be with him. He could make me feel like a princess with just a word, a look, or a smile. I desperately wanted Bonnie to be his child. But I could see the hurt on his face every time I looked at him, especially since we brought Betty back. It ate at me like cancer.

And let's face it. Sassy tells him not to make permanent decisions based on temporary feelings because he is rash. What impetuous decision would he make now?

God only knew because I sure didn't. I was afraid he would throw a Kirkworthy hissy fit and leave.

He had done that before.

Richard would never raise a hand to my children or me. Richard was a kind, loving, gentle soul. Violence was not part of his makeup. At least, I had never seen it if it was part of him. If only he would be patient now and wait as I asked. I knew what I was doing in Barbados when I asked him to be patient and wait. It was unfortunate they came in December. I asked him to wait a year. Would he now grow tired of waiting and act rashly again like he did when he left Belle Rose last year?

*Please, Richard. Don't make another permanent decision based on your temporary hurt feelings.*

# Chapter 5
# Surprises
# 1783

This time, she cut me to the core. I keep trying to believe she still loves me, but I had to face facts. I wasn't feeling the love.

There are times she hurts me so badly I am unsure if I can ever heal from the wound. Adopting Kirk's bastard was one of them.

"She's going to stay with the sorry excuse for a man." I stared out over the water in stunned disbelief after I realized she adopted his child.

"Now, *m'hijo*, you don't know that." Sassy fretted with her handkerchief, twisting the fine linen into a knot.

"Get real, Mom. What else could it mean? She married him. They are back here. There is as much a chance he is Bonnie's father as I am. It's not like we can do a DNA test to determine who Bonnie's father is. Now, Francesca adopted a child she never even met before they completed the adoption. I'm all done. I want to go home."

Mom hugged me. "We can go home, Rick. I figure we came at the wrong time."

"No, *I* came at the wrong time. And now? I want to go home."

Silent for once, Sassy nodded as she continued to hug me.

About then, Will joined us outside in the garden. "What say we head back to Virginia? I have had about all the fun and games I can endure this trip."

Wordless, I nodded.

"I think that's an outstanding idea, Will." Mom's voice was tight with unshed tears. "*Si*, it's time to go home. Let's blow this joint."

*Past time to go home*, I thought. *We should never have come. No, I corrected myself. I should never have come when I did. I arrived at the wrong time for us.*

But had I ruined things forever? Would there ever be a right time now for Francesca and me?

Hmm. I wonder if that painting still hangs in Ranscome Manor and if it says she was my wife? Or if it says she was the beloved wife of a privateering son of a bitch named Captain Kirk O'Malley?

As long as it doesn't say O'Malley murdered her in a raging fit when he realized I sired her daughter.

We left for Virginia at dawn the next morning.

. . .

"It was high time they left. Why Will, Sassy, and Richard came in the first place is beyond me." Kirk had a smug look of triumph all over his face.

Fancy stared out across the waters, silent, but Kirk could see the tears glistening in her beautiful aquamarine eyes. Finally, she nodded. "You're right. They shouldn't have come."

She sighed, and her shoulders sagged. Kirk grabbed her by the shoulder and turned her to him with a little shake. "Don't cry. Don't you dare cry over the likes of him."

Her face clouded as she pursed her lips. She frowned and pulled away from Kirk. "The likes of him? What do you mean by that?"

"Richard Winslow is nothing but a coward who won't even fight for the woman he claims to love. A man who turns tail to run every time things become difficult. He did it in Barbados, and he did it again here."

He grabbed her arm and jerked her back to him. As she balled her hands into fists and hit him, he lowered his mouth to her. "And remember, my Wee Duchess, this is the man you not only need, but you crave. A man who will take you where you want to be. A man who won't turn tail and run when things get hard. A man who loves you through thick or thin. A man who knows how to satisfy yer every desire."

He captured her lips with a savage passion as he swung her up into his arms. *Perhaps some good loving would take her mind off the damned young Dr. Winslow. If not, mayhap a new bun in her oven would.*

*It was worth a try. At least, I will enjoy trying.*

He carried her upstairs to the bedroom, locking the door after them. She wasn't crying by the time they reached the bedroom. Instead, she met him with a fierceness he dreamed about and longed for since he first met her. Aye, though she was little, she was fierce. His own fierce Wee Duchess.

. . .

I lay curled on the bed afterward as hot tears slid silently down my cheeks. I pressed my hands against my stomach, knotted with the gnawing pain Lily said was anxiety. My head pounded, and my throat felt tight as well. Oh, dear, sweet Jesus, what do I do now?

How can one man be so sweet and yet hurt me so badly, now running from me a third time when things got hard? How could I ever trust Richard after this latest betrayal?

And what should I do about Kirk now?

The Barbadian marriage was void. And yet, I still shared marital pleasures with Kirk.

Did I dare tell him I am mixed, that I am a person of color? If I do, how will he respond?

And did I want out of this marriage? Or did I want to know my mixed blood mattered not to my wild, hot-tempered Irishman?

And could I bear it if he left me, too?

Worse yet, could I bear it if he stayed, but only because I am the Duchess of Ranscome? Was that the only reason he married me in the first place?

Oh, dear Lord, what was I to do?

I was quiet for the next week. I had much to ponder. Finally, I told Marc I needed to see the solicitor again.

He nodded and patted me on the back. "We can go this morning, lass. But, you're doing the right thing."

I took a deep breath. "I guess that remains to be seen. I want to take Kirk with us..."

He looked shocked. "Are ye sure, Fancy?"

I nodded. "Yes. I have thought about this a lot. I think he deserves to learn about this void marriage from me, not from some legal document. It would be cruel to have him served papers right before he boards his ship to voyage to Barbados for six months."

Marc shook his head. "I don't know, *mo leannan*. But this is your life and your decision. You know I'll support you, no matter what you decide."

I smiled. "I know, Daddy. The one thing I can always count on is you love me."

"Now and always." He sounded thoughtful and sincere.

We both grew silent as Kirk bounded down the stairs. "Are you ready?"

I nodded as I struggled not to chew my lip.

"Then let's go to Cork." Kirk grabbed my hand and pulled me close for a kiss before starting to the door.

My heart lurched as the familiar tightness wrapped around my throat. I doubted Kirk would be so exuberantly happy once we all met with the solicitor.

An hour later, Mr. O'Halloran ushered us into his offices. I had grown increasingly nervous as Marc grew disapprovingly silent. I could no longer refrain from chewing either my lip or my fingers. I pressed a handkerchief against a cuticle I ripped until it bled. Kirk gave me a strange look, his brow furrowed with concern, but he did not question what the meeting was all about.

The attorney came bustling in a few minutes late, effusively apologetic for his tardiness. "I apologize. They held me over at chancellery court this morning."

"Th… this morning?" I swallowed hard before I squeaked out the words.

I rubbed the fabric of my Kinsale cloak between my fingers. *Feel the fabric. Focus on the material. You can lift away from this if you focus on the texture of the fabric.*

"Oh, yes, Your Grace. I am there nearly every morning. Captain O'Malley, the Duchess consulted me about a rather awkward problem. She was concerned about the validity of your Barbadian marriage. She asked me to determine if it is void or valid."

Kirk looked surprised and then grinned. "Oh? Why on earth did Fancy think the marriage might not be valid?"

"Because of fraud, sir." O'Halloran's voice remained deceptively soft.

Kirk's eyebrows lifted slightly. "Indeed? And what fraud might that be?"

"I believe your wife failed to advise you of an important fact which makes any marriage the two of you entered into in Barbados to be void."

Kirk's lips turned up as he relaxed again. "Ye mean to say you believe her Grace fraudulently coerced me into marrying her? Now, why on earth do you think she did that?"

"Kirk…" I began, but Marc cut me off.

"The lass failed to tell you she's a person of color. Whites cannot legally marry persons of color in Barbados." Marc's voice was soft, but his words were powerful.

I felt my cheeks redden at his curt words. Silent, I gulped and nodded.

Kirk stared at us for several minutes. "But, Marcus, I already knew she's mixed."

We all turned to stare at him at the unexpected twist.

"Huh? How? I mean, when did you learn that?" I gasped as I dropped the clot of fabric from my hand.

He shrugged. "I reckon it was back in '64. I heard comments on the ship about Lady Tamsin. Some o' the men were sayin' t'was likely Lord Fitz Simmons would not react well when he learned his wife was mixed. It concerned Will that Lord Fitz Simmons might beat her to death when he learned of it. I asked Mr. Jo, who confirmed Lady Tamsin and you both were mixed, but it mattered naught to him. T'was clear, he thought you were the most beautiful child ever born, with your aqua eyes, ginger tresses, and golden skin. That's when he told me 'though she is but little, she is fierce.'"

I blinked. "You knew? But you never said a word. You could have kept me a slave for life in Barbados."

Kirk shrugged. "T'was never my intent to keep you a slave for life. I just wanted to make sure you were safe. And then, by damn, I up and fell in love with ye."

I frowned. "Oh? If you just wanted to make sure I was safe, why didn't you take me to Will in Puerto Rico? The ship sailed right past Puerto Rico, going to Barbados."

"Ah, darlin', if I had done that, who would have held you when you awoke to scream sometimes two or three times a night? I had no choice. I took you home to give ye time to heal. And I fell in love with my Wee Duchess. So, what do we do now? Do we need to marry again here in Ireland to make it all legal? Lord knows it would please my Mam if we married here, in front of a proper priest. It did not impress her that we married before an Anglican minister in Barbados."

"But, the indenture..." I began.

He shrugged again and flashed me another of his devil-may-care smiles. "T'was a way to ensure you stayed long enough to ..."

"Snare her into marriage?" Marc's voice was soft, but the disgust in his tone was unmistakable.

Kirk's head snapped towards Marc. "No, Marc. Ye do not understand how she was then. A broken nose, broken ribs, beaten black and blue from head to toe. But that was the least of her injuries. Fancy would wake up screaming like a banshee two, three times a night. She would be white as a ghost, shaking like a loosened topsail in a high wind. It was as if she was somewhere else. She couldn't even see me at times. They broke the lass, through and through. She would scream like a crazed woman until I gathered her into my arms, and I would somehow calm her down. She would gradually relax and go back to sleep. I couldn't take her to Will like that. My sister would wake up screaming like that when she was young. My mam called it night terrors. She had been, well, the lass had been hurt by an Englishman. Anyway, by the time we got to Barbados, Fancy's night terrors were diminishing. She needed the time to heal."

"You… you knew?" I asked, my voice thick with shock.

He nodded. "Aye. Then, your Mam confirmed it when Wee Bonnie was born with the spot on her bum."

I blinked. "I didn't realize you knew Bonnie had the spot, much less what it means."

His eyes crinkled as he laughed. "Betty had one, too. They go away over time. Betty's spot is almost gone now."

I nodded. "Bella had one for a long time. Charles never had one."

And then he grew serious. He gathered my hands into his own as he stared into my eyes. "So, now what do ye want to do, my Wee Duchess?"

Ironic. A week ago, I wanted my freedom. But now? I gulped. I sat up straight and squared my shoulders as I held my head up. My hands stopped shaking with each deep breath I drew. "I want you to woo me. I'm a Duchess. Treat me like I'm a Duchess, like I'm the most precious woman in your world. But I don't want you to love me because I'm a Duchess. I want you to show you love me despite the fact."

I blinked the fresh rush of unbidden tears back from my eyes. *Like Richard used to treat me,* I thought.

He nodded all seriousness and then sank to his knees before me. "You already are, Fancy, my love. But to convince you of that? It would be my greatest pleasure."

He bent to kiss my hands. I giggled as the unexpected kiss washed over me like a healing balm. He looked up at me from where he was still kneeling before me, bent over my hand, grinned and winked.

I giggled again. "Yes, like that."

Marc remained silent, impassive, as Mr. O'Halloran cleared his throat. "Then, the wooing of Her Grace shall begin. Good luck, Captain O'Malley."

Marc left us outside Mr. O'Halloran's office. He looked disappointed as he headed back to Waterside. Kirk and I made a foray into a fabric shop. If there is a fabric shop, I'm always game. I oohed and aahed over all the newest designs in Spitalfields's silks for an hour, buying fabric for drapes and two chairs besides materials to make Easter dresses for the girls and myself. Finally, sated from my fabric splurge, we ate at the inn before we went back to Ranscome Manor.

"I have to admit I would never have expected you to buy yellow gingham silk for parlor chairs," Kirk said as he tousled my already windblown hair.

I leaned away from his hand. "You know I like yellow. And I like the fresh, crisp look of this fabric. It looks formal enough for Ranscome Manor and rustic enough to feel comfortable at the same time, out here in the country. Why?"

Kirk laughed. "You'll be wantin' to put burlap pillows on them next."

"Hmm. I might do that. I could stencil yellow irises on the pillows and trim them with some yellow silk. Yes, I might do that, Kirk." I grinned, happy to be teasing him.

He stopped and stared at me with a look of dismay marring his handsome features. "You wouldn't really, would you?"

I laughed out loud (something Sassy called a 'LOL'). "Maybe. You must wait and see."

He looked a bit shocked. "Well, it is your house," he stammered. "And you are the expert on color and texture. But do ye think it would be appropriate at Ranscome Manor? I mean, perhaps at home…"

I laughed again, amused he had not realized I was teasing him. "You will just have to wait and see, Captain O'Malley."

Hmm. Perhaps I would put burlap on the dining room chairs with burlap table runners, I thought, with the yellow gingham silk trim. I could put yellow gingham silk on the windows, with stenciled burlap tie-backs. I could already see the room in my mind. I realized with a start Sassy would love the unusual juxtaposition of fabrics. Maybe someday she will see it.

Richard would love it, too. But then, he would not have questioned my choice of fabrics, even with the unexpected addition of burlap. I got a catch in my throat as I thought he would have grinned and told me that I was smart with such things.

We rode in silence the rest of the way back to Ranscome Manor. As we walked inside, he pulled me close to him for a long, deep kiss. As our lips parted, I sighed. *A healing balm,* I thought again. I could feel my body yielding to him.

"Does this mean you gave up on him?" His voice grew husky with desire as his hands roamed my body.

I tried to smile. "I think Richard gave up on me."

I swear the man growled. "I'll never give up on ye, lass. Not until I've drawn my last breath."

He dropped his head towards me, and I thought he would kiss me again. Instead, he grinned as he swung me up into his arms to carry me upstairs.

Oh yes, the wooing had began.

# Chapter 6
# First Richard and Then Fancy with a Little from Kirk
# 1783

It was a quiet voyage back to the States. Even Sassy and the children seemed subdued. Perhaps Rick's depression affected them. Or probably, as Will suggested, they were all 'dad-gummed sick and tired of traveling.'

Will grew accustomed to seeing Rick stand on deck, staring out across the waters. But as days stretched into weeks and weeks into more than a month, Will finally broke his promise to Sassy and approached Rick.

"I remember once, about twenty years ago, when I stood in that same spot fussing at God."

Rick's head snapped around at Will's voice. "Why on earth were you doing that?"

Will's smile was bittersweet. "My wife died, and I thought my world was ending. I fussed at God for taking my Tennie away from me."

Rick tried to smile. "What did He tell you?"

Will stared up at the sky before he answered. Finally, he pointed upwards. "He told me to look at the clouds."

Rick looked startled. "The clouds? Why?"

Will pulled out a cheroot and trimmed off the end. He lit the little cigar and took a long draw on it before answering. Finally, he pointed upwards again. "Clouds move all the time. The Cherokees say you can see spirit people in the clouds. So, at first, I tried to see my Tennie in the clouds. Sometimes, I could see her. Sometimes, I can still see her up there, smiling down on me. And then it finally hit me. I could no more hang on to that woman than I could hang onto a cloud. You see, Rick, I couldn't own the sky any more than I could own Tennie."

Rick tried to laugh. "I take it you are reminding me the same is true about your sister?"

Will let out a string of smoke rings as he nodded. "Yep, pretty much. Let her go, Rick."

"I know. I'm trying." Rick's voice cracked with the emotion he was trying not to show.

"It's hard to let go of a woman you love. Damned hard. But, Rick, do it, so you can open yourself up to new things the Lord has in store for you."

Rick turned to face Will. "You think He has something else in store for me besides Fancy?"

"All things in His own time, Rick. It took Him fourteen years to send your mom to me. It took me a while to realize she was the promised one. And let me tell you, lad, that woman is a handful."

Rick laughed. "A handful, hmm? Yeah, I guess you could put it that way. Dad used to say she was enough to drive a saint to suicide, and he loved her something crazy, too."

Will laughed, suddenly self-conscious. "Oh, believe me, I love your mama, more than I ever dreamed possible. But, yes, Owen was right. She can be a trial sometimes. Kinda like my baby sister."

Rick quit laughing and grew silent again. "Can't own her any more than I could own the sky, hmm? Is that about Tennie? Or Mom?"

Will nodded as he exhaled another string of smoke rings.

Rick's eyes narrowed. "Or your sister?"

Will shrugged. "Well, now that you mention it, lad…"

Rick could no longer hold the tears back from filling up his eyes. Finally, he turned towards Will again. "So, what do I do?"

"I don't rightly know, Rick. That's between you and the Good Lord. However, I can teach you how to let go of some of that tension that's eating you up."

Rick looked startled. "My God, Will, I wish you would. This feeling of loss is horrible."

Will nodded. "I know. I remember. So, tighten your fist as tight as possible."

Rick nodded and balled both hands into tight fists.

After a minute, Will noticed Rick wince. "Hurt?"

Sheepish, Rick nodded. "Yes, sir."

"Then shake them out. Let all that tension go. Release all that negative energy-I think that's what Lil called it, negative energy - and let go of the pain you bottled up inside of you. Let it all out and breathe."

Rick looked surprised as he shook out his hands. "How did you get so wise? Who taught you this?"

"Shadow Wolf. The Cherokees taught me lots of things. For instance, do you know it takes less effort to smile than to frown?"

Rick nodded. "Yeah. I learned that in med school. It takes less effort to relax than to tense up. Thank you for reminding me. I wonder why I have such a hard time remembering that?"

"We all do, lad. I have to remind myself of that at least a dozen times a day, especially when your Mama gets on a rant. You need to remember that when our hands are open, we are ready to receive our blessing from the Lord. And when we clench our fists tight in anger, we reject any blessing He is trying to give us."

Rick blinked. "Wow, I never thought of it that way. But, wait a minute, are you saying I messed things up with Francesca?"

Will shook his head. "No. That's for you and the Good Lord to decide. I'm just trying to help you get yourself into a position, into a condition, to recognize it when God tries to tell you something about this whole situation."

Rick nodded. "Your son, Tom looked at me the morning we left Ireland and said, 'Rick, it's just a big ol' jumble of worms, ain't it?'"

Will laughed. "I heard that. Pretty well nailed it, didn't he?"

Rick nodded. "From the mouths of babes…"

Will left Rick standing there, clinching and relaxing his hands. *He's a smart young man. He'll figure it out,* Will thought. *Maybe not right now. But I have every confidence he'll figure it out, eventually.*

After 42 days at sea, they arrived at Belle Rose.

. . .

Each day, Kirk was more romantic. More engaging. More charming. And yes, more seductive. By the end of the week, I was blushing like a schoolgirl, smiling and giggling all the time.

My Grampa died in May. Lily thought he had another stroke and said he went quickly in his sleep. I grieved sorely for losing the sweet, elderly gentleman who became so important to me late in his life. I mourned all those years when I was in Virginia and could have been in Ireland.

Kirk was right there to console and comfort me once again. Not long after we laid my Grampa to rest next to my Gramma Meara, in the beautiful gardens overlooking the sea, Kirk asked me to marry him again.

I told him yes.

Kirk sailed to Kinsale the next day to have our banns read at the Catholic Church, and on the fifteenth of June, we repeated our marital vows. It was a small ceremony, attended only by Mrs. O'Malley. I wore the same yellow dress I wore in Barbados when we married.

I did not tell Marc or Lily what we would do. I tried to talk with Marc several times about possibly remarrying Kirk. Each time, he looked horror-stricken. He would say, "Pray about it, Fancy. You'll make the right decision."

I was not at all sure he thought my remarrying Kirk was the right decision.

Marc kissed my cheek and handed me over to Kirk as we boarded the ship to go to Kinsale. I couldn't make out what he said to Kirk, but I saw Kirk's cheeks blush red at Marc's words. I wasn't sure if his face grew red in anger or embarrassment, although Kirk laughed at whatever Marc said and clapped Marc on the back as if they were best friends. I gave Kirk a quizzical look, which he ignored as he focused on the ship. Fine. I could find out later.

. . .

Kirk's cheeks burned bright pink even as he laughed. *So, you'll kill me if I disappoint her, Marcus? Perhaps. If she dares tell ye. But one thing is sure. She'll be my wife, and you cannot undo our marriage again, you sorry bastard.*

Kirk planned to sail to Barbados by the end of July. Fancy might think he gave in to her on the issue, but he intended for the children and her to accompany him, come Hell or high water. By damn, he would show off his beautiful wife and family to his friends and acquaintances there, and it was high time his wee Betty met her grandparents again. Yes, he would be a man of importance when he returned to Barbados, married to the Duchess of Ranscome, with his family in tow.

# Chapter 7
# Richard
# 1783 and Beyond

I spent two months at Belle Rose before I told Mom and Will I would mosey on down the road and explore the New World. By then, she gave birth to the new twins, a boy, and a girl, and named them James Richard and Alinora Marie.

Mom looked shocked. She began begging me to stay. "Please, Rick, you can't leave…"

I clasped her hands close to me as tears filled her lovely eyes. It was damned hard. Dad used to say he fell in love with Mom the first time her emerald green eyes filled with tears as she fussed at him about something long ago forgotten. I think he was already in love with her, but he never could resist a woman's tears. I'm a lot like him in that respect. That was one reason we left Ireland without me telling Fancy goodbye. I couldn't bear to see the pain in her beautiful eyes, much less the actual tears.

Even worse would have been if I had just seen relief in her eyes. Or if she had said, "Oh, thank you, Richard. I'm so glad you understand."

That would have killed me.

Will gave me £200, which was a lot of money in 1783. "Use it wisely, lad. Don't be flashing your money around strangers. And know you are always welcome to come back here."

I smiled. "Thanks, Will. I know, and I'll be back one of these days."

He nodded. "I know. You'll know when the time is right. Keep your hands relaxed and uplifted for your blessings. Safe travels, Rick."

Mom stood beside him, waving to me from the big front porch as I rode away. I knew she was crying. Will had one arm around her as he waved to me, also. I gave them one last wave and headed towards Williamsburg. I planned to travel down the coast to Charleston and Savannah before turning inland to head westward to Indian Territory and the Cohutta Wilderness. I have always loved those three cities and looked forward to seeing them in 1783. It would be a lengthy trip, and I felt nervous about traveling alone, but I was eager to see some more of this beautiful, pristine, new country before I headed west into Indian Territory to go home.

Home to Atlanta. Not where my heart is. That's probably always going to be San Antonio. I wistfully smiled as I thought of the mansion a few blocks from Trinity I used to say I would own someday. I figured that wasn't likely to happen if I ever returned to the eighteenth century. Atlanta was where I belonged, at least for now. I hoped Dan would take me back to study with him like I was doing before I left. I realized I should have stuck with the residency I started years ago. If I had, now I would be a board-certified cardiovascular surgeon. Oh, well, no sense crying over spoiled milk. I just had to figure out what to make from the spoiled milk of a relationship gone bad.

I was in Williamsburg before nightfall. I had been there a few times in this century and loved the original even more than the recreation where my family spent so many summers while I grew up. I passed the jewelry store where I had Francesca's ring made in two hundred years. Oh, yeah, I told her I bought it on eBay, not that she knew diddley squat about eBay. But in reality, it was custom made for her with the big Santa Maria aquamarine I bought Beyond at the same jewelry shop where Marc told me he purchased Lily's wedding ring in 1764. I patted the ring box in the little pocket inside my jacket. Well, maybe someday she will wear it. Maybe.

Hmm. I wonder if that was why Francesca insisted on giving it back to me?

I watched the girls dyeing fabric like Mom used to do in the future. I could smell the solutions, and I knew which mordants they were using, thanks to Mom's old lessons. I flirted with the girls awhile as they stirred their large pots of dye before I headed to the Inn. It reminded me of Dad standing by the fence, flirting with Sassy as she stirred those pots years ago. I boarded my horse at the livery stable and walked into the Inn and rented a room. I ate a filling dinner of shepherd's pie and fresh hot bread, washed down with some tasty, home-brewed ale before I turned in for the night.

Yes, everything was the same and yet so different from all those years reenacting with Mom and Dad. I remembered Dad used to say he fell in love with Mom the first time they came to Williamsburg. It always amused me he had so many stories about how and when he fell in love with Mom. I always told Dad that he loved her way before Williamsburg, but Williamsburg clinched it. He would chuckle, nod, and puff thoughtfully on his pipe.

I never pointed out to Dad he had several scenarios he claimed were when he first fell in love with Mom. When her eyes filled up with tears for the first time. When they went to Williamsburg that first summer. When he saw how relaxed and happy I was with her.

I thought again how much my Dad would have loved to have had this opportunity to live through at least part of the Revolutionary War. I laughed as I thought he would have been every bit as shocked as Mom was when I told her that she is the Progressive, not the Conservative. I could imagine his face turning deep red with anger as he would have fussed and flustered at me over my rude comment.

One of the biggest arguments I ever had with my Dad was about that very subject. He about blew a gasket when I likened the Constitutional Republic established in the 1780s to a kind of New World Order. In hindsight, I'm surprised that didn't trigger the fatal heart attack he had three weeks later.

Oh well, no matter. I wasn't here to help maintain the Constitutional Monarchy or to establish the Constitutional Republic. I came here looking for the love of my life. What did that old song say? Was I looking for love in all the wrong places? Maybe so. At the very least, I was looking for love at the wrong damned time. Teach me not to do something stupid like fall in love with a woman in a painting ever again. Yeah, sure. I was still head over heels in love with Francesca despite everything.

Francesca's apparent inability to commit to me was especially ironic when you considered I had never committed to a relationship before her. The story ought to make Melanie laugh her ass off since I was never ready to settle down when I was with her. Hmm. I wondered if the pretty registered nurse would even look my way when I returned. She was fighting mad the last time I saw her.

I rode out of Williamsburg after two days. I headed for Roanoke after travelers advised me to head west instead of south.

You would have thought by then I would have remembered the roads in 1783 were pretty crappy. As I struggled south and westward, I realized why Marc and Lily caught a ship north from Charleston years before. To call these trails 'roads' was a big stretch from the highways I used to know. I had forgotten just how freaking horrible it could be to try to travel south through gator-infested swamps, and then westward through the mountains, battling some of the biggest damned mosquitoes I ever saw.

Thank God I had my immunizations against many illnesses, including malaria, before I came. Thank God they vaccinated my generation against smallpox, even though it was the last generation to receive smallpox vaccinations in the future. They eradicated the horrible disease in the future, thanks to those immunizations. If I had been born a few years later, I, too, would be vulnerable to smallpox, unless I got inoculated here. I saw lots of pock-scarred people here, including Washington. It was possible to survive the disease, but I met no one who survived it unscathed by the characteristic pockmarked scars.

Ironically, I have one scar on my belly from chickenpox that resembles smallpox scarring. Like lots of kids, I scratched a scab off one of my chickenpox lesions, resulting in the pitted scar. More than one person here thought I had survived smallpox because of the scar my mother hated so much. Poor Kathryn always related that one blemish to child neglect. She felt she should somehow have kept me from scratching the lesion. I bit my tongue and resisted telling her not preventing me from scratching the scab off was not neglectful. Dragging me from drug house to drug house as she scored heroin by selling her body was neglectful if not downright dangerous. No child should ever have to live through the things I saw.

After fifteen days, I dragged into Roanoke, exhausted. I found the inn Will recommended, boarded the horse, stumbled up the stairs to my room, and tumbled onto the bed. Somehow, I wriggled out of my jacket and tie and to kick my shoes off.

I slept 48 hours straight. Who would have dreamed I could sleep so well on a lumpy mattress covered with rough, homespun cotton in 95-degree Fahrenheit heat? It was July, and by damn, it was freaking hot.

I dreaded to think about the next part of the trip. I was out of the swamps, but now I would traverse south to Charlotte, and then westward deep into the Indian Territory. I would travel on the Wilderness Trail, through the mountains, all by my lonesome. I spoke neither Cherokee nor Creek. French might help a little. Spanish, not so much. It didn't seem nearly as daunting coming from McCarron's Corner with Marc. The problem was I didn't have Marc and his exceptional skill with languages with me on this trip.

I saw a good number of plantations as I approached Charlotte. It still rattled me whenever I saw slaves toiling under the blistering sun. I cringed every time I saw an overseer raise a whip to a slave when the damned brute thought the slave worked too slow. I would never like this aspect of living in the Old South, to which I would never grow accustomed. Maybe it was the black blood flowing through my veins. Perhaps it was my basic revulsion for the institution of slavery. I knew slavery would end in 82 years, but I chafed at the basic human rights violations occurring all around me. I hated this part of my time travel adventure the most.

Well, except for being rejected by the woman I love. That sucked toads.

After another twenty days, I made my way through the Cumberland Pass and into Knoxville. It amazed me at how tiny the village was. Travel was a lot easier if I didn't get lost like I did several times through the Carolinas and in Eastern Tennessee as I made my way through the Cumberland Pass. And this was supposed to be the *good* road? It's amazing how lost you can get on paths and primitive roads, even with a compass and the best maps available. I planned to rest several days in Knoxville before tackling the last leg of my journey on down south through the Indian Territory. I figured with luck, I could reach McCarron's Corner in another week, hopefully with my scalp still attached. Mom had told me the gruesome story of Will dragging in half scalped in '79. Lily wasn't here this trip, and I damned sure did not want to have to sew my scalp back on.

On the morning of my third day in Knoxville, I checked out of the Inn and headed for the livery stable. It was the last week in September. I was about halfway to the livery stable when a young boy from the Inn ran up to me.

"Dr. Winslow, I'm so glad I caught you. My Mama told me to catch you before you left town." The boy doubled over, trying to catch his breath.

I frowned. "Freddie, what's the matter? What does your Mom need?"

The boy's breathing slowed, and he stood up. "Mama says ol' Doc Ryland needs yo' help. I'm supposed to take you there right away."

"Dr. Ben Ryland? Why? What's wrong?" I pressed.

The boy looked up at me with eyes big as saucers. "Yessuh. They got typhus at the Walker Plantation, about fifteen miles out of town."

Well, eff me running. That was not what I wanted to hear that crisp autumn morning.

I had seen typhus before a time or two, most memorably at Yorktown. Martha Washington's son, Jackie Custis, died from it there. I would not have been disappointed to have lived the rest of my life without seeing another case of typhus. Usually caused by the Rickettsia bacteria, confirmation of typhus confirms from a biopsy of skin lesions. It produces a distinctive rash loaded with the bacteria. Stool loaded with bacteria verifies typhus, also. Symptoms are headache, fever, chills, and the tell-tale rash. Epidemic typhus can also cause severe headaches, high temperature, stupor, low blood pressure, eye sensitivity to light, and severe muscle pain. Nausea, vomiting, and diarrhea often accompany it, also. They contracted it from the bite of lice, ticks, or mites carrying the bacteria, or sometimes flying squirrels. I didn't think there were any flying squirrels around there, but God knew these people tended to have lice. It could be hard to diagnose because the symptoms were similar to those of dengue fever, malaria, and brucellosis. Dengue fever occasionally came in with slaves. Malaria came from the damned mosquitoes. And then there was brucellosis. I used to think dogs got brucellosis. We would test the dogs for it before breeding them because it is sexually transmitted among pooches and can kill a litter. Let me assure you that people can contract it, too, and without antibiotics, it can be deadly.

I sighed. It would be a long couple of days with any of those diseases. I had my microscope so I could identify whether the offending bacteria was the typhus bacteria, or one other I suspected. I had some antibiotics with me, but I didn't have enough doxycycline for an epidemic. I left most of it at Belle Rose in case they needed it. There is a good chance of survival of typhus with early treatment by antibiotics. Without antibiotics, the chances of survival dropped appreciably. I knew we would have deaths, especially among the older adults and the malnourished. Where you have slaves, you nearly always find poorly nourished people. For some reason unknown to me, children usually survived typhus. I knew the mortality rate could be anywhere from 10% to 60%. "Great. Let's go get my horse, and I'll head out there."

"I'll go with you, sir." The boy was eager to help.

I shook my head. "No, you stay here. Your mom would skin me alive if I let you go out there with me."

It took me two hours of hard riding to get out to the Walker Plantation. I was glad to find Dr. Ben Ryland already working. I quickly located him and pitched in to help. I met Ben in '81 at Yorktown. I knew he was a Tennessee man, but it still surprised me to run into him in Knoxville. He was an outstanding man to work with during a crisis. Fortunately, Ben Ryland was one of the 'modern doctors,' who understood bacteria cause disease. He also shared my low opinion of bleeding patients. He looked askance as I drew a blood sample from one of the sicker patients. Dr. Ryland frowned, his lips pursing together disapprovingly.

"What are you doing, Winslow? I thought you didn't believe in bleeding."

I chuckled inwardly at the disapproval in his voice as I put some blood onto a slide and slid it under my microscope. "I want to look at this. The bloody stools these people have concern me. It doesn't smell like typhus. Plus, not one of them has a fever."

Rydell washed his hands in the basin and came to peer over my shoulder at the slide. "I have to admit I thought the same things. Have you ever seen typhus under the microscope before?"

I nodded. "At Yorktown. Ben, this isn't typhus."

"Got any ideas about what it is then?"

"A few. Typhus might be preferable."

As an alternative to typhus, I was hoping for typhoid, which is an enteric fever caused by Salmonella Typhi bacteria. It produced very similar symptoms as typhus. With typhoid fever, they would run a fever, too. Some doctors confused the two. Those were the old school guys who didn't believe bacteria exists and still thought bleeding was the thing to do in most cases, which was why it rattled Ben to see me draw blood. He knew I was not 'old school.' The slide was not either easily recognized bacteria. I stared in dismay at the sample. Oh, hell. Eff Me Running.

"Ben, I need a stool sample. STAT."

Ben nodded. "Jimmie Lee, take some shit this slave just passed to Dr. Winslow. No, for God's sake, do not scoop it up with your bare hands, boy. Carry the dad-blasted chamber pot to him. And be sure to wash your hands well when you finish. Jesus, the dad-blamed boy was gonna stick his hands in the shit."

I quickly prepared the slide. I knew it would not be nearly as accurate as fecal occult blood tests could be, but given the look and smell of this diarrhea,

I was pretty damned sure what it was. It looked like rice water and stank to high heaven like rotten fish. Sure enough, swimming through the shit were millions of Vibrio cholerae.

Dammit, we had a full-blown outbreak of cholera.

The wonderful news was we wouldn't need antibiotics. The other marvelous news was I had plenty of rehydration salts with me. The hard part would be to get the rehydration fluids into people without iv's. If I could rehydrate people, we might stop a potential epidemic.

You usually find cholera in water or food contaminated by feces. Remember when your mom told you to wash your hands after you use the bathroom? There are reasons why she taught you to do that. Cholera comprises one of them. Good hygiene stops this disease, but try to explain that to the people who owned slaves and rarely bathed in this day and age.

You rarely run a fever with cholera.

"Mr. Walker, have you purchased any new slaves recently?" Dr. Ryland's brow furrowed with worry.

Walker looked surprised. "Why, yessuh, I bought twenty new boys last week. I bought them over in Charleston. I got a good price on them because they just had a bad hurricane over yonder, and they wuz wantin' to sell them boys fast. Why?"

Ben gave me a look that let me know he recognized the disease, too.

"Are all the sick folk from the new slaves?"

Walker nodded even as his face reddened. "Dadgummit, I think most of them sure enough is. I'll sue that sorry slave trader if he sold me sick slaves."

I felt sick. The sick slaves didn't concern the damned man. It upset him about the money he would lose if they died. What a sorry piece of crap. I took a deep breath.

"Mr. Walker, meaning no disrespect, but we need to contain this. We need to quarantine the new slaves and anyone else who is sick from the others."

Walker turned pale. "B-b-but—"

I turned towards him, impatient with the idiot man. "But what? This is very serious, sir. People will die if we don't act fast. If we can't get this under control, many people may die."

Walker was turning green. "But my son. You need to check on my son."

Wouldn't it just figure he bought a fresh batch of slaves with his ten-year-old son in tow, and now the kid had diarrhea, too? I bit back the angry, castigating words I wanted to scream at this numbskull. I rewashed my hands and then poured alcohol over them to kill any residual germs. I slid my microscope back into the case. "I'll go check on the kid, Ben. Have your helper boil a big kettle of water for 15 minutes and then put that packet into it. Start giving it to the sick men as often as they will drink it. Tell them if they don't drink it, they will shit themselves to death. Come on, Mr. Walker. I need to look at your boy."

I told the housekeeper to boil water as soon as we stepped into the house. Without a word, she nodded and ran to the kitchen. Mr. Walker took me upstairs to his son's room. I gagged as the putrid, rotten fish scent assailed me from the boy's diarrhea when we entered the room. His chamber pot overflowed and dried feces trailed down the boy's legs. I threw open the window. That helped a little. A quick check of the lad revealed he was in a critical, dehydrated condition. He had the dark blue-grey color to his skin that shows a cholera patient is dying. I cursed and quickly prepared a second packet of the rehydration salts into an oral solution. If I could get the kid to drink the solution, I might save him, but damn, this kid was sick.

"Why didn't you tell Dr. Ryland your son was ailing?" I snapped at Walker.

I will give him credit. The man looked shaken when he realized how sick his boy was. "I swear, Dr. Winslow, I had no idea Malcolm was this sick. He just had a little upset stomach and headache this mornin'…"

I was just about to chew him out good and tell him the child would have been dead in a few more hours without medical attention when the big lug cried. Dammit, I hate it when parents cry. I wanted to cry, too, but I had neither the time nor energy to spare right then if I would save his son. Not to mention the rest of the miserable souls inhabiting this pathetic excuse for a plantation.

"Fine. I need hot water and clean sheets for this boy right now. We have to clean this mess up the best we can. And keep healthy people away from the sick ones."

He looked way beyond rattled. "Will… will my boy live?"

I said nothing as I ladled water into the boy's mouth. It relieved me to see the kid could swallow.

"More," the youngster whispered.

I smiled. It was the first positive sign I had seen since I arrived at the plantation. I gave the boy a bit more. "Maybe. We will see. In the meantime, everyone has to keep clean. We need to get your son cleaned up right away. You make sure everyone washes their hands every time they use the chamber pot or the outhouse. Wash their hands if they empty a chamber pot. Wash their hands if they touch a sick person. Everyone should wash their hands every time anyone thinks about washing their hands. Got it?"

He looked rattled. "Yessuh, Doctor."

By midnight, I was sure the boy would live. We lost three slaves, but ten more were on the mend. By morning, four more were ill, but we quickly started them on rehydration fluids. By the end of the week, we had twenty-five who had experienced some sickness, but it looked like no one else was coming down with it. I quarantined the plantation for twenty days. Dr. Rydell agreed. Mr. Walker bitched and moaned but conceded the issue with little fight. I think he was so relieved his son lived that he was willing to listen to us.

On the twentieth day, I rode out for McCarron's Corner. I arrived there ten days later, on November 1st. I tended to some sick folks at the Cherokee village before I left. I stowed the remaining medical supplies I had brought in Marc and Lily's house with an itemization of what I left. Since they were not back, I made sure Rose, the Cherokee shaman, and Gentry and Michael knew where the medicine was, and how to administer each one.

Shadow Wolf and I talked about my bad timing. He agreed this was not the right time for me to have come. "You will see, Richard Winslow. You will be together again when the time is right."

I tried to smile, but all I managed was a shrug. "Well, we will see. Mom says *sea lo que sea*. It means what will be will be."

He clapped me on the back. "Exactly. It will be as the Great Spirit wills it to be. You must be patient and wait for the Great Spirit to reveal when the time is right."

Silent, I nodded. It's a lot easier to nod like I agree than to get into long, involved philosophical discussions, especially when trying to communicate with a Cherokee chieftain. We both had a rudimentary grasp of the other's language, but neither of us was fluent in the language of the other. Yet, finally, I could hold back the question no longer.

"How will I know the time is right, Wolf?"

"I cannot tell you how, but rest assured, my friend, you will know when the time is right. I promise."

And then, just before the full moon, Shadow Wolf accompanied me to the meadow where the portal to another world was located. As we said our goodbyes, we heard the ominous woofing of an angry black bear. I will never forget that sound until the day I die.

We both looked up just as the bear leaped down from a tree, landing not twenty feet from us. The bear charged towards us. All I remember seeing right then were mammoth-sized bear claws and an open mouth full of teeth. As Wolf reached for his bow and arrow, the angry bear swiped a massive paw across his head. I felt sick as bright red blood sprayed across the bear's face. Adrenaline pumping like mad through my veins, I swung my AR-15 around and aimed. By the time I aimed and shot, Wolf had already released two arrows. The bear let out a howl of pain, raised on his hind legs, and ran towards us again. I shot but the bear just kept coming. I fired again when the bear could not have been more than a couple of feet from me. We were face to face when the big black bear opened its mouth to bite me. I crammed my AR barrel into its gaping maw. As the big demon chewed on my barrel, I somehow pulled the trigger, emptying the magazine down the throat of the bear. Thank God that magazine held thirty rounds. Suddenly, the bear pulled back, moaned once, and collapsed.

It was dead.

It stunned me. It was the most massive black bear I ever saw. It must have weighed at least 500 pounds. I don't think the whole attack could have lasted over a half a minute, but believe me, and it was the longest half a minute of my life. It was also the most scared I had ever been in my life. I was sad I had to shoot the bear, but I didn't have an alternative. It was the bear or us.

I pounded Wolf on the back. "We did it, Wolf! Let me check your head wound."

Wolf winced as I examined his injury. "I thank you, my friend. You saved my life, and I will not forget. The bear would have killed me if you had not been here. I walk softly in the forest these days, always listening for the sounds of a bear. There have been many bears here this year. This wily trickster hid in the branches above us and made no noise until it was almost too late. Brother Bear will help feed our village through the winter."

I quickly assessed Wolf's injuries. The bear's claw had caught him a glancing, raking blow on his scalp, and ripped it about 4 inches long. While there was a lot of bleeding, the cut was not life-threatening. Fortunately, I still had some necessary medical supplies with me, and I could staunch the bleeding, clean the wound, and stitch it up. I helped him skin the bear before I left. Wolf offered me the bearskin, but I figured that it would have been hard to explain to the park ranger at the Beech Bottom Trailhead. They would have wanted me to take them back to the carcass, and no bear carcass would be there. Wolf was still dressing the bear, with the skin at his feet where he was placing chunks of bear meat as I left. The meat would help feed the tribe in the winter to come. We waved to each other, and I headed across the meadow.

"Watch for the Guiding Light. Send her to us!" Wolf shouted.

I grinned and waved again. "Of course!"

Halfway across, I felt the tug on my heart and my body as I came through the time hole. "Wrong time. It was the wrong time." I muttered the words to myself for the zillionth time as I blinked unbidden tears back from my eyes.

I trudged the four miles to the Beech Bottom Trailhead, where I convinced a park ranger to let me use the landline phone. I called Uncle Jim to come and get me. He arrived three hours later in a pounding downpour. He was shocked, thrilled, and, most of all, eager to hear the entire story.

I was back in the future. I knew Lily came back to learn medical skills she would need when she returned to the past. I figured like Lily, I had things to do and learn before I could go at the right time. I understood I went at the wrong time before. I had skills to learn and equipment to obtain before I could go back again. I intended to be a board-certified cardiologist if not a cardiovascular surgeon when I returned. I might not do heart surgery in the $18^{th}$ century, but I would learn how to manage a heart condition without surgery as effectively as possible. I figured I would only get one more chance to go back in time. I had better be ready, and it had better be the right time, the next time.

Too much depended on it.

# Chapter 8
# Fancy
# 1783

We had been married again for almost three months, and what a wild ride it had been.

Marc and Lily still did not know I remarried Kirk. Marc frowned when he felt Kirk was way too forward and yet he somehow always held his tongue. Lily looked puzzled.

My grandfather died shortly before Kirk and I remarried. His death had pulled the attention away from me at Ranscome Manor back over to Waterside.

I gave up trying to resist accompanying Kirk on his voyage when he agreed to take us to Bermuda rather than to Barbados. Marc and Lily, and Hattie Mae and Tobias, came with us. Marc and Lily planned to go back to McCarron's Corner via Charleston after we arrived in Bermuda. Aunt Hattie insisted she would not let me out of her sight soon. Uncle Tobias nodded in agreement.

We sailed to the Canary Islands first, where Kirk took on a load of spices. From the Canary Islands, we sailed west to Puerto Rico and then to Cuba before Kirk swung the Enterprise north to Bermuda. We arrived there in August. Kirk planned to take Marc and Lily to Charleston the first of September, from where they would return on their own to McCarron's Corner. The Enterprise would then sail southward by way of the other Caribbean islands on his way to Barbados. He would stay at the plantation for a month before returning. We hoped he would return by November, and with luck, we might get to Ireland for Christmas. In the meantime, the children and I would enjoy the warm waters and pink sands of beautiful Bermuda.

To say I was shocked to find Clarissa living at Spring Haven would be a gross understatement. She looked equally shocked to see me arrive, married to Kirk.

"What are you doing here? How did you get here?"

She held her head high as she pushed her little boy behind her skirts. "You told me I could come back here for my child. I did. You will not take him from me."

"Not take him? Oh, for the love of all that is holy, I will not take him. The family does not treat family like that. Good lord, woman, why would you think that?" I frowned, frustrated by her comments.

She cast a nervous glance at Marc. Silent, he shrugged. Finally, she responded. "They think I had something to do with you bein' kidnaped."

That rattled me. No one had mentioned Clarissa's involvement. "Why do they think it involved you, Clarissa?"

She gulped and looked at Marc again. "He don't like me none. He told them I did…"

"Nay, I did not. Don't be making up yet another story, lass. She delivered the altered note to ye, Fancy. Rick asked you to meet him at the quay at 1. The note was changed to say 12." Marc looked furious.

I could feel the color drain from my face. "Clarie, you didn't do that, did you?"

She looked uncertain for just a second, and then she straightened up. "Of course not. The family does not treat family like that. Why would I have betrayed Fancy the same day she freed me?"

I nodded. "My thought, exactly."

"Well, it looks like you came out good. You're married to a big, handsome sea captain." She eyed Kirk up and down with a speculative glance.

As Clarie eyed Kirk, I slipped an arm around his waist and pulled him close. "Yes, I did. And remember this: I never told Calvin to get rid of you, but I won't share. Understand?"

As the barest hint of a smile flitted across her lips, she answered. "Yes, ma'am, Miss Fancy."

"You will address the Duchess as 'your Grace.' Do you understand me, girl?" Kirk growled as he placed his arm protectively around my shoulders.

She eyed Kirk up and down again before she answered. "Oh, I understand, Captain O'Malley."

She turned and walked back into the kitchen, her hips swaying seductively back and forth, with the little boy in tow.

"Feckin whore."

I looked at Marc, surprised by the anger in his voice and his use of vulgarity. "Do you think it involved her?"

He nodded. "Aye. We all do. That girl may be kin, but she's nothing but trouble. I'm sorry, Hattie Mae…"

"I understand, Mr. Marc. Tobias and I will keep a close watch on her. We ain't gonna let her do nothing to our Miss Fancy, I promise."

Tobias nodded in agreement with his wife. "As you said, Miss Fancy, the family don't treat family like that. Iffen I learn that girl was involved, well, she don't want that to happen. That's all I got to say."

I realized I might be well-advised not to trust my cousin. Forewarned is forearmed like Daddy Jo always told me.

As chance would have it, Kirk and I argued that morning before they left. Kirk was still trying to get me to accompany him to Barbados. We argued about this over and over. I was adamant in my refusal.

"No. I won't go. I've told you at least a hundred times this week alone. I had that awful dream again last night. I will not go back to Barbados. That's final." My voice cracked with emotion, but I was adamant.

His face darkened with the scowl that marred his handsome features. "Dammit, Fancy, that's just a dream, nothin' more. A wife is supposed to obey her husband."

I shook my head again. "Kirk, I already told you, no. I only agreed to come this far because I thought you agreed we did not have to go on. Don't try to make me go. I know something horrible will happen. Something happens every time I have that blasted dream. And, please, please, don't leave angry like this."

He shook his head as he hoisted his duffel bag over his shoulder. "You're a troublesome woman. I don't know why I love ye so damned much."

*Oh, go on, pull at my heartstrings, you damned Irish rogue,* I wanted to shout as my stomach clenched with pain. But I just shrugged as I blinked back tears, and I held my trembling hands close so he could not see them shake. "Odd way you have of showing it. Please, Kirk, reconsider. Stay here with us, at least for a few days."

He sighed, frustrated and started down the pier towards the Enterprise. Just before he boarded the ship, he turned back towards me. He slung the duffel down again and opened his arms to me. "Fine. Stay if you must, but I canna. I have work to do. Kiss me now, woman, because you're gonna miss me when I'm gone. Who knows? I might be gone a long, long time if your damned dream comes true."

"But the sky is red this morning. 'Red sky in morning, sailors take warning.'" I clung to him, still desperate to keep him from leaving.

He smiled. "Aye. Are ye going to kiss me, or continue to fuss?"

As tears filled my eyes, I nodded and snuggled into his loving embrace. My body melded against his as we kissed. "You take care. And you come back to me, you hear?"

"I hear you, darlin'. I will come back. I love ye, lass." He bent to kiss me again.

I nodded as my hands clung to the crisp linen of his shirt. "I know, you big galoot. I love you, too."

I never meant to fall in love with my wild, Irish rogue, but it turns out he is quite lovable.

Marc, generally quiet, had less than usual to say since I agreed to travel with Kirk. I felt sure he did not approve. Marc still did not know we had married again. Every time I tried to approach the subject, he became upset and told me not to make a stupid decision. Even without words, his disappointment I considered remarrying Kirk was palpable. I could see them on deck. I waved to them and blew them kisses, but I didn't let him see me cry when the ship pulled from the dock. It hurt that I could see his frown of disapproval over the kisses at the pier. I swear it hurt me every bit as bad when he left, angry, as when Richard left without a word in February. I felt as though Daddy and Lily were abandoning me, too.

Two days after they left, the weather was odd. The temperature felt cooler than usual, with lots of clouds, occasional storms and powerful winds from the north. As the rains increased in frequency, strength, and duration, Bella fussed because I would not take the children to the beach. I grew more and more alarmed as band after band of dark, and ominous clouds kept rolling in over our island. I tried to reassure myself that Calvin swore there had never been a hurricane in all the years he lived in Bermuda. If there had not been a hurricane for 35 years that he lived here, surely there would not be one now.

"Have you ever seen the weather like this before since you lived here?" I stared up at the cloud-darkened sky with growing concern.

Clarissa shook her head. "Never. I saw weather like this at Yorktown once. We caught the tail end of a hurricane. I remember Miss Paddy said we were on the 'dirty side' of the storm. I don't rightly know what she meant by that comment, but it rained enough to fill the York River twice over. The streets flooded for a week."

Her words did not comfort me. They left me more worried.

And then in the night that followed, all hell broke loose.

As the rains grew harder and winds picked up in intensity, the servants and I locked the shutters on all the windows. It terrified me as the palm trees almost doubled over from the force of the winds. Fearing the worst, we filled every basin we could find with potable water. The servants who first laughed when I called this a hurricane quit laughing as winds walloped us so fast and furious the house shuddered. I feared the winds would rip the house apart around us.

I knew floodwaters with hurricanes in the islands could exceed depths of twenty feet. Calvin built the house fifteen feet above sea level. He often assured me no storm had ever brought floodwaters overtaking that depth on Bermuda. I moved everyone upstairs in an abundance of caution. I wanted us out of floodwaters if it became deep enough to enter the first floor of the house.

We all huddled together, praying in the hall upstairs as the raging winds screamed past the house through the night. Bella hung right beside me with her eyes wide with worry as Tobias and Hattie clung to Clarissa and her son.

I bent to kiss Bella's cheek. "It will be okay, baby. I promise."

She nodded, and her little body finally sagged against me as she dozed off. I sat there stroking her hair, soft as silk. I sighed as the repetitive motion intended to calm my child calmed me. I realized rubbing her hair affected me much like rubbing fabric soothes me. My eyelids sagged as my tension slipped from my body.

When a flash of lightning hit, we all jumped at the loud crash that followed as one of the tall palms cracked and fell, hitting the roof.

Little Betty awoke screaming and scrambled to cling tight to my neck as she sobbed. "I want my Poppa."

"I know little one. I want your Poppa, too." I bent over to kiss her cheek.

Charlie's eyes flew open, and Uncle Tobias murmured words of comfort to him as Aunt Hattie crooned to baby Bonnie. Clarissa kept patting her son's back to calm the wide-eyed, terrified child, but I could tell it scared her, too. I didn't expect that.

By morning, I knew my worst nightmare had come true. We were in the middle of a hurricane. I have never seen rain or wind before or since like I saw that day. We were alone, without my husband or my father to help us. With a lump in my throat and my heart racing, I prayed harder than I ever prayed in my life that the Good Lord would protect my precious children and keep them safe from harm. I prayed for Daddy and Lily on their journeys, and I prayed for Kirk and his crew, caught somewhere out in open seas during this horrible ordeal.

Once again, my nightmare foretold something terrible was about to happen.

Twenty-four hours later, most people sighed with relief. Unfortunately, the storm severely damaged the roof and cistern, and I could see water leaking through the ceiling. That meant in a matter of days, we would be out of drinking water, on an island with no drinkable water other than rainwater. The flooding had been deep enough in the house to get up to the first floor before the waters receded, leaving a slimy layer of mud and muck covering the first floor. I felt relief it had not been deeper, but the ruined floors and rugs, water-marked walls and damaged furniture left me dismayed and discouraged. Calvin brought beautiful furnishings from England years ago, some of which were antiques handed down in his family.

Unless I were mistaken, much of the first-floor furniture would soon ruin after sitting in three feet of water overnight. I instructed the servants to sweep the muck out of the house, to scrub the floors and walls, and to sit the parlor furniture out in the sun on the porch. Aunt Hattie set to work cleaning the kitchen while the other servants worked in the parlor and Calvin's office.

By noon, I could smell harmful vapors from the accumulated sludge and water damage. I knew black mold would likely cover the first-floor walls and furniture in a few days. Lily warned me black mold is toxic. We used vinegar as much as possible to clean everything because Lily told me it had some germicidal qualities and could stop black mold. It saddened me to realize many of Calvin's books would be a total loss. I worked at a feverish pace, wiping the books with vinegar to salvage as many as possible. I could tell hundreds of the priceless first edition books he collected over the years were probably ruined.

I will give credit where credit is due: Clarissa worked feverishly to help clean up the mess. I wasn't sure how she stayed so calm. In contrast, I was terrified, but I did not have time to fall apart. Come to think of it, maybe that was how my cousin felt, too. I struggled to take deep, calming breaths like Lily had taught me as I rubbed the fabric of my skirt back and forth between my fingers, desperate for the calm detachment which usually came from the repetitive movement.

As the staff worked on salvaging the house and belongings, I decided I should go to the harbor to seek a way off the devastated island. It was up to me to get us off Bermuda if we were to survive. I could do this. I had to. My children needed me to stay courageous.

Filthy water and rubbish littered the flooded streets. I trudged through thigh-high floodwaters to the port, to learn if any ships were fit to sail. I sighed with relief to see the Ranscome Revelation had come through the storm with flying colors and was in port.

"Captain Peavy, is she safe to sail?" I sagged against the rail with exhaustion.

Her captain stared, stunned to see me. "Your Grace, what on earth are you doing here?"

"Trying to get my family off this blasted island. Can you take us?"

"Of course, Lady Fancy. It's your ship. Can you have your family down here this afternoon?"

"I can have them here in an hour if some of your men can help me. Thank you, Captain."

The Captain turned and called out to a deckhand. "Jack, help Her Grace get back to Spring Haven. Get the children and any of her servants who wish to accompany her together to come to the ship. Take a half dozen of the men along to help haul their things back here."

The men hurried along with me back to the house. Somehow, I scribbled out a note for Kirk. My hands were shaking so hard I hoped he could decipher my near illegible scrawl. I left the note tacked to the mantel, where I hoped he would find it when he returned. I prayed again that he was safe and had come through the storm unscathed. Within the hour, we were packed.

"I'm not going." Clarissa's voice sounded tight yet determined.

I blinked, unsure I had heard her right. "Not going? Are you sure, Clarie? It damaged the cistern. You will run out of water."

"I don't care. My baby and I are free. We are stayin' here, where my little man was born. I'll try to get the place fixed up before you come back."

I pulled her to me as if to hug her. I knew I could whisper to her that way. "I'll get Captain Peavy to bring you water, and for his men to fix the cistern and roof. Now, tell me the truth. Why won't you go?"

She shook her head as tears filled her eyes. "I ain't ever goin' back to the Colonies. I'll stay here, or I'll go on to England."

I frowned. "But…"

She shook her head again. "I ain't goin' back there. Ain't no one ever gonna treat me like dirt again…"

Her voice broke.

As I hugged her tight, we both cried. "I swear, Clarie, I didn't know you were here. He never told me."

She nodded as she sobbed. "I realize that now. I realize you are just tryin' to take care of us all. But I can't go back there. Here, I'm a housekeeper. There, I'm nothing more'n a common whore. Iffen I go back, that's all I'll ever be. Just a colored whore."

"Don't talk about yourself like that…" I began.

She shook her head. "No, I done decided. Toby and I will be fine. I promise."

I left her a note that said Toby and she were both free and that she was free to go anywhere she chose. A second note allowed Ranscome shipping to transport her wherever she might want if she decided to leave. I left her a letter of reference to ensure she could find work. And lastly, I gave her £100. "I wish I had more to leave."

She hugged me tightly. "I never expected you to leave me money, Fancy. I—I—" She began to cry again.

I hugged her close once more. "They did you wrong, Clarie. Heck fire, they did us both wrong. Just tell me one thing."

She nodded as she wiped her nose with her handkerchief.

"He's Calvin's boy, isn't he?"

She looked shocked by my question and began crying again. She finally nodded.

"The sorry bastard should have married you," I whispered. "This should be Toby's inheritance."

"He told me he was gonna marry me when we first left Belle Rose, but when we got here, Calvin made it clear he bought me from Tom. Calvin said he intended to marry you when you turned eighteen. It just about killed me," she whispered as tears welled up in her eyes.

I wondered how Calvin would have reacted to learn his duplicity with Clairee resulted in such dire results for me. Would he have cared? His poor treatment of Clairee adversely affected me. It didn't affect him. He was all about appearances. It would have upset him if it made him look bad when something horrible happened to me. Tarleton would not have carried me off to try to force me to marry him if I had still been married to Calvin – unless Tarleton killed Calvin first.

It wasn't the first time I wondered if Tarleton had something to do with Calvin's untimely death.

The sailors threw a trunk up to carry on each man's shoulders and headed for the ship. The servants and I followed with the children and carried other personal items best we could. The sight of the deep water we had to wade through made little Betty cry. She clung tight to my Uncle Tobias' neck.

"I want my Poppa." Betty's voice was soft as tears welled in her grey eyes, so much like Kirk's eyes. She is her Poppa's girl, and she had missed Kirk bitterly since he left.

Uncle Tobias held her close, talking to her in a soothing voice. It impressed me once again at his easy-going, steady demeanor in the face of chaos. I reckon if my Uncle Tobias had been born a white man instead of black, he would have become one of the imminent leaders of our country with his calm temperament, quick mind, and strength of character.

Aunt Hattie held tight to little Charles, who remained silent with eyes big as saucers. I noticed she had tears in her eyes, but as stoic as ever, she pushed on with only one longing look back at her granddaughter and great-grandson.

As she stifled a sob, I hugged her. "She's tough. She'll be okay."

"I know. That girl is a regular little alley cat. She's always gonna land on her feet. Besides, she's a grown woman. I'm worried about her child. My poor baby." She stifled a sob as she turned away from watching Clarissa and Toby and started towards the docks.

I tied baby Bonnie to me in a sling. Bella refused to go with anyone else and clung tight to my arm. At times I had to lift her to keep her above the fast running water. We were both trembling from exhaustion and fear by the time we reached the ship.

Captain Peavy helped us onboard and ushered us to his quarters. He shook his head as I protested. "No, ma'am, not a word. You own this ship. You shall take my quarters. We'll be there well before morning. I will manage just fine with the men. I doubt I'll sleep much tonight, anyway."

I tried to smile, but I could see from my reflection in the window that it came out more like a grimace. "Thank you, sir. I shall always remember your kindness."

"Harrumph. Nonsense, m'dear. You take care of these babies, and we'll set sail. Cook will bring you all some dinner. Hopefully, we'll make landfall before midnight."

Hattie and I got the children into dry, clean clothes, and well-fed before we got the exhausted children bedded down. Bella and Betty huddled, whispering long after the younger babies fell asleep. They were my big girls at 5 and 4 and had a better understanding of the seriousness of the situation. I could tell our circumstances shook them both. Heck fire, it shocked me. I changed out of my soaked garments into a clean, dry shift before I laid down between the girls. They finally fell asleep, clinging to me as I stroked their hair.

Around midnight, I heard a sailor cry out, "Land ho!" I relaxed a little, knowing soon we would be back on the mainland of the United States. I gently eased away from the girls and slipped out of the Captain's enormous bed. I pulled a big shawl around my shoulders, tiptoed to the door, and slipped out without disturbing the sleeping children. I crept out on the deck to watch the men working to bring the elegant ship into the port of Charleston. Uncle Tobias was there, puffing on his pipe, watching the men bring the craft into the harbor. He wrapped an arm around my shoulders as we watched. I felt my tension begin to slip away in his protective embrace. We both knew he wasn't supposed to be so forward with a white woman in public, but by damn, it was late, it was my ship, and he was my uncle. If anyone dared to say anything, they best expect my angry reply and the pink slip that would follow.

As we slid up to the dock, the Captain spoke. "All is well, Your Grace. You can go back to bed. Get some rest. We will find you accommodations in the morn unless you want me to carry you up to Belle Rose."

I hesitated only a minute. "No. I will write a letter to my brother and let him know we are safe, but I want to head west, after my father."

He nodded. "I suspected as much when you asked me to bring you to Charleston. I'll send the men out again at first light to see if Mr. Marc might still be here. The hurricane probably slowed them down."

"I hope so. I dread to think of my parents on the road amidst heavy rains and flooding," I murmured.

He nodded in agreement.

I slept after I returned to the enormous bed. About 7 a.m., I went up on deck with the children. It dismayed me to see extensive hurricane damage to the City of Charleston. However, the floodwaters were already draining off, and people were outside, making repairs to their homes and businesses. An hour later, as I pointed out various things to the children, I noticed a sailor come running on board.

"Cap'n Peavy, I found 'em!"

I made a beeline for the sailor and Captain Peavy. I noticed they both looked gravely worried. "What's wrong?"

"It's your father, ma'am," began the sailor. "He's been hurt. Bad hurt."

My heart started beating hard, fast, and crazy. I pressed a hand to my chest and took a deep breath. "How bad? What's wrong?"

"Broke leg, ma'am. Miss Lily be havin' one hell of a hard time convincing the old sawbones there not to take his leg off." The sailor shifted nervously from foot to foot as he twisted his cap in his hands.

I felt the blood drain from my face. Hands shaking, I handed the baby to Hattie and started running off the ship. "Take me to him. Now."

The sailor hesitated only a second before he nodded and ran ahead to lead me to my father.

Lily was holding her own when we arrived, but I could tell she was on her last nerve.

"I tell you again, sir, you will not cut off my husband's leg. I stabilized the break, a simple fracture. There is not even a break in the skin. You. Will. Not. Amputate. This. Limb. Do you understand me?"

My heart lurched at the sound of Lily's voice. Her voice was loud, assertive, yet I could hear the strident, near-hysterical edge of fear in each word. I rushed up beside her. "I'm the Duchess of Ranscome. This man is my father. What's the problem, Doctor?"

The elderly doctor turned towards me, surprise and relief written all across his haggard features. "He broke his leg, ma'am. And this fool woman won't let me take the leg. He'll die unless I remove it."

Lily let out an unladylike snort. "More likely he'll die if you take his leg with those filthy instruments. I tell you again, sir, you will *not* touch my husband."

I cringed as her voice rose to a shrill note I had never heard from Lily before. I reached out a trembling hand to hers. "Is he stable?"

She nodded. "Oh, yes. Quite stable. And this quack will not cut off Marc's leg. I already splinted it, so it's stable. I need to set it. I thought this so-called Doctor would help me do that, but all this quack wants to do is lop off Marc's leg."

I could tell it took all Lily could do not to cry. I stepped in front of her. "Doctor, Mrs. McCarron is a well-known healer. She was at Yorktown. She knows when to amputate a limb…"

"Balderdash! The woman is emotionally overwrought. She is not thinking rationally. Now, if you will get her out of here…"

"No." I have to admit even I was surprised by the calm, firm tone with which I spoke.

He stopped and blinked two times. Mouth agape, he took his spectacles off and wiped them with his filthy handkerchief. Finally, he replaced them, and peering over them, glowered at me. "Now, look here, little lady, I don't care if you are the Queen of Siam…"

I struggled not to laugh. I knew the doctor intended to intimidate me, to force me to cower down to him. Not this time, buster. Somehow, I glowered back at him. "No. If Mrs. McCarron says the leg stays on, it stays on."

"But…" His face turned purple with rage.

I held up my hand as I shook my head. I pointed a finger right at him. "No, I agree with Mrs. McCarron. You will *not* remove Mr. McCarron's leg. Do you understand, sir?"

"Oh, I understand, all right. I understand you two stupid women will kill this man. Fine. It's on your heads, not mine." He spun and marched stiffly out of the room.

Lily crumpled against me as the doctor left. "Oh, thank God you're here…"

My heart lurched as she cried. I pulled her into my arms, where we both clung together, trembling. "It will be okay now, Lily. You'll see."

She nodded. I could feel her regaining her calm. That was good because I feared I was about to lose mine. I closed my eyes and leaned against her as I took a deep breath.

"I know. It's just been a horrible twenty-four hours, which culminated with that damned man trying to butcher my Marc." She struggled to control her trembling.

Marc reached towards her from the pallet on which he laid. "Aye, but ye held yer own against him, *mo leannan*. T'will be fine now. You'll see."

Marc's appearance disturbed me. He looked like he hadn't shaved since he left Bermuda days earlier. I realized grey mottled his ragged beard. He looked thin and haggard, with pain etched across his face. His hands trembled as he reached towards me as I bent to kiss his cheek. My heart lurched. I had never seen my Daddy look like this before. I quickly kissed him, hugged him tightly, and pasted a smile on my face like I had learned to do from Tamsin.

Lily wasn't much better. Her hair looked like an unruly rat's nest of tangled red curls. Her complexion was pallid with bright pink splotches on her cheeks, probably from anger or anxiety or both. Her gown was soiled, and one shoulder was torn. I noticed with alarm that her hands, ever steady, were still shaking like leaves.

"Can you help get my Daddy and Miss Lily back to the ship? I'll head out to see if I can locate an inn that is in decent enough condition to house us. We can set his leg once we get you guys situated, if that is all right, Lily."

Lily nodded as a spark of excitement flashed through her eyes. "Oh, that would be wonderful, Fancy. Thank you."

I flashed a smile at her, too, and grabbed her close for a hug. "It will all be okay, Lily. I promise."

Her eyes clouded with new unshed tears as she nodded to me, wordless.

"Oh, no, ma'am!" The sailor assigned to help me shook his head. "Captain will skin my hide if I let you wander around Charleston alone. Charleston ain't safe for a woman out by herself right now. Ye stay here, and I'll go fetch more men to help me get you and your Dad someplace overnight."

Lily nodded again. I noticed the shaking of her hands lessened as she calmed. "I guess he's right. Stay here with me. I may need you again against Dr. MacDirty. I'm sure he would continue pressuring me to let him lop Marc's leg off if you left."

"Well, that's not going to happen." It surprised me I sounded as loud as I did. God only knew I felt scared witless.

She half-way grinned. "I know. But I might hurt the damned fool."

We moved Marc to another spot, further from the saw-happy doctor and his filthy surgical field. Marc groaned as we settled him onto the new pallet, but quickly tried to smile at us both. "I'm all right. Lily, why don't you see if you can help anyone else?"

She snuffled. "I would except the doctor made it clear he has no respect for 'crazy women healers.' Besides, I would prefer to stay right here by you, given his bizarre desire to lop off your leg. I don't trust the damned man any further than I can spit."

"Nor do I," I chimed in. "And I bet Lily has set more broken legs than he has ever seen."

She sniffed again. "I don't know about that, but I bet I saved a good many broken legs the fool man would have amputated. He is damned sure not going to cripple my Marc. Not on my watch."

After we got back to the Enterprise and got Marc settled, I felt better once I knew my Daddy was safe. My heartbeat slowed down, and I felt less like I might faint or puke. *Everything will be okay*, I said to myself over and over. *Take a deep breath, Fancy girl. Everything will be okay.*

I hurried into town to hunt for plaster. It took almost an hour, but I finally found a store open that still had some good, dry plaster. I paid, thanked the merchant, and hurried back to the ship where Lily had already prepared Marc's leg for the cast. I had seen her cast limbs before at Yorktown. I knew it was a medical skill not commonly used, which would become much more common in the future, although Lily assured me better methods of casting were yet to come. She had already soaked strips of fine linen from one of my clean petticoats I gave her and had a soft layer of linen around his leg. She quickly prepared the plaster and applied the plaster-soaked bandages around Marc's leg.

"There. That should do it. It will take up to 48 hours for the cast to cure, but it is already firming up. I'm pleased with the way it looks."

The ship's doctor let out a low whistle of appreciation. "I'm impressed, Mistress. Thank you for allowing me to assist. Hopefully, I will save more of the limbs of injured sailors with this new technique."

Lily flashed him a smile. "Yes, this technique should help. It stabilizes the limb far better than splints around the leg, immobilize the limb with strips of fabric stiffened with egg whites, or even with a flour and egg mixture. Starch is an excellent stiffening agent to use in a pinch at sea, also, although it is not as good as plaster of Paris. Another method immobilizes the joint with starched strips of linen. I prefer to use plaster instead of starch if it is available. Just remember, the cast must stay on 6 to 8 weeks, and the limb will be weak from lack of use when you remove the cast. The plaster cast also allows the patient to be up and about after 48 hours, but no climbing in the rigging. The man will move awkwardly with poor balance while in the cast. And when it is time to remove it, use a handsaw, carefully. You don't want to amputate the limb you saved."

That's my Lily. She can stay calm when I would be frantic. Here she was teaching another doctor a new skill while she set Daddy's broken leg.

Once Lily stabilized Daddy's leg in the cast, I hustled around town hunting for a place where we could stay. I shook with exhaustion and dripped sweat by the time I finally located suitable accommodations at an inn just west of town. The innkeeper would even provide a decent room downstairs for Marc and Lily. My breath started coming easier as I paid half the price so he would hold the rooms. Once paid, I hurried back to the ship with a lighter step than I'd had since before the blasted hurricane.

We quickly rounded up everyone except Lily and Marc. Lily insisted they wait until the next day before moving Marc. "I want this cast to set up properly before we move him again."

I nodded and herded the rest of the crowd on to the inn. I explained to the innkeeper that my father and stepmother would arrive the next day. We got everyone settled in, although it upset me the accommodations provided to Aunt Hattie and Uncle Tobias were less than ideal.

"I thought you assured me you had rooms for everyone," I protested as my heart started beating way too fast again.

The elderly innkeeper scratched his head before he spat out his tobacco. "Well, Miss, you didn't tell me you wuz bringin' slaves."

I let out a sigh of exasperation. "They are not slaves. Both are free. Why don't you say what you mean? You won't put them up in the main house because they are colored."

The man at least had the decency to blush at my accusation. "Now listen here, little missy, I'm bein' more than fair. Most folk wouldn't put them up at all. You know good and well no self respectin' white folk would sleep in a bed they done slept in."

I huffed up again, ready to tell him we would go on then when my Uncle Tobias laid a hand on my arm. "Miss Fancy, ain't no big thing to us. I done slept in far worse than what he be offering us. We will all be jus' fine, here. Now, let me help get everyone situated. You go sit down and rest. You ain't done nothin' but run all day, and you are startin' to cough like you do when you get exhaustipated. We'll be jus' fine."

The innkeeper nodded. "Smart boy, you got there. Listen to him, ma'am. Ain't no need to go off half-cocked tonight."

I still seethed with unspent fury as they both turned to move baggage into the inn. It infuriated me when people referred to my uncle as 'boy,' when he was a better man than most men I ever knew. I sat down and tried to catch my breath as I wiped my sweaty hands on my skirt again for the umpteenth time that day.

I shook my head. I will never understand why some people treat others so poorly. I have seen it all my life. I have been the victim of it much of my life because of my black blood. I dared not tell the innkeeper my babies, and I all bore black blood. The innkeeper looked startled when he saw Betty, but after a quick look at my frowning face, he allowed her into the house.

I was still seething with anger later at supper. I noticed the innkeeper let Aunt Hattie cook, even though he wouldn't let her sleep in the house.

As Hattie served up bowls of piping hot chicken soup, she grinned and winked. "Don't you worry, honey child. The loft in the barn is dry and comfortable. We got blankets and pillows. We will be just fine. And we won't have to worry 'bout getting no lice from his beds."

"Dear Lord, I hadn't even considered lice. Dad blast it, now I will have to check everyone's hair each day for lice and nits." I shook my head in frustration and disgust.

Aunt Hattie laughed. "Child, you do that anyway. You do it every day as a matter of course. That's one reason we never see bugs in the hair of these young' uns."

The next morning, I made my way back to the ship while Hattie Mae watched my children. As men carried Marc in a litter, Lily and I hurried along beside them until I spotted a boy selling news sheets. I stepped over to the boy and pulled out a penny for the paper. I gasped, and I could feel the color drain from my face as I read the headlines.

"Thousands believed dead because of the Dreadful Hurricane, the worst to hit North America during this century. At least one ship destroyed in her wake."

"What ship sank?" I gasped as I scanned down the page. *No, no, no, no, please God, no.*

I spotted the name as the boy pronounced the word. "The Ranscome Enterprise, ma'am."

Lily rushed to catch me as I swooned.

"How on earth do they know that?" She snapped the words out as if they left a unpleasant taste in her mouth.

The boy shrugged. "They been pickin' up wreckage from the Enterprise all up and down the coast from that ship. They even found the figurehead washed up about 20 miles south of here. Why?"

"My husband captains the Enterprise. Have they found many survivors?"

The boy looked shocked. "No, ma'am. Nary a one. A whole bunch o' bodies done washed up, but they ain't found no live folk washed up from the Enterprise."

I fainted.

# Chapter 9
# Fancy
# 1783 and Then Some

I felt empty. Everything seemed to move around me in slow motion as if I were in a fog or some surreal nightmare. Lily called it 'disassociating.' I understood what was happening, but I felt nothing except emptiness. Could I bear the loss of another man I loved? Could I bear another scar upon my heart?

We planned to stay in Charleston for two weeks. But as the stores of food and freshwater grew slim, and the town had outbreaks of deadly diseases, we headed west towards McCarron's Corner.

"I feel like a coward, turning tail and running, but with these children…" Lily sounded thoroughly frustrated.

I finished her sentence for her. "We aren't taking any undue chances. It's not cowardly. We're using our God-given good sense. I must take care of my babies. I'm all they have now."

Wordless, Lily nodded.

I freed all my servants, who were not already free. Most decided to tough it out and stay in Charleston rather than travel west to brave Indian Territory. Hattie Mae and Tobias finally decided they would get passage on a Ranscome ship and headed north to Belle Rose. Aunt Hattie said the trip west to the Indian Territory sounded terrifying. They took letters to Will, Sassy, and one to post to Tam. I sent another letter to the ship captain to confirm they were free and allowed to travel to the Belle Rose Plantation. Another letter advised Ranscome captains it permitted them to transport Clarissa Selk and her son, Tobias, from Bermuda to any place they might wish to go. Tobias and Hattie assured me they would get word to Clarie about what happened and where they headed. I hated to see them go, but I knew it was for the best.

Somehow, we found a decent Conestoga wagon and a team of mules. On the tenth day, we started for the Cohutta Wilderness Marc loved so much.

It would be a significant understatement to say it was rough going.

The roads were still a quagmire of mud and muck as we headed out of Charleston. We considered traveling south to Savannah but decided the roads were far too waterlogged to try. Instead, we struggled westward for Fort Augusta.

It took a full twenty days to travel to Fort Augusta. Along the way, I grabbed news sheets in every town we passed. Each sheet bore more and more horrific stories about the storm. Each confirmed not only the devastation to human lives in the hurricane but the destruction of crops, which would cripple the coastal areas for at least the next year. We passed acre after acre of ruined rice, hammered flat by the rains, rotting in stagnant water. The overwhelming, acrid odor of rotting rice hung thick in the air like a miasma of grief and sadness. Each subsequent news sheet we obtained confirmed the loss of the Enterprise, although bits of debris were still washing up along the South Carolina and Georgia coasts. Not one survivor of my ill-fated ship appeared.

Seventy lives lost seems like a small number compared to the tens of thousands lost up and down the coast. Yet, those seventy were my men, my crew, and yes, my husband.

I finally understood what Sassy meant when she used to say she didn't know why Owen had to up and die. Owen was her first husband, and he was Richard's father. He had a heart attack and died in Sassy's arms as they were moving into the house they had just bought. She always sounded so lost, confused, hopeless when she told me about that day. Now, I understood her grief over the death of a man she ever loved and sometimes hated.

Like Sassy says, love is complicated.

Marc told me he was sorry for my loss when we first learned the Enterprise had gone down. However, I could see the light shine in his eyes, which had been missing for months since I allowed Kirk to stay with me. Marc still did not know I remarried Kirk. No one in my family knew we remarried in Ireland.

When we arrived in Fort Augusta, the news sheets proclaimed the loss of the Enterprise and all men on board in the Dreadful Hurricane of 1783. As a smile played upon Marc's lips, I confronted him.

"Don't you have a shred of sympathy for the men lost? Or their families? Must you gloat over their deaths?"

Marc looked shocked. "Aye, I feel sympathy for those lost souls, and I ken t' was a significant loss for your shipping line to lose such a canny ship. But Fancy, aren't you better off without the damned man?"

"I cannot believe you would ask that, Marc. Are his daughters better off without him? Was Fitz better off to grow up without your brother there to be his father?"

I didn't push it. Somehow, I managed not to ask Marc if I was better off growing up without him.

My voice broke with emotion. I realized I clenched my fists. I struggled to relax them.

His irises flared with specks of gold that revealed his anger as his lips narrowed. Lily says his lips disappear when he gets angry. They sure disappeared right then.

"I notice ye dinna ask if I think yer better off without him, *m'inion*. Aye, I think so. You're better off without the man. So are the babes. And for all we ken, he isna' Bonnie's Da at all."

I felt the flush creep up my neck and onto my face as my cheeks reddened. "Oh, shut up. Even a poor father is better than no father…"

"Indeed? Well, wasn't Tom Selk summat like a father to ye for all those years after Jo died? And how did that work out for ye?"

Cheeks red with shame and fury, I snapped at him again. "Dammit, Marc, don't ask stupid questions. Tom was never like a father to me, and you know it. My life would have been ever so much better if *you* had been in my life then. Instead, they left me to the not-so-tender mercies of a half-brother by adoption who hated me, judging by the way he abused me for years."

By then, my hands were shaking, my heart was beating hard and fast, and my temper most definitely flashed. I struggled to control my breathing. I pressed my hand against my chest as I tried to force my heart to slow down. "Besides, we damned sure don't know Bonnie isn't his daughter, do we? There's no way to know now, in 1783. The other man who *might* be her daddy turned tail and ran. Again. So even if Kirk isn't her daddy, no one else is around to step into his shoes. I don't even know where Richard is. God alone knows. Just like God only knows which of the two is her true daddy. Richard could be anywhere in this world. Heck fire, he could have gone Beyond."

Marc looked stunned by my words and nodded without uttering another word. We rode on in awkward silence to find an inn for the night.

The children were all thrilled to be out of the wagon and on dry land again. We stayed in Ft. Augusta for several days, to restore our supplies and rest before tackling the rest of the journey. Soon we would cross into Indian Territory and then into the Blue Ridge Mountains and the Cohutta Wilderness Marc loved so dearly. Travel would be harder with the wagon and children than it would have been with all of us on horseback, but we were nervous about letting Marc or the children ride a horse. However, Marc fussed so much over being in the wagon that Lily finally relented and let him buy a horse to ride at least part of the way to McCarron's Corner.

They no longer went by Fitz Simmons. They were back in the skin they were most comfortable in, their McCarron skin. I sighed of relief because I wasn't a Duchess here. I was once again Plain Fancy, the McCarron's Daughter. Lord knows I love being the McCarron's Daughter and never wanted to be the Duchess of Ranscome. Being the Duchess had brought me naught but pain and heartache. I didn't want this peaceful time in my life to end. I wanted to stay Plain Fancy, the McCarron's Daughter, forever. I knew it would have to end eventually, but maybe I could stay here awhile with my family in the vast, beautiful solitude of the Cohutta Wilderness. My children needed this.

I needed it more.

I remembered how much I loved it out here when Will brought me in '78. I left Belle Rose broken and wounded. As Sassy said, I was still a victim when I left Belle Rose. I was not yet a survivor. Marc, Lily, and Sassy took Bella and me in with open hearts and open arms. In the months that followed our arrival, I did a lot of healing and even more maturing. They all helped me move from being a scared little victim to being a survivor. I was afraid when we returned to Belle Rose the next year after everything that had transpired there. I did not want to fall back into that old victim role, but fortunately, the lessons I learned at McCarron's Corner held me in good stead. When we returned to Belle Rose, I had healed some. I had a new calm of spirit, a new determination, a new self-confidence I had never felt before. I have recovered even more in the years since then.

Living in the wilderness will make a girl strong and self-reliant. So will acceptance and love by the people around you. And now, I was eager to go back to McCarron's Corner.

Some time, Lily drove the wagon carrying Marc, the children, and me. At other times, she would give in and let Marc ride horseback. Marc took frequent breaks in the wagon. He may have been feeling claustrophobic in the wagon with four children, but riding tired him out pretty quickly. She would ride alongside him on her mare then, and I would drive the wagon.

It took us another twenty days to get home. By then, nearly three months had passed since the hurricane. The leaves had already turned colors, and there was a frosty nip in the air as we pulled into McCarron's Corner.

The village was dark and silent except for a lone, quacking duck. No one remained.

Marc slowly dismounted from the wagon to walk around the eerily silent and empty homes. He went from house to house, searching for the people. The settlers abandoned their cabins and took all the livestock except for the one raucous, errant duck. At last, Marc came back, worry all over his face.

"There's nary a soul here. I doona understand it. Where could they be? Where would they have gone? These families worked hard for their land. They wouldn't have just up and left…"

My heart lurched as his voice broke. Lily scrambled down from her mare and threw her arms around his shoulders. "We'll figure it out, darling. But it's late, and we're all exhausted. Let's get everyone inside our house. Tomorrow, we can go over to the village and find out what's going on."

He looked around once more, and then his shoulders slumped as he nodded. He helped the children down from the wagon and stood watching them as Lily and I began unloading the supplies we would need that night. I started a fire and put a pot on to boil water for tea and then began bustling about to prepare dinner for three adults and four children. I may be a Duchess now, but I have had lots of experience running a house. I jerked the dust covers off the furniture and began setting things right again. Finally, with a lot of coaxing, Marc and I got the children to come back in. Bonnie was already fast asleep in her cradle by the fire as we sat down for our first meal back home.

I noticed Marc rubbing his upper thigh. "Does your leg hurt?"

He looked over at me as if startled by my question. His hand dropped from his leg like a child caught with his hand in the cookie jar. As his face colored red with embarrassment, he nodded. "Aye, a little."

I figured if my Daddy admitted his leg hurt 'a little,' it was most likely paining him pretty good. I mentioned it to Lily, who took him a cup of willow bark tea and began massaging his leg.

Morning came early. As always, Marc was up at the crack of dawn. As he was about to leave to go over to Wolf's village, we heard a tentative knock at the door. Marc pulled it open and then grinned ear to ear as he pulled Shadow Wolf into the house for an enormous bear hug. Michael, my half-brother, followed right after his father-in-law. Lily rushed over with a squeal of delight to hug her son.

"We saw the smoke from the village, and we worried there might be a problem," Michael finally explained. "We came over to make sure everything was okay."

Marc's brow furrowed as he frowned. "Why? What happened? We noticed last night the other houses are empty, and all the livestock is gone."

Michael nodded. "Aye, the others all moved on, either to our village or south towards Fort Augusta."

"But why? I don't understand." Lily's brow furrowed as she frowned with worry and concern.

"The Chickamauga Cherokees are on the warpath. They intend to run the white settlers back out of the Indian Territory. They have killed a passel of settlers all across the area. We warned the folk here, and they sought protection from us or moved out." Wolf shrugged as if embarrassed.

Marc's frown deepened. "But the Cherokees wouldn't have this land if I had not given it to them. I was here first."

Wolf nodded. "Then you understand how many of the Cherokees feel. The Cherokee nation extended from the northern part of this country to the south of us, and from the east coast far to the west. Sassy thought we came from the Appalachian region, and the split between Northern and Southern Iroquoian languages began many long years ago. Our oral tradition told us the *AniYunwiya* migrated south in ancient times from the Great Lakes region, where other peoples lived who spoke a similar language. That is why they call us the people of another language. But never forget we were living here in all this land long before the white man ever came, my brother. And you must admit, not all whites understand us or embrace our people and our ways like you do."

Marc blinked. "So, the hostilities between our people have begun."

Wolf nodded. "Of course, they have. The hostilities started long ago. We saw it in Virginia before we came here. That's why we came here. Gen. Washington is a principled man, but he has not been kind to our people, even when we helped him fight the French. You know that. He plans to civilize us, to make us become like the white man. We chose to come here so we could keep our old ways. You and I have discussed how unfair it is that your people pushed mine back from the rich lands of the tidewaters. Now, I have grown to love these mountains. But my people were in this country long before yours knew or even suspected these lands existed, Marc."

Marc blinked. "So… you do not want me here? Am I no longer wanted here? Is that what you're telling me, Wolf?"

I cringed as Marc's voice broke.

Wolf shook his head and clapped Marc's back. "No. Do not talk nonsense, Marc. I did not say that. You are more than my friend. You are my brother. You are Cherokee, as are Michael and Lily. You are part of our tribe. You were all adopted into our tribe. Michael married my daughter. They are the parents of two children of our tribe with a third on the way. It is good that Lily and you have returned. Richard swore the people of our tribe would come through this safely in the days ahead of us. But I am worried it is not safe for your family to stay over here away from our village, my brother. There is safety in numbers."

My heart began beating crazily as Marc blinked twice, his mouth ajar. "But the Cohutta Wilderness belonged to me before it became Indian Territory…"

Wolf nodded but remained silent. I resisted the urge to point out the land was Indian land long before Europeans came to these shores, much less this land. If Wolf could hold his tongue, I would, too.

Marc stood up, straight and tall. His face grim, he finally answered again. "They'd best not mess with me nor mine. This land is our home. Ye know I invited you to bring your tribe here, to share this land with me. I didn't have to invite yer people here. I invited you because you are family to me. If you mean to reject us now…"

"No, Da, that's not what Wolf means. You're the Lone Wolf. Mam is the Red Moon Woman. I am the Red Wolf, and I am married to the Bright Star of Hope. I know my sister interests several men who would gladly offer her their hand in marriage if she were ready for another man. But we fear the Chickamauga's may not realize you are part of the Cohutta Cherokees if you are not living in the village. And in particular, even if they know who *you* are, they will not know who Fancy and the wee bairns are. We doona want harm to come to any of them."

Marc stood staring at them, the anger plain across his face. He was puffing, and Lily looked concerned. Wordless, she slipped an arm around his waist and pulled her body close to him.

"Yes, I am concerned about your daughter and her children. If you move to the safety of our village…" Wolf began.

"No." Marc's answer was short and concise.

Wolf frowned. "But, Marc…"

"No. We will not turn tail from our home and run." Marc glowered at his old friend. "I built this home with my own two hands. I willna' run in fear."

"Always the oak, Marc." Wolf shook his head as if he were frustrated with his old friend.

Marc nodded and remained silent.

"But sometimes we must be the willow and bend. For the oak snaps in a high wind, and the willow does not."

Marc shook his head again. "Nay. The Lone Eagle needs his own space. You know me well enough to know this. I always lived apart from the village to maintain my independence. We're close to the village. We're only a few miles from ye. If need be, we can come for refuge. But they will not force me from my home like a rat."

"Perhaps Brother Rat is wise to move when the small hunter becomes the prey." Wolf looked increasingly frustrated by Marc's refusal.

I felt scared. Lily looked like she was, too. "Marc, maybe we should…"

"No. McCarron's Corner is my home. I will not turn tail and run. I worked too long and too hard for this property. I fought in two wars for these acres. I cleared and planted this land with my own two hands. My wife has doctored your people for twenty years. We will not move from our home."

I could feel terror rising inside me. I stepped forward, clutching Bonnie to me. "Now, Daddy, maybe we need to think about this …"

Wordless, he gave me a look that silenced my voice. His green eyes were so dark they looked almost black, but I could see the gold stars twinkling from the dark pools that always meant it was the wrong time to cross him. I swallowed hard, nodded, rubbed my sweat-dampened hands on my skirt, and stepped back.

"We'll stay." His voice was low and hard.

"But, Da…" Michael began, only to let the words trail off into nothing. Michael looked stricken by Marc's words, but he knew our father well enough not to argue with him. Once Marc's temper cooled, he might come around. But right then, there was no way that bull-headed Irishman would give in. As he said, it was his land. They would not run him off his property, especially the Cherokee people he helped so many times over the decades.

I herded the older children outside to pull carrots and onions to go in a pot of soup. Lily held Bonnie close as we left the cabin. Charles stayed inside, clinging to his Poppa's leg, eyes big as saucers. I realized my son had never seen Indians before. He looked rattled.

I knew how my son felt. I felt rattled, too, and I had seen Cherokee warriors before. Heck fire, a few courted me when I lived here with Sassy.

As I looked back to check on Charlie, Michael knelt by my son to show him the tattoos across his face. I always thought the symmetrical tattoos on each side of his face resembled paw prints. I said that to him once, and he told me they represented the paw prints of a wolf. Since they inked the marks in red, his Cherokee name, Red Wolf, was written on his face. Charlie reached up, tentatively, to touch the symbols first on Michael's face and then the ones on Shadow Wolf's face. They etched Wolf's marks with gunpowder, making them look like dark shadows of paw prints. Wolf then let my son touch his slotted earlobes and run his hands over Wolf's head, shaved except for the traditional patch on the back of his head, about twice as big as a crown piece.

"Did it hurt when they marked your face?" Charlie sounded concerned.

Wolf smiled. "A bit, but a Cherokee warrior faces pain without flinching even though he feels afraid."

Michael laughed. "I flinched."

"Yes, my son, but you had not yet become a Cherokee warrior then," responded Wolf. "And sometimes, the greater mark of manhood is you endure what you fear when you know you must. Enduring the pain despite your fears is how you became a Cherokee warrior."

As I moved outside, Charlie examined the beads, feathers, coins, and other items tied or braided into Wolf's long hair.

In the months that followed, I rarely ventured far from the house without a gun. As the winter snows melted and the first signs of spring pushed forth from the ground, I became lax about carrying the heavy shotgun everywhere I went. It should have come as no surprise to any of us that a Chickamauga warrior would eventually return to McCarron's Corner.

Bella and I walked the half-mile to the meadow on my birthday. I was craving fiddleheads, one of the first greens to pop up in the spring. As we picked the fiddleheads, I stopped at the sound of a twig breaking. I raised, suddenly terrified. I knew there are only two creatures that break twigs like that: bears and men. If it were Marc or someone from the village, they would call out to me. I pushed Bella before me into the shadows beneath the trees. I slipped the dagger from my waist and slowly turned around. Once I turned around, Bella was directly behind me. I fully expected to see a bear there.

It was a Cherokee brave I did not know. As I pushed Bella further back behind me, I whispered, "Get Papa."

She backed up a few steps and then ran into the nearby woods as the leering brave approached me.

"You don't want to do this," I warned. "My father is Lone Eagle. My mother is Red Moon Rising. My brother is…"

"You lie, white girl. They have but one son. He married Bright Star. Your new man will be a brave Chickamauga warrior, and you will give me sons with hair like the setting sun and eyes blue as the skies above."

*Like hell I will*, I thought, as I crouched into a defensive pose, my dagger poised ready to strike.

He laughed. "As, yes, I like a woman with spirit. You will give me many brave and strong sons."

He lunged forward to grab my forearm, but I slashed the dagger at him, catching him by surprise. I saw shock, and then anger wash across his face. He raised his fist and lashed out at me. Somehow, I pulled back and avoid the full impact of the blow, but he stepped forward again and grabbed me tight. My heart beat wildly as he pulled me to him. I began slashing the knife at him again and again. In anger, he slapped me hard and wrenched the blade from my hands. As my hands grew slick from blood as the dagger cut into my fingers, he laughed as he twisted the knife from me, tossing it aside.

*This is it*, I thought in dismay. *This maniac will rape me and carry me away to be his woman. Is this my fate? To always be victimized by evil men?*

In an unexpected moment of clarity, I remembered Wolf's words: courage does not mean you never fear. Courage means you do not let your fear stop you. *No*, I thought, with a new determination, *I won't give up!* I realized a rape might tear me in half emotionally, but it would not end me. I would survive. But this time, I would not just survive the attack. I would fight!

Going through hell changes a person. It transforms who you are. It alters who you could be. It can make you bitter and resentful, but you don't have to let it do that to you. It can pave your way to greatness. I realized if you escape the pits of hell, you are not weak. You are not a loser. You are, as Sassy used to tell me, a survival badass.

I grabbed hold of my semi-colon, and I let all my inner badass out at that moment.

I kept struggling against the brave with renewed resolve. The son of a bitch would not force me to be his woman. No one would victimize me ever again. And then suddenly, a loud noise pierced the air. Startled, we both looked about to find the source of the awful noise. The brave loosened his hold on me just enough that I could pull away.

And then, it seemed like I was falling.

. . .

"Papa, come quick, a mean man is hurting my mommy!"

Marc had been cleaning a gun when Bella rushed in. "Where?"

"In the meadow," Bella sobbed.

"Oh, Jesus, no." Lily grabbed a pistol and powder horn to go with Marc.

Marc jumped up, grabbed his powder horn, and rushed out to follow Bella. Lily ran behind him. They all stopped in stunned disbelief. While there were signs of a struggle, Marc could only find one set of tracks leading from the meadow. For an experienced tracker like Marc, the footprints revealed the Cherokee left alone. The prints in no way indicated he was carrying Fancy with him.

Marc tracked the man about a half-mile north from the meadow into the woods before he found him. The Cherokee was kneeling on the ground, pressing his hand against a long gash across his belly.

"Shoot me, white man. But you will not get the girl back." His voice was grim with pain as he gasped out his words.

Marc strode quickly over to the man and jerked his hair upwards. The man winced, surprised, as Marc pulled out his skinning knife.

"Shoot ye? Oh, no. I'll scalp ye, pour honey over your wounds, and leave ye staked out for dead unless you tell me what ye did with my daughter."

The man barked out a surprised laugh. "You do not know, old man? She left. Your woman came from Beyond many moons ago, and now the one who claims to be your daughter has gone Beyond."

Marc's hand hesitated. "Why do ye say that?"

"Because the big noise came, and then the flame-haired woman was gone."

Lily frowned. "What big noise? What do you mean?"

"Our people know about the big noise. It marks the opening in time. She went Beyond. You will never see her again."

Bella nodded. "There was a real big noise, Papa. It hurt my ears, but I kept running to the house as Mama told me to do. But, tell me, Papa, where is this beyond?"

"It is not what or even where, little one. The question is when your Mommy will land."

Bella's eyes grew wide as Marc slit the man's throat from ear to ear. As the life flowed out of the warrior, Marc spoke. "She went after Rick."

Lily nodded. "She must have heard Wolf tell you Rick went home. That will be hard for her. God knows if she can find him, much less adjust to the future. Now, what do we do with the body?"

Marc's answer was brief. "Dispose of it."

They quickly stripped the man. Marc then hoisted the lifeless body and threw it down into a nearby ravine.

"You think they will find it?" Lily fretted.

Marc shrugged. "Not anytime soon. And not before we leave."

She frowned. "Where are we going?"

Marc smiled. "Where else, *mo leannan rua*? Beyond. After our girl."

. . .

"Ma'am? Are you okay? Ma'am? Oh, my God, Devin, I'm afraid she's hurt bad."

I slowly regained consciousness as the pretty, young, black girl patted my cheeks. "No. I'll be all right. Wh-wh- where am I?"

I struggled to pull myself up. I winced with pain as I put weight on my hands, and I looked down in shock. "What happened to me?"

The handsome adolescent squatting beside the girl frowned. He was a good-looking kid, tall and muscular. He looked mixed, with coppery skin, and short, curly, dark brown hair. "That's what we wondered. It looks like you cut your hands pretty badly. Janet, tell my Dad I will run ahead to the ranger's shack at the trailhead. They can call for an ambulance."

I stared at my bleeding hands in disbelief. Had the Indian hurt me this badly? I knew we struggled over the knife, but--

And then it hit me. The girl wore short pants with a skimpy little top that looked more like undergarments than outerwear. I turned my head in embarrassment as my cheeks flushed red. I never saw a girl clad in so little in my entire life. The youth wore loose-cut pants and a shirt with no sleeves. I saw no one dressed like either of them before. I swallowed hard as I looked around, suddenly self-conscious of my long skirt, homespun shift, stays, and apron. It looked like the meadow, but the path appeared different, more worn. And lots of people were walking along the trail. I bit back the question I wanted to ask. These people would think I was crazy if I asked, "what year is it?"

Holy Mother of God, had I somehow gone forward in time? What was it the Cherokees called it? Had I gone 'Beyond'?

The girl pulled a little first aid kit out of her backpack. She pulled some gauze out of the small box. I winced as she pressed it against my hands. I tried to smile. "It's okay. Really."

"Yeah, sure. And I have some oceanfront property in Sacramento I'll sell you cheap."

I stared at her, unsure of how to respond. I didn't want to admit I had never heard of a place called Sacramento, but I suspected there was no oceanfront property there, wherever it was.

About then, one runner slowed down and came over to me. "What happened, Jan? Where's Dev?" The tall, lanky man frowned as he gently took my hands into his. I noticed his skin was copper-colored like the boy, although his short, curly hair was darker. He looked like he was most likely about Marc's age. "I'm Dr. Dan Smith. How did this happen?"

I looked down at my bleeding hands in dismay. The survival badass did not feel very badass right then. "A man attacked me. He had a knife."

He nodded as he gently pulled the wadded gauze away from my fingers. "The bleeding has about stopped. Do you think you could walk?"

I nodded. "Yes, if you could help me get up. Oh, I guess I lost one of my shoes…"

I looked around, but the shoe was nowhere in sight. *Probably back in 1784, I thought. Or maybe somewhere between there and here, wherever 'here' is. Oops. 'Whenever' here is.*

"Jan, run after Devin and tell him I have the lady, and we are coming in."

"Yes, sir, Doc. Will do." The girl took off down the trail after the boy.

"What's your name, sweetie?" He asked as he helped me to my feet.

"Fancy Hobbs, sir."

He stopped and frowned at me. "Fancy Hobbs? Well, that's interesting. What year is it, Miss Fancy Hobbs?"

I gulped. "Um… I'm not rightly sure, sir. I still feel rather dizzy. You know, all discombobulated. I reckon something whacked me in the head."

"Uh-huh. And how did I guess that answer was coming?" The corners of his dark brown eyes crinkled with amusement as his lips curled into a smile. "Been at a re-enactment, Miss Hobbs? Maybe at McCarron's Corner?"

I gave him a funny look and nodded, but said nothing else. I wasn't sure what a 're-enactment' was, but I reckoned that sounded like as good an explanation as I could come up with for my clothing. I appeared to be the only woman dressed in a long skirt. He let me lean against him as we ambled the four miles or so to the ranger's shack, as Dr. Dan called it.

"Why do people call you 'Dr. Dan?'"

He chuckled. "Well, I'm a doctor. My name is Dan Smith, but Dr. Smith is so common. And my patients like it that they can call me by my given name. So, tell me why your lips are turning blue, Miss Fancy Hobbs."

I stopped walking as I struggled to catch my breath. "Well, sir, I have a heart murmur."

"Yeah, I was afraid you would say that. Look, take your time. Do you want to rest a minute and catch your breath?" He frowned as he took my wrist into his hand and checked my pulse. "Yeah, your pulse is a little fast, and a little thready. We have all the time you need. We'll get there. Better safe than sorry. We don't need to run any races today."

I smiled at him. I could tell my heartbeat was slowing down, and I felt a little better. "Thank you. It does that when I overexert."

Dr. Dan made me wait there until my coloring looked better to him. It must have been more than an hour later when we finally reached the building, which he called the ranger's shack, that was a little log cabin. I sighed as Dr. Dan helped me into the building and settled me onto a chair. He fetched a pan of warm water and sat my hands in it to soak the bloody bandages loose. And then, as he gently eased the gauze from my hands, he looked up and smiled at someone who came in the ranger's shack behind me.

"Hey, dude, I'm glad you're here. I have someone I would like you to meet. I found this pretty lady down the trail in the meadow. Miss Hobbs, I'd like you to meet my associate, Dr. Winslow. Although unless I am mistaken, I suspect you two met before."

I turned around in the chair, stunned by Dr. Dan's words. "Richard."

# Part II
# Beyond

# Chapter 10
# Fancy and Rick, the Present

We stared at each other at first. Mouth agape, I could not quite comprehend how I followed Richard Beyond. I thought you could only go back in time. I didn't know you could go forward.

Finally, he grinned and sauntered over to me. "Hello, sweetheart. Imagine finding you here."

Dr. Smith chortled.

Richard knelt and gently took my cut hands into his as he examined the lacerations. After an interminable pause, he nodded. "Looks like you might need some stitches, Francesca."

Dr. Smith frowned. "I thought you said your name is Fancy?"

I nodded. "That's what most folks call me. Except for Richard. He always called me by my given name, Francesca."

Dr. Smith chuckled. "Richard, hmm? We all call him Rick. Unless he's a …"

"Dick," muttered Richard. "Like you are now, Dan. Come on, sweetie. Let's all get into the car and head to Ellijay. We can talk later. Dan and I will decide on stitches when we get back to my house. If you need stitches, we can do it there, or I can run you into the clinic if need be."

My heart began beating all crazy like it does when I stress out. My hands and then my entire body began to shake. "But, Richard, my family won't know where I am…"

"We can't change that, kiddo. Let's get those lacerations stabilized. Then we can figure out what to do next." Dr. Dan sounded adamant.

Numb, I nodded. I blinked rapidly to keep the tears from falling. I was sure I did that disassociating thing Lily said I do sometimes when I get distraught.

Richard saw me sway and grabbed my arm. He and Dr. Dan helped me up. *I can do this.* I fought down the panic I felt coming on. *I can do this. What is it Sassy always says? 'You are a badass survivor.' Trust my instincts.* I was not feeling like a badass right then, but suddenly I thought about that semi-colon. *The rest of my story hasn't been written yet. I can do this. This is my future, at least for right now.* I squared my shoulders, took a deep breath, and walked to the door where I blinked at the sight of the big, red carriage of some sort waiting outside. I swooned as my heart began beating wild and crazy again. "Uh… What's that?"

Richard chuckled. "It's a horseless carriage. They call this a van. It can carry a bunch of people. I'm driving. Do you want to sit in the front with me, or the back?"

I stood staring at the big contraption he called a van and finally realized I needed to answer him. "Um… I reckon it doesn't matter. But how does this contraption move without horses to pull it?"

"You'll see, sweetie. Here, let me help you get in. I will put you in front. That way, you get the best view of the Cohutta Wilderness, 21$^{st}$-century style."

Wordless, I nodded and went to the door he was holding open for me.

"21$^{st}$-century, huh? Wow. Now what?"

He reached across me and pulled a strap around me. "Now, I fasten your seatbelt, everyone gets in, and then we take off."

I hung on tight as Richard maneuvered the big contraption he called a van, through the other horseless carriages parked at the trailhead. I reckon my eyes were as big as saucers. My fingernails dug into the soft leather of the seat cushion. This unknown world was alien to me. How on earth could Lily and Sassy adjust to my world when they came from this? How could Richard have adapted? Was that why he came back? Perhaps he couldn't cope with living in the past.

I was just about to relax a little when he sped up. I never imagined people could go so fast and live to tell about it! My eyes must have been large as dinner plates by then, as my fingers dug deeper into the comfortable seat cushion. However, I began to relax a little when we did not fly into a kajillion itty bitty pieces based on the crazy fast speed we were traveling. "I can't believe we can go so fast and live to tell it."

Dr. Dan laughed. "When trains were new, people feared that women's uteri would fly out because of the speed."

"What are uteri? And what are trains?"

He laughed. "Oops, my bad. Medical jargon for the plural for a uterus which is your baby-making equipment. Trains are another form of transportation. We will probably pass one or two on our way to Ellijay."

I felt my cheeks redden. I was unaccustomed to men talking openly about women's private parts. I cut my eyes at Richard.

He winked at me. "It's okay, sweetie. Dan never lived in the 18th century. That's the way men talk today. At least doctors do. Doctors are blunt in their speech these days."

I remembered a phrase Richard used to say back in the day. "My land a' mercy, kinda like when you used to say 'eff me running?'"

He laughed. "Exactly. Not at all correct language for the 18th century, but relatively well accepted now, as long as I say 'eff' instead of what it stands for. God knows my smart mouth got me in trouble back then."

*Your smart mouth, among other things*, I thought, but I held my tongue.

"It still does, grasshopper," chuckled Dr. Dan.

Devin, Dr. Dan's son, asked me lots of questions about back home, as did his girlfriend, Jan. It fascinated both kids that I somehow came to the 21st century from the 18th century. They grew silent as Richard and Dr. Dan emphasized; they could *not* tell people I traveled through time from the past. Jan pouted, but both young people swore they would keep my secret.

"Most people would not believe Fancy. The ones who would believe Fancy might want to conduct scientific studies on her," Dr. Dan intoned. "Or put her in a mental hospital. We would not want anything like that to happen to our Fancy."

Both teens looked a bit shocked at that. They nodded and promised again to keep my secret.

We drove in silence for the rest of the way to Richard's house. It was a beautiful log home nestled in the woods overlooking Carter's Lake. As we walked in the door, Richard laughed, as if it embarrassed him. "The furnishings are still a bit sparse. I only moved in a few weeks ago, and I have been working most of the time since then."

Richard touched something on the wall, and suddenly there were lights in the room. I jumped with surprise.

"How did you do that?" I was breathless, both excited and scared.

He chuckled. "I turned on the light switch, sweetie. Watch."

He flipped the thing he called a switch several more times as I stared in amazement.

I gasped. "And what do you call this?"

"The miracle of electricity," Richard replied.

I frowned. "What is electricity?"

"Magic." Dr. Dan sounded solemn and serious, but I suspected he might tease the ignorant girl from the 18th century. I crossed myself to be safe. Better safe than a sinner, as Daddy Jo used to say.

Richard laughed. "Oh, Dan, don't tell her that. She's from the 18th century. Magic is not something warm and fuzzy there. It is the Devil's work."

Wordless, I nodded.

Dan shrugged. "How would you explain it? Hell, I can't explain it any other way. It's magic. It's good magic, but it's magic."

Richard laughed again as he shook his head. "You're crazy, Dan."

Dan grinned. "Probably why we get along so well, grasshopper. Besides, like I keep saying, you gotta be at least a little crazy to be a cardiovascular surgeon."

Well, that made me more nervous because I'm a good Christian girl, and I don't cotton with magic, but I remained silent. Plus, I had no idea what a cardio-something-or-other surgeon was. The question must have shown on my face.

"He's a heart surgeon," Richard whispered the words to me, almost as if he could read my thoughts.

I blinked. "You mean people can perform surgery on a person's heart here?"

Both men nodded.

"My lord o' mercy, I would never have dreamed…" I didn't dare ask the question: could Dan fix my heart?

It was a handsome room designed for a man. The ceiling reached up to the sky, almost like a cathedral. Glass went down one wall, and there was an enormous stone fireplace climbed up to the ceiling. The fireplace had a rough-hewn mantle crafted from an enormous tree trunk. Dan called it a 'live edge.' Richard decorated the room with a large leather sofa and two comfortable-looking leather chairs. The great room opened into what appeared to be a kitchen, judging from the pots and pans hanging from a rack. The cabinets looked like they were hewn from oak, and the countertops were glistening black.

"It's pretty, Richard." I looked around in awe.

He looked embarrassed. "It's a hot mess. I still have boxes stacked around in different rooms. I'm sorry it isn't all put together and decorated yet."

I tried to smile. "It looks fine to me."

I sank into a chair at the dining table, where Dr. Dan and Richard examined my hands again. They soaked my hands in some solution Richard swore would help prevent infection from setting in. It stung like crazy. I bit my lips, determined not to look like a big ol' cry baby, whining over a bowl of stinging disinfectant. I let out a sigh of relief when they decided I did not need stitches because the cuts were superficial. Dan sat chatting with me as Richard applied what he called 'topical antiseptic ointment,' and he bandaged my hands. I felt better knowing I should not become septic from the cuts. Afterward, Dr. Dan and the kids loaded back into Dan's van and drove off towards their own home.

"Why did you come after me? Won't your husband be upset? Where is O'Malley, anyway?" Richard's brow furrowed into worry lines.

I had been wandering around the kitchen, thoroughly engrossed in the most beautiful stove I ever saw. My head jerked up at his words. "What do you mean? I did not come chasing after you, Richard Winslow."

He chuckled. "Well, you're here. How did that happen?"

I frowned. "I don't know. The last thing I knew, I was struggling against a Cherokee warrior who wanted to make me his woman. There was a noise, and then I was falling. It must have knocked me out. When I came to, Devan and Jan were there, fretting over me. You tell me what happened, Mr. Know It All."

He laughed until I mentioned the Cherokee. Then his eyes narrowed. "Wolf won't like that."

"He wasn't from the Cohutta tribe. He was Chickamauga. They are at war against the settlers. But he seemed to know who Marc and Lily are."

"Gosh, you have an incredible ability to attract trouble." He snickered.

I frowned. "That's a horrible thing to say. Why not just say: 'you have a real ability to attract rapists, Fancy?' That's what you meant, isn't it?"

Richard's features hardened. "Did he? Dammit, did the sorry bastard sexually assault you?"

I sniffed. "No, but not for lack of trying. That's why I pulled the dagger on him…"

Richard began laughing again. "You mean the man cut you with your knife?"

I could feel my cheeks reddening again. I pulled my arms close to hug my body as I stood up to my full 5'5". "Oh, shut up."

"Then what happened, if he didn't cut you with your knife?"

My cheeks had to be scarlet. "Oh, you are so dad blasted irritating. We were wrestling over that consarned dagger. The blade sliced across my palm and cut me. And then, I heard that horrible, loud noise."

Richard nodded. "Looks like the Good Lord was watching over you, girl. And He sent you here. To me."

I sniffed. "Yeah, sure."

He tried not to laugh. "So, where is O'Malley? Why were you at McCarron's Corner in the first place?"

I blinked twice. "I figured Sassy would have written you. Kirk's dead."

Richard looked stunned. Then he started laughing yet again. "Dead? Are you serious?"

I nodded. "Don't laugh. It's rude to laugh over a man's death. The Enterprise went down in the Dreadful Hurricane."

He stopped laughing. "I... I didn't know. I'm sorry." He frowned. "Why did you tell Dan your name is Fancy Hobbs?"

I flipped my hair back over my shoulder. "Because it *is* my name. If you hadn't been in such a consarned rush to leave, you would have known."

His brow scrunched up as he frowned again. "Known what? What the blazes are you talking about?"

"I swear, you are without a doubt the most frustrating man who ever lived. Heck fire, I almost said Selk. I could have used either. You would have known my marriage to Kirk was void if you hadn't turned tail and run. Again. Something about its initials. But you made your choice. You chose to leave. Without a word. Again."

It looked like someone lit a candle behind his face. "My God, you mean the court ruled it was *void ab initio*? Void from the start?"

I nodded. "Yes, I think that's what the barrister called it."

"How did you manage that?" He sounded intrigued.

I sniffed again and shrugged. "I told you I had grounds to get out of a marriage with Kirk, and you should trust me."

"Yeah, but how? What did you do?"

I smiled. "It isn't legal for whites to marry persons of color on Barbados. I look white, but I'm still a person of color. More than a drop, remember? My Irish barrister filed papers for a judgment to declare the marriage void. They signed it a few days after you turned tail and ran, you big dope."

"But... but why didn't you tell me you were doing that?"

I sniffed again. "I chose not to tell you. You are not very good at keeping secrets, as I recall."

He looked plumb dab shocked. "What do you mean?"

I shook my head as I glowered at him. "'I'll never tell about Tom, sweetie. I promise.' Sound familiar?"

He had the decency to look embarrassed, and he lowered his eyes. "Uh, yes, I remember. I told you I'm sorry..."

I sniffed again. "Yes, that helped a lot with my relationship with my father and my brother, not to mention with your mother. It took ages to mend fences with Will and Sassy."

He frowned, his eyes shooting darts at me. "But you adopted his bastard. Why would you do that if you intended to have the marriage declared void?"

I sighed, totally exasperated. "Oh, I swear, you are the most double-dogged, aggravating man I ever knew. *I* adopted her. Her name is Elizabeth Selk. *I* chose to adopt her. I don't want a little mixed-race girl like me to grow up hated for no other reason than she is mixed. Her Irish grandmother hated her. I could see that going bad, just like it did for me with Tom. So, I adopted her. She's *my* little girl now. If Kirk were still alive, he wouldn't have a dad-blasted thing to say about her. She's *my* child. You are always so hasty. That's why your mama tells you not to make permanent decisions based on temporary feelings. You never even bothered to ask me about it. You chose *not* to ask. You just turned tail and ran. Again. Heck fire, you always turn tail and run, Richard."

I'll give him credit. He looked plum dab shocked, if not embarrassed or ashamed. He hung his head, suddenly sheepish, and said not another word. I felt an unwanted tug at my heartstrings. Dad blast it. I did not want to feel sympathetic towards him. I tried to keep my mad on, as Sassy would say. If he had only stayed last year, we could have married and had our happy-ever-after. I thought I found my semi-colon when I met him, my reason to go on. Now, I figured, not so much. I wasn't sure what he was to me anymore.

And yet, here I was in the 21st century alone in his house with the man. I suddenly felt very unsure of myself. I ran my bandaged hands up and down my arms. I swear I felt like a possum walked right square across my grave.

"Well, you seem to have all your ducks in a row," he muttered.

I snorted. "Ducks in a row? Hardly. I don't have any ducks. Or a row. I have squirrels. And the sorry little buggers are everywhere."

He kinda laughed. "Squirrels everywhere, hmm?" He grew quiet again. "You could have told someone." His voice grated, gruff with unspoken emotion.

My head snapped up at his words. "I did. Marc knew. Lily knew. They can keep secrets."

That time, he remained silent. His cheeks flushed red. I wasn't sure if the heightened color was from embarrassment, shame, or anger. Or maybe some of all three.

Finally, he spoke again. "Okay, can we start over?"

I shrugged and flipped my hand in the way I saw Sassy do many times. "Whatever."

He cringed at the word. He swallowed hard several times. "I'm serious. I wish we could be strangers again. I could introduce myself to you—"

"That's silly."

He swallowed again and extended his hand. "Allow me to introduce myself, ma'am. I'm Dr. Richard Winslow."

I giggled and then nodded as I held out my fingertips to him. As he took my bandaged hand, I curtseyed. "I'm Fancy Hobbs. I believe I know your mama. She's my friend."

He smiled. "And I believe I know your father. He's a great guy."

We both laughed. Richard squeezed my hand. "See, we can laugh and talk. We can learn about each other all over again, in this day and age."

I nodded, enchanted by the novel idea. "I… I would like that."

His face lit with excitement. "We can come up with new inside jokes only we know."

I chuckled. "That should be easy. We're the only people here who have also been there."

"Exactly. We can create new memories."

I smiled. "Memories are wonderful. I would like that, Richard."

He beamed at me. "And maybe… we could give each other a second chance?"

My throat felt tight with longing. Did I dare risk it? Would he disappoint me again? Or would we finally be able to have our happy-ever-after? Suddenly trembling, I nodded wordlessly. I walked across from the beautiful stove to a large, rectangular box. I figured that was enough serious talk for one evening. I took a deep breath, pulled tentatively on the handle, and gasped as the frosty air hit my face. "What is this contraption?"

Richard chuckled. "It's called a refrigerator. It keeps food cool. The bottom opens to a freezer."

My eyes must have just about bulged out of my head as he pulled the lower section open. Inside were ice and packages of frozen meat and vegetables. "Oh, my merciful heaven! How can the ice remain frozen in the house?"

He laughed again as he showed me the different drawers in the refrigerator, including buttons you could press to dispense ice and water.

It amazed me. I dragged Richard from one shining contraption to the next until he explained them all to me. The gas stove, with six burners and two ovens. I hadn't even used that stove yet, and I was already in love with it. I could barely wait to cook a meal on it. There was some odd contraption coming out of the wall over the stove that Richard called a pot filler. He about shocked the daylights out of me when he turned a knob and water poured out of that thing. There was an enormous stainless-steel sink with hot and cold running water, the big refrigerator, and something called a dishwasher that cleans dirty dishes for you! He showed me a machine to wash clothes and another to dry your clothes in a little area he called a 'utility room.' There would be no more washing clothes in a cast-iron pot over a fire and drying them on a clothesline. "My lord o' mercy, I could cook meals and keep the kitchen and clothes clean in a tenth of the time it took me back home. Show me what else you have here."

He laughed, grabbed my arm, and led me to a room with another funny looking contraption. "It's a toilet. You sit on it to relieve yourself. It's a lot easier to use than a chamber pot. And this is toilet paper. You use it to wipe yourself clean. Then you press this lever when you finish your business, and the waste washes away."

"You're joshing. You waste paper like that?"

Richard laughed, his amber-colored eyes twinkling with mirth. "No, I'm serious. No emptying of chamber pots here, sweetie. Here is a sink with running hot and cold water, like in the kitchen. And the thing Lily swears she misses most of all."

He reached inside and turned more knobs. I squealed as hot water came pouring out of the contraption above my head. "Oh, my land, it must be a shower!"

Richard nodded, his eyes twinkling again. "It is. And this is just one of four bathrooms in this house. There is also a big soaker tub in here. The water runs right into the tub and the shower."

I reached out and touched his hand. "Show me everything!"

We went through the entire house. On the first floor was the big room with the fireplace, kitchen, bedroom and bathroom, and the laundry room, where the beautiful washing machine and dryer were located. We went upstairs and found another large bedroom with a bathroom, and a loft overlooking the forest through the floor-to-ceiling windows. Another bedroom was at the other end of the second floor, with another bathroom. He let me pick out my bedroom. I chose one upstairs that looked out over the trees. It felt like I was in a treehouse, surrounded by greenery.

"We can order you a bed tomorrow. In the meantime, I'll bring up a box with Mom's old clothes in it. You two are about the same size. I could never make myself give her clothes away. You might feel more comfortable here wearing modern clothing."

I felt my cheeks redden at his words. "I'm not sure I'll feel more comfortable, but I might fit in better. I can sleep on the couch until another bed comes."

I swear the man snorted at that. "Oh, I don't think so. My Mom didn't raise me to let a guest sleep on the couch and for me to sleep on the king-sized Tempurpedic mattress. You take my bedroom, and I'll sleep on the couch. It opens into a comfortable bed. I insist."

Finally, we went downstairs to what Richard called the terrace level, to see another large room with a billiards table, couches, and what Richard called a 'TV.' He turned the contraption on, and I must have jumped fifteen feet when images of people suddenly appeared on what he called the screen. My land a' mercy that must have scared five years off my future life! There was also another large bedroom and bathroom on the terrace level. There was even a little kitchen there. For the life of me, I have no idea why a person needs two kitchens, but I admit it sure is convenient.

I smiled as the dogs came running to meet us. They looked a lot like Sassy's little critters back at Belle Rose. They came over to sniff at me and began licking my legs while they wagged their tails at me. Richard introduced the girl as Shadow and the boy as Darby. Darby was colored a lot like Sassy's Hawk and reminded me of Hawk. Shadow was a dark grey, very different in color from the others I had seen. They were both friendly and ran right up to me. I could tell they had been well socialized. Richard opened the French doors to let the dogs out, and I saw chairs sitting around a fire pit. The dogs trotted into the yard to 'do their business' while I looked around outside.

"Pretty dogs. What does your Mama call them? Skyes?"

He nodded. "Yes, Mom would love them. I got them when I came back. They are only eight months old now. Great bloodlines, beautiful conformation. They are line bred, but they are not littermates. I may show them. Mom and I used to show our Skyes. I will try to take the pair back with me when I go back the next time."

I tilted my head to study him. "Do you intend to go back?"

He nodded. "Well, I did. I figured I went at the wrong time. I thought if I came back in a couple of years, maybe it would be the right time. I figure I'll- we'll-be back in the past by 1789. Why?"

I tilted my head to look up at him as I studied his face. "How do you know if it is the right time? And why do you think we will be back by 1789?"

He chuckled. "I'm not sure how you know it is the right time. I know Lily went back when she was a kid and had to return to the future to grow up and train to be a doctor. She is the only other person I know who has come back."

"Except me. I came here, too."

His head jerked towards me. "True. Hmm. I wonder why Providence allowed you to come here?"

I shrugged. "Beats me. And why do you say we will be back there in 1789?"

He blushed again as he reached into his wallet. I gasped as he handed me the worn copy of a picture of a painting—of me, dated 1789.

And on the back of the little card, it said I was his wife. His *beloved* wife. I blinked back tears as I began nibbling at my lip.

"I kinda always figured we would both be there in 1789. I left because I understood I went there at the wrong time. I don't want to muck up our future if we still have one. I love you, Francesca, with all my heart."

Mouth dry, throat aching with yearning, all I could do was nod. I could not squeak out a reply although my heart screamed, *tell him, stupid, tell him you love him!* But right then, I could not quite get those words or any other words out. I stood there, silent, blinking back tears, with my hands shaking like crazy as I handed the worn picture back to Richard. I managed a shaky smile as I nodded to him.

So much to take in. So many things here to make life more comfortable than in the world I came from. It was exciting and terrifying at the same time. We had pure, clean water at the twist of a knob. We wouldn't have to boil water to know it was safe to drink here. Chamber pots that empty themselves. You have no idea how nice it is not to have to take the refuse outside to toss it away and then have to rinse out the chamber pot after each use. Heck fire, you have no idea how wonderful this Charmin' stuff feels compared to wiping yourself with moss or leaves. I'm not sure I will ever get over the luxuriant indulgence of wiping my behind with paper and then flushing it away. I can't get over the big, gorgeous cookstove with six burners and two ovens, on which you could control the temperature. Richard rather proudly told me it was 'commercial-grade,' whatever that means, and running hot and cold water. It was all quite amazing. I had no idea why the Good Lord let me come to this day and age, but I had an inkling it might be fun to live here.

So much was different and yet the same. The rivers were the same, but lakes now existed that were not in this area years ago. Richard told me Carter's Lake was manmade within the last century. The same mountains and crisp, cool air were here. And most important, Richard was here to help smooth my way. Yet, all these new-fangled contraptions and these fabulous roads and modern methods of transportation. I mean, what is a computer? What is television? A DVD? And what exactly is this thing called electricity?

Yet, I worried. Could I ever go back home? I already missed my babies, and I hadn't been here one day. How would I survive months or maybe years without them? It almost killed me when Tarleton sold me to Kirk. I was gone from my family for seven months then. And even more critical: how would my children survive without me again? Did my family have any notion of where I had gone?

I sighed. So many questions, so few answers. All I could do was wait.

I know that sometimes when things around us fall apart, it means they are falling into place for us. Was this my place? Was this supposed to be my forever home?

Would Richard and I finally get our happy-ever-after? Was this the chance we needed?

# Chapter 11
# Fancy
# The Present

In the days that followed, Richard and I settled into a kind of routine. He arose by five nearly every day to head to the hospital to make rounds, or to see his hospitalized patients. Every other week, Dan and he would drive south on Sunday night to a big, sprawling city called Atlanta to do surgeries at an enormous hospital called Grady Memorial. They would return late Tuesday, usually exhausted from long, tedious hours of performing heart surgeries.

Richard told me that Dan and a good number of other physicians loved Ellijay and Blue Ridge and chose to office here rather than in Atlanta. They were 2 hours away from Atlanta and Grady, considered one of the most excellent hospitals in the country. Patients were a quick helicopter ride away in case of emergencies.

Dan examined me and determined I had two heart murmurs. One was in my aortic valve. I learned the aorta is the large artery carrying blood into my heart. He figured I was born with a defective aortic valve, and he just thought it was what killed Ginny years ago when her aortic valve failed. He said I had a bicuspid aortic valve, and he believed it was a congenital disability. The other was in my mitral valve, and he felt it was most likely caused by the rheumatic fever I had when I was ten. He put me on some medicine and started having me come to the office every two weeks for tests to see how my heart was doing. It didn't stop my shaking or my sweating, but it helped control the erratic heartbeat, at least from the heart murmurs.

The third time I went in, Murielle, the lady who usually answered the phones, was on what they call 'maternity leave,' meaning she had just had a baby. The phones were ringing, and no one wanted to answer them. Finally,

Peggy, the office manager, yelled, "Will someone *please* answer that damned phone?"

So I picked it up. "Hello, Doctor's Office. This is Fancy speaking. How may I help you?"

Everyone in the office turned and stared at me.

The man on the other end of the phone (however that works, I still don't know) said, "Hello, this is Dave Collier. I have an appointment this afternoon with Dr. Dan, but I'm not sure of the time I'm supposed to be there."

"Well, Mr. Collier, let me check the calendar."

Lickity split, someone handed it to me. I glanced down and saw his name. "Your appointment is at two today, sir. I see you are a new patient. Did you download your papers through the patient portal?"

I felt quite clever that I thought to ask about his paperwork.

"Oh, darn, I forgot. Can't I fill the papers out when I arrive?"

"Of course, Mr. Collier. Could you arrive about 15 minutes early to complete the papers?"

"Sure, that will be fine. Thank you, Miss."

"Wonderful, Mr. Collier. We look forward to helping you."

As I sat the receiver back down into the cradle, I realized everyone was staring at me like I'd grown a third head. "What? Did I do something wrong?"

"Not at all. You handled that beautifully. Uh, would you mind helping with the phones today?" Peggy looked embarrassed.

I laughed. "No problem. I believe I have read every magazine in here at least three or four times. Doc works me in, so it would thrill me to help you all a little bit."

Peggy smiled. "Thank you, Fancy. Here's the calendar. You can check their appointments for them, but pass the call to the nurse if they are a potential new patient wanting an appointment or if they are having some urgent health problems. Susan knows how to screen them based on the severity of their condition. And don't be afraid to tell them to hang on while we call 911 if they think they are having a crisis like a heart attack."

I took a deep breath and smiled at her. "I can do that."

The morning and the afternoon passed quickly. At 1:45, Mr. Collier came in, and I gave him the papers he needed to fill out. A few minutes later, he came up to the front desk. I noticed he had a worried frown on his face.

"Is something wrong, Mr. Collier?"

He kept glancing back into the waiting room, with a look of concern on his face. "Fancy, my dear, there is an elderly man out here who doesn't look too good—"

I looked out the window and blanched. "Peggy, Mr. Hensley is turning blue! We need a doctor out here, stat!"

I didn't wait for anyone. I grabbed a stethoscope and hurried out front to Mr. Hensley. Lily taught me how to use one at Yorktown. That was where she taught me to say 'stat' if something was an emergency. Mr. Hensley's pulse was fast, and what Lily called thready, and he was gasping for breath.

"Can you breathe?" I asked.

He nodded. "But my chest hurts. And down my arm…"

And suddenly, the poor, dear man flat dab keeled over.

"We have a crisis here!" I shouted. "Call an ambulance and get me a doctor out here, STAT!"

I started CPR, as Lily had taught me. Richard ran up as I began the second set of chest compressions. "Oh, thank God."

I noticed he had some machine with him.

"Get back," he said, his voice tense and worried.

I moved back, and Richard placed two pads on Mr. Hensley, one on his right breast and one on his left waist. He then administered a jolt from the machine, which appeared to make Mr. Hensley's heart beat again.

"I didn't mean to be rude, but time was of the essence." He smiled at me and patted my trembling hands.

"It don't matter to me." I winced. I lapse into what Calvin called 'poor grammar' when I get stressed out, and believe me, I felt stressed then. "I mean, it doesn't matter."

"Thanks, sweetheart." He flashed me another one of his beautiful smiles.

Mr. Hensley opened his eyes and took a big breath on his own. He grabbed my hand. "Thank you, little lady. I reckon you saved my life."

Richard smiled. "Yes, I believe she did, Mr. Hensley. I will take you over to the hospital. I think we can get you feeling much better by morning."

The old gentleman grinned tremulously. "I already feel much better, young feller. Thank you for helping that little gal. She's a crackerjack. Jumped right in and did that CPR stuff when she saw me going south."

Richard looked up at me. "Yes, she's a treasure, Mr. Hensley."

I felt guilty. "Aw, that wasn't so much. Richard used that machine to make your heart start again…"

"The defibrillator," Richard explained. "But you saved the day when you spotted the problem and started CPR before anyone else got to Mr. Hensley."

About then, the ambulance crew came in. They talked with Richard briefly and then loaded Mr. Hensley onto the gurney to take him across the street to the hospital.

After Richard and the ambulance crew left with Mr. Hensley, I realized Dr. Dan was standing in the doorway, watching me. When he saw me watching him, he nodded his head to me and turned away.

As things quieted down, I took Mr. Collier's paperwork and handed it to the nurse. She smiled at me, glanced at it, and then took Mr. Collier to an examination room.

Richard got back from the hospital about six that evening. He went into Dr. Dan's office, where the two men talked for a good half hour, if not longer. They call that 'debriefing the cases.' Finally, Richard stuck his head out and invited me to come in. I had been ready to leave for over an hour by then. The muscle by the side of Richard's eye was twitching like it does when he is upset. I moaned. *Oh, Lordy, I hope I didn't get him in trouble for starting CPR on that sweet old man! I didn't know a defibrillator thingy even existed, and sure enough, I didn't know how to use one.* I pasted a Tamsin-worthy smile on my face, took a deep breath, and walked into the lion's den, as the girls all called Dan's office. They all swore you only got called in there if you were in trouble. Heck fire, could I get in trouble for volunteering to help?

As Richard closed the door behind me, I settled into the oversized chair in front of Dan's desk.

"Is anything wrong?" I could hear more than a tad of trepidation in my voice.

Dan smiled. "I don't know. That's why I wanted to chat with you. How did you get cornered into handling the phones today?"

I blinked twice, surprised by the question. "Oh, no, it wasn't like that. The phones were ringing so I answered it when everyone was busy. Wasn't that okay? I promise I won't do it again if—"

"Oh, no, it was quite okay. I didn't want the other girls pushing work off on you."

I shook my head. "Oh, no, sir. It wasn't like that at all. I was plum dab bored to tears. When the phone rang, everyone was busy, so I just answered it. It seemed like a polite thing to do. Peggy seemed pleased by my, what did she call it? Oh, yes. My initiative. She commented I handled the call well. I offered to help while I was sittin' around waiting. Did I do something wrong?"

I realized I was trembling. I held my hands tight in my lap so Dan couldn't see my hands shaking as I waited for his response.

Dan smiled. "Kiddo, you did great. And I never had a receptionist who knew when to call for backup, much less jumped right in and started CPR when a patient was in cardiac distress."

"Oh." I wasn't sure if that was good. My voice sounded tight and low.

He chuckled. "Look, Murielle won't be back for six weeks. I wonder if you would work here, even part time, to help with the phones. Every patient I saw after about ten this morning raved about the wonderful new receptionist. I was a little shocked because I damned sure I knew I had hired no one. And then, a little before two, I realized *you* were the wonderful new receptionist, and at that, you were in the lobby doing CPR on a patient."

I swallowed hard, and my mouth suddenly dry as sand. "I'm sorry, Dan. I promise I won't do it again."

"No, no, no, Fancy. You don't understand. You saved that man's life today. So, tell me where a girl from the 18th century learned to do CPR?"

I blinked, totally surprised by his unexpected praise. "Lily taught me."

He frowned, and his eyes narrowed. "Who is Lily?"

I smiled. "Oh, she's my mama. Lily McCarron. Why?"

"How did she know CPR?"

I shrugged. "I don't rightly know. I reckon I thought everyone knew it. Do you know where Lily learned it, Richard?"

"I imagine she learned it in med school." Richard grinned.

Dan looked surprised. "Med school? Do you mean to tell me there is a med school in the 18th century that takes women? And teaches CPR?"

Richard grinned. "I never said she learned it in the 18th century, Dan. I think she graduated from the same school as you, around the same time. She's one hell of a woman, and one hell of a doctor."

Dan sat there looking perplexed until a startled look crossed his face. "You don't mean...?"

Richard nodded. "Yeah, I do. She went back in time, just like I did. She was a doctor here before she went there. She told me once God knew what He was doing because she had no one here, and she found love and a life worth living there."

Dan looked puzzled. About then, there was a knock at the door, and then a lady peeked inside.

"Dan, darling? I wanted to see if you were ready to go to dinner."

Dan stood up and hurried over to the lady. "Oh, precious, I'm sorry. I didn't realize you were here. We can go in just a minute, but first, let me introduce you to Rick's fiancée. Fancy Hobbs, this is my wife, Delia. Delia, Fancy."

She was a sizeable woman. I don't mean fat, but big, like I would think Viking women were big. She was every bit as tall as Lily, in fact, taller, but must have weighed a good 40 or maybe even 50 pounds more than Lily. Lily is stick thin. Delia Smith had jet black hair, which was turning grey, and sparkling, dark brown eyes.

I smiled and held my hand out to her. "It's a pleasure to meet you, Mrs. Smith. Richard tells me you have been very kind to him since he rejoined the practice."

She made a funny sound and pulled me into her arms. "Oh, honey, Rick has talked and talked about you. I'm so glad you're here. But you must call me Dee. All my friends do. Now, when are you two men going to fix this girl's heart?"

As my cheeks reddened, Dan laughed. "That's my girl. She always cuts right to the chase, don't you, my love? We will probably operate on Fancy in two months. I'm trying to convince her to fill in for Murielle until she comes back from maternity leave. She helped today. Did a damned fine job and even did CPR on a patient who went into cardiac arrest until Rick could get out there. She then helped him until the ambulance crew got here."

Delia's eyes grew wide with surprise. "Really? How wonderful! Oh, Dan, that would be great if you think Fancy's heart will hold up."

He nodded. "We need to repair Fancy's heart, but it is holding steady. Fancy, if you are interested, I would love for you to work here until Murielle comes back."

"I think it's asking too much of her, Dan." Richard sounded worried. His voice was low and controlled, but I could hear the concern in his words.

"Nonsense, Rick. She'll be right here. We'll keep a close eye on her," Dan replied. "How else could we keep watch on her all day long, every day?"

Rick shook his head as he shrugged. "Whatever," he muttered under his breath.

I bit back the laugh at his comment.

"What do you think, Little Bit?" Delia asked.

My head whipped around at her. "What did you call me?"

She chuckled as if suddenly embarrassed. "I called you 'Little Bit.' I apologize if it offended you."

"Oh, not at all. It's just ironic. My older brother is married to Rick's mom, and Will calls Sassy 'Little Bit.' It kinda rattled me."

"Oh, good. You are just so little next to me. Oh, well, it is my combined Cherokee and Viking blood that made me so big. Anyway, it's late, and I could eat a horse. Come on, guys, it's time to take your ladies out to dinner. You promised me steak tonight, Dan. We haven't had steak in a month of Sundays, and I refuse to eat another chicken dinner tonight. Let's go."

I laughed as she pulled his hand and batted her eyelashes at him. Dan laughed, too, as he let her pull him up.

"Yes, I did. Okay, Fancy, you think about the offer. Now, let's all go eat those steaks."

I was bone-tired, but I reckoned it would not bode well for Richard if we begged off dinner with his boss. Richard could see I was exhausted and shook his head. "If you two don't mind, we will take a rain check. Francesca looks like she's about to drop. We need to head on home and let her turn in early. Especially if she's coming back to handle the reception desk tomorrow."

"Oh, I'm okay, Richard. Really."

He shook his head. "No. You need to turn in early if you want to come back tomorrow. You can hardly stand up. We're going home and turning into pumpkins tonight."

He helped me gather my things together, and we started for the door. Just as we were almost out, Dan said, "I don't think I caught your mom's maiden name, Fancy."

I turned back and laughed. "Oh, you would ask that. I'm never sure I have it right. What was it? I remember it sounds like Vanda Poutin'."

"Her maiden name was Van Der Houghton," Richard interjected. "Ginette Liliana Van Der Houghton."

As Dan paled, Delia looked at Dan with a grin that looked like she won the lottery. "Told ya she went somewhere special and had a wonderful life filled with fabulous adventures."

He shook his head. "Damn, Dee. Who would'a thunk it? Well, it sure explains how this sweet girl knew CPR."

"It explains a lot, Dan. Just rest assured Lil has had the life she was supposed to have. Just like we have." She slid onto his lap and laid her head on his shoulder.

He smiled as he pulled her close to kiss her. "She could not have had a life half as wonderful as ours."

She laughed as she kissed him again. "You always were a sweet-talking man."

Richard pulled my arm. "Come on, sweetie. Let's go."

I nodded. "Okay. Did you notice Dee was speaking Cherokee? I would swear she told him 'gv ge yu hi,' which is Cherokee for 'I love you.'"

He nodded. "Yeah, they are both part Cherokee. They speak the language together sometimes. Every once in a while, he mutters something to himself in Cherokee, and I answer him. I think I shocked the fire out of him the first time I did that."

"Huh. I didn't expect that. I figured Dan was mixed."

Richard nodded. "He is mixed black and Cherokee. Dee is mixed Scandinavian and Cherokee. The combination made some pretty babies. Dev is a handsome kid, and Baylie is drop-dead gorgeous. She's away at college right now. Dev is still in high school. Dan and Dee can both trace their lineage not just back to the Baker rolls, but back to the late 1700s. They say the Cherokee connection was what first attracted them to each other. Why?"

I shrugged. "I reckon it doesn't much matter. Let's go. I'm plumb dab tuckered out."

I was so tired I didn't even ask what the 'Baker rolls' were. I figured I could find out later.

I wondered if Lily ever knew the man she lived with when they went to medical school was Cherokee. She never mentioned it. She told me his name was Dan once, but never talked much about him. She told me the best thing that ever happened to her was 'ol' Dan dumped her, so she went up the Jacks River Trail, fell through a hole in time, and found the man she was destined to love. I reckoned I would have to tell them that, eventually.

Isn't life funny sometimes?

At Richard's urging, I petitioned the court to determine that Kirk was dead, and that Kirk died at sea over seven years before. Uncle Jim knows the actual story, and he was the judge who heard it. Richard and Jim said this would tidy up the details, and there would be no issue about Richard and me getting married. I could not for the life of me imagine what details could have proven problematic. The poor man was long since dead.

I took the test for my GED. It shocked me when I passed the test on the first try. Don't ask how I managed that. Richard told me he knew I would pass the test. I shook my head and laughed, but you don't reject faith like that. He always has faith I can do whatever I set out to do. Maybe that's some sort of privilege. Perhaps it's the result of growing up in this era, with parents who always encouraged him. He continually encourages, motivates, and inspires me. He says, 'you can do anything you set your mind on.'

# Chapter 12
# Rick
# The Present

I still couldn't believe God brought her here to me.

Every day, when I awoke, I tiptoed to her room to make sure she was still there. Every morning, I felt like dancing with joy when I found her sleeping in that brand new, queen-sized bed.

"Wake up, sleepyhead. Time to rise and shine."

And every morning, she would yawn and then stretch like a cat before opening her beautiful, aqua eyes and smiling at me. 'Good mawnin', ' she would say with her charming Virginia drawl, every single morning.

But that morning was different. Francesca reached up to me. My heart jumped up somewhere between my Adam's apple and my tonsils as she said, "Come make love to me, Richard."

Hot damn, she only had to ask once.

I tried to take it slow and give her time to make the first move. Oh, yeah, we argued like cat and dog, especially at first. But as weeks passed, we argued less and kissed more. She would snuggle up against me on the couch while watching old movies. She would entwine her fingers with mine and would smile up at me like I was something special. She often fell asleep like that, curled up against me, rubbing the fabric on my shirt, with a smile flitting on her lips. I love the way she smiles in her sleep. I would kiss her cheek, pick her up, and carry her to bed.

That happened many nights. Francesca would moan as I laid her down on her bed. She frowned as I pried her fingers off my shirt. Then she would sigh, roll over, and soon be snoring softly. I would slip out of her room once I knew she was fast asleep.

That morning, Francesca was wide awake when I came in. She wanted me. My mouth went dry with desire. I started slowly, but she wasn't having it. She rolled on top of me and took charge.

Hot damn, as much as I hated O'Malley, it seemed like he taught her how to let go of her inhibitions. I pulled back for a second, but she dragged me to her open mouth. She moaned and arched into me as I began kissing her. I moaned as I melted right into the woman who owns my heart. Eff me running, I didn't care where she learned this or who taught her how to do it. I was trapped in her spell. I began pulling my t-shirt off for her to still my hands.

"Let me."

I laid back down, terrified and excited by those two words. I let Francesca take the lead.

She never had before.

It was magic. Hot, silken sex magic. I wondered if I died and went to heaven because this was my idea of paradise.

An hour later, bathed and dressed, we headed out for the day. We drank our breakfast smoothies in silence as we drove to the hospital. My heart overflowed with a joy I hadn't felt in years. *This will work this time*, I thought in wonder. *We will make this work.*

Jim helped us get a birth certificate for Cessie. I began calling her 'Cessie,' short for Francesca, although everyone else calls her Fancy. The birth certificate helped Cessie get her driver's license. She enjoyed driving around Ellijay. She would drive me to the hospital where she let me out after a sweet, long kiss, and then she would drive back to the house. She didn't need to be at the clinic for hours. The woman never ceases to amaze me. She would clean the house top to bottom and then bake some yummy treats to take to work.

When I arrived at the office after my hospital rounds one morning around 9:30, everyone gushed about her homemade chocolate chip banana bread. Dan sat eating his second slice with a look of pure rapture written across his face.

"You know, if I didn't adore my wife, I'd give you a run for your money for that young lady. She's a gem."

I nodded as I grinned, grabbed a piece of banana bread, and checked the roster for the day.

You never slow down in a cardiovascular clinic. They booked us solid all day. The phones rang non-stop. Yet, every single patient I saw raved about the sweet girl at the front desk.

I beamed with pride. *That's my girl. I love her with every fiber of my being. I'm going to marry her. And yes, she is something extraordinary.*

The whole week, every week, went like that.

We settled into a routine. Fancy loves to cook, so she brings lunch for the two of us every day, usually salads with chicken or fish. She also brings daily treats for everyone. Staff and patients rave about her heart-healthy yummies, as they dubbed her goodies. She puts out little plates with her treats around the waiting room and the offices, with copies of her recipes. Clients and staff clamor for more.

After lunch, she takes a quick power nap. That always energizes her for the afternoon. She's bone-tired by evening, but she seems to cope pretty well with the crazy pace.

We started planning our wedding. The forged birth certificate helped us get a marriage license. Cessie felt sad her family would not be there, but she seemed excited about our plan to marry in the meadow on the Beech Bottom Trail. We figured that was as close as we could get to them.

My Uncle Jim is a district court judge and can marry us. He's excited we asked him to perform the ceremony. Heck, it seemed like the least we could do after he has helped us so much. Aunt Sue, their kids, and a bunch of the people from the office and their families will all be there. It was looking like it would be the Cohutta Wilderness event of the year.

Fancy found a pretty rose-colored gown for the ceremony among Mom's re-enactment gowns. I could never make myself throw out the dresses Mom used to wear at Williamsburg. Fancy squealed with excitement when she discovered the exquisite confection of rose silk and handmade bobbin lace. She teared up when I told her it was a gown Mom particularly loved.

"Then it will be my something borrowed. And I will have to take it back to Sassy when we go back someday."

I smiled as she sashayed around the room, holding the dress up to her bosom. I didn't tell her it was the gown Mom wore when she and Dad repeated their vows at Williamsburg years ago. Fancy spotted the photo of Mom and Dad one day and asked me about it. When I told her I took the photo the day they repeated their vows, Fancy said she hoped she would look as pretty wearing it at our wedding as Mom did in the picture. I told her she would be even more beautiful. So, she cried over that, too.

When I asked about the color, she said, "Mama Belle said, 'Belle Rose brides always wear rose-colored gowns.' I may not be at Belle Rose, but this makes me feel closer to home. Connected, somehow. And it is a beautiful gown. Besides, I plan to make this marriage work. I didn't wear a rose-colored gown either time before. Those didn't turn out well, not that I ever intended the marriage to Kirk to succeed."

When she said wearing the rose-colored dress would make her feel connected to the past, it was the first time I felt guilty that we were here, Beyond, not back there, Before. That's what we call back then, in the 18th century. I know she misses her family. I catch her sometimes crying over the children. But we both agree we won't consider going back until after Dan repairs her heart, and she has fully recovered.

And then, two weeks ago, she surprised me again. She came in one Saturday afternoon, all excited. She clutched a hanging bag, the kind you bring nice clothes home in from expensive stores.

"Hey, sweetie. Whatcha been doing?" I looked up from the case file I was reviewing and smiled at the woman I love.

"Richard, would you mind if I didn't wear your mama's dress at our wedding? Baylie and her Aunt Bay and I went shopping and, well, I found somethin' else, if you don' mind…" Her voice trailed off.

I started laughing. "Honey, it's your wedding dress. You will be the bride wearing it. You pick whatever you want. I don't mind. Need some money?"

She shook her head. "No, I had plenty. Dan pays me a decent salary, you know. I saved it for something special. I just wanted to be sure it wouldn't hurt you."

I pushed back from the desk and went over to her, where I pulled her into a hug. "Not at all. Now, what does this new dress look like?"

She pulled the hanging bag out of my reach. "It's a surprise. Aunt Bay says you can't see it until the wedding."

I laughed. Dan's sister, also named Baylie, was called Bay by most folk. She was called that way longer than 'Bay' was used to signify 'girlfriend'. Bay was about 5'5", slender, with long, jet-black hair and dark brown eyes, so dark they glowed like orbs of obsidian. Bay was a lawyer with the Bureau of Indian Affairs and worked with the Cherokee Nation in North Carolina. She told me the Eastern Band of Cherokee Indians is a federally recognized Native American tribe. It is a sovereign nation within the borders of the United States. It is not and never has been a 'reservation.' Aunt Bay gets testy when asked about the 'Cherokee reservation.' We heard her jump a man out in Publix the other day when he called the Cherokee nation the Cherokee reservation. The members of the Eastern Band descended from the small group of Cherokees who remained in the Eastern United States after the Indian Removal Act forcibly moved over 16,000 Cherokees and approximately 60,000 Native Americans in total out west in 1837. One out of four Cherokees died on the trip. If you wanted to know about the forced removals and the infamous Trail of Tears, Baylie Smith was the person to ask.

Aunt Bay was smart as a whip, and as Dan put it, as stubborn as a Missouri mule. Beautiful. Strong-willed. Clever, if moody at times. Dan always said in that respect, she was more Cherokee than their mom or dad had ever been. I told him I wasn't sure if that was a Cherokee trait or a womanly trait. Most women I know are clever, if moody at times. Dan laughed when I said that and warned me most women would view that statement as misogynistic. Bay would, for sure.

My Cessie - I call her Cessie more than not these days - adores Aunt Bay. She looks up to Bay. Dan's daughter, Baylie, often says she wanted to be just like her Aunt Bay someday. I figured if Bay told Cessie I couldn't see the dress before the wedding, Cessie took the advice of her mentor to heart.

"Okay. I guess I'll see it at the wedding then." I hugged her again.

She nodded and turned to take the hanging bag holding her new dress upstairs. About halfway there, she stopped and looked back down at me. "Now, don't you go prowling around to see this, you hear? A girl needs some surprises for her wedding."

I struggled not to laugh and put on a serious face. "I wouldn't dream of it, Duchess. But tell me, is it rose-colored?"

"Yes. Well, maybe. We'll see." She started chewing on her lip, a sure sign I was making my girl nervous.

I bowed to her. She stared at me as if unsure whether to laugh or hit me. She finally smiled, curtseyed, and went on up the stairs, hugging the garment bag to her chest like it contained something precious. Come to think of it, I guess it did.

Part of the reason we are marrying now is her heart condition. We need to marry so the insurance will cover her surgery. If we marry before the surgery, my insurance carrier agreed to cover it. I'm still not sure how Uncle Jim pulled that one off. We told them we have been 'married at common law' for two years. It turns out Georgia doesn't have common law marriage but recognizes them from other states. I told them we met and held ourselves out at common-law while we lived in Texas. Okay, I lied. It would have been damned hard to explain we were betrothed in 1782 and considered ourselves married… kinda sorta. I assume they bought it. I'm sure it helped that Dan, the surgical team, and the hospital wrote their bills off. Now that Murielle is back from her maternity leave, the time is right to proceed with the wedding and the surgery.

Fancy's surgical workup is finished. Dan has practiced the procedures over and over, as he always does before performing open heart surgeries. And we all know the longer we delay, the more nervous Fancy becomes. It has become a matter of 'now or never,' and 'never' is *not* an option.

We planned the wedding for Memorial Day weekend. On the following week, we would confirm there were no hiccups with the insurance, and barring some unforeseen problem, the surgery would take place the Monday after Memorial Day, at Grady Memorial Hospital in Atlanta where Dan prefers to perform his open-heart surgeries.

Dan offered to give Cessie away since Marc was nowhere near. I never saw Dan blush like he did that day when Cessie threw her arms around him and kissed him soundly.

"Aw, kiddo, it's no big deal. Besides, you're almost the same age as our Baylie. I suppose I need to get in some practice." Dan patted her back as if he was suddenly rendered shy.

Cessie hugged him again. Her eyes shined bright with a mix of excitement and unshed tears of happiness.

We drove to the Beech Bottom Trailhead on Friday before the ceremony. We hiked to the meadow and camped out overnight. It gave us a chance to spruce up the area a bit and get it ready for the ceremony. On Saturday morning, Jim, Sue, Dan and Delia joined us. By noon, as guests arrived, everything looked picture perfect. Fancy slipped into the tent with Baylie, Sue and Delia so they could help her fix her hair and makeup and get into her pretty 'maybe-it's-rose-colored' gown. I heard the women laughing.

Sue said, "I sure am glad it isn't so much trouble to get dressed anymore. What a pain it must have been every day!"

"Oh, not really. You get used to whatever you have. It was normal to me. I had to adjust to wearing less. Sometimes, I still feel half naked without shifts, stays, petticoats and panniers. But you have to admit this is a gorgeous dress. I never dreamed I would find a modern dress I loved this much. That was why I planned to wear one of Sassy's re-enactment dresses until I found this one."

I swear my heart leaped right into my throat when my beautiful bride stepped out of the tent. She smiled at me, and I melted to a big, man-sized pile of mush. The designer made the gown of pale pink cotton batiste in a style I would call Modern Renaissance. The bodice especially emulated a gown she might have worn back in the day, absent the stays or panniers, mind you, with a sweetheart neckline, cotton lace, and ribbons, but the style and fabric were modern. They designed the gown to show off the shoulders. The sleeves fell into three gathered tiers, each tied with matching ribbon. They covered most of her arms with the delicate, sheer batiste. There was a slight train of the layers of gauzy fabric. The effect made my beautiful bride look like a renaissance fairy. It was elegant while still looking somehow appropriate for a forest wedding. To add to the fairytale illusion, the women braided miniature pink roses, little pearls, ribbons, and baby's breath into her beautiful, long hair. She wore pale pink pearls around her elegant, swan-like neck, with matching pearls in her earlobes. She borrowed the pearls from Dee. I trembled as she smiled at me. Was this finally going to happen?

Our friend, Jason Gunn, played Mairi's Wedding on his bagpipes. Fancy asked him to play that tune. It's one of her favorites, and she loves the way Jason plays it on his pipes. She heard him play the tune at the Georgia Renaissance Festival and begged him to perform at our wedding. Jason is a popular piper, but he squeezed us into his busy schedule.

Dan stepped forward, and took my girl by the arm, to lead her over to Uncle Jim and me.

And just then, there was an ear-bursting, loud boom. At first, I speculated it was gunfire. My first thought was 'incoming!' as my mind flashed back to gunfire at Yorktown. I realized I had covered Cessie with my body. Cessie ducked and covered her head. Dan said the boom sounded like a cannon. I have to admit he was right. Other people looked skyward, wondering if it were a sonic boom or a loud clap of thunder.

As we all looked about in shock, we heard a voice we had longed to hear but had not expected to hear soon.

"Papa, look, Mommy and Rick are getting married!"

Fancy wheeled around so fast she dropped her bouquet. She let out an excited squeal and ran to the beautiful little girl standing there. As Cessie pulled Bella into her arms, they both began sobbing tears of joy. I joined them and pulled 'my girls' into my arms.

"Aye, lass, it looks like we arrived at the right time," came the emotion-roughened voice of Marcus McCarron, carrying a sleeping toddler.

I arose and wrapped Marc in an enormous bear hug. "It's great to see you, man. How did you manage?"

Marc thumped me soundly on the back, no minor feat while holding a sleeping child. "Ah, lad, Wolf told us sometimes t'was heard ye could go forward if needed. So we tried repeatedly. Here, please take yer daughter. She's heavy as a load of bricks. Now, where's my Lee? Surely she made it with the other two weans."

"My… my daughter?" My heart lurched. Was this beautiful child mine? My heart went all mushy as I held the sleeping toddler Marc had thrust into my arms. "But… but how do you know she's mine?"

He grinned. "Wait until she wakes. One look at her amber eyes and ye'll ken who her sire is, lad. She didn't get those peepers from O'Malley. Now, where's my Lee?"

He looked around and his face lit with joy as he realized Lily had come, with the other two children in tow. Charles let out a squeal and ran to throw himself into my arms as Lily and Betty ran to Marc.

I turned to the crowd, holding the still sleeping Bonnie in my arms as if she were the most precious treasure I would ever hold while I somehow managed to balance Charlie on my hip. "Now, you all know the surprise. Fancy's family has come for the wedding. Uncle Jim, please ask who gives this woman again?"

Jim grinned and asked the question. My eyes misted with unshed tears as everyone there shouted, "We do!"

Marc laughed and shook Dan's hand. "Thank you, sir, for standing in for me until we arrived…"

"Dan?" Lily sounded shocked or stunned or maybe both. "Dan Smith?"

Dan grinned as he nodded and hugged Lily. "It's good to see you, Lil. We often wondered what happened to you."

She stood there, mouth agape, as Delia came up beside them. "I told you she was fine, Dan. And here she is with her beautiful family. Oh, Lil, it's good to see you after all these years."

Lily's eyes filled with tears as she grabbed Delia and pulled her close. "Oh, my God, Delia, I was so horrible to you both back then. I'm surprised you two ever gave me a second thought."

"Oh, nonsense. We were all friends. Best friends. We found your car after you disappeared. We still have it in storage. Dan swore you would come back some day. Dan should have told you about us months before he did. He didn't want to say anything until finals were over. That wasn't fair to you—"

"Fair to me? Oh, girl, let me tell you, Dan breaking up with me allowed me to find the man destiny meant for me to find. Marc is the love of my life. He has my heart. I might never have found my Marcus if Dan hadn't broken up with me. You have no idea how often I thanked God for letting Dan break up with me and for God leading me to Marc." She slipped an arm around Marc's waist and leaned her head against his chest.

Uncle Jim cleared his throat. "Perhaps we could hold off on the reunions until I complete the nuptials."

Lily and Delia both looked embarrassed and laughed. Lily said, "I apologize. Please proceed. We have all waited a long time for this."

"Some 230-odd years, I reckon." Marc's voice was barely above a whisper.

Jim stifled a laugh and proceeded with the ceremony. In short order, I slipped the beautiful aquamarine ring made for Cessie onto her ring finger, and Jim uttered the words, "I now pronounce you man and wife. You may kiss your bride."

And kiss her I did. I swept my lady into my arms for one of those old movies, swoon-worthy kisses. As we finally surfaced for air, I realized everyone was clapping and cheering. I grinned and kissed her again as she laughed ecstatically.

We all danced in the meadow until nearly midnight. We danced Irish step dance that would have put River Dance to shame, with the women lined up on one side, the men on the other. Then Chad Tangaroa led the other doctors and me in a Maori Haka dance he taught us. He told me part of the chant meant "it is our time, our moment!" I learned that crazy dance for my bride just to tell her that. Francesca laughed and clapped at our raucous dance. At midnight,

Marc sang an old Irish song in Gaelic, which he swore Josiah Selk sang years before at his wedding to Lily. The tonal quality of his rich, baritone voice amazed me. I had never heard shy Marcus McCarron sing before. We all danced as he sang the old tune. By then, my amber-eyed baby girl clung to me, calling me Da.

Yes, it's true. Life is good.

# Chapter 13
# Fancy
# Now

It began as a beautiful week.

We camped out in the meadow so we could swim at the falls the next day. Marc's mouth fell ajar at the sight of everyone clad in swimming attire at the falls. Bella blinked, and then calmly sat down, pulled off her shoes and stockings, pulled off her dress, and scurried into the water in her shift. As she played in the shallows with other children, I relaxed. My children would adjust here.

I wasn't so sure about my Daddy.

Bonnie already attached herself to Richard's hip, who could barely stand to let her down for an instant. Charlie clung to him as well. Only little Betty clung to her Papa, unwilling to go to the strange man, and she still cried sometimes for Kirk.

By late afternoon, we packed up to head to the house. The original plan was Richard and I would go to Williamsburg. He called the Inn and told them we would not come because the family had come at the last minute from out of town. Instead, we would introduce my Daddy and my children to this unknown world.

Marc fared well until we reached the parking lot. His eyes wide in dismay, he looked like he was caught in a sniper's crosshairs as we began walking to the car. "But… Where are the horses, *mo leannan*?"

I chuckled. "No horses needed, Daddy. This newfangled carriage has an engine with the power of 450 horses. Now, sit down, put on your seat belt, and we'll head home."

Lily helped him buckle his seat belt. "It will be okay, darling, I promise."

He turned about 20 shades whiter as Richard started the SUV. I knew how he felt. I remembered experiencing those same feelings a few months ago. I gave him a reassuring smile and reached over to pat his hand. "It's scary at first, but I promise we will be okay."

He tried to smile and nodded.

The children all squealed with excitement as Richard eased the car out onto the road. The children were beyond themselves with excitement as the vehicle moved effortlessly down the road. Charlie stayed glued to the window watching all the cars go by, and when we passed a train, he pointed in excitement. "What's that, Mama?"

"It's a train, sweetheart. It goes choo-choo!"

The children all laughed, as Richard and I chanted, "chugga-chugga choo-choo!"

But Marc remained silent as he held little Betty tight. *My children may be young enough to adjust to this, but I'm not so sure my Daddy can adjust,* I thought with dismay. I reached over and squeezed his hand again. "I understand. It's overwhelming at first."

He looked at me and smiled, but I noticed the smile didn't quite reach his eyes.

An hour later, we were at our house. I love the sound of that: our house. I showed Marc and Lily from room to room. Marc reacted much like I had a few months before as he saw each recent creation. He was most fascinated with the refrigerator and the toilet and most nervous about the electricity. I knew how he felt about electricity. I figured it would always scare me. I remained adamant in my refusal to plug anything into an outlet. I made Richard do it.

After dinner, Lily helped me get the children bathed and bedded down on pallets. We could buy beds for them the next day. In the meantime, they thought it was a big adventure to be sleeping on pallets in the loft. As they all fell asleep, I slipped downstairs to go outside to what Richard calls the terrace level, where Richard, Lily, and Marc sat by the fire pit.

"They are all bedded down. Daddy, we have the bed made so you can turn in whenever you like."

"You tryin' to get rid of me, lass? I'm enjoyin' sitting out here this evening, listening to the katydids and watching the fireflies flit about in the night air. Tis most pleasant watching the lights reflecting off the water in the lake. Aye, this a beautiful home you have here, Richard. A man could get accustomed to living like this. I'm just not sure I could ever get accustomed to those contraptions you use to get about in. Give me a good horse any day."

Richard nodded. "I understand. There's a lot to take in. It was quite an adjustment for me going back in time, and I knew what to expect. Still, nothing prepares you for having to operate on people with no anesthesia, the stench of burning and rotting bodies, or fighting cholera. God, that was horrible."

"Cholera is never good, lad. 'Tis always a horrible shock. T'will always be awful to have to hold a man down to saw off his leg while he screams in agony. God, the first time I saw that was during the Seven Year War…" Marc's voice trailed off.

"Were you in the Seven Year War, Daddy? I never heard you talk about it before."

Lily laid a hand over Marc's side. "He doesn't like to talk about it."

He nodded. "Aye, I don't even like to think about it. What would ye like to know, *mo leannan*?"

"How did it start? I've heard various stories, but if you were there…" My voice trailed off into an inviting silence designed to get Marc talking.

He nodded again. "Aye, I was there when it all started. They selected George and me because we had surveyed for Governor Dinwiddie. In '53, the French began acting more aggressively towards British-held lands. They sent 2600 troops into the region, built a fort on the shore of Lake Erie, and another fort at the headwaters of Le Boeuf Creek. British officials in Virginia and their Indian allies in Ohio were alarmed. I went with Washington in late '53, to take Gov. Dinwiddie's demands to the French commandant. I speak fluent French, and George knew he could use me as a translator. The French commandant refused us in the politest verbiage I ever heard. Aye, he sent us packing, but not before we collected valuable intelligence about the area. We learned the French were assembling a flotilla of small boats to carry them to the Forks of the Ohio, where the Allegheny and Monongahela Rivers meet to form the Ohio River, and where the British planned to build a small but strategic fort."

He took a long draw on his pipe before he continued. "Then, in early '54, they promoted Washington to second in command of the Virginia Regiment and sent with a contingent of soldiers back to the Ohio Valley. Will and I went with him. Our assignment was to finish building the fort at the Forks that would anchor Britain's control over the Ohio Valley. He was not told to start a war, mind you, but he had the authority to restrain any French interlopers and to 'kill and destroy,' if necessary."

Richard looked shocked. "Kill and destroy? That's powerful language."

Marc nodded as he puffed on his pipe. "Aye, it was. En route, we received stunning news. The French had already claimed Trent's Fort, our intended destination. We heard they had hundreds of French troops and over a dozen cannons. But did George turn back? Nay. Never. He is not one to admit defeat, as ye well know from Yorktown."

"On the night of May 24th, we camped in the Great Meadows, one of a rare few open clearings in those bleak, dark woods. I recall the conditions were horrid. The night sky was black as pitch. The unceasing rain made the dark woods impervious to soldiers and warriors alike. You couldn't see yer own hand in front o' yer face. And then, Washington received word from Tanaghrisson, called the Half King of the Ohio Iroquois, that an army of Frenchies was coming to attack us. I spotted French tracks a mere five miles from us, so George sent out 75 of us to search for the French party.

"Did you go?" Marc telling this old story from his viewpoint fascinated me.

"Aye, I did. I spoke both fluent French and passable Iroquois, so Washington asked me to go in case we needed to communicate with either. Hell, I was young. It seemed like a grand adventure. I said I would go. We found the French camp hidden in a glen near the crest of a nearby mountain ridge, exactly where the Indians had told us it would be."

"And then what?" Richard leaned forward, eager to hear every word of this exciting tale.

"I rode back and told them we had found the French upon Chestnut Ridge. Early on the 27th, Washington and the rest of us headed out to take the ridge. Seven men got lost along the way. The remaining 33 of us climbed straight up Chestnut Ridge with Washington at the head of the column. As directed by the Iroquois, we went up the hill, not more than 50 yards above the French, who were in plain sight directly below us. About seven that morn, as the sun began to rise, burning off the mists, we could see the French were right below us. Thanks to our Iroquois friends, I led George and his stalwart men to a rocky precipice overlooking the French camp. The Half King and his warriors went to the left to intercept the French if they should go that direction, and Monacatootha and Cherokee Jack went to the right."

I blinked. "Cherokee Jack? Was he the one who used to take settlers up the Jacks River?"

Marc nodded. "Aye. He came with us from Virginia. He was very young, mayhap 15 then. T'was his first battle. Anyway, Washington was at the head of our column and took the first shot. The French scrambled for their muskets. I swear, the battle lasted no more than 15 minutes, beginning to end. At least ten French soldiers fell. I confess our Indian allies killed most. One dead was their commander, Ensign Joseph Conlon de Villiers de Jumonville. T'was said later the Half King killed him with a tomahawk through his skull, but I did not see that. They had transformed the mountain glen from a place of idyllic beauty to a macabre scene of unburied and scalped French corpses, with one Frenchman's head stuck upon a pole."

I saw a look of shock wash over Richard's face. "Jesus, that's the battle that sparked the whole French and Indian War, Marc. And you were there?"

"Aye. At the beginning of the war, the French had significant holdings on the continent. At the end of the war, they held naught in what became the United States of America some 20-odd years later. Even New Orleans went from French-held to Spanish-held. As Voltaire said, 'so complicated are the political interests of the present time that a shot fired in America shall be the signal for setting all Europe together by the ears.'"

"When was Monongahela, Marc? Were you there, too? My dad used to talk about Monongahela and Fort Necessity." Richard leaned forward, eager to hear more.

Marc nodded as he stood up abruptly. He walked over to the fence and stared out over the lake. Finally, he spoke again, his voice raw with anguish. "Aye, I was there."

Lily hurried to his side. "It's okay, darling. You don't have to talk about it."

"I know, Lee. Monongahela was why I turned from soldiering, Richard. I could never bear to soldier again after that day."

"You've fought in battles since then, Marc. You fought against the Creek in '63." Lily sounded defensive of her man.

His face softened as he pulled Lily to him. "Aye, but that day against the Creeks, I fought for family. For you. For Michael. And God knows I raged with a fury that morn as we attacked the Creeks."

He bent to kiss Lily. I would have loved to hear the story, but he said nothing more about either fateful battle.

When he spoke again, he resumed talking about the present, as if the entire conversation about the Seven Year War had never occurred. "Still, there are so many things here, Richard, the likes of which I never dreamed. 'Tis all so different."

Marc's voice fell off as he again tamped tobacco into his pipe. I felt a wave of disappointment as I realized my Daddy would not be talking more about the Seven Year War that evening. I sat down on the edge of the chair by Marc and rubbed his neck. He smiled as he finished with his pipe and reached up to pat my hand.

"It gets easier with time. It does. All the new machines, the noise, the crowds, even all the smells, all get easier to cope with the myriad changes. Well, maybe except for the crowds and smells. You know I never was much for big, stinky cities." I laughed.

"I remember New York bothered ye. But this town isn't so bad. New York was bigger, more congested, even back then. Ellijay isn't much bigger than Williamsburg, except it is cleaner and has better streets."

I nodded. "Yes, But I wasn't thinking of Ellijay. I love it here. I was thinking of Atlanta. I'm scared every time we go there. We go Friday again."

His eyes narrowed as he took a puff on his pipe. "Lee mentioned Atlanta before. Tell me about it."

I chuckled. "It's enormous. There are so many people, houses, buildings. And so many cars! Oh, my land, Daddy, there are cars everywhere. The traffic is horrible. I won't drive in Atlanta. I sit in the passenger seat, terrified, the whole time we are on the road."

Marc tilted his head at me. "Then why do ye go there, *mo leannan*?"

Silent, I glanced at Richard. I realized my hands were shaking, and I was unsure of how to explain the surgery to Marc. "You explain."

Richard nodded and then answered for me.

"She's having surgery there next week. We have had several trips there about it."

Marc paled beneath his sun-bronzed skin. "Surgery? For what?"

Lily came out about then and handed Marc a glass of whiskey. "To replace the damaged valve in her heart."

Marc had just started sipping the drink when she said 'heart.' He began coughing as he choked on the amber fluid. "Her heart? How in the blazes do they operate on a heart?"

"Daddy, they do it all the time. I'll be fine." I tried to sound confident, but my voice sounded shaky, unsure.

"I'm sure surgeons do heart surgeries on every street corner. For God's own sake, Fancy girl, to let someone operate on your heart. Is there any chance at all you'll live through the surgery?"

I cringed as his voice broke, heavy with emotion.

"Of course, there is a chance she will survive, Marc. We wouldn't be doing the surgery unless we were sure it would be successful." Richard snapped out the words as if offended by the question.

I hurried to his side and wrapped my arms around him. "Behave, darling. He doesn't know about all the wonderful medical advances since the eighteenth century."

Richard looked embarrassed and bent to kiss me. "You're right, sweetie. I'm sorry, Marc. I didn't mean to sound rude."

Marc untangled his long frame from the chair and strode over to stand by the fence and look out over the lake. It was a pretty night, with the lights skittering off the surface of the lake as if fairies were dancing across the water. He took another long draw off his pipe, and then he shook his head, and his shoulders slumped. "So, God let us come because you're having an operation on your heart."

I nodded. "Yes, Daddy. They will fix the damaged valves and make me good as new."

"Aye, surgeries always work the way they are supposed to. My God, girl, have you given serious thought to this?"

I nodded. "Every single day since I arrived here and learned Dan is a famous cardiovascular surgeon. That's a heart surgeon. I'm lucky Richard works for Dan, and I have access to the best doctors and hospital. Richard is studying to become a board-certified heart doctor, too."

Marc laid his head down on his upraised hand. "Fancy, you have children to think about."

"I am thinking about them, Daddy," I retorted. "My heart has worsened in the past two years. It is much worse. Without the surgery, my heart will continue to deteriorate until I die, just like my Aunt Ginny did. I have a miracle here. No one is going to grab my miracle away from me or thumb their nose at it. I don't want to die of an untreated heart condition at 24, as Aunt Ginny did. I have a husband I adore, four precious little souls I love dearly, besides Lily and you. I wound up here for a reason. I think God let me come so I could get my heart fixed. Think about it, Daddy. Why else would God send me to this day and age?"

He didn't answer me at first. I could tell he was pondering my words because his eye was twitching like it does when he is thinking. Finally, he nodded. "You may be right. Could Lee and I go with you Friday to talk to the doctors?"

I nodded, excited he seemed to be coming around. "That would be great, but I bet we could get you in to confer with Dan before then. His office is here in Ellijay. He has a video you could watch."

"What's a video, *mo leannan*?" Marc sounded tired, no, defeated.

I gulped. I reached over and grabbed Marc's hand. "It's kinda like the television. Dan can show you how they do the surgery."

My words fell off as I could not explain the concept better. I looked at Richard and Lily. "One of you explain it to him."

Lily smiled. "They made a movie of them doing the operation and show it to patients and families. You could see exactly what they do. Fancy, are they going to crack your chest, or can they do a minimally invasive procedure?"

"I'm not sure. I think Dan will do an open heart. That is one thing they will tell us Friday. There has been major concern my valves are too deteriorated for a repair, and they need replacements. I told Dan I would rather plan on the open heart and do the replacements if he fears repairs won't hold."

"He's leaning to a mechanical replacement, especially since it involves two valves, and considering her age. They will last longer. With the mechanical replacement, they will crack her chest." Richard sounded eager to share his knowledge of the field he loved.

Marc's eyes were as big as saucers. "They would what? Crack her chest? Why?"

"They have to open the covering over her chest wall to access her heart, darling. But what's this about two valves, Rick?" Lily began rubbing Daddy's neck as I had earlier.

Richard nodded. "Both her aortic and her mitral valve need to be replaced. Aortic stenosis. Dan thinks the aorta has been bad since she was born, while we're pretty sure her rheumatic fever damaged the mitral valve."

They sat talking technical, medical stuff I didn't understand while poor Marc looked sicker and sicker. I reached out to him again. "How about we go inside, and I fix you a nice cup of tea, Daddy? Maybe with a healthy dollop of the bottle of McCarron whiskey you brought."

He looked a bit startled as his eyes refocused on me. He smiled and reached to cup my face with his big hands. "All right, *m'inion*. You do know I love you dearly, right?"

I took his work-roughened hands into mine and gently kissed them. "I know, Daddy. I love you, too. I'm so glad you're here. But it really will be fine, Daddy. I promise."

He tried to grin. "It had better be, lass, or I'll kill ye."

I chuckled and pulled him by his hand. "You've got a deal. Come on. Let's go get that tea."

Richard looked up long enough to frown and wag a finger at me. "No whiskey for you, Mrs. Winslow."

I smiled and gave him my best salute. "Yes, sir, Dr. Winslow. Would you two like a cup? With or without the hair of the dog?"

"Oh, with, most definitely," Lily said with a smile.

Marc followed along behind me, silent as usual. When the kettle whistled, I poured the boiling water over the tea leaves. "It's hard at first. Getting used to being here. But it does get easier. I'm so glad you are here. I'm so glad you know where I am, and that Richard and I are married and —"

"That the doctors are going to operate on your heart next week. Ah, *m'inion*, I could have gone my whole life without knowing this. What keeps you from bleeding to death when they cut open your heart?"

My heart lurched at the raw pain in his voice. "They have marvelous equipment that can keep you alive, Daddy. Let's talk to Dan tomorrow. He can explain it better than I can."

"Nonsense. You show the video to our surgical patients all the time. You can explain the procedure to Marc as well as Dan can," Richard interjected.

My head snapped up at his words. "I didn't realize you two came in. But, Richard, most people I am talking with understand the rudiments of heart surgery when they come in."

"Balderdash. That's why you should explain it to Marc. Here. Tonight. Let's all sit down here together and explain the procedure to Marc," Lily said.

"You do a great job of explaining the surgery to patients, sweetie." Richard reached over to rub my back.

I took a deep breath. "Okay. Well, I usually have the video, and we don't have it here. But heart surgeons in this country do over 100,000 heart valve operations every year. The aortic valve and the mitral valve are both on the left side of the patient's heart. The left side of the heart works harder than the right side, and those valves are more prone to wear out. I have severe valve damage, which means my valves must be replaced. Before they start, they will give me a medicine called anesthesia, which will make me sleep through the surgery. I won't feel a thing."

"I understand about anesthesia. Lily has made some before. It's a miracle." I could see the tension begin to ease out of his body.

I smiled. "Yes, it is. Patients tell me they don't feel a thing, and they don't remember the surgery at all."

"Excellent," Marc said.

I took another deep breath. Now on to the hard part. "With a mechanical valve replacement, the surgeons have to open the chest wall. They call the procedure a medial sternotomy. That means they will open my chest by cutting through the sternum, which is my breastbone. They cut it right down the middle. They found doing it that way is easier to heal and less likely to become infected."

Richard smiled and patted my hand. "You're doing great, sweetie. Go on."

I flashed him a quick smile and then continued. "Once in, the surgeon deflates the lungs and stops the heart. Then, they put the patient on the heart-lung machine."

"What's that?" Marc frowned.

"It's a machine that will recirculate the blood and put oxygen back in the blood after cleaning it while the surgeons perform the surgery," I explained.

Marc frowned. "How in the name of all that is holy do they do that?"

"They open a vein here," I said, pointing to my groin, "So venous blood can go through the machine to be cleaned and given fresh oxygen before it is returned to the body, here, in the femoral artery."

He gulped. "Jaysus."

"We call on Him often." Richard's voice was droll.

"They stop the heart right before they start the heart-lung machine, right, Richard?"

"Right."

"Well, then they cut into the non-beating heart which has been emptied of blood, and they replace the valves. Friday, they are going to decide whether they will be using biological replacements or mechanical replacements. Dan and we are leaning to mechanical replacements for when we go back home. They can do a minimally invasive procedure with a biological replacement, but the mechanical valves last longer than the biological. We figure once we go back in time, we might not be able to come here again. I told him I'm fine with the mechanical replacement since it will last decades longer, although the minimally invasive procedure would be an easier surgery and recovery. They can do the minimally invasive procedure only with biological replacements."

"Wow, I didn't realize they could do either replacement by a minimally invasive procedure," said Lily.

I nodded. "Oh, yes, it's a big deal. Dan does almost all his repairs and a lot of his replacements by the minimally invasive procedure. Anyway, once they decide which to do, the hospital will also do some last-minute tests on me again. An EKG, which will check the function of my heart, in addition to some blood tests, a urinalysis, and an x-ray."

"What is an x-ray?" Marc asked.

"It is a picture they can take with a special machine of the insides of your body. It shows where bones are located, which will help the doctors on Monday."

Lily and Richard both nodded. Marc looked impressed.

"An x-ray comes in handy with broken bones, too. It would have shown your leg fracture, and I could have used one to confirm the bone was set with good alignment. It could have shown me how advanced Belle's cancer was, too. Although I doubt, I could have successfully excised it then." Lily choked up as if she were about to cry.

"Then, when the valve has been replaced, they sew the little incision in the patient's heart back up. They take you off the heart-lung machine once they re-inflate the lungs and re-start the heart. They make sure it works okay before they pull the sternum back together as close as possible with wire. That helps cut down on possible infections. They sew up the tissue and skin, and then voila! C'est finis."

Marc stared at me. "Why do ye keep sayin' the patient instead of sayin' 'me'?"

I gulped. "I'm used to telling other patients about it, Daddy."

Let's face it. I couldn't quite manage to say my sternum, my lungs, my heart. I didn't want my father to know it, but the whole process scared me. Who wouldn't be scared? They were going to cut open my living heart in less than a week. The reality scared me witless. But I didn't want him to realize that. I didn't want anyone to know it.

That was one of the reasons I began talking to patients about their surgeries. I understand their fears. Dan and Richard both say I had a lot of empathy with the patients. I know how they feel scared about all this. I try to help them understand it so that they can cope better.

So, I can cope better, too.

I think he realized about then I was scared. He stared at me a long time before he nodded. "Yer a brave girl, lass. I'm not sure I would be brave enough to do this."

I sat up straight. "Of course, you would. You're the bravest person I know. It's like what Sassy and Lily always said. What doesn't kill you makes you stronger. And I'm not goin' to die. I intend to be one badass survivor."

My heart was beating fast and hard by then, pitter-pat, pitter-pat. I took another deep breath and forced myself to crack out a little smile.

He smiled back. "Aye, that ye are, lass. One badass survivor."

Thursday morning, Richard drove to Atlanta to check on surgical patients. He planned to be back by evening to take me to Atlanta on Friday morning for my last tests before my surgery on Monday. Thursday afternoon, we all went into Ellijay and ran by the office. Marc still had some questions, and I had the brilliant idea to show him the video while Lily took the kids for ice cream.

Did I say brilliant? Not so much.

When we arrived at the office, Dan's face lit up with pleasure. "Hey, Fancy, could you show the video to these people, too? They are all having surgery soon, and there is no one to show them the film."

I sighed. Showing the video is not a problem. Fielding the questions afterward is the time-consuming part. But Dan was always kind to me. I nodded. "Sure. Are they all here yet?"

He took us into the video room, where there were already three other people waiting. "Mr. McDaniels, Mr. Bryant, Mrs. Silvestri, you are in for a pleasant surprise. Fancy Winslow is here this afternoon, and she will be showing you the video. Fancy is married to our own Dr. Winslow."

The little, grey-haired lady's face lit up. "Oh, you are the girl who Dr. Rick told me about two weeks ago. Congratulations." She smiled at the men. "They just got married last week."

"Thank you, Mrs. Silvestri. This is my dad, Mr. McCarron. He's going to watch the video today with you guys."

Mr. Bryant tilted his head at Marc as he held out his hand. "Nice to meet you, sir. Are you having surgery, too?"

Marc laughed, nervous and ill at ease. "No, my daughter is. On Monday. She wants me to understand the procedure."

Mr. Bryant frowned. "Fancy, do you have a sister?"

I chuckled. "No, sir, I'm having heart surgery. Mitral valve and aortic valve are both going to be replaced Monday."

He turned pale. "Oh, my dear, I had no idea. You're so young."

I laughed. "Yes, but I was born with a congenital defect to my aortic valve. It is a condition called aortic stenosis. My aortic valve has only two cusps instead of three. That's called a bicuspid aortic valve. My congenital condition worsened, and the mitral valve was also damaged when I had rheumatic fever when I was a child. That caused scarring on both valves. The damaged, scarred heart valves don't open or close properly, so Dr. Dan is going to replace them both next week."

Everyone started talking at once. Like I say, my squirrels were once again all over everywhere when all I wanted was a nice, orderly row of well-behaved ducks.

"Next week?" Mrs. Silvestri squeaked.

I nodded. "Yes, ma'am, Monday. It's time. Anyway, let's pop this video in and let you guys see what Dan and Richard will be doing to fix my heart next week."

Mr. Bryant looked surprised. "Dr. Rick will be on the team?"

I nodded. "Yes. Richard is in the residency program to become a board-certified cardiovascular surgeon. Dr. Dan has warned he might have to put Richard out if he's a problem."

Mr. Bryant appeared relieved. "Oh, well, good. I was afraid your husband might be the surgeon in charge."

I laughed. "No, I don't think Grady Memorial would approve a surgeon operating on his wife as the primary surgeon. Plus, Richard is excellent, but he is not board certified yet. He will be one day. Now, I can stop the video at any time if you have questions."

The video had not been playing very long when Marc became agitated. "Oh, for the love of -- Fancy, stop this video. I canna watch it. To think they will be doin' this to ye in a matter of days. Nay, lass, I canna..."

I glanced at everyone as I jumped up. "Uh... I'll be right back..."

I ran after my father.

He ran outside, breathing in deep gulps of air. As I came up beside him, he wrapped his arms around me. My heart lurched as he began to cry.

He shocked me. I never saw my Daddy cry before. My arms crept up to console him with awkward pats to his back.

"It's okay, Daddy. It will all be fine." I continued to pat his back, and I tried to console him.

"I thought I could watch it at first. I swear I did. And then, he started prying that man's chest apart. All I could think was, 'this could be my girl. This might be my Fancy.' I had to leave. Oh, lass, are you sure? Are ye confident about this surgery?"

I took a big breath. My heart shattered by his pain. I never heard such anguish in Marc's voice before, and the unexpected tears were killing me. "Yes, I am sure. I will die without surgery. Oh, not right now. Maybe not for another year. But my heart function is slipping. I can do less than I could six months ago. I can't walk as far. Heck, walking has become a serious chore for me. I used to walk five miles a day, if not more, without breaking a sweat. Now, it's hard to make a half a mile without having to rest along the way. It was pretty tough for me to walk to the meadow the other day, and you saw how hard it was for me to walk back to the car. I will live a long, happy life if I have this surgery. Without it, my days are numbered. I may have a year or even two, but I won't have the length of life much less the quality of life I want. Yes, I gave this a lot I prayerful thought, and I am quite sure my decision to have the surgery is the right decision. I don't want to die. I choose life over death."

It took me over three hours to walk to the meadow last week. It should take about an hour.

He looked so rattled, unnerved, so downright frightened. I never saw that look of panic in his eyes before, even when my Grampa died in '83. I suspected he looked like that when Jay attacked Lily and kidnapped Michael all those years ago. I sidled close to him and slipped my arms around his waist. "I'll be fine, Daddy. I promise."

My heart lurched as I realized tears were again clouding his dark eyes. "You better be, *m'inion*, or I'll kill ye."

I chuckled as I stretched up to kiss him. He has said that to me as long as I can remember. "I would expect nothing less, *m'athair*."

I could feel the tension ease from his long frame. "I do love it when ye call me father in the Irish, lass. It softens my heart to ye every time ye say it. Fine. Let's go watch the blasted video."

He averted his face a few times but stuck it out until the end. The other patients were all quite sympathetic. They understood my father's worries. They shared them. Although these patients were used to the idea of cardiovascular surgery, it is always scary to contemplate someone cutting into your living heart. After the video, they all asked questions. Marc remained silent, but I saw he paid close attention.

It was getting late when we finished. What should have taken an hour had somehow stretched into nearly three. I was dog tired. Lily and the children still played in the playground across the street when we finally left the clinic.

"Everything okay?" Lily asked as she pushed an excited and squealing Charles again in the swing.

I nodded. "Yes. Dan convinced me to include three other people in the video. Marc had a hard time with it, and we took a break so I could talk to him alone. Then, after the video, Dan joined us for questions. He doesn't usually do that, but I figure he realized Marc might have questions."

Lily shook her head. "No, Dan figured you would have questions. He realizes you are scared."

I frowned. "Not scared exactly. Nervous. What's that word? Trepidatious? Is that even a word?"

Lily nodded as she tried to keep me from seeing her grin. "I'm not sure, but I understand what you mean. You feel trepidation. So is Marc. It's logical under the circumstances. Heck, even Rick and I are nervous, too."

That startled me. "You think Richard is scared, too? But he helps Dan do this surgery all the time…"

Lily nodded. "Yes, but you are the woman he loves, the mother of his child."

I blinked. "The DNA results aren't back yet…"

"Honey, all anyone has to do is look at that baby girl, and they know she is his child. She not only has his bone structure; she has his eyes. He has the most beautiful eyes I ever saw on any man other than your daddy. That amber color is rare. Rick tells me his mom's eyes were that color, too. The DNA test should be back tomorrow. I am confident it will confirm Rick is her father. You need a will. The one drafted in Ireland in 1783 will not suffice. A new will can say what happens to the children, just in case."

Her voice broke.

I grabbed her hands close. "Nothing bad is going to happen."

She nodded as she clung to me. "I know, honey. I know. But, you two should try to talk to a lawyer tomorrow."

Throat dry with new anxiety, I nodded. "That's the plan. We will, after my tests. Rick called in a favor."

I felt her sag with relief. "Oh, good. One less worry."

I nodded.

It was after five when we left the office. Lily had the bright idea to take the children to Chic-Fil-A for dinner. After a reasonably nutritious dinner of grilled chicken, fruit salad, and milk, we let the children play on the indoor playground for another hour before we headed home. I fell asleep in the car as Lily drove the ten miles to the house. She and Marc herded the kids upstairs to get them ready for bed, and Lily commented it was like herding cats. I laughed as I collapsed on the couch. I was exhausted.

I must have fallen asleep there. About 9, Richard called.

"I thought you would be home by now," I said with a big yawn.

"I thought so, too, but things went a little haywire here today. Look, could you drive down tonight? O'Banion asked to change your appointment from 1 until 10 in the morning. I figured you wouldn't mind."

"You figured I wouldn't mind? Richard, I can't drive to Atlanta now. I'm exhausted. It's been a helluva long day. Why can't we come in the morning as we planned?" I yawned again.

"You'll need to leave by 7. Look, sweetie, I thought we could have the evening alone if you come on down. Lily and Marc could come down tomorrow."

I let out a sigh of exasperation. "Richard, that is plain silly. Why didn't you call me about this hours ago? I am way too tired to drive 3 hours to Atlanta tonight."

He was silent. I could almost see the wheels working in his head. At last, he spoke again. "What if Lily…"

"No. She would have to turn right around and come back for Daddy and the kids. And we are not dragging these babies out of their beds. Not at this time of night."

I was proud of myself. It's hard for me to stand up to people, especially people I love, but I held my ground this time. Even so, my hands sweated enough that I had to wipe them on my jeans.

"Hmm. Well, what if I send an Uber driver for you? Come on, sweetie. We can be alone tonight. You know, uh, special time. Just you and me. We haven't been alone since the wedding."

"Oh, for the love of -- no, Richard. We will be there in the morning. If you want, I'll stay in Atlanta with you tomorrow night. I am not coming tonight."

I realized Lily impatiently waited there, reaching for the phone. Her lips were pressed so thin they were white, and she stood tapping her foot as if angry or frustrated. "Let me speak with him."

I hesitated a minute and then handed it to her. I hissed, "I already told him 'no.'"

She nodded as she snatched the phone from me. "Rick? This is Lily. No, she is not coming tonight. Period. The poor dear is done in. We went to the office for Dan to show Marc the video, and he wangled her into showing it to Marc and three other patients. In case you forgot, she's having heart surgery Monday, most likely open-heart surgery. She tires easily. We will be there by 10. You should have called hours ago if you wanted her to come tonight. It's a hard 2 ½ hour drive at best from here to Grady. If she left right now, it would be close to midnight before she got there. As your Mom would say, not gonna happen, dude. Not Gonna Happen."

With a look of triumph, she handed the phone back to me.

"I guess she told me." Richard sounded subdued.

"Sounded like it. So, I reckon we'll see you in the morning. I'm gonna turn in now. I love you. Don't be mad."

He paused before he answered. "I'm not mad. She's right. It's just been a God-awful day. I, uh, I just needed to hold you…"

His voice broke. My heart lurched.

"Richard, what's wrong? What happened?" And then, a horrible thought crossed my mind. "Oh, no. Is my sweet Mrs. Delaney all right?"

"She'll be okay. It was pretty touch and go for a while today, but I think she has stabilized now. It rattled me. I never had a patient go south on me like this before. I have to admit, I didn't need it right now, days before your surgery. It rattled me bad. I need to hold you, but I can wait until tomorrow."

His voice broke, and I ached for him. I almost relented, but I knew I was far too exhausted to try to drive to Atlanta then. Heart in my throat, I could not bear to ask what went wrong with Mrs. Delaney. She was one of my favorite patients, always sweet and smiling. "We'll be there on time, I promise."

Marc was watching me with a curious expression on his face. "What's wrong?"

I shook my head and forced myself to smile. "Nothing. He misses me. After all, we haven't been married a week yet."

I wasn't about to tell Daddy one of the heart patients was having post-surgical complications. It would freak Marc out. Heck fire, it freaked me out. It even freaked Richard out.

"Harrumph. That man needs to start thinking about you first instead of himself," Marc muttered with a shake of his head.

I struggled not to tell him what upset Richard. I put on a serious face and nodded. "Absolutely, Daddy."

Lily nodded as well. "Sometimes, I wonder where his head is. But then, Sassy says he acts before he thinks."

I choked back the retort. While he can act rash at times, I realized this was not one of those times. I knew he would have called hours ago if he had not been dealing with an emergency. "Look, I realize we could stand here and talk about Richard all night, but I am exhausted. I'm heading to bed. It looks like we have to be up early to head out, so I'll set the alarm clock for six."

Marc snorted. "Six isna' early, lass. I'll be up before then. I can rouse everyone."

I reached up to pat his cheek. "Thank you, Daddy."

I set the alarm clock anyway.

# Chapter 14
# Fancy and Rick
# Now

True to his promise, Marc roused everyone at six the next morning. We left the house by 6:30 and pulled into the parking lot at the professional building next to Grady at 9:30 on the dot. Richard looked relieved as we walked into Dr. O'Banion's offices. He wrapped me into a big bear hug.

"Is everything okay?" I felt my brow furrow with worry, and I quickly forced a Tamsin-worthy smile.

He nodded. "She's much improved today. She'll be fine. It rattled me horribly."

"You mean it scared you? I understand," I whispered. "Me, too."

He pulled me close and held me tight. "It will be all right. I promise."

"I know. Trepidatiousness is normal."

He chuckled. "Trepidation. Yes, it's quite normal. You must remember, you have the best surgeons, the best team, the best hospital."

"I know." I cringed as my voice quivered.

"It will be fine." He kissed the top of my head. "Come on. You can come back now. His office manager said to bring you back as soon as you arrived."

They drew my blood and had me pee in a cup for the umpteenth time. Afterward, I underwent another EKG and chest x-ray. Once they completed the tests, we expected Dr. O'Banion would give me the once over again before signing the release to Dan for my surgery on Monday.

But a stranger walked into the examining room. As my hair stood up on end, Richard sidled in front of me.

"What the hell are you doing here?" my husband growled.

The doctor looked up from his papers and smiled. "Oh, I'm sorry, allow me to introduce myself. I'm Dr. Killian O'Malley."

My jaw must have hit the ground. "Um… You look like someone we used to know. He came from Ireland, too."

"You're a dead ringer for him," Richard muttered.

The Kirk O'Malley lookalike tilted his head at that. "Oh? And who was he?"

"No one you would know." Richard's voice sounded stiff and unfriendly.

The doctor stared at us both, uncomfortable with our hostility. "Indeed? Hmm. Interesting. Ah, well, probably not. Most of my family is in Ireland. I've only been here for a few years. Most of the O'Malley's are seafaring men. I'm the first doctor."

My heart was beating hard and fast. "How long has your family gone to sea?"

He shrugged and grinned. "Hundreds of years. An ancestor founded O'Malley Shipping. The family followed his footsteps ever since. I'm the renegade heathen son who chose medicine instead of the sea. Now, let's look at your test results."

Richard bristled as Dr. O'Malley picked up my file with my newest test results. "Where's Kevin? I thought he would be here."

Dr. O'Malley shrugged. "Called back to the hospital. He asked me to see your wife. Let's take a listen to your ticker, pretty lady."

He put the stethoscope in his ears and held it to my chest. He frowned and asked me to cough. He listened again and shook his head. "Your heart is beating fast and furious. Is that typical, Dr. Winslow?"

"No." Richard was curt in his reply.

I forced myself to smile. "Excuse my husband, doctor. Sometimes, my heart beats erratically, like it is now. Why?"

His face softened as he looked at me. "Ah, there's a pretty *nighean rua* if I ever saw one. I would swear you were Irish if I hadn't heard your lovely southern drawl. So, why do you have this horrible heart murmur, lass?"

"Born with the defective aortic valve. I have a bicuspid aortic valve causing aortic stenosis in addition to mitral valve prolapse. It damaged both valves when I had scarlet fever as a child. And my Daddy is Irish. I understand I look a lot like my paternal aunt. He says we both are red-haired beauties. Thank you for the compliment."

"I figured there was an Irishman in the woodpile, with that hair and complexion. So, you understand the Irish? I must say, I did not expect to walk in to meet such a beautiful young woman today, much less that she would understand Gaelic. Yes, your heart sounds like you need the surgery. There is a good bit of regurgitation there. Otherwise? You seem as fit as is possible with that bum ticker. You're cleared to go. I understand from Kevin that Dr. Smith and he agree they prefer the mechanical replacement. Kevin said he thought you both agree."

We both nodded.

"Good. Do you know the surgery entails the open-heart procedure?"

Wordless, we both nodded again.

"Well, the secretary will email the release for the surgery to Dr. Smith." He signed the release with a flourish and winked at me with a lopsided grin I remembered all too well. Richard took the release from him when Dr. O'Malley held it out.

His outright flirtatiousness rattled me. He looked and acted so much like Kirk. It was exceptionally discomfiting. I could tell it shook Richard as well.

We were almost out of the door when I could contain my questions no longer. "So, where are you from in Ireland?"

He flashed that damned smile at me again, making my heart lurch once more. "From a village near Sligo. Our family has lived there since the 1700s. My ancestor was once married to a beautiful young woman from Cork. She disappeared without a trace in '83. I think it was after a big hurricane. You remind me of a painting I saw of her once."

I felt the color drain from my face. "What was your relative's name?"

"Captain Kirk O'Malley, ma'am. Her name was Fancy O'Malley. I never met anyone else named 'Fancy' before."

I gulped, not at all comfortable with the unexpected twist. "Uh… Fancy is an old family name. Maybe it was more common in the past."

His eyes narrowed as he studied me. Could he tell I was lying? Richard says my face is like an open book, but Lily says I can 'schmooze with the best,' whatever that means.

O'Malley finally smiled and barked out a laugh. "That must be it, Mrs. Winslow. Or perhaps we're distant cousins. Best wishes for a successful surgery next week."

He bowed with a flourish, and then left the examining room.

"Un-freaking-believable," Richard muttered.

I tugged on his arm. "Come on, darling. Let's go."

We ate lunch with Marc, Lily, and the kids, and then hurried to the appointment with the lawyer. We did my will and other papers, 'just in case.' The attorney assured us he would prepare a lawsuit to establish Richard was Bonnie's father, since the DNA test done at the first of the week was back, confirming his paternity of our amber-eyed daughter.

Next, we headed out for a trip to the zoo. Richard snapped lots of photos. The exotic animals enchanted the children. Bella loved the elephants, the giraffes captivated Betty, Charles adored the hippos, and little Bonnie beamed at the penguins. "Bird, Mama, bird!" Four hours later, I felt exhausted, but I knew we made beautiful memories for my children.

Richard arranged for Marc and Lily to stay overnight in the apartment next door with the children. After eating out, we all turned in about 9, although Marc fussed it was too late for little children to be still awake.

Saturday, I fixed pancakes with powdered sugar and fresh strawberries at the apartment for everyone. Afterward, we went to the Atlanta Aquarium to make and record more memories before we ate lunch. It fascinated us to watch the fish swimming beneath the surface from the observation deck built below ground level. The sea otter encounter enchanted the children. Richard promised them that the next time we come, they could go to the penguin encounter. As always, Richard captured lots of memories with photos.

The plan was Marc, Lily, and the kids would return to Ellijay Saturday evening and would come back Monday morning for my surgery. Among the children, Bella alone seemed to comprehend the seriousness of the situation.

"I don't want to go. I need to stay with my Mommy. She needs me." She struggled not to cry as tears welled up in her eyes.

Bella rarely fusses or whines. We call her 'Mommy's little soldier.' Richard calls her the 'brave big sister.' My heart lurched at the fear in her voice. I knelt, wrapped my eldest child into my arms, and hugged her close. "It's okay, sweetheart. Mommy will be fine with Richard until my surgery. The doctors won't start it until you get back. I promise."

She looked unconvinced and wrapped her little hands tight around mine. "Are you sure? Because I need to be here with you. Please, Mommy, let me stay. I promise I'll be a very good girl if you let me stay. You'll see. I won't be a bother at all. You'll hardly know I'm here."

My heart lurched again. Bella's little body trembled like a leaf in a high wind as she struggled to contain her tears. I didn't want her to leave crying, 'just in case.' I looked at Richard, imploring him with my eyes. "What do you think, darling? You know she'll be a good girl. She always minds. Can't she stay?"

I could tell it frustrated him. He still wanted some 'alone time' before my surgery. But I'll give the man credit. He did not disappoint the terrified child. He shut his eyes and took a deep breath before he bent down and took her little hands into his big ones. "I tell you what, Bella Boo. How about you all stay? I'll call Miss Dee and see if she can take care of the dogs for a few more days."

"Oh, you are the very best daddy a girl could ever have!" Her little face lit up, and she threw her arms around Richard to hug him tight, just as the rush of tears began.

"Hey, now, hold on there, girlfriend! What's with the tears, little bit?" He asked, as he pulled his starched and neatly ironed handkerchief out and handed it to her.

She smiled through her tears, hiccuping as she tried to get control of her emotions. She wiped her tears and blew her nose into the immaculate linen. I bit back laughter when Bella neatly refolded the handkerchief and handed it back to Richard. "Thank you, Daddy."

He somberly tucked the soiled linen back into his pocket. "You're welcome, Bella Boo."

She gave him a shaky smile. "It scared me you would say 'no.' And I'm so happy you answered 'yes'!"

He hugged her again as tears misted his own eyes. "Now, when have I ever told you 'no,' Bella Boo?"

"You told me 'no' in Ireland. You wouldn't stay, and you wouldn't let me go with you. I cried, and I cried." She struggled to contain her crying.

His brow wrinkled as he frowned. "Now, you promised me you would never tell your Mommy about that, Bella."

She nodded. "I know. I'm sorry. But you did tell me 'no.' You did, Daddy."

It hit me like a ton of bricks. "You knew Richard was leaving?"

Wordless, my child nodded.

"She did. She caught us that morning as we headed down to the pier, but she promised not to tell you she saw us." Richard looked embarrassed and a bit defensive.

I stared at them both. I always told Bella to never keep secrets from me. She admitted she kept a whopper of a secret from me in Ireland. Thank God Richard was not the man Tom was. "You don't keep secrets from me, Bella. It's one thing if it's about a present. Or Christmas. But you must never keep important things from Mommy. Do you understand?"

She nodded, her eyes wide as she stood silent and solemn.

That night, we all snuggled on the big couches and watched Disney movies. The children were undecided whether they liked *Moana* or *Frozen* best. I guess I'm 'old school,' as Richard calls it, because I preferred Cinderella.

After the children turned in for the night with Marc and Lily in the apartment next door, Richard and I finally had our alone time. He surprised me in the shower where he slowly soaped my skin beneath the steaming hot water. We kissed and caressed each other's soap slickened bodies until Richard lifted me to make love in the shower. I threw my head back, exulting in the flood of emotions to be so cherished by the man I love. After we toweled off and retired to the bed, I laid in his arms for hours, making love again, then talking, and then making love one more time before we finally drifted asleep, safe and secure in each other's arms.

How is it that every time we make love, it is better than the last? And how does he always make me feel like a princess -- or maybe a duchess?

I asked him that, and he grinned. "Well, sweetheart, you *are* a duchess."

I sniffed and shrugged in disdain. "A reluctant duchess. You know I never wanted the title."

He laughed and pulled me into his arms again. "I'm just glad *my* Reluctant Duchess is here with me."

Sunday morning brought unexpected rains to Atlanta. We headed to IHOP for pecan waffles, bacon, eggs, all the high-fat foods that heart patients should avoid, and I was craving. I swooned over the rich flavors of the biscuits and gravy.

"I don't know how you eat that stuff," Richard said with a grimace of disgust. "I could never force myself to taste it. It looks like something you would feed the hogs."

I laughed. I had heard my husband say this before. "He's a Yankee."

He frowned. "I am not. I lived in the south most of my life. Heck, I was born in Texas."

"Maybe, but your mother conceived you in Boston. You lived there for almost ten years. You. Are… A… Yankee."

"I'm 32. I lived in Boston for six years. I lived in San Antonio eight, Virginia, eight, and Georgia for ten years. I am *not* a Yankee. I don't like the looks of biscuits and gravy."

Marc looked dumbfounded. "You think biscuits and gravy look like… like hog swill?"

Lily finally responded. "I know it's not heart healthy, but you do not understand what you are missing, Rick. It tastes great and will fill you right up. Come on, try a bite."

She extended a small bite on a clean spoon.

He laughed and shook his head. "I think I'll stick to my French toast."

"Coward," she teased.

Afterward, we took the children to the Children's Museum. I moved slowly, with frequent stops to rest and catch my breath. I could tell I moved slower each day. Calm little Betty realized I was tired and came to sit close to me. She leaned against me, patting my arm.

Bella frowned. She put her hands on her hips, with her little foot tapping with impatience. "Are you okay, Mommy?"

I made myself smile. Thank heaven, Tamsin taught me how to smile on command. "I'll be fine. I'm a little tired today. Go on. Finish your art project. I'll watch from here."

She hesitated, still frowning. "Yes, ma'am. But you call me if you need me, okay?"

I struggled not to laugh. My daughter looked so serious standing there in her little sundress and apron, her brown hair braided down her back the way mine was braided, her hands and her face smudged dirty from working with the paint and clay.

"Yes, ma'am, I promise. Now, go on back and finish your project and make sure the other children don't get into any mischief. Betty, go with your big sister."

Betty frowned but nodded and rose to accompany Bella back towards the craft table.

*They grow up so fast. My Bella is growing before my eyes*, I thought. *She's only six, but my Bella loves to help. She takes on all responsibilities with such an air of maturity.*

Bella nodded and turned to go back to the project table. About halfway back, she stopped, turned back to me again, and blew me a kiss. I caught it, pretended to tuck it close to my heart, and then I blew a kiss back to her.

I know I'm not supposed to have favorites, but I will always be closest to this girl. She is my unique child, my angel, my gift from God, who saved me from myself at my lowest hour. If any man ever hurts her, I would kill him. If anyone hurt her the ways Tom hurt me when I was a child, they would beg and pray for the sweet release of death long before I gave it to them.

I quivered with exhaustion by the time we left, but I realized we created plenty of happy, positive memories to help my beloved family withstand the rough days ahead. I knew the remembrances of the children's sweet, laughing faces would encourage me to survive the surgery and to recover. *My babies need me*, I told myself. *I can do this. My babies need a healthy mother.*

"I'll get all the pictures developed and bring you copies," Richard said.

I beamed up at him. "I'm counting on it."

We knew those photos would help me cope in the days to come.

Everyone accompanied me to the hospital that afternoon. Marc and Lily stayed in the lobby with the children as Richard took me upstairs since the children could not enter the cardiac wing. Bella stood somberly watching me as the elevator doors began to close. Her eyes shone bright with unshed tears as she raised her hand to blow me another kiss.

I pretended to catch it and pressed my hand to my heart. I smiled and blew a kiss back to Bella. "I'll be fine."

She nodded. I could see moisture welling up in her beautiful blue eyes, so much like my mother's eyes.

"I know," she mouthed as she struggled not to weep.

It didn't take too long to get me settled into the room in the cardio surgical wing. As I settled onto the bed, we heard a knock at the door, and an attractive, older, black lady with steel-grey hair stuck her head into the private room. "Excuse me. I'm Olathe Roberts. I'm looking for Dr. Winslow ..."

Richard rushed across the room to gather the lady into his arms. "Gramma, I didn't know you were coming. How sweet of you! I want you to meet my wife, Francesca. Sweetheart, this is my Gramma. She was my Mama Kathryn's mother."

I slipped off the bed and walked over to her, extending my hand. "It is a genuine pleasure to meet you, Mrs. Roberts. I had no idea your Gramma lived in Atlanta, Richard."

He laughed as if he were suddenly embarrassed. "Really? I thought you knew…"

"Richard Winslow, you know good and well if I had known you had family nearby, we would have been visiting them. My heavens, she could have come to our wedding!" Tears welled up in my eyes at the unexpected and unknown slight to his Gramma.

Her eyes narrowed. "Now, child, don't you cry. But I must admit, I wondered if my Ricky was ashamed of his old black Gramma."

Richard looked horrified. "Oh, no, Gramma, not at all!"

I shook my head. "Not at all, Mrs. Roberts. My Great-Gramma came from Nigeria, where she was a slave. I'm mixed, too. I have black kinfolk I dearly love. My Uncle Tobias and my Aunt Hattie, well, they are my family. The color of our skin does not affect the love in our hearts. We are all the color of the water. It comes in different shades, but it is all H2O. I figure since people are comprised of what? Sixty? Seventy percent of water? Well, I reckon the same holds for us. We are all the colors of water. We all bleed red. I reckon it doesn't make a lick of difference to the Good Lord which shade we are."

I did not explain Sassy taught me 'the color of water' analogy. Sassy read a book called *The Color of Water* in a college class, and the phrase touched her heart. It stuck with her. Sassy replaced Richard's mother, Kathryn, after Kathryn died from a drug overdose. I figured Gramma Roberts might not have fond feelings about Sassy.

I did not explain that my Granny Ebony came to the Colonies in the 1720s as a slave. Richard told me slavery was legal in Nigeria until the 1930s. I reckoned Mrs. Roberts would think my Granny came from Nigeria before it abolished slavery. It was logical.

Time travel? Not so much.

She grabbed hold of my hands. "Oh, you dear girl. You must call me Gramma O, child."

I smiled. "You wouldn't mind? Both of my Grammas passed long ago."

*She could not imagine just how long ago*, I thought.

She beamed at me as she patted my cheek. "Oh, child, you and I will get along fine."

About then, Richard's cell phone rang. "Oh, hi, Marc. Sure. Just a minute." He turned to us and grinned. "Ladies, come over to the window."

We both hustled over to the window where Marc and Lily stood outside with the children, who waved up to us when they spotted our faces. Then, they unfolded their art project and held it up for me. "Get well quick, Mom!" It proclaimed in large, block letters written in Bella's identifiable scrawl.

"Mrs. Roberts, there's my Daddy, my step-mama, and my children. My Daddy is holding little Bonnie. She is your great-grandchild."

She turned to me, beaming. "Oh, you dear girl, I am delighted I got to see them! But you really must call me Gramma O. All the family call me that. Now, Richard, you tell them to wait right there because we are comin' downstairs so I can meet them. Francesca, I will see you again, my dear. And I will pray the Good Lord guides the hands of your surgeon tomorrow."

Tears welled up in my eyes. "Thank you, Gramma O. Would you pray with me now before you leave?"

I think that's when she discerned how frightened I felt. She clasped my hands into hers and prayed one of the most potent, most heartfelt prayers I ever heard. Unshed tears glistened in my eyes as she finished and pulled me into her arms.

"I'll be praying for you, child. Trust in the Lord. He's got this covered."

I nodded as she kissed my cheek and turned to hurry downstairs with Richard.

I felt a little lost as Richard and Gramma O hurried from the room to go outside so she could meet my family. I took a deep breath and turned back to stare out the window at the meeting of Olathe Roberts and her great-granddaughter for the first time. "I hope Richard remembers to take photos of this."

And then I chuckled as he pulled out his camera and began snapping shots. Of course, he photographed them. He takes snapshots everywhere he goes.

Just then, I heard the door swing open. "How are you doing, kiddo?" Dan said.

I turned around to greet him. "I'm okay. No dirt in my face."

He laughed at the office line. "You must be fine if you woke up with no dirt in your face."

"Isn't that what you told me? 'Every day you wake up without dirt in your face is a good day.'"

"Yes, ma'am."

We both laughed and then lapsed into an awkward silence. I blinked rapidly to keep those unwanted tears back.

Dan tilted his head as he studied me. "It'll be fine, Fancy. I promise."

I nodded, too overcome with emotion to speak. If I spoke, I knew I would cry. I didn't want to weep in front of Dan. It would not help matters and would make me look weak. I forced a smile on my face and finally squeaked out an answer to Dan. "I know."

Lily told me she had her tonsils removed when she was 7. She thought the doctor would cut off her head to remove the tonsils from her throat. As the doctor prepared to roll the gurney carrying the little girl into surgery, she turned a flip on it, sat up, grinned, and announced, "Well, here I go to get my head cut off."

She thinks it was hilarious that she was so naive back then. I figure it was the statement of a terrified little girl who didn't want her family to know how scared she was, so she joked while presenting a brave face.

I know how she felt. It's one of those 'facts versus feelings' things. I know the procedure. I know they won't cut my heart out to fix the valves, sew it up, and then put it back in my body. But sometimes it is hard for an $18^{th}$-century girl to wrap her mind around the intricacies of $21^{st}$-century medicine. It felt like I was about to have my heart cut out.

It scared me witless.

About ten that night, a new nurse came in. She was a pretty young woman, about 5'7", taller than me, shorter than Lily, with a statuesque figure, blonde hair, striking brown eyes, and a beautiful smile. "Mrs. Winslow? My name is Melanie Henderson. I'll be your special duty nurse following your surgery. I wanted to come by and meet you beforehand."

I blinked and sat up straight. "I'm sorry, I dozed off. I'm pleased to meet you. But my name is Fancy. I might not respond to you if you call me Mrs. Winslow."

She gave me a funny look. "You wouldn't mind?"

I shook my head. "Of course not."

We talked a few minutes, and then she said something about Rick that brought me up short. With a sudden lurch of my heart, I realized who Melanie Henderson was.

"Melanie, if you don't mind me asking, why did you agree to be my special duty nurse?"

I saw a look of sadness flit across her face for just an instant, and then she smiled. "Rick asked for me. Why?"

"Does it bother you? Having to help his wife, I mean?"

She looked stunned. She swallowed hard a couple of times before she answered. "No, of course not. Rick and I broke up before he ever met you. I'm glad he found a person he could love. A person to whom he could commit…"

Her voice broke.

I reached out and touched her hand. "Are you sure?"

She nodded, but I could see the tears in her eyes. "I wish you both all the happiness and long, healthy lives. So, what's this I hear about you starting college this fall?"

*Excellent recovery*, I thought. "Yes, I work at the clinic with Richard and Dan Smith. They are both encouraging me to go to nursing school. I reckon they don't want any grass to grow under my feet. They want me to start college this fall. I've been accepted, so it looks like I will attend college to become a nurse with a renovated ticker."

"I'm sure you will do fine. I have heard Dan and Rick both raving about how well you do in the office."

We talked for a long time that night. She told me how Richard could never commit in the past because he always obsessed over Sassy's whereabouts. She was with him when he found the letters from Sassy at the Smithsonian. She could not believe he wanted to go back in time.

I laughed. "Well, I'm glad Rick let go of that pipe dream. We met in Williamsburg…"

"Fancy, Rick told me." She kept her voice low.

I blinked. "H-h- he told you?"

She nodded. "I thought Rick was crazy when he first started talking time travel. But let's face it. He disappeared from here for what? Six months? And he came back a different man. With photos of a different place and time. And photos of a beautiful woman he told me he loves."

"Oh." I cringed. I sounded like a little mouse squeaking. "Wait a minute. He only left for six months?"

She nodded.

"But he was there for eighteen months. Weird. Well, the Cherokee say time does not move in a straight line."

She smiled and patted my hand. "That's interesting. No wonder Rick matured so much in his absence. I want to stress to you Rick could never commit to me. We weren't right for each other. He didn't love me. My mother says it isn't love if only one of the two feels it. It's infatuation. I see you love each other dearly. I wish you both every happiness, every success, including successful heart surgery tomorrow. Now, are you okay with me being your private duty nurse after your surgery?"

I nodded. "Richard chose you for a reason. He must trust you. If you can handle it, so can I."

. . .

The surgery went off without a hitch. Afterward? Not so much.

For starters, Francesca awakened slowly and with difficulty from the anesthesia. It scared me out of my mind she might never awaken when she roused and struggled.

We restrained her from pulling the ventilation tube out of her throat. Thank God Mellie was with Francesca. She immediately called for me. Mellie knew I could calm Francesca if anyone could. Francesca looked terrified as she struggled to breathe. You cannot breathe normally while intubated. I stood beside my beautiful, terrified wife, urging her to calm down and to relax so she could be de-intubated. Yet, even after we removed the tube, she still suffered from a state of heightened anxiety, or what physicians call emergence delirium. She begged the staff not to hurt her, as tears coursed down her cheeks.

Mellie looked shocked the first time Francesca said that. "Why does she think anyone wants to hurt her?"

"She doesn't fear you. Two men brutally raped her a couple of years ago. She suffers from flashbacks. It's okay, sweetie. I'm here. No one can hurt you now. I promise."

When my Cessie realized I was there, she clung to me as she sobbed, still begging the staff and me 'not to let them hurt her anymore.'

"No one will hurt you. Try to relax. Everything will be okay." The blunt, older, anesthesiologist sounded aggravated by Cessie's fears.

I continued talking to her in my best bedside manner, as I rubbed her hands and face. She gradually relaxed and drifted off to sleep, still clinging to my hands.

Poor Mellie looked stunned. Shocked. Horrified. "Oh, my God, Rick, I had no idea. Thank heaven you were close when she awoke."

"Thank God you called me. We don't tell everyone about it. She calls it 'her shame.'"

Mellie's face revealed a flash of anger. "That's ridiculous. Doesn't she know we no longer view rape like that? You must tell her it's not her fault."

I nodded. "I do. Quite often. Objectively, Francesca knows it. Emotionally, it's been tough for her to let it go. As she says, facts and feelings don't always fit together as they should."

"If you love her like you claim you do, you must help her with this. For heaven's sake, Rick, get the poor girl some counseling. She just had heart surgery. You expect her to begin college in two months. She must get some help. Otherwise, you set her up for failure. And after all she has been through, she needs failure like she needs, oh, let me think. Like she needs a brand new hole in her heart."

The hysteria continued every time Cessie awoke over the next 24 hours.

We knew Cessie had flashbacks after the rapes by Tarleton and Darlington two years earlier. One of us stayed with her all the time. By then, Dan and even the gruff anesthesiologist voiced concerns about the lengthy agitated emergence delirium she experienced.

"It sometimes happens, Rick. We evaluated her for delirium using the Confusion Assessment Method. This prolonged agitated emergence shows she is still suffering from emergence delirium and may show postoperative cognitive dysfunction," Dan said.

I felt the blood drain from my face. I reached out to the desk to steady myself. "But that can last for months."

The anesthesiologist nodded. "And in some extreme cases, for years. It occurs more often after cardiac surgery."

Dan cleared his throat. "One more thing. Patients suffering from POCD pose a significant risk for long-term cognitive problems. It could adversely affect her in college. And, I hate to tell you, but these patients are at an increased risk of death for the first year after their surgery."

I sank into the chair by Dan's desk. My mind suddenly went blank. I should know why, but my brain was all mush. I gulped. "Okay, I already worried about her starting college. The school understands she underwent heart surgery this summer and will let her take a reduced load this first semester. But why is there an increased risk of death once we repaired her heart?"

"Suicide. Some people can't cope with cognitive problems. I am quite concerned about her since she has these recurring flashbacks. I want to call in a psychologist to work with her."

I nodded. "Yeah, I agree. I want to call Brian Tanikawa. He works a lot with sexual abuse victims."

I didn't mention I met Brian in Virginia after my sexual assault when I was fifteen. Once he finished his residency, he moved back to Atlanta. He was one reason I came to Atlanta to attend med school. I refused to lose my psychiatrist.

Dan nodded. "Tanikawa would be an excellent choice if Fancy will work with a man. Brian is a great psychiatrist. He worked with a couple of my patients who suffered from POCD."

I frowned. "I thought they consider this to be an inflammatory response to the surgery?"

Dan sighed and nodded again. "Yes, that's why we strive to moderate inflammation throughout the surgery with temperature control and beta-blockers. After surgery, optimal pain management and infection control are important. Which brings us to another problem."

I felt my heart drop to my toes. "Jesus, Dan, what else?"

"She has an elevated white blood count. I started her on antibiotics. I also increased her pain meds to make sure we control her pain. I will ask for Brian to help us decide if she needs anything extra for anxiety now. I'll admit it, Rick. I'm worried about our girl."

Wordless, I nodded my head. Tears were welling up in my eyes, and I damned sure didn't want to cry in front of these two doctors, one who was my boss.

"We'll get her through this, Rick," said Dr. Royston, the anesthesiologist. "We're here for you."

I tried to smile. "Joe, I know it's not your fault…"

"I know it, too. But this can be damned rough. The poor girl has gone through hell and back. Shit, can't she ever catch a break?"

I shook my head. "She says if it weren't for bad luck, she'd have no luck at all."

"Gloom, despair, and agony on she. Deep, dark depression, excessive misery. If it weren't for bad luck, she'd have no luck at all. Gloom, despair, and agony on she," said Dan, modifying the words to a song from the old Hee Haw television show. The grammar was incorrect, but the meaning came through loud and clear.

I sighed. "Yeah. Pretty much."

Damn. Dan sounded as depressed as I felt.

. . .

I groaned. Did a freight train run over me?

As Dan promised, I suffered significant post-surgical pain, but I could bear it with the medication they gave me.

The harder part was the awful onslaught of memories attacking me without ceasing. Lily and Richard called the repetitive assault of memories "flashbacks." I'm not sure the word adequately describes the God-awful terror of reliving the trauma over and over and over again.

The flashbacks caused emotional pain, anguish, and raw, unmitigated, psychological pain. The flashbacks went beyond horrendous, yet was not the 'run over by a freight train' pain.

The physical pain came from me, struggling against people trying to help me. I struggled against the restraints used to prevent me from hurting myself. Coupled with the pain from my heart surgery and the emotional/psychological pain I suffered, and combined with fresh injuries from struggling, I felt pretty dad-gummed crappy.

Then add to the mix the staph infection. Everyone seemed mighty relieved I did not have 'MRSA staph.' Believe me; this version hurt more than enough. I found out later in nursing school how lucky I was the infection was not antibiotic-resistant MRSA. MRSA staph is harder to treat than other strains of staph because it has become resistant to some commonly used antibiotics like penicillin. If I developed MRSA with mechanical valve replacements, that would more than likely have been 'all she wrote.' It felt like the blood coursing through my veins poisoned me, scalding me from the inside out.

So then they gave me more pain meds in addition to the antibiotics for the infection. With increased pain meds came increased flashbacks. And all those combined to make me feel like a freight train ran over me.

Trains fascinate me.

I have been intrigued by trains since I came here, to the Beyond. How they can carry such enormous loads. How long it can take big trains to stop. The hypnotic rhythm of the wheels turning on the tracks.

An old-fashioned steam engine train runs from Blue Ridge up through the Chattahoochee National Forest to McCaysville, Tennessee. Richard and I rode it one weekend. I love the rhythmical, clickety-clack sound the wheels make, especially over the bridges. I love to hear the whistle sounding to warn the train is rounding a bend. The train went north from Blue Ridge, through the mountains and over the Toccoa River. The train ride was magical. While considered old-fashioned now, here in the Beyond, the steam-powered train seems cutting edge to me, a girl from the Before.

Yet, as much as I love trains, it terrifies me to think of one running over me.

I sat propped up in my bed, sipping a cup of tea on Thursday after my surgery when a handsome man entered my room. I tilted my head at him. I didn't know him. He looked similar to Indians I have known, but not quite.

He extended his hand to me. "Mrs. Winslow, my name is Dr. Brian Tanikawa. I'm a psychiatrist."

I grabbed his hand. "Oh, you're Richard's friend, the 'Japanese vase' man. Richard told me the story. Does he know you are here?"

He smiled. "Yes. Rick asked me to visit with you if you don't mind."

I tried to smile, suddenly self-conscious. "That's probably good. I'm not doing too well since my surgery..."

I broke off as tears welled up in my eyes. Mellie got up. "I'll step out while you two talk alone."

I nodded towards her. "If you don't mind, thank you, Mellie."

"Buzz if you need me."

I waited until she left the room. By then, I could feel the emotions rising in my chest, threatening to choke me or make me burst into tears. I took a deep breath. *Do this, Fancy.* "I'm so broken, Dr. Tanikawa. Please, help me get fixed."

His dark brown eyes softened at my words. "We'll get there, Fancy. May I call you Fancy?"

I nodded. "Of course."

"Well, Fancy, it can take time, but you will get better. I understand you're having some awful flashbacks?"

I nodded, unable to speak at first. Finally, I choked out, "Yes. These flashbacks must stop. I can't stand it. It's like the sexual assaults occur all over again."

"Want to talk about it?"

"I'm not sure I will ever *want* to talk about it, but I think I *need* to talk about it." I took a deep breath, and we started talking.

We talked at least an hour, if not more, maybe two. About my childhood. Tom. Calvin. Simon. The kidnapping and rapes two years ago. About my feelings of worthlessness before Richard. And about the Japanese vase which Richard often used as an example to me.

Dr. Tanikawa explained the Japanese repair broken things with gold. They call the process Kintsugi. Instead of hiding the flaws and cracks, they are accentuated and celebrated as they become the strongest part of the pottery. They fix the shattered pottery with a strong adhesive, and then they sprinkle the repair with gold dust. The Japanese say the resulting, mended piece is more beautiful, stronger, and more interesting, once broken and then repaired.

And then he explained how the concept applies to people. He said I could also become stronger, more beautiful, more interesting when I become restored after I broke. For the first time in a long while, I felt hope. Maybe I could be fixed.

"I'm sure you have Post-Traumatic Stress Disorder or PTSD for short."

"Richard and Lily both say I suffer from PTSD." I nibbled on a nail.

He nodded. "It induces these awful flashbacks. We say you have been 'triggered' when you have a flashback. Unfortunately, it feels like you are right back there, but experiencing the event again when something triggers you. It's not merely a memory."

"It's like it's happening all over again." I batted at a tear.

He nodded. "Exactly. Let's face it. You have a severe case. You've been through hell and back. However, I can help you get past all this, Fancy. And I can help you cope with the flashbacks, so you feel less like the world is controlling you and more like you can manage your life."

"That would be wonderful." I felt a glimmer of hope at his words. "I never told anyone before, but I have serious holes in my memory. Things I can't remember, or perhaps something I won't let myself remember. I tried to tell Sassy I don't want to remember. It frightens me."

"It isn't easy to work through these issues. It can be very frightening. You must embrace the struggle, and you will become stronger," said Dr. Tanikawa.

"Like the vase." I drew in a ragged breath.

He nodded. "Yes, like the vase. And while the struggle can be complicated, it won't last forever. You work through those terrible memories, and you improve. You become tougher. It will be worth the struggle and hard work."

He taught me some breathing techniques and a meditation to practice until I saw him again the next day. He also left me with a CD of music designed to help me relax and sleep better. I soon noticed the breathing techniques calmed me, and I felt more in control without needing to rub the fabric to distract me. When I told him I do that, Dr. Tanikawa said the distraction of rubbing the fabric might help in the short run, but it would not teach me how to cope.

My hand stopped rubbing the fabric and fell to my lap. "Oh. Well, I like to rub fabric."

"Oh, it's okay. I didn't intend to make you self-conscious." He looked embarrassed.

I felt exhausted when he left. I turned on the CD he gave me and dozed off to sleep. I awoke startled, when Richard entered the room and bent to kiss me.

"What? Oh, it's you. Your friend came to see me. I like him. I believe he can help me." I returned the kiss, and then I reached over to turn the CD off.

Richard blinked and then beamed at me. "What did you like best about him?"

"It's easy to talk with him. Richard, Dr. T knows how to apply the Kintsugi process to humans. I, too, can be a human Japanese vase."

He glowed as he bent to kiss me again. "Yes, you can, sweetie. I promise. Brian knows what he is doing. He fixed me. He can repair you, too. I have confidence you can do this."

"No, he helped you fix yourself." I squeezed his hand.

I explained about the breathing exercises and the meditation Dr. Tanikawa taught me. Afterward, I turned my CD back on, and I fell back asleep, clutching my husband's hand, more relaxed than I had been in ages.

Interesting. I wasn't rubbing fabric as I fell asleep. God only knows how long it had been since I drifted off to sleep without rubbing cloth to and fro between my fingers.

# Chapter 15
# Fancy
# Now

I saw Dr. Tanikawa every day. At his suggestion, Lily brought my journal, and I began writing in it again. I planned to fix this broken vessel called Fancy Winslow.

I knew Richard and Dan both divulged that I came from the past. Even so, he looked shaken when I let him read about Tom and Calvin. "Damn, girl. They were a real pair of rat bastards."

I nodded. "Yes. I reckon they were both what Richard calls narcopaths."

"If not absolute psychopaths. Did Tom sexually assault other women at Belle Rose?"

"Oh, yes. Tom assumed the slave women were his playing field. His attitude was common at many plantations then. Daddy Jo and Will didn't behave like that, but Tom sure did."

He frowned. "Hmm. I wonder what caused him to behave differently from his father and brother?"

"I heard he spent a lot of time in his teen years in Louisiana with the Broussard's, Miss Belle's kinfolk. Maybe they had different feelings about women," I suggested.

"That could be the answer. They probably viewed women as property."

"Well, at least the slaves, but you have to remember that slaves were considered to be property then."

Dr. T shook his head. "I guess we will never know. Hmm. Maybe your Dad or step-mom would have some insight into the secrets of Tom Selk."

I paled. "I don't want to ask them. I know Marc and Tom didn't get along. Marc carries a ton of guilt that Tom abused me as I grew up. Please, don't discuss Tom's abuse of me with them."

Doc stared at me for a minute before he responded. "You know, Fancy, it could be cathartic for Marc to talk about those issues—"

"No! Please, Doc. Leave Marc out of this. Please." I realized I was trembling. *Please, no confrontations. Please.*

He nodded, but I could see he was not excited about my decision. "Well, perhaps you will change your mind about it later when you are further along in your treatment."

I blinked. "Maybe."

But I doubted it.

Even without involving Marc in my therapy, I grew stronger day by day. I told Richard and Doc I loved being a human Japanese vase, stronger, more beautiful, and more interesting than before it tore me apart. However, I often lapsed into tears over the least little thing. Everyone said my tearfulness was a combination of the heart surgery and all the garbage I endured over the years. That didn't make me feel any better, but I would survive. I have to survive. My children need a mother upon whom they can depend. My husband needs a helpmate, not an invalid. He needs a wife, not another child. If I want to go to college to become a nurse, I better figure out how to get in control of my emotions and my life.

Gramma O often came. We played cards, sewed or knitted, and she always prayed for me. I think her prayers and her 'occupational therapy' as she called it helped me heal, too. We made plans that she would come and visit us in Ellijay once Dan released me from the hospital.

Dan discharged me to go home on the fifteenth, with a powerful warning to take it easy a couple of weeks before tackling the world. I had been in the hospital for ten days. It felt more like a month.

The children were as delighted to see me as I was to see them. I could barely go to the bathroom without four children and two dogs tagging along with me. We started taking short walks down to the lake. As I regained my strength, we began venturing up the Benton McKay Trail a couple of times a week to hike a mile or two. We drove to Amicalola Falls one Saturday right before the Fourth of July and walked almost five miles around the beautiful park. I felt exhausted but exhilarated. I stood up to the task. I made it. I could practically see the gold shining on my skin, helping to bond me back together. With each step forward, I felt physically and emotionally stronger. My thoughts were lucid. I communicated competently. I could focus on what I was reading or working. I felt confident I could face the world and tackle college.

Richard came into our bedroom one night after I had been home for about two weeks as I sat at my dressing table, brushing my hair. He bent to kiss the top of my head. I reached for his hand, but he slipped away from me and moved to the bed, where he settled against the upholstered linen headboard to read a medical journal. I frowned and moved to stand beside the bed next to him.

"Why haven't we made love since I came home? Does my scar repulse you?"

He dropped the journal. "Are you kidding me? Hell, no. It's just… Well…" he began stammering.

I tilted my head at him as I unbuttoned my nightgown. "Oh? Show me."

He turned white as he tried to restrain himself. "Cessie, sweetie, I don't want to hurt you…"

I pulled his head to my bosom. "I'll tell you if it hurts. Show me you still want me."

God bless him; he showed me. He fell on me as a starving man might fall on a plate of crispy fried chicken. Later, sated from our lovemaking, he trailed a finger down my scar.

"Does it hurt if I touch it?"

I shook my head. "I told you I would let you know if it hurts. It doesn't. Do it. Again."

He grinned. "Really? You sure?"

I nodded and pulled his head to my chest. As he began to rain kisses down my scar, I trembled with passion. "Oh, yes, I'm sure…"

Dee and Dan invited our family to their home for the Fourth of July. Odd. The original Fourth of July was all so fresh in my mind, and yet it was in the distant past. The Fourth was a month to the day after my surgery. I hummed with enthusiasm to be out and about, visiting friends and experiencing a modern celebration of the founding of our nation.

People packed the Smith home. Dee and Dan have this gorgeous log home up in the Chattahoochee National Forest just outside of Blue Ridge in the Aska Adventure area that overlooks the lake. Dev and Jan were there, Baylie was home for the summer from college, and Aunt Bay came from North Carolina. Even Gramma O came along with our brood.

We arrived a little early. Gramma O and I brought trays of baked goods we had made for the party. Dan and Dee oohed and aahed over the goodies as Gramma and I both laughed. Gramma O loves to bake as much as I do. She reminds me a lot of my Aunt Hattie. She is warm, nurturing, accepting, and tolerates no mess in the kitchen. We get along great.

As Bay and Lily stepped outside to talk medicine and politics with the men, an unlikely combination if I ever heard one, I wandered into the den where I settled onto the big couch to watch the movie already in progress. I frowned as scenes reminiscent of home flashed on the screen before me. I leaned towards Dee. "What is the name of this movie?"

"It's called *The Patriot*. You'll love it. We do. It's a brilliant movie about the founding of our country. We watch it every year on the 4$^{th}$." She picked up a handful of popcorn from the bowl before passing the bowl to Gramma O.

'Love' was not the word I would have used to describe the movie. I ached with longing for my family in Virginia, as my nervousness grew while the battle scenes unfolded. I alternated between nibbling on popcorn and nibbling on my nails at scenes reminiscent of Belle Rose and the life I used to know.

And then it happened.

They called him Tavington in the movie, but I knew right away who he portrayed. He looked enough like Tarleton to have been his twin brother. Or maybe his identical cousin.

Suddenly, I thought I was choking. I arose unexpectedly, knocking over the popcorn. All I could see was the face of a man I never wanted to see again in this or any other lifetime. And then, as he abused the woman before him, I screamed. I threw my hands up as if to ward him off from me. Lost in a nightmare over two centuries old, I was oblivious to the people around me as I sank to the floor sobbing like a quivering mass of crazy. I finally regained my wits as Richard rushed back in and pulled me into his arms.

"It's okay, sweetheart. It's a movie. It's not him. He can't hurt you. I promise the sorry bastard can*not* hurt you. God damn it, turn that effing thing off, Dee. She's having a damned flashback." Richard lifted me onto his lap, where I clung to the man I love as I sobbed like a terrified child.

My meltdown frightened Dee. She turned the movie off when she realized the film triggered my flashback. She wasn't the only one rattled. So were Marc and Lily, not to mention Richard's grandmother and my babies. Bella sat close to me, stroking my hair. Bonnie clung to me, sucking her thumb.

"What's wrong with her?" Gramma O sounded subdued.

"The guy in the movie looks like the man who raped her, Gramma." Richard held me tight in his arms.

"Oh, dear Heavenly Father, help this precious child." She lifted her hands heavenward and began to pray.

Bay looked shocked. "Who raped her? Was he convicted?"

I shook my head. "They convicted him of raping other women, but he escaped and was never brought to justice."

And then Dan pulled Bay aside to whisper something to her. She paled under her tan. "You're not serious, Dan. Such things aren't possible."

Wordless, he nodded and coaxed her out of the room. Bay is never at a loss for words. She's a lawyer and makes her living with her words. She appeared stunned speechless by whatever Dan told her.

Richard called Dr. Tanikawa, who talked to me by phone for about an hour.

"Doc, I never dreamed it would be this difficult," I sobbed.

"Fancy, remember I warned you that you would have to embrace the struggle. You still fight it."

I struggled to control my crying. "What do I do? I can't live like this."

"What do you want to do?" His voice remained soft, calm, and collected everything I wished I could be right then.

I took a big breath. "I want to get better and grow beyond all this. I want to become stronger. I want to become human Kintsugi."

I bared my soul that night as I told him things I never confided to anyone before. He urged me to write it all in my journal. "This story is important, Fancy. This information is worse than anything you told me before. You may be the only person who knows the real Tarleton. You owe it to posterity and to yourself. Don't let that sorry bastard get away with this, even if it happened over 200 years ago. This is horrible."

"I don't want to remember it. I want to forget all of it. I want these memories to stop. To be gone." My voice was soft but determined.

"I know. It's damned hard to embrace your struggle, to face your monsters, and then to conquer them. But you have to face them to exorcise them. You can do it, I know you can do it, and this will let you put Tarleton where he belongs: in the past."

I shook my head. "But I'm so angry. I don't like harboring this much anger towards other people."

"Fancy, it's okay to be angry. Allow yourself to walk away from toxic relationships. Allow yourself to leave people who hurt you. You can be angry with all of them. Hell, you're allowed to feel selfish, to put yourself first for once. You need not forgive and forget. Allow yourself to be unforgiving of these assholes. Do you understand?"

"Yes, I think so. But understanding is a lot different from doing it." I took a ragged breath.

"I know, but once you do this, you will control your memories. None of them will control *you* any longer. Not Tarleton or Darlington. Not Simon. Not Tom or Calvin. Not even Kirk, and I know you have very mixed feelings about him." Brian sounded firm.

"I do, Doc. He wasn't a bad man. Not all the time, anyway. And remember, it was a different day and age." I cut my eyes over at Richard.

"It's especially difficult to cope with your feelings when you loved a man who hurt you."

Zing. Brian Tanikawa nailed it again.

I gulped and glanced at Richard again. Doc and I had talked about Kirk several times. He wanted me to discuss Kirk with Richard, but I was nowhere near ready for that conversation. "Uh-huh."

He chuckled. "Rick must be there. Don't worry. We don't need to discuss Kirk tonight. Back to the subject. You owe this to yourself. You must do this to heal. It will put you in charge of your memories and control of your life. This will help you to never be a victim of Tarleton or any asshole ever again. It will allow you to become the badass survivor you want to be. Remember what we discussed? Fit the pieces together to know where to put the epoxy and the gold. It is not always easy to fit jagged shards together. You must embrace the struggle to get better."

I sighed as another tear slid down my cheek. "I'm not sure I'm courageous enough to do this, Doc. I'm terrified to confront these memories."

"Courage doesn't mean you don't feel fear, Fancy. It means you don't let your fears stop you. You feel like you're stuck in a tunnel. You told me you don't even care if there is light at the end of the tunnel anymore, you're just sick and tired of being stuck in that damned tunnel."

I blinked as I recalled Shadow Wolf telling Charlie that centuries ago.

I nodded. "I do feel stuck in the tunnel. I want out."

"Well, there *is* light at the end of the tunnel. Keep pressing on. You owe this to yourself. And you owe it to other women who are facing their own Tarleton. That's what the #MeToo movement is all about. Helping other women know they can stand up against sexual abuse so they can become badass survivors, too. Can you do it?"

"I'll try."

He shook his head. "Don't try. Just do it,"

I swallowed hard and then straightened my back and squared my shoulders. "I'll do it."

I made my promise with a new resolve. I might not do it for *me*, but I would write my story for other women and my daughters.

I would write it for history.

I wrote with a new resolve when we went home that night. Page after tear-stained page. With each new page, my determination to inscribe it all grew stronger. 'I need my Daddy,' it began with the aftermath of Simon's 1780 attack, as I struggled to reconstruct the journal I destroyed so many years before.

I composed all I could remember in far more graphic details than I put in the first version. I finally fell asleep, exhausted from the effort, still clutching the pen in my hand.

I slept hard. Sound. Dreamless. I didn't even need to play my sleep music. For the first time in how long? Oh, yes, since those awful days in 1780. It might feel like I had scoured a wound raw with salt, but I knew I exorcized the sorry bastards from the holds they held on me for far too long. Never again would I be a victim. I deserved better than that. So did Richard. So did my children.

The next morning, after breakfast, I resumed penning my story. Around noon, Richard asked me what I was doing.

"I'm writing." My answer was brief.

He looked perplexed, maybe even worried, with his brow furrowed with concern. "Yes, I can see that. On what are you working?"

"The diary of Lady Francesca Selk Winslow, the First Duchess of Ranscome."

He chuckled. "You ought to call it Diary of the Reluctant Duchess."

I looked up at him, startled by his words. "Hmm. Diary of the Reluctant Duchess. It has a nice ring. I like it."

And then I resumed putting down my story.

I relented and agreed that Marc could be part of the counseling. It was hard, but somehow, I survived it. Marc seemed shaken after the first few sessions, but he grew even more protective of me than ever before. I realized he understood for the first time the extent of the horrific abuses I suffered for all those years. It grieved Marc that he could not help me when it occurred. Marc wept during one session and said it just about killed him to think of all the horrible things they did to me. But, our relationship was sounder, stronger than before, as if some of that epoxy and gold helped to mend breaks in our relationship, which we had never seen before.

In the days that followed, it surprised me to see Richard drawing. He views photography as his art. At first, he wouldn't let me see what he drew. As his picture took shape, I realized he was painting a copy of the postcard of the painting he purchased at Ranscome Manor.

"Are you copying it?"

"Something like that," he replied with a sheepish grin.

When I started writing, my diary was probably 50 pages long. Like a fool, I destroyed the original in New York. I regretted that rash act many times. I began re-writing it after I arrived in Barbados, where I would not describe the horrors I endured at the hands of Tom and Calvin, much less Simon. I wrote about Tarleton and Darlington. I didn't want Kirk to know about the others, much less how Tom and Simon abused me because of my mixed blood. I didn't dare write a word about being mixed when I was in Barbados. It could have had disastrous results for my Bonnie and me if it had somehow fallen into the wrong hands.

After the marriage to Kirk was determined void, I wrote in my journal some, but not as much. I carried the journal with me when we went to Bermuda and then on to McCarron's Corner after the hurricane. I composed a lot about my feelings when Richard left me. I described Kirk wooing me and remarrying Kirk. I penned how we would fight like night and day, and then make wild, passionate love. I authored my feelings upon learning Kirk had died, and my anger, my grief, and my heartache over losing Kirk and his love. I journaled off and on until I catapulted through time to the present.

I didn't have my diary with me the day I fought with the Chickamauga warrior and came crashing through time to wind up here in the present. Lily brought the journal to me when they arrived, along with the packet of my jewels. Since then, I penned some more in it, but I never sat down and composed like this, hour after excruciating hour, baring my soul.

This time, I wrote despite my fears about everything. Tom. Calvin. Simon. Tarleton's attacks on Sassy and other women. I wrote about him and Darlington kidnapping me and their repeated attacks on me before they sold me to Kirk.

I described it all. I wrote how Tom trained me-groomed me-as a child to do as Tom wanted, and to not be aware of healthy boundaries between men and women. I described in significant detail about the unrelenting sexual abuse and how Tom held me in sexual bondage for all those years. I cried as I wrote how Tom sex-trafficked me to Calvin. I discussed how I would 'zone out' to detach from what happened. I described how I would cut myself, so I could feel something, anything while I struggled to numb myself emotionally to the men who hurt me. I included every sordid, dehumanizing incident I could remember. I wrote about the drugs, restraints, whippings, and the demands I beg for more. I cried as I detailed how Tom would make me give more when I least wanted to give anything. I wrote about every sensation, all the tastes, each hurt. I wrote about all the years of unwanted pleasures no child should endure.

Every Paltry Thing.

Hell, what could they do to me? Not a damned thing. They all died long, long ago. So, I wrote about it all. I would get healed. I would get past their evil. I am alive. I shall survive.

The only thing I didn't include was remarrying Kirk, although I talked to Dr. Tanikawa about Kirk more than once. I never quite admitted I fell in love with Kirk or that I remarried him in my journal. Richard did not need to know those things. It was irrelevant. I included my complicated feelings for him, and the dreadful grief I felt when I learned he died in the hurricane. How I wondered then if I could ever dare love again.

Hmm. Maybe I revealed I fell in love with Kirk. I wonder if Richard realized it? But what kind of woman could somehow love two men at the same time? Especially when the two men were so different from each other?

Then I put down how the Duchess of Ranscome battled her way back from the bottom, determined to be an example of kintsugi, like a human version of a Japanese vase, more beautiful and stronger than before once repaired with gold from the refiner's fire.

I composed night and day in every spare minute. I went back to work, so I had less time, but still, I wrote in every extra minute, like a woman obsessed. Heck fire, I guess I was.

In August, just before I started college, Richard brought home an iPad Pro for me. I used one at work, and he figured I could use it in school and in my writing. With it, I graduated from writing by hand to writing on the electronic treasure. Eyes wide with delight, I began transposing all I had written by hand onto the tablet.

Bella started first grade in August, also. She loved school. Bella's old-world manners amazed her teacher, but Bella's naïveté concerned her. I told Mrs. Black we limited her exposure to television, and we did not allow Bella to play on electronic devices. The teacher expressed surprise. She commented Bella could read better than most of the students in her class, and that her math skills were terrific, but she urged me to let Bella learn to use the computer. "She needs the skill for school. Please don't get me wrong. She's an exceptional student, even if she is rather shy."

I didn't bother to explain to her teacher that Bella wasn't shy; she was introspective. She is introverted, like her Poppa and me. It's not that we don't like people. We feel better when not too many are around us. Her teacher was a classic extrovert. She is always bubbly, with hugs and sweet touches for everyone. The person I wish I were, but I will never be, no matter how repaired this human Japanese vase might someday be. I figure I will always cringe when strangers touch me, at least on the inside. I am learning how to hide those cringes from the outgoing people who seem to need to touch and hug me. I pasted a smile on my face as Tamsin taught me, and I nodded.

Richard and I talked about it and started allowing Bella to work on the iPad for up to one hour a day. She enjoyed reading stories on it. It amazed her teacher, who said Bella was soon reading at the third-grade level. She loved a book she found on-line called *Misty of Chincoteague*, a story about a wild pony on one of the outer bank islands. Bella plays some game Bella calls Geometry Dash. She began playing little tunes on a music app. Soon, she could play a dozen songs by ear.

However, I intended for my children to run, jump, play, and practice their music on an actual instrument more than fiddle around on an electronic device. Since she loved the piano app so much, we rented a piano, and she began taking piano lessons twice weekly. Lily was delighted by Bella's musical talent and Lily worked with her to help my child learn her fingering, chords, and essential tunes. Bella practiced playing her rental piano so much we had to make her stop to play outside. I never met a child before who would fuss about being forced to go out and play. It soon became apparent making music on the piano comprised her heart's desire. Bella loves music, body and soul.

Betty began dance classes. She fell in love with ballet the way Bella fell for the piano. Richard installed mirrors and a barre in the terrace room for Betty to practice. She cried for hours when she learned she could not dance on pointe until at least age 10, and perhaps as late as age 12. Her teacher has tried to explain the dangers of dancing on pointe before the foot growth is completed to no avail. She is considering sports dance in the interim.

Charlie discovered soccer and fell in love with competitive sports. He was only four, but he was a phenomenal forward. If he was not at practice, he was bouncing a soccer ball or a hacky sack from foot to foot while Betty danced.

I began college with a lot of encouragement from Richard and Dan. I took essential hours the first year before I started my nursing studies. I was relieved I didn't have to jump right into the hard stuff. I took most of those classes online. Dan and Richard both insisted I had all the makings of a badass surgical nurse. I laughed each time they said it.

In the evenings, I wrote or studied while Richard drew, Bella practiced playing her piano, Betty danced, and Charlie dribbled the soccer ball. Bonnie sat and watched, although she often tried to emulate Betty as she danced. She lacks Betty's natural talent, but makes up for it with hard work and something their teacher calls 'true grit.' Richard grins every time the dance teacher says it.

And then, my Bonnie began singing with a clear, pure voice which Lily swore could make angels weep with joy. I figured that was infinitely better than Sassy and Charlie's singing, which could make angels scream as they writhe in agony. That boy could not carry a tune with a bucket. He's worse than Sassy if that is possible.

And then one day, Charlie dragged a scroungy little puppy home. "He's mine. The Lady gave him to me. He's mine, and I'm keeping him."

It seems a woman threw the puppy out of her car to my child and told Charlie he could have the puppy. He and the pup are now best friends, and Charlie has become a vocal advocate for dog adoption. Who would have dreamed the prospective Duke of Ranscome would become a powerful advocate for 'adopt, don't shop?'

# Chapter 16
# Fancy
# Now

I sat writing on my iPad one day at the office when Bay came to see Dan. She looked upset. Her eyes appeared red and puffy, and I could tell she had been crying. I hugged her and handed her a clean tissue. "Dan's with a patient, but I'll let him know you're here."

She nodded as tears filled her eyes again. She and her husband argued a lot, and I knew they were talking about a divorce. We spoke several times about the problems in her marriage.

I fixed her a cup of coffee, and then I left her at my desk as I helped a patient into the examining room. When I returned, Bay bent over my iPad, immersed in reading my manuscript. My heart lurched when I realized what she read.

"That's private, Bay." I kept my voice soft.

She looked up, startled. "Good lord, Fancy. It's true."

Wordless, I nodded.

Tears welled up in her eyes again, this time for me, and she pulled me into her arms. "Dan tried to tell me on the 4th of July. I didn't believe him. I thought he was blowing smoke. My God, I thought I had problems with my lazy husband refusing to work until he finds the 'perfect career.' How do you cope?"

I struggled not to laugh as she made quotes in the air as she said 'perfect career.'

I pasted a smile on my face. "Lots and lots of therapy. And I write in my journal."

"Dan claimed you were from then. Before. I told him he lost his pee piddling mind. People couldn't... well, you know. I thought those stories were nothing more than old legends passed down through our People. But it's true. It's all true."

I nodded, nervous lest anyone else hear us. "You can't tell. You must promise you won't tell."

She nodded. But I noticed her eyes twinkled for the first time in months. My eyes narrowed as I studied her. "What are you thinking, Bay?"

She looked guilty and shook her head and then gave a furtive look around. "Can we talk in private?"

I looked up. "Peggy, Bay needs to talk. We'll be in Conference Room 1 for my break."

"Okay, Fancy."

I pulled her into the empty conference room, with my iPad in my hand. I figured I better not let it out of my sight again until I installed password protection. "So, what do you want to know?"

"Oh, nothing. It must have been amazing to be alive then. To know those people." She sounded stunned, or perhaps a little star-struck.

I chuckled. "I can assure you even Washington and Jefferson put their pants on one leg at a time, Bay."

She shook her head. "Oh, no, I didn't mean them. Washington was not kind to my people. He viewed the indigenous nations as 'vanishing people who would die out, migrate, or assimilate soon.'"

"I heard him say that," I murmured.

She gave me a sharp look. "You knew George Washington?"

I nodded. "Mount Vernon was close to Belle Rose. I gave birth to Bella at Mount Vernon. Miss Patsy- that's what most people called Miss Martha- was always exceedingly kind to me."

She shrugged. "Freaky. You must tell me about them sometime. Anyway, following the English victory over the French in 1763, the English King, George Whoever-It-Was…"

"George the Third," I interjected.

"Yeah, I think that was him. King George issued a Royal Proclamation, which set a boundary line from Nova Scotia to Florida, roughly following the Appalachians. This boundary line was supposed to separate the Indians from the colonists. The Royal Proclamation reserved a vast western territory as exclusive Indian hunting grounds and curtailed colonial charters at the boundary. The European colonists could not settle west of the boundary line.

But the settlers were eager to obtain rich lands and soon moved into Indian Territory, like Marc."

I shook my head. "No, Marc moved west before the '63 proclamation."

She looked puzzled. "How do you know that? I mean, that makes little sense."

"Marc surveyed the area now known as the Cohutta Wilderness for Daddy Jo and Washington from '58 to '60. He loved the area and bought part of the land. It became McCarron's Corner. He lived out here in '60 when I was born. He urged the Cherokees he knew to move from Virginia and settle in the Cohutta Wilderness. He knew the land west of the Appalachian Mountains was supposed to become the Indian Territory. Marc gave part of his property to the tribe when they migrated here. Daddy Jo gave the tribe an additional 2000 acres. Marc tried to get my mother to come here so they could marry."

She tilted her head at me. "Why couldn't they marry?"

"My mother was ¼ Black. They called her a quadroon. She was a free woman of color, but she couldn't marry a white man in Virginia. If she went west with Marc, they could marry, at least at common law. She refused."

Her eyes narrowed. "Oh, that's right. Blacks and whites couldn't marry then. You mean she was pregnant, out of wedlock, and she chose *not* to marry in 1760? Why on earth would she do that?"

"She refused to go in '59. I was born in March of '60. Marc didn't believe I was his baby when she told him she was biggin'. He would marry her anyway if she came west with him. She refused. She wouldn't marry a man who thought she cheated on him. Truth be told, she feared to move to Indian Territory. As a result, my grandfather and his wife adopted me when I was an infant."

"Why do you put it like that? Wasn't she your grandmother?"

I shook my head. "No, but she adopted me. I loved my Mama Belle. She was an exceptional woman."

Baylie waited for an explanation, but I did not offer it. She shrugged and began again. "Washington viewed the proclamation as a temporary expedient to calm the Indians. He believed various Indian nations, including the Cherokees, would be displaced by the growing wave of European settlers who would soon cross the Alleghenies seeking to establish themselves on Indian land. As you know, the European settlers ignored the new line. They continued westward to settle on Indian land, to build homes, daring the Indians to force them out."

"The Chickamauga Cherokees worked diligently to drive settlers back east when I lived in the Wilderness, although one of their warriors tried to force me to become his woman. Providence sent me hurtling through time to this time and place. Ask Marc about the Chickamauga." I realized I was rubbing the scar from the knife wound on my hand.

She nodded. "Yes, I know about the Chickamauga Cherokees. Further west, the settlers caught a lot of resistance from the Indian tribes who refused to become 'civilized.'"

I frowned. "Civilized? I never met a civilized Indian back then. Oops, my bad. I meant Native American. What was 'civilized' supposed to mean?"

She nodded again. "Ah, no biggy, Fancy. I work for the Bureau of Indian Affairs, not the Bureau of Native American Affairs. Washington cooked up the ingenious idea to 'civilize' us, to Westernize us to be more like Europeans. To make us more like the settlers via assimilation. When they ultimately pushed us to Arkansas and then further west to Oklahoma, the Cherokee had assimilated so well the whites called us one of the 'five civilized tribes.'"

I never heard people speak of General Washington in less than glowing terms unless it was the British who always called him Farmer Washington, or modern people complaining that he owned slaves. I knew he owned a passel of slaves. "Oh. I didn't know about that. I hear people say negative things about him because he owned slaves, but many people did then. It was common among planters."

Her eyes narrowed. "Your dad didn't own slaves, did he?"

"Marc? No. Barbary pirates captured and enslaved him when he was a kid. Daddy Jo freed him. Marc never owned a slave, and he refused the job offer to become the Belle Rose overseer. Daddy Jo owned slaves."

She looked shocked. "You're kidding, right?"

I shook my head. "No. Marc was a slave for about five years, I think. My great-grandmother came from Africa as a slave. So did her son, my Uncle Tobias. My grandmother, Maisie, was born in Virginia. She was half-white, conceived of rape on Barbados. She was also a slave until Daddy Jo freed her. Daddy Jo began freeing his slaves in the '30s with my Uncle Tobias."

"Why did he free your uncle?"

"Uncle Tobias saved Will when he was a toddler. Will fell in the Potomac, and Uncle Tobias jumped in to save him. Tobias was eight years old. Daddy freed him as a reward for saving Will. You could free slaves for exceptional bravery above and beyond normal expectations. After he freed Marcus, Daddy Jo began to free slaves regularly, as fast as the law allowed. Will says Daddy Jo realized slaves were as human as he was, no matter what their color."

"What do you mean, as fast as he could?"

"Virginia law was not very open to freeing slaves before 1782. For a long time, you could only free slaves for excellent service or heroic acts, such as saving your life or things like that. Daddy Jo began freeing a few slaves every year if the Virginia Legislature would permit it. He freed quite a few before he died in '70. My brother, Tom, never freed anyone. Will began freeing slaves after Tom died at Saratoga. It was costly to free slaves when the law changed in '82 to allow planters to free their slaves."

"Why?" Bay looked curious.

"The law required the property owner to pay taxes on the slave to be freed. The property owner also had to guarantee the former slave a job and an income."

She frowned. "How do you know that?"

"Richard's mom worked as a historian before she went back in time. She told us the requirements before the law passed. By '82, Will freed the rest of the slaves. I remember he told Marc and my Grandfather Fitz Simmons about it."

"That's fascinating." She shrugged again. "The Cherokees owned slaves, too. That was one reason Washington considered us 'civilized.' Go figure."

"I saw nothing about slavery I would call 'civilized.' Who were the other civilized tribes?"

"The Chickasaw, Choctaw, Creek, and Seminole in addition to the Cherokees comprised the five civilized tribes. That meant they became Christians, they had centralized governments, they traded with the settlers, and they became literate," Bay explained.

"Really? The Cherokees I knew back then could not read or write, and I never knew a Cherokee back then who professed to be a follower of Christ." Her knowledge fascinated me.

She grinned. "Sequoyah had not created the Cherokee syllabary when you left. Anyway, the five civilized tribes learned to read and write in English. They developed written constitutions. They took part in the trade market with settlers. They owned slaves. Many became Christians. And, they intermarried with settlers."

"Like my Aunt Ginny."

"Exactly. Like your aunt. Oh my God, you're a Selk. You must be related to Ginny Blue Eyes. Gosh, it freaks me out that you're related to Ginny and Bright Star. How amazing it must have been to have known the Bright Star of Hope." She gushed with excitement, her eyes shining bright, and her cheeks flushing with color.

"Ginny was my aunt, but she died when I was a little girl. I never met her. At least, I don't remember if I met her. I know my birth mother, Tamsin, resented Ginny. She viewed Ginny as the spoiled little white girl who had everything and married a wild savage."

"I wonder if Ginny's eyes looked like yours. And you knew the Red Wolf …" Her voice faded to a whisper.

I smiled. "Ginny's eyes were Selk blue. Mine are blue green. Michael, my brother, is Red Wolf. His eyes are like Lily's eyes, the eyes of a red wolf."

She raised her eyes from my iPad to me. "Born to be the protector of Bright Star. My God, you mean Lily and Marc are…?"

I nodded again. "They call Lily Red Moon Woman. Marc is Lone Eagle."

She looked stunned. Finally, she spoke again. "You knew Shadow Wolf."

I realized with a start, Bay said his name like a caress. A prayer.

"Again, Bay, one leg at a time. They were people. He was a man. An honorable man, but just a man. He wasn't an epic hero…"

She shook her head. "You're wrong, Fancy. He is an epic hero to my people. My people call Shadow Wolf and Red Wolf the 'Cohutta Wolves.' They saved many of our people from the horrors of the Trail of Tears. It is an epic tale of courage, bravery, and valiant effort to lead our people to a safe place before the time of the great trials."

I narrowed my eyes, studying her. "Then perhaps you need to write their story."

She looked at me, surprise all over her face. "Maybe so, Fancy. Hmm. Did you know Guiding Light?"

I tilted my head at her. "Guiding Light? No, I never heard the name before. Why?"

"I'm named for her. It's my Cherokee name. My people say she helped Bright Star guide the Cohutta Cherokees to the place of safety in Arkansas before the Trail of Tears. They were part of the Old Settlers. Later, she showed them where to go when Indian Territory was pushed further west again. She helped them settle in the Arbuckle Mountains."

"Maybe she hadn't been born yet. When I left, I mean."

Her eyes jerked back to mine. "No, she should have been, oh, heck, my age, more or less. Maybe she wasn't with the tribe yet. The old stories say she came from afar with an uncanny knowledge of the lands to the West. She was old when she led them to the Arbuckle Mountains. She's always been my heroine. I wanted to be like her when I was a kid. She motivated me to go to law school and to work for the Bureau of Indian Affairs. I wanted to help my people, to guide my people, as she did. Instead, it seems I can never quite help them enough to matter. I am nothing more than a paper pusher for the government. The BIA helps the government far more than it helps the AniYunwiya."

I chuckled. "Shadow Wolf asked Sassy to marry him."

Bay looked shocked. "Sassy? Who is she?"

I laughed out loud. Her jealousy was palpable. "Richard's mom. She married my brother, Will."

I could see the tension ease out of her body. "Interesting. So, Guiding Light hadn't arrived when you came here. Hmm…"

I swear, I could see the wheels turning in her brain, but I had no idea what those wheels were churning out.

By the time I finished writing at the end of September, I had over 300 pages. At Lily and Richard's suggestion, we edited it to read as if it were from a diary I found written by my long-dead, distant ancestress. I converted my journal into a manuscript interspersed with things about my current life. It read like present-day Fancy learned and grew from reading her ancestor's diaries. Ironically, modern-day Fancy was learning and growing from writing her memories of her life Before.

Lily called the result a memoir, as Richard suggested months earlier. "Memoirs are hot, Fancy, and this is damned good. It might become a best seller."

I laughed, more than a little apprehensive at the idea lots of people might read my diary. I joked about a title in the first place, but I never thought publishing my journal was something I would consider, or that I might send it out to a publisher. "I doubt that, Lily. Why would this sell? Even assuming a publisher would want it."

She laughed, incredulous at my words. "You joke, right? With all the brouhaha over this #MeToo stuff? This is the story of a woman who overcomes all sorts of horrors in her life to become the first Duchess of Ransome. A powerful Duchess, in control of her own life, who chooses her path, walks away from her title, fortune, and riches, to follow her heart and her love. What did Kirk call you? Oh, yes. His Wee Duchess. Well, Wee Duchess, you are one badass survivor, kiddo. This story needs to be told. It is a story you need to tell, not just for you, but for all women. It's a story you alone can tell."

I blinked. Her reference to the #MeToo movement rattled me as much as Brian Tanikawa shook me the first time he referred to it. "You must be kidding."

I tried to act like it didn't matter, even though I knew better.

Lily knew better, too. She gave her head an impatient toss as she snorted. "Yeah, sure. You do not understand how badass our Wee Duchess is becoming. You are not just a human version of that dratted Japanese vase you always talk about. You are one kick-ass survivor. One badass survivor. You must tell this story of how this Kintsugi process applies to people, sister girl. There are thousands of women out there, desperate to hear how a woman who has been beaten, raped, and sex trafficked could overcome it all and could become, well, become you."

"I can't call it Becoming. Michelle Obama's book is entitled that, and it's already a best seller." I chewed on my thumbnail as I pondered her words.

"Fine. Call it *Becoming Fancy* or call it *Diary of the Reluctant Duchess*. Now, are you ready to send it out to publishers?"

I shook my head. "*Becoming Fancy*. That seems pretentious. I tell you what. You and Richard think so much of it. You two send the manuscript out. I double-dog dare you."

I tossed the iPad to her. I saved the manuscript to the cloud, so all she needed to do to send it out was attach a link to the manuscript with a cover letter. I would not admit I couldn't bear to send the manuscript out and have it rejected. I could almost hear publishers saying, 'things like this don't happen in real life.' I couldn't bear it if anyone told me that. I knew everything cited in the manuscript could happen. It happened to me.

That was two months ago. Today, Richard rushed in from the clinic. He grabbed me, swung me around, kissed me as he danced around the room with me, and claimed a publisher wanted to buy it. My story will be a book.

"Sweetie, Black Rose Writing wants to publish *Diary of the Reluctant Duchess!*"

# Chapter 17
# Diary of the Reluctant Duchess

I didn't know whether to be thrilled or horrified.

I stared at my husband in shock. "What do you mean? How do they have a copy of my story?"

Richard grinned. "Lily sent it to them. We told you we could publish it. As I recall, you double-dog dared us to try. You said 'there ain't a publisher in the country who would want my silly ramblings.'"

I blinked a couple of times as I tried to process what Richard was telling me. "But how did you do it?"

He laughed, kissed my cheek, and handed me the email from the publisher. My land a' mercy, *my* publisher. My hands trembled as I quickly scanned the letter. "My God, Richard, this is a contract."

"You bet your cute little butt; it's a contract. Come on. We need to get this witnessed and send it back."

"You don't think your Uncle Jim needs to review this first?" I continued to read the legal document in my hands, not comprehending half the words in it. The words all ran together in a blur.

He laughed as he pulled me back into his arms. "He read it this afternoon. Sweetie, you will be famous."

I snorted. "Yeah, sure. Now, in all seriousness, Richard, tell me who on earth would want to read the inane ramblings of a little ol', uneducated gal from Virginia. I only have the equivalent to a fifth-grade education. You know that."

Richard grinned. "Don't put yourself down. You got your GED on the first try. You have the equivalent of a high school diploma."

He never expressed it in those terms before. "My lord a' mercy, I reckon I do."

"You're going to college to become a registered nurse. Heck, you wrote the book in three months. You are an exceptional woman -- a badass survivor. Who would want to read it? At least half the world, sweetie, the female half. After all, it's the ramblings of the First Duchess of Ranscome, discovered by her namesake descendant. It describes so much about the incredible changes that occurred during her-your-lifetime. Heck, the publisher thinks it might become a movie."

"A movie? Are you sure he said that?" I was wondering if this was all a dream. Or even more likely, I thought, a cruel joke. "Come on, Richard, admit it. You made all this up."

Richard shook his head. "No, sweetie. I'm serious."

I looked up at him, both shocked and thrilled at his words. Who would ever have dreamed my diary could become a published work, much less a movie someday? But then, who but I could have written the story of the reluctant duchess? After all, I am her.

"You need to sign the contract before two witnesses, and then we need to email it back to him. Dan and Dee are coming over to witness your signature, and my Gramma is coming. I told her we had a big surprise."

"She probably thinks I'm biggin'. Hey, wait a minute. You told Dan and Dee before you told me?" I put my hands on my hips and pouted.

Richard laughed. "Dan was at the office when I got the email. You had already left for your class. He heard me whooping and hollering about it like a chicken with its fool head chopped off. They all know. Everyone is super excited for you. Dan and Dee are bringing pizza and beer. It's a book signing party, sweetie. Hey, we could call this your first book signing party!"

He pulled me into his arms for a deep, long kiss.

As the kiss ended, I looked outside.

"Red sky at night, sailor's delight," I mused.

Richard nodded, eager to sell the book and for me to have my chance to tell my story. "That's right, my sweet girl. The sky is red tonight. That's a wonderful sign. That's what Will always said."

I stared outside at the soft red glow over the lake. "It is supposed to be a good sign at night. Lily always says, 'the solution for tomorrow is in the bosom of the present.' Okay. If you and Jim say it's a legitimate contract, I'll sign it when Dan and Dee get here."

Dan and Dee arrived a few minutes later. They brought the promised pizza along with Dan's favorite IPA. Gramma O came shortly after them with an unexpected celebratory bottle of bubbly. We all giggled as we dined on pizza and champagne. Well, except for Marc, who was unusually reticent, even for Marc.

After dinner, Dan, Dee, Lily, Gramma O, and Richard looked excited as I signed the legal document. They clapped and cheered as I signed my name with a flourish, but I noticed Marc remained silent. As they walked to Richard's study to scan the document to email it back to the publisher, I hung back with Marc. "You okay with all this?"

He shrugged. "I dunno. Red sky in morning, sailors take warning."

I looked up at him, my throat suddenly dry. "What do you mean, Daddy?"

He shrugged. "You ken what I mean. The sky was red this morn, lass."

I swear a possum must have run right across my grave then. "The last time I heard that Kirk said it."

He stared at me before answering me. "I recall. T'was on the way to Ireland in '82 that I heard him say it the first time. And then, the sky was red on the morning of the hurricane. So, now what?"

I ran my hands up and down my arms, now covered with goosebumps. "I reckon I publish a book. I sure hope we should take delight and not warning."

Wordless, he nodded.

I thought about my book and all the people in it. Suddenly, I felt plum dab scared witless. Did I dare share my innermost soul with strangers? What did I think I was doing, anyway? Why the bloody hell was I doing this?

Marc often asks, 'Are your next steps heading where you want to go? If not, step off the path and do something unexpected.'

Red sky at night, a sailor's delight. It was night. The sky was crimson red. There might be no sailor living in this home, but I knew the red sky at night meant safe, smooth sailing the waters ahead.

I reckoned this was my chance to do something unexpected. I had to believe the solution for tomorrow was in the bosom of today. The opportunity presented for me to take the solution for all my tomorrows with one fell swoop of the pen. I took a deep breath and turned to go back into Richard's study.

· · ·

I woke up from the dream in a cold sweat. I had not dreamed about it in ages. God knew I rarely dreamed of Kirk any longer. I forced myself to quit dreaming of him after one too many dreams he was alive and searching for me. How could a dead man search for me? No, that was merely wishful thinking. I compelled myself to remember the dream. As it came back to me, in vivid Technicolor, I sat up, huddled beneath the quilt, and wrote all I could remember from it. I figured something was in it, which I needed to know, something I needed to remember, if I dreamed this again, after all this time. Something I needed to help me here in the Beyond.

In the dream, the sky was red that morning.

"Always be grateful for the bad things in life, Fancy. They open your eyes to the good things you noticed naught before." Kirk sighed as he lowered the spyglass.

"Isn't that kind of like saying, 'if it weren't for bad luck, I'd have no luck at all?'" I retorted.

Kirk flashed me his sexy, lopsided grin as he tousled my hair. "Ah, lass, I would hate to think I have been naught but bad luck for you. Right now, you might well be correct. I meant perhaps things are not so bad as we first think. Get below deck with Lily and the bairns. This could get nasty before it's over."

I shook my head. "No way. Do they want to take this ship? We will meet the sons of bitches fighting. We won't go down without a struggle. They are fools if they think taking this ship will be easy, especially with them flying the red sail."

Kirk frowned as he shook his head. "Stubborn wench. Jo was right. You may be little, but by damn, my Wee Duchess is fierce. Then arm yourself, my badass lass, and hang on for the ride. It will be a rough go before we're done if we outrun yon scalawags."

I have to admit it, I always loved it when my wild, Irish rogue called me his Wee Duchess, but I couldn't remember him ever calling me his badass lass before. I circled the phrase.

In the dream, I chewed my thumbnail as I stared at the enormous ship looming on the horizon. We spotted her behind us most of the last two days. Kirk was concerned but not too worried until the warship began gaining on us that afternoon. And then they hoisted the red flag of death. We knew they were pirates from the Jolly Roger they flew. The red flag meant they would give no quarter, and they would take no prisoners. They wanted the Enterprise, reputed to be the fastest ship on the seven seas. If they could breech her, we were good as dead.

Some days, I wondered if life was worth the effort. I remember thinking, we should have gone to Belle Rose. We would be home by now.

"Who do you think captains her?" I asked as I hung on to Kirk's waist. Odd how I can still recall the feel of his taut muscles beneath my skin, the crispness of his linen shirt, the tooled leather of his belt. The man had a remarkable twelve pack.

Kirk shrugged. "I don't know. I expected no encounter with pirates off the coast of Ireland. We will run hard, darlin'. Marc tells me there's a deep-water pier at Waterside. I'm hoping to sail straight there. Now, let's pray yon blaggard is not Captain Johnny England of the Flying Dutchman."

But wait. Who was this Johnny England fellow? From where did he come? I frowned as I circled the second discrepancy I discovered.

"Why not the Flying Dutchman?"

"She's a frigate with 30 guns and a crew of 180 of the bloodthirstiest bastards who ever roamed the seas."

My heart began to beat hard and fast. I pressed a hand to my chest as if to calm the heartbeats. "Oh, dear."

"Aye. Oh, dear, indeed. If it is the Dutchman, she'll travel with four other warships. He took those ships the way he hopes to take this one."

I gulped. "Can they outrun us?"

Kirk was silent as he studied the ship on the horizon. "I pray they can't. We're going to find out if our Enterprise is as fast as we hoped. But raising the red flag means he's going to try to take us." He bent over to kiss me. "You sure you want to stay on deck with me?"

I nodded.

"Then kiss me quick because you'll miss me while I'm gone, lass. Hold the Enterprise steady for a few minutes while we adjust the rigging. Creeps, help me. We need to get the sails trimmed right away if we're to outrun that one."

I frowned again. Kirk said, 'kiss me quick cause you'll miss me while I'm gone' the morning he left Bermuda. I sighed, frustrated, and exasperated. This dream was a hot mess, all jumbled up like a creel of worms. Why?

With another sigh, I resumed writing the dream.

"The sky is red this morning," said Marc.

'Creeps' nodded and hurried to help Kirk and a half-dozen other sailors as they trimmed the sails to catch more wind. Soon, our sleek ship edged away from the ship following us.

It didn't surprise me. I knew the Enterprise was an adaptation of a schooner, a design Sassy said would be created in the mid-nineteenth century and would be called a clipper. She told us clippers like the Enterprise would be the fastest wind-driven ships on the seven seas. The Enterprise was our experimental design. She delivered top-notch performance since first put into the water eighteen months ago.

This would tell the tale whether this ship was the fastest and most maneuverable ship on the seas. If she won this race, we would live. If she lost, we would lose our lives, including the lives of my Bella, Charles, and the precious cargo in my womb.

And then, just like every other time I dreamed this blasted nightmare, I awoke with a start, my heart clamoring, my breath fast and furious. Why on earth am I dreaming this tonight, I thought? Was it because of Marc's comment about 'red skies at morning, sailors take warning?'

But things altered in the dream this time. I couldn't figure out why. I reviewed it all again in my mind. I caught several, which I marked, but there was something else right there in plain sight that I missed. What were the differences? I knew there were other changes there I could not spot. What was I supposed to catch? What was the significance of the alterations?

And who the blazes was Jolly Johnny English?

I arose from the bed, and rubbed my arms again, surprised the little hairs still stood upright like an entire family of possums had walked across my grave. I tried to shrug it off, and I headed to the kitchen. Once there, I stopped and stared out the window over the lake.

The sky was red that morning again. Two days in a row. Did it count as three with my dream? Kirk always insisted three were an omen. And if so, about what was I being warned? Was I wrong last night? Did the red skies the preceding night signify nothing? Should I refuse the contract? I swallowed hard. Oh, well, it was too late now. I already stepped off the path to do something unexpected. Now I had to wait for the shoe to fall, for better or worse.

Why the differences in the dream? Why did it seem like those alterations might be meaningful?

# Chapter 18
# Interlude

We received the galleys for my book the week before Christmas. Richard printed them, and everyone poured over the pages, hunting for typos, grammatical issues, and inaccuracies. I insisted the story must be historically correct.

I also approved a proposed cover. I was awestruck by the artwork. The artist took a copy of the painting from Ranscome Manor and tore it into sections. He pieced it back together and traced over the rips as if mended with gold, the way the Japanese fix pottery. I was over the moon.

"It's perfect." I marveled in amazement.

Richard grabbed my shoulders and hugged me. "No. You're perfect, but this is the ideal cover for your book."

I laughed. "You should know better than anyone I am *not* perfect."

He shook his head. "You're perfect in my book. Beautiful, interesting, stronger than before. Sounds good as gold to me. Ready to head back to college?"

I nodded, suddenly apprehensive about the ginormous adventure I would continue in January. "I reckon. If you still think I can do it."

He kissed me. "You can do anything you set your mind on accomplishing. You made it through the first semester with straight A's. That should eliminate any lingering doubts you might suffer from post-surgical cognitive dysfunction. I am so proud of you. I believe in you 110%, sweetheart. You know, I do. You'll finish your preliminary courses this spring and then start nursing classes in the summer."

It amazed me how fast I finished courses through on-line classes. I eliminated a year of actual time in my preliminary studies by taking most of my introductory courses on-line. As an introvert, I loved the private studies, but I knew I would have to get into the classroom when my nursing studies commenced.

One night, at the big department store in Ellijay everyone loves, my husband pulled the stunt of the year. The children again showed me the toys each hoped Santa would bring for Christmas in a few days. As the kids started giggling and pointing, I looked up and realized some crazy person was dressed in a pink Fortnight bear costume, dancing in the aisle. The pink bear twirled, pirouetted, and did the splits. It then did the minuet before doing the Charleston, the twist, the floss, and some crazy dance Betty called the orange justice. I knew when he did the minuet who it was. Who else would do the minuet dressed in a pink bear costume at Wally World in Ellijay but Richard Owen Winslow?

"Go, Dad, go!" Charlie giggled as he clapped.

Bella and Betty laughed so hard they slumped together and slid to the floor. Bonnie just watched it all, sucking her thumb, serious as the day she was born. As Richard finished dancing, she looked around, pointed at Richard, and announced, "My Da."

I nodded. "He likes to dance, but sometimes your Da is silly."

Laughing, Richard pulled off the heavy mask that covered his head and grinned. "Yes, but you like me silly."

I reached my arms around his big bear neck and smiled as I pushed his hair out of his eyes. "I do. I love you silly. I think you're this week's President of the Silly Club."

My husband bowed with a flourish. "Thank you, my lady."

"Can I have a pink bear costume, too, Daddy? Please?" begged Bella.

"Yes! We all want teddy bear costumes!" shouted Charlie.

Richard beamed. "A family of pink bears. What a fabulous idea! That will make the greatest Christmas card ever. Let's go see what we can find."

I drove the car back to the house, loaded with five bears that evening. A sixth bear costume was in the back for me, along with bear costumes for Lily and Marc. I was afraid to drive wearing the big bear head. One poor lady drove right off the road when she glanced over and saw me driving a family of pink bears towards Carter's Lake. Richard saw the woman staring at us and reached over like he would choke me. I laughed so hard I cried. When we got home, we took photos of everyone dressed in their bear costumes. The one with all of us decorating the Christmas tree was our Christmas card that year. It is my all-time favorite. The video of the pink, dancing bears singing "I'm a Gummy Bear" at the house on Carter's Lake became a U-tube viral hit.

We shared a magical Christmas that year. Marc and Lily were still with us, and all the children were old enough to enjoy Christmas.

Bella loved her piano lessons and wanted a piano for Christmas. Each time she mentioned it, Richard teased her about buying some old junk piano he found advertised in the Greensheet. Bella would put her hands on her hips, stomp her foot, and told him again about the piano she wanted as tears welled up in her beautiful eyes. Of course, she received the walnut, Queen Anne-styled, baby grand piano of her dreams, despite my protests she hadn't earned it yet.

"Richard, she has played the piano for less than a year. The rental model she uses is lovely. She could play it awhile longer until we know she will stick with the piano. Or we could buy a decent piano without making this ridiculous investment in the walnut baby grand."

Richard leaned closer and lifted a strand of hair from my face before he kissed the tip of my nose. "Sweetie, Bella plays the piano every chance she gets. You know as well as I do that she plays tunes far beyond what we expected at this point."

"But, Richard, this piano costs a fortune. My land, the price of that blasted piano could be the down payment on a bigger house. Are you sure you want to invest so much money in a piano?"

He nodded. "It is the only thing Bella ever asked me to buy for her. That piano will last her a lifetime. If she quits playing, we can sell it. Steinway pianos hold great value. Our house is plenty big enough for now. We don't need a bigger house. Besides, Christmas comes but once a year. It serves to remind us we don't deserve the blessings the Good Lord gives us. We give things even when the gift is 'unearned.' It's a time of unconditional love. We are giving her the piano of her dreams."

Well, he had me there. We humans never deserved the gift of Jesus come to save us. Richard made my child happy with that beautiful baby grand. It looked like it came straight out of the 18th century. Bella loved it from the moment she laid eyes on it. Once my child put her hands on the keys in the store, it was all she could talk about owning.

We saw the attorney again and asked him to proceed with paperwork for Richard to adopt Bella, Charles, and Betty. They all would be the children of Richard and Fancy Winslow for everyone in this world to know, and they would all have the Winslow surname. That was a present we gave all of them. It was the present Richard gave me.

Richard hired a publicist for my book. He swore everyone would hire a publicist if they could afford it. We could. The woman began sending articles about my book all over creation. Soon, the news interviewed me, not just in Ellijay or Atlanta, but across the nation. I couldn't believe magazines, newspapers, and television celebrities interviewed me about my book. When the book released, I could not believe over 1000 advance copies sold through pre-orders. I feared no one would like it. It stunned me as five-star reviews began rolling in, one after the other. Kirkus loved it, as did BookBub. Was this happening to little ol' me?

Huh. I reckoned Richard was right. Maybe I could do anything I set my mind on doing.

Once my studies resumed, I realized again I loved going to college. I knew my classes would be more difficult that semester. I had my hands full, with the children, the house, a part-time job at the clinic, book marketing, and my college studies. Yet I was happy. Challenged. And people were proud of me.

Life was wonderful.

In May, I completed my first year of college. It stunned and thrilled me to learn I earned straight A's all year and made the Dean's List. My book was in the top ten memoirs on Amazon. A big Hollywood agent negotiated with Jim Suarez for the rights to market the book as a movie. *Not bad for a little girl from the 18$^{th}$ century with a fifth-grade education. Not bad at all.*

That summer, as planned, I began my nursing curriculum. The same day my nursing studies commenced, Jim finalized negotiating the contract to make my best-selling book into a movie.

I cried when Marc and Lily decided the time had come for them to return to McCarron's Corner. Richard gave Marc the painting of me he copied from the picture on the postcard. Richard kept a color xerox copy he framed and placed on the mantle in our living room. Daddy wiped a tear from his eye, touched by the gift.

"Thank you, Rick," came Marc's gruff reply. "I will treasure this."

"We'll write you, Fancy," Lily promised. "Just like Sassy does to Rick and Jim. I promise."

I nodded, unable to speak. I could not believe how bad it hurt to be losing Marc and Lily. I finally gasped out an answer. "You better. I love you both."

Aunt Bay surprised me when she insisted on accompanying us to the meadow. I knew Lily and Aunt Baylie had grown close. Before they passed back in time through the portal, Lily pulled Bay close. They whispered a few minutes and then embraced like old friends saying goodbye. Lily said something to Bay in Cherokee. Bay responded in the same language.

"What did she say to you?" I asked.

Bay struggled not to cry. "She said she would see me again."

My heart leaped. "Are they coming back someday?"

Bay shook her head. "No. I shall go there when the time is right."

I frowned. "Are you sure? That will be a hard adjustment for a modern girl."

She nodded as she struggled to hold back her tears. "I am sure. Once my divorce is finalized, I shall go. It is my destiny."

We waved as they stepped away to go back to the 18$^{th}$ century.

I could not stop the tears. I understood, but I thought my heart would break as they disappeared in the meadow that summer afternoon. Could I manage if my family went back in time?

And then it hit me. My family lives here. My life is here. I squared my shoulders. *Put your big girl panties on, Fancy. You can do this. Like Richard always says, you can do anything you set your mind on doing.*

I began my second year of nursing school the same week I submitted my second manuscript to my publisher. He grabbed it. "My God, girl, everything you touch turns to gold."

I laughed. "Not hardly, but thank heavens, I have a wonderful publisher and a fabulous publicist. Let's see if she can work the same magic this time."

She did. My Wee Duchess came out the week the movie released. Once again, the pre-release sales amazed us. Thankfully, my publicist maintained my Facebook, Twitter, Pinterest, and Instagram pages. I rarely ever made a post, although Richard ensured she received daily photos of me working at the clinic, studying, writing, cooking, and with my family. My man loves photography. They enabled me to focus on my work, school, and on my family.

During my last year, one of my classes covered heart problems and discussed cardiovascular surgeries. My teacher knew I worked in a cardiovascular clinic, and my husband was a surgeon. It fascinated her I had open-heart surgery to replace not just one but two valves.

"Hey, did I tell you one of my professors had me show my scar to our class? I showed them the video, too, and told them about the surgery as I do with patients."

"Really? How did the students react?"

I laughed. "One big guy had to leave the room at the part in the video where they crack the man's chest. I thought the poor fellow would puke. Two girls looked kinda sick when they saw my scar."

He grinned. "Those big guys are always the first to fall."

Dan's mentor died that year, also. We accompanied Dan to Mr. Brown's funeral. It surprised me to learn the man Dan loved like a father had not been a doctor but had been a grocer in Almond, the little town in North Carolina in the Qualla where Dan grew up and still owned property.

"I used to go into his store, and I would trade potatoes and corn for other produce. When my dad died, we had a full crop of potatoes and corn in the ground. I was only 12, but my Mom and I harvested those potatoes and corn. They carried us a long way. Once a week, I took a sack of taters and corn down to Mr. Brown. I swapped my corn and potatoes for other food from his store. Finally, the day came when I only had a half dozen seed potatoes left, ready to plant. We also had seven ears of corn, which Mom refused to sell. She insisted you always kept seven ears of the old crop to plant. The potatoes were already sprouting from the eyes. They were the last of my dad's potatoes. It about killed me to take them to Mr. Brown, but I had nothing else to swap, and we were hungry. I asked Mr. Brown if he could trade some eating potatoes for the seed potatoes. He took the potatoes out one by one and studied each with care. He finally took off his glasses, rubbed his nose, and sighed. 'These some of your dad's taters, Danny?'

"I nodded. 'Yes, sir.'

"My heart lurched as he glowered at me and shook his head. 'Well, boy, you need to cut them up and plant them. It looks like you can get eight plants from each seed potato.'

"My throat tightened with shame. I hung my head. 'Mr. Brown, that's the last of them. The little kids are hungry. We can't eat the seed potatoes. Mom says they are poisonous since they are already sprouting. Mom kept some corn, and we'll plant it soon. You know how Cherokee women are about their corn.

Anyway, I can make do until the corn comes up, with what I get at school. I get a free breakfast and lunch. But the little kids, Baylie and Tim, well, sir, they are hungry. Tim's only 5, in half-day kindergarten, and Baylie's just a baby, so she isn't even in school yet. We need food now…'

"I remember I couldn't finish my sentence. I felt so ashamed.

"He nodded, and then he put his glasses back on. He walked over to the vegetable bins and gathered up some things for me. 'Here you go, boy. But here's my condition. I want you to take those potatoes home, cut them up, and plant them. When those potato plants sprout, you'll have a load of taters along with the corn from the ears your mom kept back. I'll buy all the corn and taters your family can't eat. Jim Smith was a damned fine farmer and grew some mighty fine taters. Your mom always grew the best corn east of the Mississippi. I can send some seed out, too. Your mom grows the best-damned heritage tomatoes I ever tasted. I can sell all of those big purple Cherokee tomatoes she can raise."

I protested, 'Oh, no, sir, my Mom said I could take no charity.'

"Mr. Brown frowned. 'I ain't giving you no charity, Danny boy. I'm giving you an advance. And one thing more. You ask your mama if you can come here every afternoon, after school. You can do chores around here. I can pay you no money, but I can keep you in food and seed.'

"I remember my heart leaped at his words. I stood up as straight as a twelve-year-old boy can, with the first modicum of pride I had felt in weeks. 'I believe she will agree to that, Mr. Brown.'

"He smiled. And son, this ain't 'charity.' But always remember: charity is another word for love."

"Jim Brown was a fine man. He saw to it my family stayed together when my Mama feared she might have to place us in foster care. He pushed me to finish high school and to apply to college and later to med school. Whenever tuition was due, I received a check in the mail. The note on it always said, 'payment for the corn, tomatoes, and potatoes.' If it were not for Jim Brown and his kindness to a young, hungry Cherokee boy, I doubt I would have finished high school, much less college or med school. I am sure I would not be a cardiovascular surgeon today.'

"But his kindness did not end there. He helped my brother, Tim, go to college. Tim became a teacher. Today, he's the principal here in town. Then Mr. Brown helped my sister, Baylie. He saw to it she also finished high school, and then went to college and law school. Today, she works for the BIA here in the Qualla. Mr. Brown helped lots of kids in our little town. At last count, I believe he sent at least 20 of us to college. We each have passed along his legacy. His death is a devastating blow to each of us and our community. We lost a man who knew the true meaning of the word 'love.' I cannot even envision what would have happened to all of us if he had not been there to lend a helping hand to each of us. Jim used to lament he never had kids of his own, but I tell you, Jim Brown stepped up to the plate like a father to every one of us. I know the angels danced for joy to be joined by Jim Brown, while we grieve over the loss, to ourselves and our community, of this wonderful man."

Dan's words astonished me. I knew Dan's father was mixed, black and Cherokee, and that he died of a heart attack while working in the fields when Dan was a kid. Working in the fields used to be the work of Cherokee women. His mom, a full-blooded Cherokee, never allowed their dad to maintain the corn crop. Dan told me his mom was very old fashioned. She insisted corn epitomized the spirit of women, and only women should tend it. His mom contended that corn was 'her' crop. She felt shamed her husband insisted on working in the fields and always believed his insistence to farm contributed to his early and untimely death by performing 'women's work,' yet Vernon Smith had been an outstanding farmer from a family of exceptional farmers. His father and grandfather before Vernon Smith also farmed.

The death of Vernon Smith motivated Dan to become a cardiovascular surgeon.

I never heard the story about Mr. Brown before the funeral. It stunned me to think about what might have happened if that kind gentleman had not helped Dan to become a surgeon and if Dan had not chosen to mentor my Richard after Owen died and Sassy disappeared. I thought, *what if Dan never became a cardiovascular surgeon who could repair my heart as well as the hearts of countless others?* It boggled my mind to think of how many ways the kindness of a childless grocer positively influenced so many lives, including mine and the lives of my children. I thanked God for the exceptional gift Jim Brown gave to his community and me by helping and encouraging a young, fatherless boy named Dan Smith to become a surgeon.

Not long before I graduated, we were boating on the lake one sunny afternoon. I grinned when Richard jerked his t-shirt off to jump in the water. "Looking good, Dr. Winslow."

He circled in the water as he laughed. "I guess that gym membership is worth the cost?"

I nodded as I smiled at my husband. Rock hard abs are difficult to maintain when you work the long, arduous hours he works, but he somehow managed it, between the home gym and membership in the Fight Club, where he studied mixed martial arts. "Ooh, yes, Dr. Winslow!"

He laughed again and swam back to the boat. I bent over the side to give him a quick smooch, and he pulled me in the water while he kissed me. The kids roared with laughter.

"Better watch out, Mama. He'll be wanting to make another baby." Bella laughed.

"Not a half-bad idea, Bella Boo." Richard kissed me again while I giggled like a schoolgirl.

I finished nursing school with two successful books under my belt, a hit movie based on my first book, negotiations for a second movie based on *My Wee Duchess*, and a nursing job I loved at the busy cardiovascular clinic of Smith and Winslow. It had been a busy and productive four years. My family and friends cheered as I received my diploma. At least half the staff from the office were at my graduation to cheer for me.

Richard sat for his board certification in cardiovascular medicine right after I graduated. We realized that Richard might have to retake it. It elated us to learn he passed it the first try.

Dan made Rick a partner, and they changed the name of the practice to Smith & Winslow, Cardiovascular Surgeons. I don't think I was ever as proud in my life as I was of my Richard then.

In June, I told Richard I was expecting a new baby. I had my IUD removed earlier at the Christmas break. We knew our family was big enough, but I am from an era in which couples desired large families. By damn, I wanted a big family, and I knew Richard would love to have a son, related to him by blood. We were both elated with the news of my pregnancy. Our lives were as close to perfect as we could imagine.

But with increased publicity of both books and the movie came haters and people who loved me. And while most haters leave a bad review, one did more.

Dr. Killian O'Malley became a man obsessed with me. Even before the first book came out, he began turning up all the time. At first, it had seemed rather sweet when he would drop by the hospital with flowers or a cup of coffee.

Disconcerting, but cute. However, when my first book came out, Killian began stalking me. Killian appeared places where I gave interviews, no longer friendly, but usually screaming that I was a 'fecking liar.' He had decided I was the original Fancy, not her descendant. I couldn't admit he was correct. I wanted people to take me seriously. Who would, if I said, 'Hey yeah, damned straight, I'm a freaking time traveler. So what?'

I figured that would have cost me my nursing credentials and maybe would have earned me a trip to the loony bin. I didn't want either. So, we maintained poor Killian O'Malley was 'off his noodle,' as Richard irreverently put it, that the books were based on Fancy Selk's diaries, which they were, and that only a crazy man would think time travel was plausible.

I highlighted my hair with blonde streaks and got contacts to help change my appearance. I cut my long hair into a shoulder-length pageboy. I cried like a baby when my waist-length hair fell to the floor, which I donated to Locks of Love. I always wanted Selk blue eyes, and for the first time, I had them. I looked like I might be related to the girl in the picture, but it was no longer obvious I might *be* the same girl.

And then, the movie became a box office hit, and they nominated it for an Oscar for best drama. We were ecstatic, but Killian's stalking went to the next level of insanity.

We were at Grady, where I had been assisting Dan and Richard as they performed minimally invasive surgical procedures one morning in August. As I came out of the OR, I saw Melanie Henderson whispering to Ollie, another surgical tech. Ollie frowned.

"Mellie, you need to tell her. This sucks toads."

I proceeded to the wash station to clean up, waiting to see if either would speak up. Both shifted nervously from foot to foot. I grabbed a paper towel and frowned. "What is it? Tell me. Now."

Melanie gulped twice and then got the words out. "Uh, Fancy, Dr. O'Malley ..."

"Is off his effing rocker," I snapped, using Richard's favorite obscenity. "You know that. What has he pulled this time?"

"Uh... Killian claims you are a bigamist."

I frowned. "He did what? Oh, for the love of all that is holy. Well, for the record, if the 'Balls to the Wall Nutcase' was right, and I were by some freaky chance a time traveler, his alleged ancestor to whom he says I was married is long since dead. My ancestor's diaries are clear. O'Malley died in 1783. If the man died, how could I be a bigamist?"

Now, remember, Mellie knew I was a time traveler. She nodded, winked, and grinned. "Damned straight, girlfriend. You got that right."

Ollie looked embarrassed. "Preaching to the choir, Fancy. We believe in you. You are preaching to the choir. But, Ol' Nutcase is downstairs giving a press conference claiming *you* are a bigamist."

My head whipped up at that one. My eyes narrowed, I pulled my surgical cap off and shook my hair. "Oh, for heaven's sake. Okay, I'm done with all this BS. Tell Richard and Dan I'm heading downstairs. I'll handle this."

I grabbed my cell phone from my bag and headed to the elevator. By the time I reached it, I had the hospital administrator on the phone. I told him this bull had to stop, STAT. I headed to the front door to the press conference. By the time I got there, I had Jim on the phone, and he was preparing paperwork to force O'Malley to shut the eff up. As I walked up, the press saw me and swarmed around me.

"Mrs. Winslow, what do you say to these bigamy charges by Dr. O'Malley?"

"I think Killian O'Malley is either trying to grandstand on my success, or he is totally out of his ever-loving mind. It is insane to suggest I am a woman born in what? Something like 1760, right? And that I am married to his, what? Great-great-great-grandfather, or something like that, a man who died in 1783? If he were correct, and I was Fancy Selk O'Malley, which I deny, then I would be a widow, not a bigamist. But here's a news flash. That man is dead. She is dead. Killian O'Malley needs to shut up, or he is about to lose not just his job, but his medical license. He might wind up getting deported back to Ireland at this rate. He's here on a work visa. Dr. O'Malley isn't a citizen. I will not put up with him harassing and slandering my family and me like this. I am all done."

Killian turned to me, rage written across his face. "You bitch, you know you're lying to them. You know you're the Duchess, and you know damned good and well Kirk O'Malley did not die in 1783. He didn't die in that blasted hurricane. Captain O'Malley thought *you* died in the hurricane. He didn't die until 1812. Here's a copy of his death certificate."

I felt the blood drain from my face. I snatched the paper from Killian. "I don't believe you."

But the document, sure enough, looked like a death certificate. It said Captain Kirk O'Malley died in a sea battle in the fall of 1812. I struggled not to let anyone see me as I began to shake. I crumpled the paper and threw it in his face. "That in no way proves I am who you claim. So, your ancestor lived for what? Another 30 years? Good for him. He's dead *now*. If I could have been his wife somehow, I'm not married to him *today*. He's dead, Killian. Kirk O'Malley died over 200 years ago. How the bloody hell can you come in here today and claim I am a bigamist? That's insane. Now, you stay away from me. You stay away from my family. I have had it with you. My attorney will get a court order to make you stop making these insane accusations."

About then, Richard rushed up to me. He pulled me into his arms. "Ladies and gentlemen of the press, I ask you to be kind to Dr. O'Malley. He is seriously out of touch with reality, but his continual harassment of my wife has to stop. Please don't feed into his insanity. Please. Let's end this nonsense today. Francesca is alive. It is not medically possible that she could be the woman he claims she is. Jesus, she would be over 260 years old if she were Fancy Selk, and I don't think Francesca would be pregnant if she were that old."

Members of the press laughed as Richard ran his hands over my slightly rounded belly.

"Dr. Winslow, are you giving us a spoiler?" one reporter asked.

Richard chuckled and bent to kiss my cheek. "No spoiler, but we are excited to announce Francesca is expecting a baby. Our little Valentine present to each other should arrive in February. So, how about we let all this jizz go, okay, dude? If my wife is your, what? Great-great-great-gramma, or something like that, I have to admit, she's looking mighty fine for a woman her age, but we probably shouldn't upset her. Considering her delicate condition and her age and all."

With that, the press guffawed. Several reporters began putting their things away to leave.

Killian turned red in the face and began blathering on and on in Irish. All I could make out was *mhac na galla*, which I knew meant 'son of a bitch.'

I smiled. "Talkin' about yourself, O'Malley?"

He stopped mid-sentence. "Ye see? She kens the Irish. Tis her, I say! It is!"

"Oh, for the love of all that is…" Richard began.

I smiled and laid a hand on my husband's arm. "I know enough to know what *mhac na galla* means. And you are a sorry *mhac na galla*. And I can say *feis ort*. I believe that means eff off."

Killian puffed up like an angry toad. "*Rafter, ye striapach*."

I blanched. Richard moved in front of me. "Did you tell my wife to go f— herself? And did you call her a slut? Why, you dirty little *tuilli*. Who the hell do you think you are?"

"*Diul mo bod*," Killian said.

"Suck your dick? I don't think so, O'Malley. Why don't you *teigh transa ort fein*? Better yet, *diul mo maglairi*," Richard retorted, telling O'Malley first to go eff himself and then suggesting Killian do something indecent with Richard's bollocks unless I were mistaken.

"Suck yer bollocks? Is yer dick so small ye figure I couldna' find it?" Killian retorted.

Richard smiled. "That's not what your Granny says."

I shut my eyes and shook my head at that one. And that was when I reckon you could say the fertilizer hit the ventilator.

Killian started shouting in Irish, with Richard yelling back. The next thing I knew, they started swinging at each other. Jesus, this was shaping into a better show than the movies up for an Oscar! I never dreamed I would live to see two doctors swinging at each other during a press conference in which one claimed I was a 260-year-old pregnant bigamist. Even if I am technically 260-years-old and pregnant, I refused to accept I was a bigamist. How could I be?

By then, security showed up and dragged Richard and Killian apart. They 'escorted' us back inside and straight to Dr. Holloway's office. Killian's nose was bleeding, and Richard had the beginnings of a black eye. I was having contractions.

Dr. Ryan Holloway functioned as the hospital administrator, so we all knew we were in Big Trouble with a Capital T. As we entered his office, he glowered at the three of us. "Would any of you three people care to tell me what the meaning of this little fiasco is? What the hell is wrong with you two gentlemen? You are doctors, and yet you brawl in the street in front of the hospital."

Killian and Richard both began talking at the same time. Holloway put up with it for a minute or two before he whistled. "Time, boys! Enough! Fancy, what the hell is going on?"

I explained that Dr. O'Malley believed we were related because I look a lot like a painting of his ancestress. I told Dr. Holloway that Killian read my books and saw the movie. Based on those, and the physical resemblance between the Duchess and me, he decided I must *be* her, mainly because my books about my ancestress were a big hit. "And, sir, that's impossible. I swear I am not hundreds of years old. I am 28-years-old."

"Killian is effing nuts," Richard interjected. "He would have to be nuts actually to believe this bull hockey."

At which point, security had to pull Killian off Richard. Again.

"Enough!" Holloway bellowed.

Both men dropped their fists. They didn't look happy about it as they shuffled from foot to foot like two schoolboys in trouble before their principal. They stood with their shoulders hunched, muscles flexed, alternately glowering and sneering at each other. Holloway pressed his thumbs to his temples to massage it. I had seen him do that before when he got a nasty headache. I figured this cluster was giving him one helluva migraine.

"Dr. O'Malley, were you giving a press conference claiming Mrs. Winslow is your ancestress, and she is a bigamist?"

Killian's eyes lit up. "Aye, sir, I did…"

"Have you lost your ever-loving mind? Are you insane? Must I order you to undergo a psych evaluation? Killian, this is ridiculous. This bird-dogging Mrs. Window must stop. If you can't control yourself, I will have to suspend you. I can't have doctors running around the hospital accusing our surgical nurses of being 260-year-old bigamists. Maybe your ancestress was a bigamist. I don't know. I don't even care. I will tell you this one time only. There is no freaking way Mrs. Winslow is your ignoble ancestress. This crap has to stop today. You can't hold press conferences at this hospital, or anywhere, claiming this young lady is your ancestor, or that she is a bigamist. That is slander. It has to stop today. Right now. Do you understand?"

Killian nodded. "Aye, I understand. Your siding with the fecking whore…"

Security stepped between Richard and Killian as soon as the word passed Killian's lips. Richard's fists balled up, with one arm drawn back, as he crouched into position to land the punch, ready for the next round. Holloway frowned and shook his head.

"That's it, Ryan. I want him away from my wife. Hell, I want him psyched, stat. The man is freaking insane. This whole accusation is crazy. I won't put up with him calling my wife a bigamist, much less him calling Francesca a whore. I want it stopped, now, or else I'll be looking for a new hospital. I will not be affiliated with a hospital that allows staff to insult other staff members in this manner." Rick sounded furious.

"Nor will I. I refuse to tolerate any further abuse of Fancy or Rick. This insanity has gone on far too long. It must stop right here and now, or we will take our cardio surgical team to Emory. They have been after us for over a year now. They can get credit for the Smith-Winslow valve and procedure, and all the business that is coming with the procedure and valve." Dan came in about the time Killian called me a whore, and he looked livid.

Dr. Holloway paled and stammered. Dan and Richard patented a new mechanical valve that summer, which could be inserted like a biological valve through a minimally invasive procedure. Once inserted, the little valve could somehow expand to fit as needed. Don't ask me how it worked. There's a reason they get the big bucks. Richard says I inspired the new valve and procedure, but I do not understand how they ever came up with it except they are both cardiovascular geniuses. It was being called the most important cardiovascular advance since bypass surgery. No one else in the country had the right to use the Smith-Winslow valve and procedure yet. If we took the team to Emory, or anywhere else, Grady Memorial stood to lose millions.

Ryan Holloway stood up and cleared his throat. "That will not be necessary. Dr. O'Malley, you are suspended immediately, pending a full investigation. Part of that investigation will be into your mental capacity. You will present yourself to undergo a complete psychiatric evaluation within 48 hours."

O'Malley's face lit up. "And you'll require her to submit to DNA testing?"

Dr. Holloway sighed with impatience. "Oh, yeah, Killian. Absolutely. After all, that will to prove to us she's your great-grandmother, right? No, we are not collecting DNA to see if Mrs. Winslow is somehow magically related to you. This investigation will not determine if Mrs. Winslow is your great-great-great-granny, or in any way related to you. That is a wild allegation. You are prohibited from entering this hospital other than to see the psychiatrist for the evaluation or to discuss the results of the investigation. Dan, Rick, Fancy, security will see you out. I apologize again for this ridiculous brouhaha. It will *not* happen again."

Killian was still in the office as we left. We could hear his voice rising as he continued to assert his 'proof' that I was his ancestress. We hurried to Dan's office, where we could talk freely.

"Now what? My God, he has a death certificate that says Kirk died in what? 1812? Oh, dear God, is he right? Am I a bigamist?" I struggled to contain my tears.

"Of course, you aren't a bigamist. It's the 21st century now. Kirk has been dead for over 200 years. The whole idea is ludicrous." Richard sounded angry as he pulled me into the comfort of his arms.

I turned to him, trembling. "But if he wasn't dead in 1784…"

"It doesn't matter. Kirk is damned sure dead now. He might feasibly have been alive when you left there, but Kirk was damned sure dead when you arrived here. That's why we had him declared legally dead, remember? Now, we need to let this mess go. Killian can *not* prove that you are a 260-plus-year-old woman who time-traveled from 1784 to the present."

I stared at him for a minute and then reached up to caress his cheek. "But, Richard, darling, we both know I *am* a time traveler from 1784 to the present. So, what do we do now?"

"You play it straight. Killian sounds like a lunatic making crazy allegations." Dan's kept his voice low and calm.

Richard nodded. "I agree. And, I don't mind throwing a few punches at the sniveling little asswipe when he talks smack about my Cessie. I will *not* tolerate that little turd calling my wife a whore."

"I understand, Rick, but at some point, we have to diffuse this situation. The man is unbalanced. I fear he is becoming dangerously unhinged." Dan looked worried.

My heart lurched. "So, what do we do, Dan? I love my life here. I would be happy living the rest of my life here. God knows I was always the Reluctant Duchess. I never wanted the damned title. I don't want to go back. Oh, I miss my family back there, but not other people. But we can go back if need be."

Dan reached over to pat me on the back. "Hold on, kiddo. No one is suggesting you turn tail and run. I want the man psyched. He's starting to get on my last nerve."

"He's already on mine," Richard grumbled.

"Well, he's sure as hell on my last nerve. In fact, he is way past it. So, like I said, what do we do? He has already pointed out that Richard and I have the same names as his ancestress and the man she loved in the 1780s. He already commented our children have the same names as her children had back then."

"I thought we covered that pretty effectively," Richard smirked.

Dan grinned and nodded. "Yes, it is more plausible that the two of you met through Ancestry.com than that you are both time travelers. And it is more plausible that you named your children after her children than that the kids time-traveled here."

"I'm so glad you legally adopted all three older ones, and that we had Bonnie determined to be your baby. There is no way Killian descended from Kirk and me. We never had a child."

"Yes, those adoption records are sealed, and this way, they all have Georgia birth certificates and Winslow as their surname. I am rather pleased I suggested that clever idea." Dan grinned again.

We all jumped at the knock on the door. I opened it, and one of the security officers stepped in.

"Doctors, ma'am, I wanted to let you know Dr. O'Malley left the building. We will be happy to escort you to your cars when you exit today. I don't recommend you leave the hospital without one of us walking you out. That man is nuts." He shuddered.

I tried to smile. "Thank you, Woody. I think the medical term is 'Crazy Mac Cray-Cray.' We will come to your station for an escort before we leave."

He nodded. "Excellent, Mrs. Winslow. I don't know how a person gets that messed up. My God, to think that man is a doctor! Maybe he's taking illegal drugs. He must read too many of those cockamamie time travel books. I mean, I love sci-fi, and the Outlander series is great, but I know time travel isn't real. How could it be?"

I shrugged at the officer. "Beats me. I figure if it can happen, the Duchess of Ranscome needs to tell me what happened back then. The diaries I found went to 1784, after the hurricane she said killed O'Malley. We don't know what happened to her after that, whether she remained here, in the US, or returned to Ireland. I would love to locate her later diaries and find out what happened."

"I agree, ma'am. Maybe someday one of your relatives will find the later diaries. My wife loved the books, and we thoroughly enjoyed the movie. It's a humdinger. I hope it wins the best movie award. Well, I'll leave you people to your post-surgical talks now. And you have a good night."

I stood in the doorway and watched him walk down the hall to get on the elevator. After the doors closed, I leaned my head against the door for a minute as I rubbed my tight, contracted abdomen. After a few deep breaths, I turned back to Richard and Dan. "I can't handle much more of this stress."

"You won't have to, sweetie. Uncle Jim is getting a Protective Order to stop him from harassing you." Richard gave me another consoling rub down my back.

I tilted my head at my husband. "I thought you could only get a PO for domestic violence?"

Richard nodded. "Usually, but in this cockamamie case, O'Malley thinks he's a relative. He's stalking and threatening you. Interfering with your work and your reputation. Hell, he's slandering you. Jim and I think the Judge will grant it."

I felt a twinge of alarm. "But, Richard, he's not slandering me. He believes what he is saying."

"And that is why Jim believes the Judge will sign the P.O. If it's not slanderous, the man must be nuts, right?"

I frowned. "But—"

"Let Uncle Jim handle it, sweetie. There isn't a judge in the country who will believe you traveled through time to come here, much less that you are a 260-year-old pregnant bigamist. Hell, a judge would have to be as crazy as O'Malley to believe that crap," Richard chortled.

But that was the problem. I was a time traveler. Since I was born in 1760, I was 260 years old, although I had only lived 28 years. Worst of all, if O'Malley was right, and Kirk still lived in the Before, then by damn, I was a bigamist.

# Chapter 19
# Fancy
# Now

Things were better for a while after the incident at the hospital. My contractions stopped after my obstetrician hospitalized me overnight. The Judge granted a Protective Order for my family and me for the next three years. Judge Masterson sternly admonished Killian to stay at least 500 feet away from me at all times, 'or else.'

We felt so relieved by the ruling that Richard and I took off for a weekend and hiked to McCarron's Corner. Richard purchased the old site of the village after his mother disappeared. Sassy headed there when she vanished without a trace. He hoped he could find where she went, never imagining she fell through a hole in time in the meadow. The remnants of the town once called McCarron's Corner was a little 20-acre track in the middle of the national forest, which never became part of the national forest. Don't ask me why or how. We knew part of the big house still stood, and Richard wanted to see if we could rebuild it.

We left early one Saturday morning. We each carried a backpack, and Richard dragged a little wagon behind him, in case we found anything we wanted to take home. McCarron's Corner is only about 4 miles from the trailhead to the site of the village. We veered north about a mile from the meadow where we married. We were at the remnants of McCarron's Corner by 9 a.m.

Richard made this trip many times in the past with his Uncle Jim, but I never went to the Corner since I arrived in this era. Marc and Lily refused to go as well. We were unsure how we would handle seeing the once lively little village we loved in ruins.

It shocked me.

The only remnants of a building still standing was the house where Marc and Lily lived when I visited there both times. It was a shamble. Time had weighed heavily on the condition of the old log home. I blinked back tears of dismay as we approached the cabin. Heck fire, I was plum dab mortified.

"Is it safe to enter it?" My voice quivered with dismay.

Richard nodded. "Yes. It's a hot mess, but we can enter the cabin. Part of the roof caved in years ago, so I don't want either of us to go upstairs. The parlor isn't too bad. Come with me."

He took my hand to guide me into the darkened room. "The locals who used to live in the area tell stories about 'haunts' who occupied the property. They claimed they could see people dressed in 'old fashioned' clothing at times. Some recounted seeing Cherokees clad in Revolutionary War-era garments. I talked to people who swore they heard blood-curdling cries from the village, only to find it empty of human life upon investigation. Gradually, fewer and fewer people wanted to live here. Even after the Cherokee Removal in 1837, when this land was worth a fortune, no one would buy McCarron's Corner until I came along."

I frowned. "But wait. We are in the national park. Why was this land for sale? What happened to Michael and his family? Why didn't Michael or his children inherit the land?"

Richard turned to stare at me. "Cessie, Michael married Bright Star. She was half-Cherokee. Mike and Star lived with the Cherokees, as Cherokees. Their children may have been ¾ white, but they were more than a drop Cherokee."

Well, that depressed me. My shoulders sagged as I sighed. "So, they were considered Cherokee, too. Just like me with my black blood. More than a drop, right?"

Richard nodded. "Exactly, sweetie. And as you know, the settlers were not kind to the Cherokees."

I sniffed. "As I recall, the Chickamauga Cherokees were not always kind to the settlers."

Richard arched a brow at me. "Do you blame them? This was Cherokee land at one time. They tried to share it with us. That bit them in the ass. Besides, Michael's job was to protect and help the Bright Star of Hope relocate her people, the Cohutta Cherokees, to another locale where they would not be adversely affected by the prophesied Trail of Great Sorrows. Today, they call it the Trail of Tears, the genocidal travesty imposed on the Cherokees in 1837 by Pres. Andrew Jackson. Four thousand Cherokees died from exposure along the way."

I grimaced. "At least that many died along the Trail of Tears. Baylie's aunt works for the Bureau of Indian Affairs. She swears most of the Cohutta Cherokees moved west before then and settled in the Arbuckle Mountains of Eastern Oklahoma at the time of the Trail of Tears. She swears they went with the 'Old Settlers' in 1829 before Congress signed the Removal Act in 1830."

Richard nodded. "Many say the Cohutta Cherokees went west before 1829. They supposedly went with Sequoyah. He went to Washington in 1828 with a group of Old Settler Arkansas Cherokees to sign a treaty. I believe Mike and Gentry were part of those Old Settlers, who relocated to Arkansas well before 1828."

"Aunt Bay says they traveled by steamboat up the Arkansas River." I hated to think about any of the people I knew forced to walk that far.

"I hope she's right, and they were already out west at the time of the Trail of Tears. I hate to think of Shadow Wolf's people having to endure it. But I know Cherokee people from this area were rounded up, herded like cattle, and forced to walk hundreds of miles through the cold of winter and the heat of summer to Oklahoma." Richard's voice was little more than a whisper.

I nodded, silent, as I thought about the extended, horrible march west. I prayed that my brother and his family lived to relocate safely. "She swears the Cherokee voices they hear up here are the ghosts of the Five."

Richard's head whipped up. "The ones who took the five million dollars and sold the land to the US government under the Treaty of New Echota? Why does Bay think it was them? Don't the Cherokees think the Five were traitors?"

I shrugged. "Bay says the opinions vary. Some swear they were traitors. Others think they felt they could relocate all the remaining Cherokees out west to the newly redefined Indian Territory easily with the money. Five million dollars was an enormous sum in 1836. She says the voices are the voices of the Five crying about their innocence and trying to tell where the money is."

Richard's eyes narrowed. "But weren't the Five all murdered for signing the Treaty? Weren't they considered to be traitors, who sold out their people?"

I nodded. "Yes. Bay could not figure out if they sold out the remaining Cherokees or if they were trying to save them. If they sold them out, who got the money? And if they meant to use the money to save and move the rest of the Cohutta Cherokees, who got the money? Either way…"

"The big question is, who got the money? Why wasn't it used to save the remaining Cherokees who refused to move out earlier?" Richard looked lost in thought.

I nodded as I lit the Coleman lantern we brought for light. "Exactly. Okay, help steady me. This floor looks rough."

Richard took the lantern with one hand and helped me grasp his other hand as we wound our way with caution through the room that was once Lily's parlor.

I was glad they had not come to see their old home. The condition of the old log cabin broke my heart.

The curtains I made for Lily in 1778 hung in tatters from the window. The large dining table Marc built lay balanced on three legs, the fourth having long ago broken. The sofa, imported from France, lay tipped over on its back, the fabric shattered by mice and other varmints over the past two centuries. And then my heart leaped to my throat.

There, before the long-dead fire, was the cradle in which my Bonnie once slept.

I must have let out a little cry of amazement as I rushed to kneel by the old oak cradle. As tears coursed down my cheeks, I traced my fingers over the ancient carving by my Grandfather as he made this cradle for my Aunt Dara.

Richard knelt beside me and pulled me into his arms. "Want to take it home with us?"

I nodded, unable to speak.

I reached inside the cradle and gasped as I pulled out the little bundle wrapped in the remnants of the tattered quilt which used to sit on Lily's settee. I carefully unwrapped the small figure as my tears began anew. "It's Bella's doll. She used to beg me to come up here and fetch her dolly."

Richard nodded. "I remember. It survived pretty well. Her little china head is still intact. Jeez, this doll must be worth a fortune. You might have to make her a new body and a fresh dress. Look, there's something wrapped up with the doll. What is it?"

I picked up the folded paper and lifted it open with care. I gasped. "It's a letter from Daddy and Lily. My God, I'm amazed the mice didn't eat it."

Richard crouched down beside me, peering over my shoulder. "Smells like she wrapped mothballs with it. Mice hate mothballs, but were they even invented yet back then?"

I shook my head. "No. I don't think so, but Lily probably knew how to make them, or she took some back when they went home."

"What does the letter say?" Richard leaned over my shoulder as we both struggled to read the letter.

It was hard to make out. The ink faded over the years, and no one ever accused Marcus of having pretty handwriting. If handwriting was a qualifier, he should have been a doctor. "Daughter, it has become too dangerous to remain here. We are moving to the Cherokee Village. If we aren't there when you come, we will have gone to Belle Rose. Michael and the Cherokees will help you travel safely to Augusta. Don't head north. The Chickamauga Cherokees are on the warpath and will kill any white settlers they come across. Tell Dan Guiding Light arrived and is thriving. Travel with care. All our love, Daddy and Lily."

Richard frowned. "Guiding Light? Who is that? Wasn't that the name of an old soap opera?"

I shrugged. "I don't know. I never heard of the show, and I sure met no one named 'Guiding Light.' Bay says she will know how to lead the Cohutta Cherokees to a safe place in the Arbuckle Mountains where they will supposedly build a 'castle.' Huh. Can you imagine a castle in Eastern Oklahoma? Or that any self-respecting 18th century Cherokees would live in one? I'm surprised Lily didn't say to tell Bay hello. This Guiding Light woman fascinates her."

They left the doll in the cradle with the note because they figured my girls would find the toy and give me the letter. I clutched the precious message to my chest, unable to hold back my tears. "Do you think they are all right?"

Richard nodded. I noticed his own eyes burned bright with unshed tears, yet he grinned. "Yes. He told me if they had to leave, I would know they made it away safely if the portrait of you still hangs at Ranscome Manor."

I frowned. "Why on earth would he have said that?"

"Because I painted it. Marc took it to Ranscome Manor."

I gasped again. "Do you mean *you* are the artist who painted the original?"

He chuckled. "I'm not sure if 'artist' is the right word, but yes, I painted it. Your dad took it back."

I stared, stunned by his words, remembering how Richard struggled to get the portrait perfect. He fussed over the rose in my hair alone for days. I must have told him a dozen times to leave the rose off the painting. He insisted it would look 'just right.' "Then, that means Kirk would know…"

"We married? Probably so, unless Marc and Lily took the painting to Ireland after 1812. I doubt they waited until 1812 to go. Marc would be 80-years-old then. The sign on the painting says it was from 1789."

I frowned. "So, you think even if we don't get there by 1789, the painting will be there?"

He nodded and grinned, his golden eyes twinkling. "That was my plan when I painted it."

I took a deep breath. "Well, aren't you a clever man! Should we go back? I have to admit, I thought Ellijay would be our forever home."

Richard looked shocked at my suggestion we leave. "Go back? Now? Hell, no. You've got to be kidding. And you know your dad and Lily already left when-if-we go back. It's too dangerous there. You know what Marc wrote."

I shrugged. "This has been our home for four years. I love it here, but Killian terrifies me. I am afraid he will do something crazy, maybe violent. Richard, he will hurt us if this crazy situation continues to escalate. The man is becoming unhinged. You wait and see. He will pull some stupid stunt. I'm scared. I don't want him to hurt any of us."

Richard pulled me into his arms. "No, sweetheart. He's all bluff. No substance, just a lot of hot air. He's crazy, but he won't hurt us."

I leaned against him, breathing in his confidence, praying my husband was correct. I realized I was rubbing Richard's shirt back and forth between my trembling fingers. I still catch myself doing that sometimes when I am especially stressed.

We sifted through a few other things and tucked some into the cradle. A long-forgotten tobacco pouch and a meerschaum pipe, which I often saw my Daddy puffing, brought another round of tears from me. It seemed like I could smell Marc smoking his pipe when I opened the old leather pouch and caught the scent of the old tobacco inside. They wrapped the family Bible in oilskin. I found it on the mantle, as if they forgot it as they left. I placed the Bible beneath the doll in the cradle. An old china cup from which I often saw Lily drink tea also lay on the mantle as if they overlooked it as they left long ago. A wooden spoon Daddy carved for Lily one year for Christmas still hung on the wall in the kitchen. I sat those things in the cradle, also. Finally, we lay the cradle filled with all the treasures in the wagon by the door and finished our inspection of the structure.

Yes, they could repair the cabin, but it would be difficult. We weren't sure it would be worth the effort. We would find an architect to go back to assess the cabin and to help us decide what to do.

We spent the night at the trailhead where we tucked our treasures into the back of the car before going home the next morning. The children rushed to see what we brought with us. Bella grabbed the beloved doll and began to cry as the filling sifted out of her shattered body.

"She's broke, Mommy." Bella sobbed as she clutched the doll to her chest.

"It's okay, baby, we can fix her. We will work on it this afternoon."

"But my Papa bought her for me, and you made the blue dress for her. You and I had dresses that matched." She sobbed, and soon all the children were crying.

We all missed her Papa and Grammy. I missed them most of all.

Unless it was Elizabeth. She was Kirk's girl until the hurricane. She adored Kirk. She saw him as her savior from Siobhan O'Malley, who she still talked about with horror in her voice. After we learned they presumed Kirk dead, lost at sea, she became Marc's girl. She called him Papa, like Bella did, and she made it apparent she was her Papa's girl. That did not change when Marc and Lily left. Elizabeth loved Richard and me, but she swore she would always be her Papa's girl.

At 8, she told us she no longer wanted us to call her Betty. She insisted her name was Elizabeth Selk Winslow, and she dared anyone to call her anything but Elizabeth. Bella would shrug and often called her Liz. Elizabeth allowed us to call her Liz, because 'Liz Taylor was an outstanding beauty.'

Oh, yes, she is definitely Kirk's child. Every bit as beautiful, hard-headed, and stubborn as her sire, even if she does call Richard 'Daddy.' She is a female version of Kirk O'Malley.

I believe she must be Killian's ancestress. I see the same stubborn tilt of their heads. The same dark brown, curly hair. The same fiery flash of temper in their cool, grey eyes. They both fidget the same way, tapping fingers to thumb when agitated. When she would become angry, I could hear traces of the Irish accent she had when she was small. Fortunately, I see no signs she may possess the same extremes of temper, which affected Killian. Likewise, I never saw her manifest the obsessive, compulsive behavior which got Killian labeled 'crazy.'

Would we all go back someday, or would only Elizabeth return? Would she become the next Duchess of Ranscome? If we all returned, would Kirk be alive? If so, how would Kirk react to my marriage to Richard? Did he ever find another love? Would he be able to accept my marriage to Richard?

I shuddered. I already knew the answer to that question. Even if Kirk found another love, Kirk would never willingly give up what he believed was his to another man.

And while Richard might know my first marriage to Kirk was declared *void ab initio*, he did not realize I remarried Kirk. I never intended to tell him. After all, if Kirk was dead in 1783, there was no reason to tell Richard, even if we returned to the 18th century. But if Kirk somehow survived the Dreadful Hurricane, I trembled with fear contemplating the two men meeting again. How could I tell Richard?

I wasn't sure I could survive if either killed the other. And wouldn't it comprise a perfect irony if we survived Killian to return to the past to die at Kirk's hands?

Can you say, 'caught between a rock and a hard place?' I sure felt caught in that unpleasant spot.

Yet, I couldn't stop thinking: why did Richard insist on having Kirk declared dead before we married if he believed Kirk died in the hurricane? Did he somehow know I married Kirk again? And if so, why had he never uttered a word about it to me?

I lacked the courage to ask him.

Richard came in whistling the next evening. He grinned when I gave him what he calls the 'what's up' look. I stopped and stared until he spilled the beans.

"I had a young fellow in my office today in need of a valve replacement. He told me the valve failed because he's in 'the carpal tunnel of love.'" Richard laughed as he pulled me into his arms for a much-needed kiss.

I frowned. "What does that mean?"

"'The Carpal Tunnel of Love' a song from 2005. It came to be a cult favorite among young people."

I tilted my head at him. "Are you suggesting we are no longer young?"

He laughed and shook his head. "Not at all, sweetie. Anyway, you know the carpal tunnel is this muscular tunnel through which the carpal nerve runs into the hand?"

I nodded as I smirked up at him. "Well, duh. I am a registered nurse, you know."

He grinned and leaned over to kiss the tip of my nose. "The young man told me he recently broke up with his girlfriend. He feels like he's in 'the carpal tunnel of love.'"

I shrugged. "I still don't get it."

"Cessie, they do carpal tunnel release when the carpal tunnel restricts on the nerve. He felt like the musculature around his heart constricted as if unrequited love cut off his blood flow to his heart."

I made an unladylike noise. "Did you tell the patient that's not from bad love, but the bad valve?"

Richard nodded. "Yes, but I'm not at all sure he believed me. He wants to believe everything would be fine if his girlfriend still loved him. I told him love could do a lot of things, but it can't fix a bad valve."

I smiled. "Unless the one you love fixes the valve, darling. You know that."

He laughed and pulled me back into his arms. "Dan did most of your surgery, sweetie."

I leaned my head against the chest of the man I love. "You helped. And you brought me here."

He looked down at me, startled by my words. "What do you mean?"

"I couldn't have come here to find you if you weren't here. Providence had a plan. You were the lodestone that pulled me here from Before. Without you, I would more than likely be married to that sea captain, assuming the rascal somehow survived the hurricane. Or I'd be dead."

I blanched. *Oh, sweet Jesus. Did he realize what I just said?*

He kissed the top of my head. "I'm glad you're here and not dead. Thank you from the bottom of my heart, Providence."

I let out a sigh of relief. Richard didn't catch my slip.

The hospital performed the psych evaluation on Killian. He refused to accept their findings he presented with obsessive, psychotic behavior. Worse, he refused to take the antipsychotic medications prescribed. He insisted he was the only individual who was *not* crazy. The rest of us were all nuts, according to Killian. The hospital permanently terminated his medical privileges at Grady when Killian refused to follow the psychiatrist's recommendations. We figured the hospital would suspend his license to practice medicine unless he complied and began taking his medications. The foolish man continued ranting and raving I was a 260-year-old bigamist. His story was so outlandish the National Inquirer picked it up with an 'in-depth interview' of Killian. Richard framed the story and hung it up in the office. I cringed each time clients voiced delight to meet the '260-year-old, pregnant bigamist' who wrote best-selling books. I was less than thrilled.

Ultimately, after several more scenes at the hospital and elsewhere, the court warned Killian not to come back around us again, or his work visa would be revoked, and he would be deported. I felt disappointed. I thought he would be deported when he lost his job. It is a lot harder to deport someone than I initially thought. Dammit.

The next scene occurred in late September. Killian walked out of the psychiatrist's office as we left after a long morning in surgery. Killian appeared thoughtful as he departed their office. Dan grabbed my arm and whispered for me to hold back. About that moment, Killian spotted us. His face turned red with rage, and he stormed over to begin scolding me.

"Are you satisfied now? You destroyed my life, you know?"

He was so close I felt the spray of spittle hit my face as he shouted at me. I made an exaggerated motion to wipe it off my skin. "Not by me. If anyone ruined your life, you have no one but yourself to blame. Take your damned meds. Follow the doctor's advice. Then you can resume your medical practice."

"Ah, you damned woman…" Killian scowled at me as he mumbled something unintelligible in Irish.

"Don't talk like that to your Granny." I snapped the words with more starch than I intended.

Killian's face turned purple with fury, the veins bulging out on each side of his neck. Killian shook his fist in my face as he shouted something else at me in Irish before he stormed out, slamming the door as he left.

The encounter shook me, more than it should have upset me. I was so distraught that I sat weeping and trembling for over an hour. My physician hospitalized me with premature labor. I was about 20 weeks along, and it was far too early for my baby to survive. After three days, they released me with a stern warning to avoid stress and conflict.

"Avoid stress and conflict? Yeah, sure. Tell Dr. O'Malley," I snapped.

"Yes, tell Dr. O'Malley. Warn him if he pulls anything like this again, I'll have his medical license. They won't just pick his stupid ass up and jail him for 30 days the next time for violating the Protective Order like Judge Masterson did today. I will get his sorry ass deported. O'Malley is the only stress or conflict Francesca has. Hell, I swear if this asshole causes Francesca to miscarry our baby, he'll have hell to pay. Dammit, if he hurts my Cessie, I'll kill the sorry son of a bitch." Richard pulled me into his arms in a protective stance.

I grabbed his arm. "Richard, don't talk like that. You frighten me."

He pulled me nearer to his chest and kissed my cheek. "I'm sorry, sweetie. The sorry bastard makes me crazy."

"Well, don't permit him to make you crazy. You're better than him. Don't let some consarned, crazy varmint like Killian O'Malley reduce you to his level of insanity. I'll be fine." I realized I trembled like a leaf. I swatted at him as I tried to pull away.

He kissed me again and pulled me back into the comfort of his loving embrace. "I'm sorry. I shouldn't have said it. It terrifies me he might hurt you and our baby."

While I rested at home, I did an online investigation to find information about Kirk. I felt physically ill when I confirmed he did not die until 1812, as Killian claimed. My heart fell through my toes when I discovered the painting of the famous sailing captain. I recognized Kirk, although he had aged. I had not expected to see the broadened girth, or the silvered hair. Age was not kind to my wild Irish rogue. I sauntered over to Richard and handed the photo to my husband. "The next time Killian asks me why I am with you and not Kirk, I'll show him this."

Richard frowned. At first, he speculated the picture upset me. When he realized it portrayed Kirk O'Malley, he laughed. Soon, we both hung together, laughing.

"I want to be there when you show Killian the picture, yet Kirk must be at least 70-years-old in this painting. People showed their age faster then. Seventy was an old man. And while any man would look bad if he lost the best woman he ever had, he was a pretty good-looking older man. I hope I look that good when I'm seventy."

I reckon I should have been ashamed, but right then, all I could do was laugh.

And then it hit me. Kirk lived after the hurricane. It wasn't conjectured anymore. My wild Irish rogue survived.

I stopped laughing.

"What's wrong, sweetie?" Richard asked as he wiped the tears of laughter from his face.

"Dammit, Richard. Killian's right. I'm a bigamist."

Richard flashed his devil-may-care grin at me. "Nah. They declared the marriage void. But think about this for a minute, hypothetically. Say you were married at the time of the storm. You wouldn't be now, unless we went back to the 18$^{th}$ century, sweetie. Like I've been saying, we married four years ago. O'Malley died over 200 years ago. The court declared him to be dead before the wedding. You couldn't be a bigamist. You were a widow when we married."

I nodded as I looked at Richard, desperate to believe him. "That's correct, isn't it?"

He chuckled as he pulled me into his arms. "Yes, my love. He died in 1812. He's long since dead. The court declared him dead, and we married four years ago. You're good."

I still couldn't shake the whisper of concern that maybe, somehow, I was married to two men at the same time. I damned sure realized I would have significant problems if we ever went back. Dammit, should I tell Richard? I could feel tears biting at my eyelids, threatening to spill over anew. Should I admit my own impetuous decision to remarry Kirk after Richard left Ireland? How would Richard react? He can be rash, although not nearly as much now as a few years ago. All I could think was, 'don't make permanent decisions based on temporary feelings,' but that was what I did when I remarried Kirk after Richard left.

How does the poem go that Lily recited sometimes? 'Oh, what tangled webs we weave when we practice to deceive.' Well, I wove a danged tangled web this time. I was not at all sure what to do to untangle the strands to this web. I admit I feared even trying to untangle this mess. It was, like the minister said in Barbados, quite a kerfuffle.

Two weeks later, I returned to work. My ultrasound revealed the baby was the boy Richard wanted. The information thrilled us. Modern medicine amazes me. No more smallpox or polio. Inoculations to keep children healthy from mumps, measles, chickenpox, tetanus, and whooping cough. Medicine for Rh-negative moms like me to carry our babies to term. Antibiotics. Medicine to stop premature labor. Medication to help heal a damaged heart. Not to mention all the other miracles of modern medicine we worked with every day in cardiovascular surgery! Not just valves, but pacemakers, stents, bypass surgery, even heart transplants, a myriad of heart procedures to help people live healthier, more productive lives. It delighted me to be having this baby boy now instead of in the 1780s.

Richard took an architect and a general contractor to the cabin, and they agreed they could salvage the cabin. The architect drew up plans, and the general contractor began working on it. We hoped to have a functional cabin by early summer.

I decided this would be my last pregnancy. We had four children. This boy would be our fifth. Plus, I wasn't getting any younger. I would turn 29 the month after our baby would be born. Richard snickered when I declared I was getting too old to be having babies. I believe I could never have carried Baby Boy Winslow to term in the 18$^{th}$ century. With me employed full time in cardiovascular medicine, plus my writing, I was at my limit. Heck fire, I was at my breaking point.

"Richard, I want to take off a while after I have Richard, Jr.," I announced one day as I stood rubbing my aching back outside the OR after a long morning of surgeries at Grady.

Richard laughed. "You mean, our son, Marcus. I wondered when you would figure that out."

I chuckled as I shook my head. We had been trying to agree on a name for months. I wanted to name our son after Richard. He was adamant that he hated the whole 'Senior-Junior deal.' He thought we should call the baby 'Marcus, ' after my dad. We would continue around that mulberry bush a while longer, trying to sort out the right name for Our Baby Boy.

"Richard Marcus?"

He laughed again. "How about Marcus Richard? No 'Junior,' remember. Come on, sweetie. I love your dad. I know you do, too. Let's honor him this way."

I sighed. "I'll think about it."

Richard laughed and kissed me again. He knows I usually concede once I tell him, 'I'll think about it,' but I wanted our son to be named Richard Owen Winslow, Jr.

I always experienced uncomplicated pregnancies before this, once I passed the threats of miscarriage. Any stretch of the imagination suggesting this pregnancy was uncomplicated was false. By the end of November, I had returned to the hospital two more times. Each time, we ran into Killian. It seemed he knew when we would be at the hospital, and he intended to cause me grief. He always encountered us outside of the ob-gyn's office, in the professional building adjacent to the hospital. Everyone commented he seemed to know when I would be there. Usually, he would stand outside and nod to me as I passed.

"How the hell does he know when we are coming?" Richard fussed. "Someone must give him the heads up."

"I agree. Daddy Jo always said there is no such thing as coincidence."

He looked surprised. "My dad said that, too. Hmm. I wonder who snitches to him."

Try as we might, we had no luck figuring out who was giving Killian the information when I would be at the hospital.

He waited until the week of Thanksgiving to pull another stunt.

At Thanksgiving, I was in the hospital for three days again with premature labor. Each time my doctor hospitalized me, Richard insisted I go to Grady. They considered me high risk because of my Rh-negative blood, previous heart surgery, and two prior miscarriages. The first two times, my ob-gyn hospitalized me from his office at my visits. The third time, Richard rushed me to the Ellijay Hospital, and they airlifted me to Grady. It cost a fortune. I fussed it was money we didn't need to spend. Richard says I pinch pennies. I reckon I do. He is a lot freer with money than I am, but then, I have been dirt poor. Growing up to be a servant teaches you to be frugal. I insisted a local Ob-Gyn could have handled my whole pregnancy in Ellijay. My husband maintained only the best would do for his wife and baby. I didn't know whether to beam with pride or scream in frustration. I settled on both and threw a regular ring-tailed tooter of a hissy fit.

Upon discharge, Richard and Gramma O picked me up and helped me downstairs. The hospital requires patients to exit to their cars in a wheelchair, the standard operating procedure in most hospitals. That way, the patient cannot fall until they are out of the hospital. We were doing fine, but as Richard helped me into the car, Killian showed up again. He stood across the street, just a tad over the requisite 500 feet from us, leaning up against a telephone pole.

"He's here," I whispered to Richard and Gramma O. I began trembling. What would he pull this time? Why was he doing this to me? I wrapped my hands around my twenty-five-week baby belly as if I could somehow ward off harm to my unborn child from Killian by the simple, protective act.

Richard's head snapped up. "How the eff does he know where to show up? Who tells him where we will be? This whole situation is beyond ridiculous."

Gramma O climbed into the back seat beside me and put an arm around my shoulders. "Oh, most precious Lord, wrap your arms of protection around our Fancy and her baby and keep them safe from this evil man."

Richard shut the car door and stood up to stare at Killian. When Killian made eye contact with Richard, he smirked and held up a sign that read, "WHORE."

Richard's lips thinned into an angry slash. My husband snapped a picture with his phone before he made the eye motion Daddy used to make at Kirk, the one that says, 'I've got my eyes on you.' Killian sneered, made the same sign right back at Richard. By then, Richard was on his phone with the hospital security, alerting them Dr. O'Malley was stalking us, again. Almost immediately, security rushed out. Richard strode across to Killian with security.

"I'm telling you, O'Malley, this crap has to stop," Richard shouted.

Killian's sneer broadened. "Why, Winslow? Afraid your whore doesn't like it? What are ye goin' to do about it?"

Richard's fist lashed out to connect with Killian's jaw. "It stops now, or else I'll kick your crazy ass like no one ever kicked it before."

I gasped, shocked by Richard's threat of violence. "No, Richard, no!"

But fortunately, security quickly pulled them apart. I couldn't hear what they said, but security dragged Killian into the hospital. Richard returned to the car, shaken and furious.

"I swear, I will kill that asshole yet." He looked and sounded furious, as he clenched and unclenched his hands while he struggled to control his breathing.

I sobbed as I clung to his arm. "No, you can't. You can't let yourself make permanent decisions based on temporary feelings. If you did something rash and wound up in prison, it would kill me. What would I do without you? What would the children do without you? Killian is not worth it."

"These are not temporary feelings," he growled.

Olathe reached over to touch Richard's shoulder. "Now, Rick, honey, you need to calm down. You can't go off half-cocked like this. They'll be thinking you're as crazy as he is."

"I don't care. I've had it with this asshole. Killian can not keep harassing my Cessie like this. I swear he's trying to make her lose this baby. If she miscarries, I swear I'll kill the sorry little bastard."

"That does it. I refuse to come back to Atlanta again. Someone tells him when we are coming. I can't cope with any more of this, Richard. I'll have my baby in Ellijay. I won't come around Grady for him to harass me like this." I sobbed in frustration as I clung to Richard and his grandmother.

Richard wrapped me into his arms. "It will be okay, sweetheart. I promise. He's a bully. He means to break you. We can't give in to him. It would empower the sorry little worm and encourage him to continue. We'll be safe, sweetie. I promise."

"Richard's right, Fancy. The man is nothing more than a bully," said Gramma O, but she sounded less sure of her words than Richard did. I thought she stated what she wanted me to hear, but she didn't quite buy the song and dance Richard was peddling.

I shook my head with a new resolve as I struggled to stop crying. I pulled a Kleenex out of my purse and wiped my face and blew my nose. "I… I don't care. I won't come back. I'm all done. Like your Mama says, stick me with a fork because I Am All Done. This has gone far enough."

My hands shook halfway back to Ellijay. I struggled to use my coping skills as I rubbed the fabric of my coat back and forth between my fingers.

The next week, I found an Ob-Gyn in Ellijay who would take over my case. I met Dr. Elise McClintock at a yoga class while I attended nursing school and I often saw her around the Ellijay Hospital. I liked her and used her in the past for my well-woman checks. After several lengthy conversations, Elise agreed to take my case. After more discussions, Richard decided it would be good for me to have a doctor in Ellijay 'just in case.' My 'just in case' would be that I would not tell him I was in labor until it was too late to go to Atlanta. Like I told him at Grady, I was All Done with a Capital D.

I stopped working at my new doctor's recommendation. Dr. McClintock agreed that this should be my last pregnancy. She could not believe I worked as a surgical nurse as long as I had, standing on my feet for long hours in the Cardiovascular OR with Richard and Dan. She fussed Richard pushed me too hard. Richard looked shamed after their talk. For once, he did not try to convince me to go back to my Atlanta doctor. It relieved me Elise convinced him I needed a local doctor. It thrilled me she was my new doctor.

We had searched for a bigger home since we learned of my pregnancy last summer. It might not keep Killian out, but we hoped a new, unknown address in a gated community would help. We both wanted to stay in the mountains despite the lengthy drive into Atlanta. We looked as far north-eastward as Young Harris but agreed it was too far. We looked around Lake Blue Ridge, where Dan and Dee lived. We love the area, but it is damned expensive around the lake. We finally decided we wanted to stay closer to Ellijay, the hospital and clinic. The hospital in Ellijay is better than the one in Blue Ridge and is across the street from our clinic.

Once we decided we wanted to stay in Ellijay, we searched around Carter's Lake, at Coosawattee, Walnut Mountain, Buckhorn Estates, Black Ankle Mountain, and Rainbow Ridge. I swear we must have seen every big house available in a 20-mile radius. When I despaired that we would never find the right house, Richard upped the budget. Once I quit gagging and choking about the money, we finally found a beautiful, new home in the Pine Mountain gated community located minutes north of Ellijay in Cashes Valley.

The beautiful Craftsman-style log and stone home was more than twice as large as the house at Carter's Lake. The attractively landscaped home nestled beneath the towering pines of North Georgia. The luxurious, custom-built home possessed six bedrooms and six baths in the main section of the house. It thrilled the children they would each have a bedroom of their own. The stacked stone fireplace seemed to reach up to the sky in the great room. Unlike many log homes in the mountains, it provided us with a formal dining room where Bella's baby grand piano would look beautiful. It also had a private office for Richard. The formal living room became an office for me with the addition of French doors. If I loved the kitchen at Carter's Lake, I swooned over the kitchen at Pine Mountain. It had the biggest commercial-grade gas burning stove I ever saw in my life, with six burners, two ovens, two warming ovens, and a built-in rotisserie grill. The house also boasted a gym in the basement where we could all exercise, plus a full bath with a sauna and hot tub. We installed mirrors and a barre down one wall for Elizabeth. The house had a fully decked-out apartment over the garage for the nanny, with a small living area, kitchenette, bedroom, and private bath. The house was freaking ginormous. It sat on five acres, overlooking a private lake, and it straddled the boundary of the Cohutta Wilderness. It provided a private, in-ground swimming pool in the back yard and stables. We all love to ride and swim, and I wanted the kids to be expert equestrians in case we ever went back to find our futures in the past. Three of the five acres were fenced. I loved the beautiful, long-range, layered mountain views of Cohutta Mountain, which helped me feel closer to my family. We all agreed the house was perfect for us. As soon as we walked into the house, ten-year-old Bella announced, 'this is it!' We could do everything except practice medicine in the new home. To make it even better, we could move in before Christmas. Once I found a nanny, I would be ready to give birth to our baby.

Richard convinced me to take the children to the Atlanta Aquarium to celebrate the following week. We would not go to Grady. The snitch would not know we would go to Atlanta. The school dismissed for the Christmas holidays, and we had closed on the house. We would begin moving into our new home the next day. We felt comfortable going to the Aquarium since we were packed, and no one at the hospital knew we would be in Atlanta.

Gramma O met us to tour the Aquarium. As usual, the children rushed to her waiting arms with hugs and kisses. As we stood watching the marine animals beneath the surface, we heard the voice we had all learned to hate.

"Ah, how endearing. The whore out cavorting with her lover and her children. Have you no shame, Granny? When are you going back to your true husband?"

I grabbed Richard's arm as he bristled at the words. I turned to face Killian and forced myself to laugh. "I *am* with my true husband. Even if I could have somehow time-traveled from 1784 to the present, and even if your ancestor lived until 1812, he is long since dead. I *am* with my true husband."

Bella's eyes grew wide as Killian pulled a knife out. She remembered Marcus often carried one like it in the past. Bonnie screamed at the sight of the skinning knife. Elizabeth pulled Bonnie close to her as Gramma pulled Bella and Charles to her. I pushed all of them behind me. I heard Gramma O begin to pray.

"Killian, this isn't funny. What do you want?"

"I want you to admit you are my great-great-great-grandmother. You're married to Captain Kirk O'Malley. Admit it, bitch, admit it!"

I stared at the foam of saliva on his lips. "You know you're insane, don't you?"

"Wrong answer, Granny."

I sighed and shrugged. "Admit I'm married to Captain Kirk of the Enterprise, right? Fine. Whatever. Here we go. I'm Francesca Marie Selk, known as the Reluctant Duchess, born to Tamsin Selk in 1760 at the Belle Rose Plantation. Josiah and Belle Rose Selk adopted me as an infant. I married Sir Calvin Hobbs, third Earl of Spring Haven, in March 1780. Calvin died at Yorktown in October 1781. I agreed to marry Richard Winslow in April 1782, but Tarleton kidnapped and sold me to Captain Kirk O'Malley. He transported me to Barbados against my will and forced me to sign Articles of Indenture. I married him in November 1782…"

"Aha! I knew it!" Killian shouted with a look of triumph.

"The marriage was judicially determined to be *void ab initio* in January 1783. The court ruled it void because Kirk couldn't legally marry a woman of color in Barbados."

He blinked. "Void? But you aren't colored—"

I smiled. "You're wrong. I am one-eighth black. People with more than one drop of blood could not legally marry whites on Barbados then, any more than they could marry in Virginia. With more than a drop of black blood, they considered you black, just like in the Southern Colonies, where I was born. Right, Gramma?"

I didn't bother to explain Olathe was Richard's grandmother, not mine.

She nodded. "That's correct, my darling girl."

I smiled as I held my head up high. "I thought you read my books. Didn't you realize I'm part black?"

"I don't believe you. You made it up. I have no black blood."

I laughed. "Maybe not, Killian. You aren't related to me. With no black blood coursing through your veins, I can safely say you aren't related to any of my children. If your DNA is on Ancestry.com or 23AndMe, it doesn't show me to be related to you. Didn't you check?"

"You're lying." He responded with false bravado, but I heard an inkling of doubt creep into his voice.

"I guarantee you my granddaughter is part black," Gramma O said.

I bit back my grin and nodded my head. I would not snicker at his fluster. "I speak the truth. My Captain O'Malley died in a shipwreck off the coast of the Carolinas in 1783 during the Dreadful Hurricane which destroyed his ship. All the men on board died. Bodies washed up for weeks. The news sheets all up and down the coast, and as far inland as Augusta, reported they all died in the hurricane. I loved Kirk. I grieved for him when he died. But even if he survived somehow, he is dead now, Killian. I legally married Richard."

I didn't mention we had Kirk declared dead before we married. We could always drag out those papers if we needed to in the future.

"I... I don't believe you." He continued to deny the obvious, but I could hear the uncertainty in his voice as clear as I could see it on his face. "And I don't believe that a black woman is your grandmother. Nanny to your children perhaps, but she's not related to you."

I didn't quibble with him. Gramma O was Richard's Granny, not mine. Instead, I smiled. "I tell you what, Killian. You pick the DNA center. We can both be tested. I bet you $10,000 it proves we are not related. If it shows a relationship, you get $10,000. But when it proves we are not related, then you agree you will go back to Ireland. I'll even buy you a one-way, first-class ticket back to Dublin. They need talented doctors in Ireland. How's that?"

He stared at me. "But when it proves we are related..."

"It won't," Richard said, his voice firm. "Bonnie is my child, not Kirk's. Hell, we'll give you a copy of the DNA test that proves she's my child if you want it."

Killian blinked. "Fine. As long as he'll pay up when it shows we're related."

"Oh, for the love of -- just let me pitch him in the shark tank." Richard shoved his hair out of his face with an exasperated sigh.

I touched Richard's arm again. He didn't need to push Killian too far while Killian was holding a skinning knife. "Hush, Richard. Be nice. Look, Killian, I'll sweeten the deal. If it shows you and I *are* related, we'll give you $25,000. On the condition that you go back to Ireland and never bother us again."

"Francesca..." Richard began, but he stopped when I gave him a dirty look.

"Our lawyer can write it up as a contract. But I expect you to leave whether I prove to you we are related or not."

"Maybe you haven't given birth to my ancestor yet. Ever think of that?" he asked.

I smiled. "I thought you told me your ancestress died in a hurricane, and she was never heard from again?"

I could see the indecision in his eyes. He didn't want to risk being disproven that I was his ancestor, or that I abandoned my loving, Irish sea captain for another man. You have no idea how badly I wished I had the painting of old Kirk with me right then. I would have loved to have handed it to him and asked, 'do you blame me?' But there was no need to add fuel to the fire, especially with him holding the damned skinning knife. In this day and age, it would be no big deal if I divorced Kirk to marry Richard. Divorce was an enormous deal in the 1700s. I would have lost custody of my children over adultery back then. And this man was unbalanced. He could not think clearly.

Killian rubbed his forehead. "You make my head hurt."

"Well, think about it. The offer is on the table for 48 hours. After that, you can *feis ort;* you can eff yourself. I am sick to death of your stalking and harassing and threatening my family and me. Do you understand?" I snapped the words out at him, suddenly sick to death of coddling him.

About then, two armed security guards approached with their weapons drawn. "Drop the knife, mister."

Killian looked rattled, but he complied and dropped the knife. "I wouldn't hurt her. I just wanted her to admit who she is."

"Yeah, sure, buddy." The security officer looked unimpressed. The men quickly handcuffed him and took Killian away.

I sagged against Richard. "Oh, my dear lord, I thought they would never arrive."

"You were magnificent. Are you okay?" He hugged me close as he stroked my hair.

I nodded, but I clung to him, still trembling. The children huddled around Gramma O and us. Richard lifted Bonnie as she began to cry again.

"It's okay, baby, Daddy has you. Everything will be okay." He patted her back as he gently rocked back and forth, holding his little girl.

But would it ever be okay? What could we do to get this man out of our lives? How could we get him out of our lives? Was it time to return to the 18th century to find our futures? Or did we stay here, in the present we loved, and somehow cope with Killian's lunacy?

# Chapter 20
# Back Home on the Ranch, or to be more specific, the Belle Rose Plantation 1786

Springtime at Belle Rose plantation was always beautiful. The cherry blossoms and the roses bloomed, the birds sang their sweet melodies, and the sky burned a bright, clear blue. Kirk O'Malley saw none of it.

Will cleared his throat. "No, we haven't seen or heard from her in a coon's age. The last we heard from her, she was headed to McCarron's Corner in '83. I have no dad-blamed idea what happened to her after that. I heard there's a lot of friction with the Indians out there."

Kirk frowned. "I can't imagine they survived the damned hurricane to wind up dead in the wilderness. I've gone out there hunting for them time after time. The settlers abandoned the entire village. I tried to talk to those damned savages in the nearby Cherokee village, but I got no information from them. It's as if Fancy and the bairns fell off the face of the earth."

He sighed, his shoulders sagging as if he were exhausted.

Sassy handed him a cup of tea. "Kirk, it's time you face the facts. You must let her go. I fear you cannot find her. Perhaps the Chickamauga Cherokees captured them, God forbid. Maybe they died of some horrible disease. We heard cholera was in Tennessee close to McCarron's Corner around the time they returned there. But we haven't heard a word from her in years, Kirk. I would be shocked if we heard from her."

He looked sick. "So, you think Fancy won't return?"

Sassy laid a hand on his arm. "Honey, I think she's gone. Let her go. It's time."

Sassy's heart lurched as Kirk's grey eyes filled with unshed tears. He sat the cup down and lowered his head between his big hands. "Oh, God, I feared you would say that. We argued the mornin' I left Bermuda, but before we left, I told her I loved her. She told me she loved me. And the bairns. The poor wee bairns. I swear, I canna bear to think they died. Wouldn't I know it in my heart if they were dead?"

"It's been more than four years since we last heard from her, Kirk. It's time to get on with your life. You must let her go. Fancy wouldn't want you to grieve for years on end like this," Will coaxed his old friend.

Kirk looked up at Will as tears began to spill from his eyes. "I canna, Will. I love the lass. I love the bairns. I canna give up on them."

Will patted Kirk on the back, the movement awkward and clumsy. "You have to let them go, Kirk. Fancy's disappearance eats at you like cancer. It's eating you alive."

Kirk shook his head. "I told her to kiss me when I left because I might not see her for a long time. It looks like I was right."

"I believe she missed you, Kirk. She thought you died in the storm. She sounded heartbroken in the letters she sent us before she disappeared."

Kirk shook his head. "You don't understand, Will. I miss her so much. My heart has shattered. How do I survive this? How did you live through the loss of Hortense? Jaysus, man, what would ye do if ye lost Sassy and the wee bairns as well? I've lost the only two women who ever captured my heart. First Anya, now my sweet Fancy. You say 'find another love.' Good women don't grow on trees. It is even harder to find a woman willing to put up with the likes of me. Think how long it took you to find Sassy after Tennie died. How do I go on? Hell, why should I? I've lost the love of my life, and my children in one fell swoop."

Sassy's heart ached with pity for Kirk. She could see the big lug's heart ached. She realized over the past few years, he loved Fancy, but she had not understood the depth of his love until now. She began chewing her lip, casting nervous glances at Will. "I will leave you two men to talk business. I know Will wants to talk ships with you, Kirk."

As the two men began talking about ships and Ranscome Shipping, she slipped from the room and hurried upstairs.

"Could you hear all that?" she asked Lily and Marc.

Marc nodded. "Aye. Well done, Sassy."

"I agree, Sass. I loved it when you told him she's gone, and when Will told him it was time for him to get on with his life," Lily whispered.

"Now, if only he will. I never thought I would live to say I feel sorry for Kirk O'Malley, but I do. This poor man needs to get on with his life. He should find another woman and get married again. Maybe have a passel of kids. He was good with Bella, Charlie, and little Bonnie. I have no doubt he'd make a decent husband and father for the right woman." Sassy shook her head, aching with sympathy for a man she once hated.

"I agree. Kirk has his faults, but we all do. God knows he has a bad temper. But the bottom line is he's a decent fellow. And he genuinely loved her." Lily shook her head.

"He breaks my heart, still hunting for her. Poor, dear man. How many times has Kirk gone to McCarron's Corner now?" Sassy's brow wrinkled with concern for Kirk.

"I'm not sure. I wonder why Kirk keeps going there?" Lily replied.

"Kirk said he's sure the answer to Fancy's disappearance is there, right in front of him, if he can only find it."

"As it is," said Marc.

"Yep, right in front of his nose. If he knew where to look," Lily said.

They all grew silent as they heard steps coming up the stairs. When Will walked into the room, Sassy rushed to her husband. "What did he say? What are you going to do?"

"He's gone for the day, but he'll be back tomorrow. I will sell Kirk a partnership in two of the ships. I know he wants to own a shipping line someday. This opportunity to co-own a ship will head him in that direction. Dammit, Ranscome Lines needs him right now. I'd rather have him associated with Ranscome Lines than not. Besides, I miss the rapscallion. Fancy was right. He was the best captain I ever had, even if he lost the Enterprise." Will looked thoughtful.

"Well, in his defense, that was one helluva storm, Will. I'm still stunned the man survived it," Marc said.

"Yes, it was the worst hurricane I ever saw. Kirk never explained how he survived other than to say another ship rescued him. I think he sailed on that ship for a while. He says he found a letter she left at Spring Haven. In it, Fancy wrote that she regretted their argument. My baby sister wanted Kirk to know why she left." Will stared out the window as he watched Kirk riding away from the prosperous plantation.

"That must have been some quarrel," Sassy mused.

Marc nodded. "Aye, it was a honey of a quarrel, even for those two. They argued like cats and dogs the entire trip. She surprised me when she agreed to travel with him from Ireland to Bermuda in the first place. He often behaved overly affectionate with her—"

"Well, Marc, they were married." Will looked grim.

Marc looked startled by Will's comment. "Nay, the court annulled the marriage in Ireland. It's illegal for them to marry in Barbados because she is mixed. Whites canna marry persons of color there."

Sassy's mouth fell agape. "Say what?"

Marc nodded as a wry grin spread across his face. "Aye. Just like it was illegal for Tam and me to marry here in Virginia all those years ago, or for Will to marry Tennie here. We were waiting for the chancery court to hand down its ruling when you left. She hadn't told you because she feared Richard would blow up and tell Kirk."

Will's eyes narrowed in speculation. "Are you serious?"

Marc nodded again. "Aye. She felt devastated when Rick left without telling her. I tried to warn her, but she swore he would stay after you came so far. She took Kirk with her to the solicitor the week after you left, and he explained the void marriage. And then Kirk began wooing her again. T'was soon clear, she considered remarrying the rogue."

"Jesus Christ, she didn't, did she? Surely, she wasn't that stupid?" Will looked shocked.

Marc and Lily both shook their heads.

"Not to my knowledge, and I think she would have told me," Lily said.

Marc nodded. "I agree. She would have told Lily if no one else. She talked to me about the possibility of marrying him several times, but I don't think she did. She could tell I wasn't keen on the idea. He often seemed a bit fresh with her to me. You ken a bit unduly forward. But she didna' complain. She seemed to enjoy his attentions."

Will shifted, uncomfortable by the unexpected turn in the conversation.

"Aye, it concerned me as well. And after the hurricane, she saw the news sheets proclaiming the ship sank, and they believed all on board dead in the storm. The poor girl fainted. She cried at times. We weren't sure if she wept for losing Kirk or the loss of Richard."

"She mourned the loss of both of them, and for all the men on the ship. She told me her feelings for Kirk were complicated. She said she knew how you felt when Owen died, and then you fell in love with Will." Lily's soft voice could not hide her sympathy for Fancy.

"Conflicted?" Sassy asked.

"Exactly. Fancy said, 'love is complicated.' Anyway, she grieved when Rick left and then again when she thought Kirk died. She lost both men she loved in less than a year."

"And then Providence took her forward in time to my son." Sassy cracked a little smile.

Lily nodded. "Yes. They repaired her heart in more than one way. They replaced both damaged valves. She attended therapy and became much stronger emotionally. Writing her book proved cathartic for her. And she fell head over heels in love with Rick all over again, and he with her. I must confess I never mentioned Kirk survived in my letters to her."

Sassy nodded. "Neither have I. Kirk needs to understand she's gone, and she's not coming back. There is no reason for him to know she lives over 200 years in the future. I doubt he would even begin to comprehend that one."

Will laughed. "It takes a bit of adjusting to come to terms with that concept. But Kirk isn't stupid. He might surprise you."

Marc cleared his throat. "Aye, it takes an adjustment. And she could come back someday."

Will looked startled. "Do you think they might come back?"

"Mayhap. Charles is the heir apparent to her title as well as an earl in his own right. All the girls could make brilliant marriages here."

"Or have wonderful careers there." Lily glared at Marc.

"Aye, Bella has a genuine gift for music. Betty loves ballet. And sweet, wee Bonnie sings with the voice of an angel." Marc smiled as he thought of his grandchildren.

"All three girls demonstrate impressive talents. Charlie is a whiz at sports. But in the future, they might become doctors. Nurses. Hey, did we tell you Fancy was going to college? She wants to become a nurse," Lily said.

"A nursemaid? Why in heaven's name—" Will began.

Lily shook her head. "Not that kind of nurse, William. She wants to become a surgical assistant to doctors. She has a genuine gift for working with

Rick's patients. They adore her. And she provided fabulous help at Yorktown. She'll make a crackerjack surgical nurse."

"Oh. Gotcha," Will mumbled. "Marc, was the Spring Haven house damaged in the storm?"

"We had left and gone to Charleston, but she said it sustained substantial damage. Why?"

"Kirk said he didn't get back there until the next summer. The house suffered flood damage, and the roof collapsed when a palm tree fell during the storm. The storm also damaged the cistern, and they had no drinking water. He found Fancy's note nailed to the mantel. It said she went to Charleston and planned to find you two. He tracked you all to Charleston. He knows Marc broke his leg, and Fancy helped you guys return to McCarron's Corner. Yes, he touched me when he asked me how he could get over Fancy. He loved two women and lost them both. Dammit, the man cried. I hate it when men cry. I never know how to respond. The poor bastard has no luck at love."

Lily rubbed her hands over her arms. "Oh, my, Will. Isn't that pretty much what Fancy used to say about herself?"

Will continued staring out the window after the lone figure riding away from Belle Rose. Kirk's shoulders slumped in defeat as he rode towards Albatross Alley. Will felt another tug at his heartstrings watching Kirk riding away. "Yes, Lil. Pretty much."

They were all silent for a few minutes as they watched Kirk ride away. "That last day in Bermuda, he told her to kiss him because it might be a long time until she saw him again," Marc mused.

Will turned back towards his friend. "He told me that. What had been going on?"

Marc shrugged. "As I said, they argued a lot. God alone knew the source of their arguments. They fussed all the time. They had another row that morning, and Kirk told her she'd best kiss him because it might be a long time before she saw him again. I think about that from time to time. T'was as if he had a foreboding something bad was about to happen."

"That's pretty much what Kirk told me," Will said.

"The Dreadful Hurricane," Lily murmured.

Marc nodded. "Aye, t'was dreadful, indeed."

Sassy cleared her throat. "Enough of all this depressing talk. Tell me again all about the wedding. It kills me we couldn't be there, too."

Lily's face lit up. "Oh, Sassy, it was beautiful. We arrived just in the nick of time."

"Now, what was this about some high falootin' surgery to fix Fancy's heart? How the blazes did they do that?" Will asked.

"Ah, William, I tell you, it was the most amazing thing I ever saw. I knew it would kill her. But save her, it did. That world is purely amazing. Let me tell ye about it…"

"About everything. But start with her surgery," Will coaxed.

"Well, they start by giving you anesthetic, so you're asleep and feel nothing while they cut on ye. Then the doctors cut the breastbone open. They hooked her up to a contraption called a heart and lung machine. It served as her heart and lungs while they operated. Once they connected her to that contraption, they stopped her from breathing and stopped her heart while they repaired the valves. That machine kept circulating her blood, cleaning out the impurities, and infusing it with fresh oxygen. Then, once they repaired her heart, they sewed Fancy up, started her heart and lungs, took her off the machine, and roused her."

As Marc explained the intricacies of open-heart surgery and lung-heart machines to Will, a look of astonishment replaced the scowl on his face.

"Now wait just a gosh darn minute. Do you mean to tell someone cut into Fancy's heart? How can a person live while they do surgery on your heart?"

Everyone laughed except poor Will, who scowled again, his brows furrowed. "I'm serious."

"I know, honey. Guys, we shouldn't laugh. Lily, explain how it works to him." Sassy struggled to stop laughing.

Lily began explaining how the heart-lung machine worked as Will paid rapt attention.

"All right," Will said, still with a puzzled look. "Just one question. What in the blazes is a gosh darn machine?"

# Chapter 21
# Rick and Fancy Now

Killian remained locked up since the Aquarium Incident, but they would release him any day. They took his DNA sample while he incarcerated at the county jail. I already saw the results. As expected, Killian O'Malley was *not* related to Francesca Winslow. To say I would have been surprised if we were relatives would be a vast understatement.

Now, as long as he did not ask to compare his DNA to that of my kids. As it was, the test showed he was 1.5% Black, or approximately 1/64$^{th}$ Black. I suspected his DNA would show he was related to Elizabeth if her DNA were in the system, which it was not, and never would be if I could prevent it from happening.

We agreed Killian would return to Ireland whether or not he was related to me, but it terrified me Killian would injure us when he learned that I wasn't his relative. I had recurring nightmares of red skies in the morning and red flags. I knew those meant beware; they would take no prisoners. I did not want the red skies and red flags to extend to a red pool of blood in which any of my beloved family lay dying at the hands of this madman.

"I've been thinking. Maybe we should leave." My voice trembled.

Richard looked shocked. "Are you serious? I thought we worked through this."

I took a deep breath. "Richard, Killian terrifies me."

"Now, sweetie, be practical. We have a written contractual agreement with Killian. Surely, he'll honor the contract. We worked damned hard to get where we are today in our careers. Even if you take off some additional time from work after you have this baby, don't you intend to return to work at the clinic at some point? You're a damned fine surgical nurse. I would hate for you to have to give that up to become the Duchess of Ranscome again. Hell, I'd hate to lose you as a surgical nurse. And I love my job. I love performing the surgeries we do. I could never do these surgeries Before. It would be impossible, even if we took a team and all kinds of equipment with us. Without electricity? No heart-lung machine. Without the heart-lung machine, no heart surgeries. We could take a generator, but it would not be sufficient for adequate lighting, the computerized programs, and the heart-lung machine itself. I would have to walk away from my career if we went back to the 18$^{th}$ century. We bought this big, gorgeous house…"

"Okay." I was exhausted from arguing about this. We talked about going back in time off and on ever since the trek up to McCarron's Corner in September. Now, Killian was due out of jail any day from his latest incarceration for violating the Protective Order again. I had a sick, hollow feeling in the pit of my stomach. Our baby was due to be born in a few weeks. All I wanted was for this birth to come off with no more hitches. Thank God I got Richard to agree to the change in my attending doctor and hospital.

We titled the house in the corporation's name, at the suggestion of Uncle Jim. That made it harder for Killian to find us than if we titled the house in our names, and if I still went into Atlanta for my medical care. Killian knew we lived near Ellijay, and we both worked at the Smith-Winslow Cardiovascular Clinic. He could find us, with a little good, old-fashioned, elbow grease.

"Are you sure?" Richard sounded relieved yet surprised by my unexpected acquiescence.

I nodded. Once again, Richard's calm, common sense prevailed. We both worked too hard for our live here, in the Beyond, to turn tail and run back to the Before. Heck, I didn't know if we could go back. If we returned to the 18$^{th}$ century, I didn't know if we could readjust to living in the past. I needed to put on my big girl panties and quit worrying.

However, I continued to fret. While I told myself we did not need to turn tail and run, my stomach roiled as I waited for the other shoe to drop.

Three nights later, I awoke with a start as the phone rang. As Richard reached to grab the phone, I struggled to sit up, rubbing the sleep from my eyes. "Dammit, I had that consarned nightmare again."

Richard frowned and motioned for me to be quiet. "Okay, thanks for calling. No, no problem at all. I'll head out as soon as I pull some clothes on.

Oh, she's asking for Fancy, too? Fine, we'll both head to Atlanta. It will take us a couple of hours at least to get there. Please tell her we love her and we're on the way. And, if Dr. DeAngelo Barajaz is on call tonight, I'd be very grateful if he would look in on her."

I frowned. "What's wrong?"

Richard bounded out of bed, pulling his scrubs on. "Gramma had a stroke. She's asking for us."

I could feel the color drain from my face. "Oh, sweet baby Jesus."

I figured this was why I awoke dreaming of the red sky in the morning dream. Richard might laugh at me, but I swore the nightmare always seemed to warn of something terrible about to happen. I hustled out of bed and into my clothes, too. We told Shirley, the nanny, we would head to Atlanta and why. She assured us she would be okay with the kids and could get them off to school in the morning. We loaded into the Range Rover and headed south in the darkness.

We talked about my recurring nightmare on the drive. I pointed out I dreamed it before several traumatic experiences, such as meeting Tamsin again after 20 years, and before the Dreadful Hurricane hit. I also suffered it before a couple of Killian's crazier antics, including the last one at the Aquarium.

I didn't tell him I dreamed about red skies and red sails the night before he left Waterside, or how it broke me to find him gone the next day. I told him I dreamed it when the hospital called about Gramma O.

Richard frowned. "So, you this dream this often?"

I shook my head. "No, just those times. Usually, right before something bad or difficult happens."

"Tell me about your dream. The whole nightmare. All the details."

"Everything?"

He nodded. "Yes. Everything."

So, I told him about it. Again.

"In the dream, the sky was red that morning. Kirk says, 'Always be grateful for the bad things in life, Fancy. They open your eyes to the good things you weren't noticing before.'"

Chills went down my spine when Richard replied. "Isn't that kind of like saying, 'if it weren't for bad luck, you would have no luck at all'?"

I swallowed hard. "That's what I always ask Kirk when he says that."

Richard glanced at me quickly. "Well, that's rather creepy."

I nodded. "Yeah, just a tad. Then he says he would hate to think he had been nothing but bad luck for me. But then again, considering all the BS we have put up with from Killian, maybe he was nothing but bad luck for me. I've noticed things change in it from time to time."

He frowned. "Was anything different this time?"

I thought for a minute. "Something. I can't quite put my finger on it."

"If it's important, it will come to you," Richard said.

"I guess. Weird. I wonder why I keep dreaming about it."

We rode in silence for the next 30 miles or so as I remembered the red skies, red sails, and my recurring fears of red blood pooled around our inert bodies.

"In my original dream, I remember Kirk referred to the pirate by one name, I think Davy Jones. In my later dreams, Kirk calls him Johnny English. In the early ones, he calls the ship as something-or-other Robert. I think he now calls it something else."

Richard gave me a sharp look. "The Bonne Homme Robert was Davy Jones' ship. What does Kirk call it now?"

I shrugged. "I can't remember. I know it's a different name than before."

"Well, Davy Jones had more than one ship."

I nodded. "I remember Kirk told me that. Oh, well, I guess it isn't important."

Richard rubbed my neck. "Probably not, sweetie. Look, we're here."

Richard was parking the Land Rover in the physician's lot when the call came. "Hey, DiAngelo. How is she? Oh, splendid news! I'm parking the car now. We should be there in five minutes." He turned to me and grinned as he caught my hand. "DiAngelo says it looks like it was minor. Probably a TIA instead of a full-blown stroke. She's still asking for us. Come on, sweetie."

I laughed as I started behind him. "Hey, slow down, dude, I can't waddle that fast!"

He turned to me, laughing, and pulled me into his arms. "Sorry, sweetie. I didn't mean to make you run…"

He pulled me close for a long, lingering kiss. I sighed as our lips parted, still clinging to the man I love more than life itself.

"Look, Richard, it's starting to snow!" I love the snow.

"Just for you, sweetheart. Just for you." He grabbed my hand, and we hurried into the hospital.

Once inside, we learned they transferred Gramma O to a private room, to observe her overnight.

"She looks pretty damned good, Rick. If she continues to improve, I'll cut her loose tomorrow or the next day," said DeAngelo.

Richard grabbed his friend's hand and shook it. "DeAngelo, you will never know how glad we are to hear that. Thanks for coming out tonight. The weather looks downright nasty."

DeAngelo frowned. "Yeah, they say it will be awful. I'm on call, so I'm here for the duration. You guys better hole up somewhere around here. I wouldn't try to drive back to Ellijay tonight. The news reports say we may get a foot of snow by morning. They canceled school up north."

Richard nodded. "That's what we heard on the way here. The kids are safe with their nanny. She'll keep them home. We'll crash at the apartment."

"Great. Your grandmother is one tough old bird. She wants to see you both when you arrive."

"It's late. Will the nurses let us in to see her?" I frowned.

He nodded. "Yes, I left orders they should admit you. Please don't stay too long."

We checked in with the nurse before we tiptoed into Gramma O's room. She appeared to be sleeping. I felt shocked to see how frail she looked, and then I thought, my heavens, she's 87, the woman is entitled to look delicate. I hung back as Richard bent to kiss her cheek.

Her eyelids fluttered open. "Oh, Ricky, honey, I'm so glad you came."

He took her hands into his own. "Of course, I came to be with my favorite Gramma. How do you feel?"

She smiled. "Much better. The nice young doctor friend of yours told me I'd be fine. And then I had the sweetest dream…"

Her voice faded off as though she fell asleep while talking to us.

Richard smiled and patted her hand. "What did you dream, Gramma?"

She blinked her eyes into focus. "I dreamed my Kathy and my RoRo stood right here by my bed."

Richard paled. I laid my hand on his shoulder. "Did they talk to you, Gramma?"

She nodded. "RoRo told me I could come and be with them any time I want. I told him I still have things to do, but I'll come along as soon as I finish my chores here."

She chuckled. She loves the country-western song that says that.

I knew Gramma O called Kathryn 'Kathy' and often referred to her late husband as 'RoRo.' "What did they say to you then?"

She smiled again. "RoRo told me he loved me, and he would wait for me as long as it took. Then he kissed me right as my Ricky came in the door."

Richard cleared his throat. "I have to admit, sweetheart, I love having you here. I'm in no hurry for you to leave."

She beamed at him and squeezed his hand. "I'm glad. I intend to be around a while longer. After all, I must meet this new baby. Which leads me to why I wanted to talk to you."

"What would that be, Gramma O?" I looked at her quizzically, puzzled by her words.

She leveled her beautiful amber eyes, so much like my Richard's eyes, on me. "You two never agreed on a name for our baby boy, did you?"

I shook my head and chuckled. She had listened to Name the Baby Discussions for months. "No, ma'am. Not yet."

"Well, I have the name." She sounded smug.

Richard frowned. "Gramma, I will not name this baby RoRo Winslow."

She laughed. 'Of course not. You'll name him Ronan Roberts Winslow. You will honor your grandfather, and by doing so, you will honor your mother and me. And the next one can be Kathryn Olivia Winslow."

I laughed. Gramma O knew we did not plan to have more children, but she still wanted another girl so we could name her Kathy. "Ronan Roberts Winslow. I like it. Richard, isn't there a character on that sci-fi show you like named Ronan?"

He nodded. "Yes, on Stargate Atlantis. Ronan is a cool dude. Okay, Gramma, Ronan Roberts Winslow it is. On one condition."

She tilted her face toward him. "What's that, baby?"

"We won't call him RoRo."

Gramma roared with laughter. "Oh, baby, there was only one RoRo. This baby will be his great-grandson, but he will never be my RoRo." She continued to chuckle. "Ain't never gonna be no RoRo but my RoRo. You can call him R2, like that little robot in those Star Wars movies."

Richard laughed. "Now, that's funny, Gramma."

We visited a few more minutes before we headed out. Richard told the nurses we would spend the night at the doctor's apartment and give them our cell numbers. The snow came down fast enough that we decided to leave the car in the parking garage, and we caught a cab to take us the two blocks to the apartment.

"I haven't seen snow like this in years." Richard helped me walk across the icy sidewalk into the building. He held my arm with one hand and supported my back with the other as we carefully crossed the icy walkway to enter the elegant hi-rise apartment building where the clinic maintained an apartment for the doctors and their staff.

"It snowed nearly this much last year. At least I won't have to go out in the snow to avoid listening to Bella struggle with that Chopin passage from the Nocturnes." I grinned.

Richard groaned. "Oh, sweet Jesus, I never dreamed I could learn to hate a song she studied. How many times could she hit the same wrong notes?"

I shrugged. "How many times will it take her to reach perfection? Who knows?"

"It couldn't be as bad as when she learned that Pachelbel Canon, could it?"

"Oh, God, I wish it weren't, but I think it was. You just had to remind me of that experience. I'll never forget standing outside in the cold for an hour to escape the damned passage in the song. I may never fully appreciate the song again. It used to be one of my favorites."

"But you still love snow?" Richard grinned at me.

I nodded. "Of course. Almost as much as I love my sweet Bella." I stopped and turned back towards him. "The Scaramouche."

He frowned as he tilted his head to study me. "What?"

"He called the pirate ship the Scaramouche this time."

Richard laughed and pulled me into his arms. "You've been listening to 'Bohemian Rhapsody' again."

I laughed. "Probably so. I do love me some Queen. I wish I could have heard Freddie Mercury in person."

"You and me, both. I was small when Freddie Mercury died. But we heard Queen last year when the band played in Atlanta."

I nodded. "Yes, but just imagine if Freddie had been there, too."

We must have talked an hour about the baby, the kids, our lives. It was almost four by the time we fell asleep, nestled in each other's arms. I remember thinking the sky was red as I drifted off. I never saw a red sky when it snowed before. I didn't know if it was beautiful or foreboding to see the red light spread across the snow.

Or perhaps both beautiful *and* foreboding.

I woke up before Richard. *Poor darling must be exhausted*, I thought as I fixed a pot of coffee. He's always up before me. I soon heard the shower running, proof my morning-person husband was up and at 'em. As I sat the just-baked pan of biscuits down on a trivet, he came up from behind me and wrapped me into a big hug.

"Mmm, that smells good." He bent to kiss my nape, and I turned around to hand him a cup of coffee and a hot buttered biscuit.

"Thank you. I think you smell pretty wonderful, too." I reached up to kiss him.

"Oh, you naughty minx. Are you trying to have your way with me this morning?" He wiggled his eyebrows like Groucho Marx.

I giggled. "Anytime, handsome."

I kissed him again.

He sighed. "No can do, pretty lady. Dan texted me a list of patients who I need to check before we go home. I need to run over to the hospital. Did you eat? Or do you want to go with me?"

"I didn't eat. My tummy is a little upset. I would prefer not to barf on the road back to Ellijay. But sure, I'll come with you. Give me 10 minutes, and I'll be ready." I turned to go to the bedroom.

He grabbed my arm. "Later?"

"Absolutely."

He grinned and kissed me again. "Go, get dressed, gorgeous."

"Huh. If you think this is gorgeous, wait until I give birth to this baby. I'll show you gorgeous in a few months!" He laughed as I ran my hands over my enormous baby belly.

Eight minutes later, I came out, freshly showered and dressed. Richard grabbed my hand, I grabbed my handbag and my down puffer jacket, and we headed out the door.

The snow had stopped. Almost a foot of snow lay on the ground, and the town looked like it was at a standstill. There were no cabs out front, so we decided to walk the two blocks back to the hospital. Thank heaven I brought my puffer jacket and my Uggs. We took our time to avoid me falling, but I lost my balance and slipped as we approached the hospital entrance. I lay in the snow laughing as I made a snow angel. Richard bent to help me up. I grabbed a handful of snow and tossed it at him.

"You're full of piss and vinegar today." He grinned as he wiped the snow from his face.

I giggled as I reached up for him to help me. "I'm sorry. Here, help me up."

"This reminds me of another time when you fell in the snow." He lowered his head to kiss me like he did that long-ago Christmas Day when Charlie was born and then grinned as he gave me a hand.

"I remember more of the dream—" I began.

Suddenly, other hands were there. I turned to thank the man, and then the words froze on my lips.

It was Killian. "Hello, Granny."

I jerked my hand away from him and struggled to pull myself up. "What are you doing here? Get away from me."

"What the hell are you doing here?" Richard snapped.

"I wasn't talkin' to you, Winslow." Killian never took his eyes off my protuberant belly.

"You say you weren't talking to me? Kiss my lily-white ass, Killian. And get your effing hands off my wife."

Killian turned and slowly raised his eyes to Richard. "What did you say?"

Richard's laugh sounded menacing. "You freaking maniac, get your hands off my wife. Right now."

Killian didn't reply to Richard. Instead, he smiled this weird smile. In retrospect, I would call it an evil grin. He eased his long knife out of his coat. I gasped and tried to pull further away from him, but he caught my arm again. "I think I'll be relieving you of the wee lad, Granny."

Before Richard or I could do anything, he slashed the knife at me, again and again. I screamed as the blade slashed towards me.

*The sky was red that morning*, I thought. All I could see were the red sky and red blood. I still screamed as my world faded and then grew dark around me.

# Chapter 22
# Red Sky in the Morning

Rick struggled with Killian for the knife. He felt sick with terror O'Malley would kill Francesca. *Dear God, surely you did not give her to me for a few years, for her to die like this!*

Security ran out when they heard the screams and saw the attack on the monitors. When Killian would not stop his vicious assault, the security guards knocked him out with something Rick swore looked for all the world like a gun. Rick guessed it was a taser by the way Killian's body jerked and twitched. Rick regretted they didn't merely shoot the sorry rat bastard.

Rick sobbed as the men pulled Killian off Cessie. "Please, dear God, please let her live. Please, God!"

An ambulance pulled up just as security stopped Killian's attack. Two paramedics jumped out, Johnny On the Spot, with a stretcher. They loaded Cessie on it and rushed her bleeding and battered body inside, with Rick clinging to her hand. "Hang on, sweetheart. It will be okay. I promise. Hang on."

Her eyes fluttered open, and she tried to smile. *Thank God, she was only passed out.* He felt her wrap her fingers around his hand.

"I'll be okay."

He glanced down and realized his hands were bleeding. For the first time, he understood why she didn't realize she suffered injuries until Devin pointed her injuries out to her.

The ER staff took over as they entered. A nurse tried to pull Rick into a separate room to clean his hands, but he shook his head. "Oh, hell, no. I can wait. I need to stay with my wife."

"Doc, you are bleeding like a freaking stuck pig. Her Ob-Gyn is heading down here right now. They'll take care of her. Let me see your damned hand…"

"Then do it right here. I stay with my wife," he snapped.

"Oh, for the love of-okay. Fine. Better?" She jerked the curtain open so he could be right next to Cessie but in a separate area and then returned to his injured hand. "Jessica, Call Dr. Roland Morton. Tell him what's going on, and we need a hand surgeon here pretty damned quick. Dr. Winslow's hand is a hot mess. He needs to get to surgery ASAP."

"Not until I know about my wife and our baby." Rick winced from the sting of the Betadine on his raw wounds.

"Jesus, save me from jack ass, crazy doctors. Fine. Dr. Markham, how's Mrs. Winslow?" She called out to the ER doctor working on Cessie.

"We're taking her to surgery. Her Ob-Gyn will meet us there," Victoria Markham said.

"Vicky, is Cessie okay?" Rick yelled.

"She will be, Rick. Baby will be fine, too. Hang in there. We'll take care of her. I gotta take her up there, STAT."

He knew it was not good if they immediately rushed Cessie to surgery. *My God, how bad are her injuries?*

Roland Morton came rushing into the ER minutes later. He carefully checked Rick's hand. "Yeah, that one tendon looks damned nasty. You need surgery, but we controlled the bleeding, and I want to hold off until my team arrives. Let's bandage you up for now, and then Harrison says you may join them in surgery with Fancy."

Rick's heart lurched. "What are they doing?"

"Emergency c-section. She's bleeding a lot, her blood pressure dropped, and she has an irregular heartbeat. Harrison says she's conscious now, and she wants you there. It won't take fifteen minutes to do the c-section. We can wait that long. Hell, it will take me longer than that to get my team here. But once they complete her surgery, I need you in prep. We'll work on those hands within the hour."

Rick glanced down at his hands and cringed. The right wasn't too bad, just a few superficial cuts, but he could see the tendon exposed along his left wrist, extending down to his thumb. Rick knew he would have months of occupational therapy to regain the full function of his left hand. Fortunately, he also knew he had one of the best hand teams in the country being assembled.

The nurse bandaged his hand to stabilize the wound so he could hustle to the Ob-Gyn surgical arena. She accompanied Rick to help him scrub his right hand. She assisted him to gown up before she held the door as he slipped into the OR to sidle up to Fancy. Rick's eyes lit up to see Cessie prepped for surgery. She reached out for his right hand and gasped when she saw the bandages.

"It'll be okay, sweetie." He bent over and kissed her cheek.

Her lips trembled. "I know, but I have to admit, I'm scared."

"It'll be okay. You ready, Joe?"

Joe Harrison, the anesthesiologist, nodded. "Yes. We gave her an epidural. It's taken effect. Her heart stabilized, but we don't want to dawdle. She's ready, Harvey."

Her original Ob-Gyn nodded and raised his scalpel. Rick felt relief to know they could take the time to do the epidural. Likewise, it pleased him to see Harvey make a low transverse incision. Also called a bikini cut, the low transverse incision is a side-to-side incision made in the lower, thinner part of the uterus that contracts less during labor. Ob-Gyn's make the incision when the baby presents head first. Rick remembered from his Ob-Gyn rotation in med school that the low transverse incision is the preferred cut, but sometimes they can't take the time to do it in an emergency. The chances of hemorrhage or rupture during future pregnancies in a low transverse delivery are much lower when compared to that of the vertical cesarean. They didn't plan on having another baby, but there were other reasons to use this cut. First, there is less blood loss. She already lost enough blood. The incision is easier to close, and there is less risk of uterine infection. There is also a lower risk of gastrointestinal complications. There were other stab wounds from Killian, but they appeared to be superficial mostly. At least, Rick hoped so.

"I think O'Malley tried to cut the baby out of her," Rick told Harvey Greenville.

Harvey nodded. "He probably would have, too, if she hadn't been wearing that puffer coat. Fortunately, the material deflected his knife, and she wasn't cut too badly by him. Now, let's get this baby delivered."

Once the incision was made, the caul bulged through the incision. Once it was outside Francesca's body, the doctor ruptured the caul, and eased Rick's son out. Rick helped deliver Charlie and Bonnie, but he never stood by her side to hold Cessie's hand as he watched her give birth, and he had not witnessed a c-section delivery since med school. It boggled his mind to observe the talented surgeon make the incision, ease the caul out of his wife's body, and lifted their baby's head out of the caul. Rick choked up with emotion when he heard his little boy screaming with rage before the babe was out of her body. Rick began laughing and crying at the sound. "He's okay, Cessie. Our baby is okay."

Cessie began laughing and crying, too. Harvey Greenville handed little Ronan to Cessie to hold as Rick cut the umbilical cord, no small task with one hand. Cessie stroked Ronan's little face and frowned at the cut over one eye. "What's this, Harvey?"

"That, my dear, is from one of the stab wounds. It penetrated your uterus, which was why we hurried to do the c-section. Killian came damned close to delivering this baby outside. Thank God you were here when the maniac attacked you. There was such extensive bleeding that we worried you hemorrhaged or had a placenta previa. Fortunately, neither occurred. I'll mend the uterine injury and the other cuts as I stitch you. I already started you on doxycycline. You don't need to develop a nasty infection."

Cessie gulped and nodded. She kissed Ronan and then held him out for the nurse, who whisked Ronan away to clean the infant.

"Kiss your wife, Rick, and then get out of here. I'll stitch up the knife wounds and her c-section incision. She's damned lucky. It looked much worse than it was. She will be fine. Let's make sure you will be, too."

Cessie gave him a nervous smile as Rick kissed her again. "See you soon."

Rick lifted his right hand to his lips, kissed his bandaged fingers like he had seen her do hundreds of times, and blew her a kiss. She caught it with one hand, touched her hand to her heart, and then blew a kiss back.

"See you soon. I love you to the moon and back." He turned to leave the surgical suite.

. . .

I couldn't believe we both survived. I was safely delivered of a healthy baby boy. My cuts healed well. I figured my new scars would make me more interesting. Lord knew if we ever went back to the 18$^{th}$ century, I would be the only living person with one scar from open-heart surgery and another from a c-section.

The cut on Ronan's face healed, but he would always have a scar above his eye. The physicians repaired Richard's hand, and he began occupational therapy.

Killian went back to the county jail, where he awaited deportation to Ireland.

We received a letter through Jim from Sassy. She admitted Kirk somehow survived the hurricane and came to Belle Rose from time to time to learn if they heard from me. They told him I was 'gone.' He thought they meant I died. They did not tell him anything different. They debated whether to tell me Kirk survived but finally decided to 'spill the beans,' as Sassy put it.

Lily and Marc arrived at Belle Rose and were deciding whether to head to Ireland or return to McCarron's Corner one more time. Lily's description of my surgery fascinated Will, and he wanted to know what machines were.

"Can you imagine Will studying plans for various machines?" I chuckled at the mental picture of my brother studying plans to build machines.

Richard nodded. "I sure can. Let's take pictures and plans with us if we ever go back."

I tilted my head at him. "I thought you never wanted to return to the 18$^{th}$ century?"

His face reddened with embarrassment. "Well, maybe someday. After 1812."

I grinned. "We'll be getting old by then."

He shook his head. "Nah. Piece of cake. We're pretty badass."

We got a letter from Marc and Lily at the same time. They were going to Ireland to turn the power of attorney of my lands over to Fitz, per my instructions. Once done, they hoped to return to McCarron's Corner. They knew it would become unsafe in the Indian Territory, but Marc hated to admit defeat.

Lily admitted she empathized with Kirk when Will and Sassy told him I was 'gone' and that it was time for him to let me go. She thought Kirk needed to move on with his life. And once again, they sent regards from Guiding Light.

I frowned. "What is this 'Guiding Light' business all about?"

Richard shrugged. "I don't know. Dan looked stunned the first time I sent the message. He changed the subject and started muttering something about his 'crazy' sister."

I giggled as he made air quotes around 'crazy.' "I know she went through a difficult divorce that took forever. Her ex-husband appealed the property division. But why on earth does Dan think Bay is crazy?"

"I don't know, sweetie. I told him you miss her. Her phone number changed, and she never gave it to anyone since the divorce."

I felt my brow furrow as I frowned. "That's not like Bay."

Richard nodded. "I know. Dan and I suspect she took a job somewhere else. Maybe the Bureau of Indian Affairs transferred her to Oklahoma. She talked about that possibility the last time we saw her. Dan thought perhaps they transferred her, and she forgot to give anyone her new number and new address."

"Yes, but she didn't want to go. I had the distinct impression she would quit before she accepted that job. She insisted she would not go to Oklahoma to be a paper pusher."

"She told Dan she wouldn't take it, but she must have gone somewhere. Surely she still has the same email address."

"You would think so." I frowned until Richard put an arm around my shoulders. I felt the tension ease from my body as I gazed at our baby, sleeping in my arms.

"Well, it looks like Bay won't be Ronan's godmother. Who do you want to choose then?" He smiled as he gently stroked down the side of our sleeping baby's face.

I smiled up at my baby's daddy. "Since we asked Dan to be Ronan's godfather, we should ask Dee to be his godmother. She's a wonderful friend, too."

Richard kissed my cheek. "Sounds like a plan."

We cornered Dan at the office the next afternoon to talk about it.

"We'd be honored to be Ronan's godparents. I'm just sorry my crazy sister disappeared, and we can't find her. I know you two are close, Fancy. And when are you two coming back to work? You've both been gone for months. We need you guys."

"How about next week? Oh, I forgot to tell you. We got letters recently found at Suarez house in San Antonio. One is from Daddy and Lily. Lily says to tell you someone named 'Guiding Light' arrived at the village. She sends her regards. Any idea what she meant?"

Dan paled and grabbed the letter from my hand. "Sweet Jesus, she did it."

I frowned. "Did what, Dan? Who are you talking about?"

He started laughing and pulled me into his arms for an enormous hug. "You inspired my crazy sister, kiddo. After she learned you came from Before, she was bound and determined to go back in time. She tried month after month to access the time portal in the meadow. I told her she wanted to run away from her problems here. The terrible marriage, the job she hated. The whole basket of negativity those entailed. She swore she could help get our people where they are supposed to go in Oklahoma. And by damn, it sounds like she made it."

"Y-y-you mean—" I stammered.

"I mean Bay went back in time to help the Cohutta Cherokees relocate *before* the Trail of Tears. We always thought they named her *after* Guiding Light, although our Gramma swore she named Bay after an old soap opera. Dammit, she *is* Guiding Light." Dan sounded elated.

"What is the significance of this Guiding Light person?" Richard's voice filled with curiosity.

"The prophecy said Bright Star of Hope would lead our people to safety. You know Lily is Red Moon Woman and Marc is Lone Eagle. Lily's job was to see Ginny safely delivered of Bright Star so she could lead our people from the eastern lands here in Georgia to a land far to the west, where they would enjoy peace and prosperity for many years and avoid the trail of many tears. Red Moon Woman had another part in the prophecy, also. She was to bear a male child who would be known as Red Wolf. That's your brother, Michael. The way of Red Moon Woman would be difficult, marked with much pain and adversity, but from this adversity would come exceptional strength for Red Wolf."

"My half-brother," I murmured. "Yes, that sounds like Michael. He is physically and mentally very strong."

Dan nodded. "They would need his strength to help Bright Star convince the villagers to move west and to accomplish the move. The prophecy said that one day a Guiding Light would come from afar to show Bright Star of Hope the path to the place of haven and prosperity for our people. This Guiding Light would literally be their guide. By damn, my baby sister did it! She used to pretend to be Guiding Light when she was little. And now, she satisfies that part of the prophecy. She took some corn and seed potatoes with her."

"You still have corn from your Mom and potatoes from those your Dad used to grow?"

He nodded. "Oh, yes, I plant some of them every year. She planned to take some of each with her. You've eaten the potatoes at our house before."

"Best potatoes I ever ate," Richard said. "And believe me, I love me some praties."

Dan's eyes narrowed in speculation. "Hmm. I wonder if she can pull off the rest of it."

"What's that, Dan?" I asked.

"The prophecy said Guiding Light would find her true love among the Cohutta Cherokees. Her true flame. It sure wasn't her ex. That slug wasn't fit to wipe the mud from her boots. I guess time will tell. At least, now she has the chance."

"You can't change your beginning, but you can start where you are and change your ending," Richard said.

"C. S. Lewis. One of Bay's favorite sayings." Dan looked lost in thought.

And then we all smiled. I found my happy-ever-after. I hope Bay found hers, too.

# Epilogue
# Bay's Journal
# 1788

I made it. I still cannot quite believe it, but I finally made it.

I tried last Saturday again. I hoped it would work this time. I finished my divorce, after four long, hideous years. My house sold and closed. I quit my job. I refused to go to Oklahoma to be another paper pusher. I was ready for my Grand Adventure. It was now or never.

I hated to go now on one level. I will miss my family. Heck, I already miss my family. And I miss my young friend. Fancy taught me much about the Before. Her baby is due any time. I hate missing the birth of her child. I never had a child of my own. I was always too busy with work, not that my idiot ex-husband ever wanted a child. He enjoyed being the child in our relationship. If I stayed, Fancy wanted me to be his godmother. I could never leave once I held that baby in my arms. I know I would have stayed. I left then because it was 'now or never,' and I was not meant to stay.

My destiny is not Beyond.

I hiked the four miles from the trailhead to the meadow the week before Valentine's Day. It was cold, but not at all bad. I hiked in colder weather many times. I love to hike with the crisp feel of cold against my skin. It wasn't cold enough to snow when I started, although by the time I got to the meadow, I smelled snow in the air.

I shivered and pulled the hoodie on my puffer jacket over my head, happy I wore my long john's, wool socks, and my Timberland boots. I continued walking.

I didn't bring a lot of clothes. Two changes of jeans and long-sleeved t-shirts, and a dozen pairs of socks and undies. I can do a lot of things, but I doubted I could go without panties or socks. I took an extra hoodie made of sweatshirt material and two pairs of warm, woolen gloves. I also brought corn and seed potatoes. I brought maps of the route westward to Arkansas and the Arbuckle Mountains and a half-dozen compasses. I brought as much old money as I could buy from the sale of my house. What money I couldn't spend in old cash and coins I spent buying gold and unset jewels. A couple hundred thousand is not much in the era I left, but I would be one wealthy Cherokee gal going back in time. With the money, gold, and jewels, my tribe would possess the funds to move westward with ease.

I know where we will go. With the help of the Great Spirit, I will guide my people safely west to the Arbuckle Mountains, as the prophecy foretold. For I am the Guiding Light, sent from Beyond to guide my people to an unknown land, a safe land, where they can live forever in peace and harmony.

It felt strange to hike along a path I know so well, and to hear The Big Noise. I knew at once what the sound signified. Unlike Fancy, I did not fall. I stopped to savor the sound as it rang out loud and true, like a beacon calling me home.

I smiled when it stopped. I adjusted my heavy pack and said a quick prayer to the four directions. I pulled sage from my pocket and blew it into the air to give thanks to the Great Spirit for guiding me to my new home. I walked on to the springs, where I knew I would meet Bright Star.

I arrived there first. I bent to drop my pack and scooped a handful of the fresh, clear spring water into my hands. I said a quick prayer of thanksgiving for pure water, untainted by pollution, and sipped the water from my cupped hands.

I never tasted water so pure, so clean before.

I heard her before she arrived. Her deerskin moccasins did not make much noise, but I listened for the faint scuffle of the deerskin on the pine needles. I looked up to find a beautiful young woman clad in deerskins, carrying a baby on her back.

She stopped as if stunned when she saw me, and then her face burst into a smile. "Welcome, my sister. I wondered when you would come."

I smiled and arose, crossing quickly to gather Bright Star of Hope into my arms. "I came as soon as possible. It is good to arrive finally, my sister. My friend, Fancy Winslow, sends her greetings."

It was a fib. I know Fancy well, and she was my dear friend, but she did not realize I came.

Star kissed me on each cheek, and I kissed her the same way, the standard greeting among our people. Her face lit with a smile. "She found her Richard? I am so glad. The Great Spirit meant them to be together. She merited some happiness. She had much sadness in her life. I did not expect her to send the Guiding Light to us."

I laughed. "I am not sure she knew who I am, or that she told me how to come."

We talked as we strolled to the village where she took me into the warmth of her snug and cozy asi. I pulled out maps and was showing them to her when he rushed into the asi.

I knew at once who he was. Who else could it be? Richard showed me photos he took of many people when he was here Before. It could be no one else, although grey was beginning to show in his ebony hair. I held out my hand. "It is a great honor to meet you, Chief Shadow Wolf."

His gaze did not waver. He nodded as he took my smaller hand into his big ones. "I am glad you have come at long last. We feared you would never arrive."

I smiled and lowered my eyes in the way girls do to flirt, letting my eyelashes flutter across my cheeks. "I understand you thought Sassy Selk was me?"

He blushed and glanced aside as if embarrassed. "At one time, yes, I thought Sassy might be the one. How do you know about that?"

I tilted my head. "Richard told me. Let me ask, do you still play stickball?"

Stickball is a game played among the Cherokees, especially the young ones. Warriors learn fighting skills playing the game. Boys and girls learn to flirt. A girl knows a boy is an outstanding warrior based on his stickball skills. She also learns if a man has a sense of humor and a strong sense of self-worth without undue ego if he can be beaten by the woman and not become angry or bitter at the loss, if he is a man who can withstand teasing and jokes.

Would he know I was flirting? Would he care?

He stared at me for a moment before answering. "I have not played stickball for many years now, since I won the hand of my Ginny Blue Eyes playing the game long ago. It is a game for young warriors. I would play again for the right woman, perhaps a woman who came from afar."

"I waited until the Great Spirit would bring me, until it was the right time." I felt my cheeks burn bright pink, and I held my head a little higher.

"Timing is important. Yes, I would play stickball for such a woman." Then he smiled, and as his smile warmed my lonely heart, I knew I was in the right place.

Hemingway once said, 'the world breaks everyone, and then some become strong at the broken pieces.' Fancy told me the Japanese repair broken things with a special process which they call Kintsugi. They repair broken pottery with a strong adhesive and sprinkle the adhesive with gold dust. The resulting repaired piece is stronger, more beautiful, more interesting, once repaired after it broke. She wanted to be a living piece of Kintsugi.

So do I.

I am being bonded with spiritual epoxy sprinkled with the refiner's gold. I will become a living example of Kintsugi. I realize this process is not about being perfect. I try every day to be the best person I can be. That's when transformation occurs. It's when the change happens, that's how it occurs. Some days, it's damned hard. I force myself to keep going, to embrace the struggle, and to let it strengthen me in the places where I broke. With each passing day here, I am stronger. More interesting. More beautiful. I continue because I am the Guiding Light. I am with my Wolf and together we shall lead our people to safety.

I found my destiny among the Cohutta Cherokees.

# NOTE FROM THE AUTHOR

Word-of-mouth is crucial for any author to succeed. If you enjoyed *Diary of the Reluctant Duchess*, please leave a review online—anywhere you are able. Even if it's just a sentence or two. It would make all the difference and would be very much appreciated.

Thanks!
Sharon

# ABOUT THE AUTHOR

Sharon K. Middleton is a fourth generation Texan. Her first relative to the Colonies came in 1742 as a 12-year-old Irish indentured servant. Her great-grandmother immigrated from Mexico in the 1890s. Sharon is a graduate of Trinity University, Texas A&M, and South Texas College of Law. She is an attorney licensed to practice in Texas. She enjoys writing, quilting, showing and raising Skye terriers. She loves the wilds of North Georgia and hopes to retire there soon.

Thank you so much for reading one of Sharon K. Middleton's novels. If you enjoyed the experience, please check out our recommended title for your next great read!

*Beyond McCarron's Corner: Sassy's Story* by Sharon K. Middleton

"A tale with an intriguing historical setting and time-travel premise..."
*-KIRKUS REVIEWS*

And be sure to read Baylie's Story, *Path of the Guiding Light*, which will release December 23. If you pre-order it, you can have it in time for Christmas!

View other Black Rose Writing titles at www.blackrosewriting.com/books and use promo code **PRINT** to receive a **20% discount** when purchasing.

Lightning Source UK Ltd.
Milton Keynes UK
UKHW011013210820
368606UK00001B/48